entropy

/ˈɛntrəpi/

n A measure of disorder in a closed system. {EN- *en* + Greek- *tropē* transformation}.

K M HARBUTT

First published by Busybird Publishing 2018

ISBN 978-1-925830-92-7

While there are historical references to events and periods of time, this is a work of fiction. Similarities between characters are a coincidence.

Cover images: Karen Harbutt, Canva
Cover design: Karen Harbutt, Megan Low
Layout and typesetting: Megan Low, Busybird Publishing

Busybird Publishing
2/118 Para Road
Montmorency, Victoria
Australia 3094
www.busybird.com.au

Contents

1.

[Wednesday, March 23, 1949. Adelaide.]

Its fur was smattered with scarlet shock, its hips crushed against the concrete, its eyes narrowed and unknowing. Forcing himself to assess the damage, Mandelson was not convinced the fox was dead. He had a sinking feeling that if he took hold of its tail to drag it to the back of the rectory, there could be shudders.

A painfully thin bachelor whose wardrobe had changed little during the seven years he had been chief organist in the Walkerville parish, Mandelson was a lonely man. He was happiest in the hour when he was seated with his back to a congregation, his fingers variously floating over and resting intimately on particular keys, a creator of moods that helped his community transcend their special and sad affairs. His pride in underscoring these moments was matched only in intensity by the anxiety he felt if his musical preparation for them was interrupted.

Oblivious to this, the Reverend Avery Holbrook had responded to the surprising discovery on the church steps that morning by frowning at Mandelson and, with only a cursory sweep of his hand, assigning his tardy underling the task of cleaning it up. It was infuriating, even contemptuous, Mandelson thought. Worse, it could imperil the double funeral awaiting them both.

A child has lost both parents and he seriously can't find anyone else to do this?

Mandelson was running out of time to practice the piano piece requested by the estranged sister of one of the deceased. Not that he needed much of a run through; the piece was easy enough but, because he also thought it frivolous and inappropriate, he feared he might add 'clumsily played' to its flaws.

He opted for a shovel and slid it easily under the fox despite the flattened pelvis. The animal had not yet stiffened, or perhaps the neck was broken, but either way its head rolled backwards. Though the movement assured the organist there would be no tremors, he had not anticipated his own.

*What scumbag would drag it here? Why not leave it in the gutter? Perhaps the driver was drunk. Maybe they did it as a kindness. Or maybe the animal dragged **itself** here – truly one of God's creatures!*

Mandelson's unanswered questions were abruptly dismissed with the sporelifting stench that encircled his nostrils as soon as he raised the body. He resisted the desire to spit until the bile rose so full in his throat he was forced to rid himself of it in one offensively fluid motion.

The Reverend, who had come to the fore of the vestibule at that moment, looked at his organist with something resembling disgust. Mandelson caught it with disbelief.

Hard to imagine that man in the Army.

He withdrew the shovel and then forced it under again, the harsh sound of metal scraping concrete being an adequate enough response, he thought, as he balanced the weight of the fox across the broad blade.

He headed for a rear corner of the grounds where he was accustomed to storing unwanted material in the narrow gap between a garden shed and the fence until he had time to incinerate it.

Or in this case, cremate it.

A large square of cardboard left there earlier, its bottom abutting the foundations and its top resting against the splintering palings, would do the job nicely. Mandelson rammed his heel into the middle of it, unintentionally jolting the carcass so that it slid into the newly formed cradle but also pinned his foot underneath. He withdrew it quickly but not quick enough to avoid the burnish of blood that now stained the soft leather of his shoe.

This was definitely not the morning Mandelson had planned and it wasn't going to get any better. The grimy task had somehow moved his thoughts on the requested music irrationally from dislike to loathing. It had none of the resonance of the meticulously chosen scores he usually brought to life on the small pipe organ and he would enjoy playing it almost as much as having to deal with the morning's roadkill.

The organist found himself turning to his own musical preoccupation – as if filling his head with a piece he had been obsessed with since he was a young man, might drown out the ditty. He knew the last movement of the suite so well – its gothic throngs, its swings, its spirals, its chase – that he could summon it at will. It was a momentous, muscular composition – at times water laden and at other times a warbling baritone of menace. He liked to play it in defiance of inanity, as a rejoinder to the Reverend's condescension and sometimes simply to challenge the man's omnipresence in the chapel. Inviting the music in now made Mandelson feel instantly better even as he knew it could be a costly distraction.

Get hold of yourself man! Can you imagine a spirit knocking on Heaven's door with Boellmann's Toccata swirling around it? You'd be lucky if Pergatory took you in.

Grumpier than ever, Mandelson walked back down the pathway abutting the church, rolling his ankle every now and then to swipe his shoe against compact tufts of grass in an effort to remove the blood. To the quietening (but not yet dismissed) rolling rhythms only he could hear, he saw with alarm that mourners were already gathering.

He would have to turn the sister's request into a respectable offering or defy the family and play a traditional piece that both he and God were familiar with in order to restore the balance. He was sure if he took the second option – taking his seat with confidence and avoiding all eye contact – no one would be disappointed.

Hastily, he rinsed his hands over a tap well. Looking up as he did, he noticed a teenage girl standing almost on the spot where the fox had been discovered. She wore a skirt of fawn and forest green plaid which came down well below her knees, a plain white shirt which looked like it would suit a school uniform and stockings and shoes which looked similarly like academic attire. The girl's sun streaked hair was braided in a single plait, with an extraordinary number of strands having escaped bondage.

It was easy now for Mandelson to dispel the toccata. The girl had captured his imagination and he was happy to compose his thoughts around the few visual clues available to him. She was staring obliquely at the stairs, with their worn and rolled over edges. She had the look of someone who was alone in knowing that what lay ahead was a house of plague.

Mandelson entered the church through a side door that gave him access to a discrete vantage point. Sometimes as a congregation arrived, he would watch through the gaps of an elaborate cane screen which camouflaged a sideboard only a little to the left of the altar. The position afforded a line of sight through the nave, down the wide middle aisle, all the way to the street if the doors were open. From here he could indulge his voyeurism while appearing to be reviewing his sheet music.

Through the screen, Mandelson looked across the shoulders of the Reverend in the vestibule, where he was greeting mourners, and searched for the girl. He found her, standing on the last heartbeat of the fox.

In a thought as lightly conceived and transient as a falling whisp of hair, Mandelson wondered if death was lingering there still.

A portly, middle aged man in a double breasted suit moved across his vision, blocking sight of the girl. Even from a distance, Mandelson could tell from his mannerisms that he was of a gentle disposition. The man turned from the Reverend toward the girl and put his arm around her. The organist did not have a clear enough view to know how the girl responded, but assumed it was poorly as the man did not hold the position long, shifting his hands to his pockets and resting his chin on his chest.

The man's companion, a woman with more bluster than height, was animated with conversation, though Mandelson was too far away, with too many chatting huddles in between, to make out the words. The woman overheld the Reverend's hand, every now and then leaning in with a private communiqué. Mandelson could not determine her mood or relationship to the girl. On the one hand she seemed – quite offensively given the occasion – to be flirting with the Reverend and on the other, determined not to take his lead to move into the church because she was tied in some way to the girl.

Behind the shed, death shifted its weight and the cardboard crib collapsed. In front of the church, the girl remained transfixed.

Mandelson had run out of time and excuses to stay engaged any longer. But he had made a decision and he took his seat at the organ with renewed purpose. He pulled out a stop, and pumped his foot to begin. At first, the sound could not be heard over the subdued but constant talk billowing at his back. Mandelson gave the organ more air and more heart, rolling his back and shoulders into nuancing the simple melody as the aisles cleared and the somewhat surprised gathering settled. It was neither the requested piece, nor the sounds of the organist's alter ego that reached out to the girl. Instead, Mandelson had chosen the naïve lilt of a little known hymn his mother had sung to him as a child when his father was succumbing to throat cancer and he was consumed with fear that it might be contagious.

Had he been able to turn around, the organist would have seen the girl look up on the second bar of the melody. Her adult companions were now able to cup each of her elbows and gently move her inside –crumpled between them, without opposition.

Avery Holbrook made his way to the front of the chapel. As the girl was walked to the empty pew reserved for immediate family, he took his place at the lectern, consciously straightening his back and clearing his expression.

His eye was drawn to the stragglers whose entrance was being impeded by a woman pacing with the aggression of a swimmer eager to turn into the next lap. Avery recognised her immediately as Katherine Westcott, the girl's aunt. Despite knowing that compassion was the right response, he felt only disappointment in her conflicted display.

There are plenty of seats; why doesn't she take one? Damn Mandelson, why didn't he play her request. Wait, is she leaving?

Avery tied his words tightly and threw them like a boomerang to the back of the church: 'Salvation is in the name of the Lord, who made heaven and earth.'

It was a familiar signal to the gathering to come together. Those who had been polite about getting to a preferred seat now attempted to move into pews by pushing past compacted knees. Voices collided in short sentences: 'Excuse me; thank you; if you wouldn't mind.'

The aunt was now still and seemed poised to leave before the service even began. With something resembling indigestion rising in his gut, Avery realised that this woman may genuinely have no regard for her dead sister's wishes and no desire to be guardian to her niece. He watched as Miss Westcott turned her back and knew that the girl was, right now, being abandoned by her only remaining relative.

Avery would wonder over the years whether it was the extraordinary empathy that engulfed him in that moment that led him to take responsibility for the girl. He would also wonder, at times, whether Katherine Westcott would have felt compelled to do the right thing if Mandelson had played the song the sisters had learned together as children.

As for the girl, she would be unsure of many things in her life, not the least of which was whether she was ever truly loved by anyone who touched her from that day on.

2.

Petals & Diamonds.

[Six days before. Morning, March 17, 1949.]

T here was nothing in the unfurling of the platinum sky, its skin drained of hue by the feverish heat, nothing in the rhythmic returns of the steering wheel guiding the car through corrugations, or even in the strawberry blotches softly rising on Felicity Muldoon's neck, to suggest the drive would be anything but mundane.

Felicity wasn't aware that she was stressed, despite the rash her husband had noted but chosen not to mention. She sought distraction through the car window but saw nothing but an endless expanse of dirt, broken only by random profusions of bluebush. Occasionally her eye could be drawn by stock feed tins posted as letterboxes at the edge of the highway, or a hapless mound of roadkill, a bird lifting reluctantly from its meal and floating back down before the gust of their passing had even left its feathery fingers.

Felicity stared absently at a brochure. She rubbed her thumb across the images of smooth skinned children in straw hats, perfect lawns, sandstone buildings. The Anglican School for Girls was undeniably impressive, but somehow, now that the day was here, she found herself fantasising that they might arrive to find it a deserted shell behind a For Sale sign, hanging by one corner from a padlocked gate.

It's the right thing to do; there are no jobs in Kimbanyon. She's lucky to have the one she does, considering how difficult she can be.

Without ever acknowledging it, not even to Jim, Felicity was tiring of worrying about Helen, tiring of the intolerance and ignorance of others – of hearing how blessed they were as parents that their daughter was 'happy in her own company'.

They had never felt they had to rescue Helen from her community, until Jim had disgraced himself at the pub that night. Helen had stayed home, caught up in a book. They had nodded at Mick and Belinda Paton, sitting with their twins, their oldest daughter showing them a proud smile as she had walked past with meals for the Browns, who had already been seated when they arrived. The Browns had invited the Patons to join them, at a table just one removed from where they had sat down.

The conversations from each table wafted, indecipherable to the other from the general noise from the bar and the tables around them. Then, as the Muldoons' meals arrived and they fell quiet, and the Patons, whose meals were yet to come, chatted with the Browns while their plates were taken away, she and Jim had been subjected to a horrible clarity of dialogue. It was Mick.

Despite mixing with some of the roughest men she had ever met on the railways, Felicity had never seen Jim hit anyone before; it was those words – 'not quite right', and Mick had been happy to repeat them. She had bristled as well, but it was Jim who had broken a man's nose and been dragged out of the hotel while she had done nothing about the knowing smirk on Belinda's face prior to that but pretend to be interested in her food.

It was true that Helen was stubborn, defiant and a little dark at times – the Muldoons had conceded that much to each other when their daughter was quite young – but Felicity had wondered after that night whether Jim's concerns went deeper than that.

She has to have a fresh start, away from these people. Perhaps we all should.

Jim usually drove the old Holden with one hand, resting his elbow out the open window. Today the windows were up in order to keep his freshly pressed shirt in pristine condition and to prevent the wind turning his wife's elegantly twisted French roll into a hay bale. His annoyance at having to drive this way was nothing compared to his wife's discomfort Jim thought, noting how crumpled that brochure had become in her grip.

'Honestly, love, there's nothing to worry about. She's gonna love it and they're gonna love her.'

Jim gave Felicity's hand a reassuring squeeze. She smiled at him, grateful for the attempt. She thought of the school uniform already hung in their wardrobe at home – one fawn and green check skirt, one white shirt, taupe stockings and black shoes.

Flick kept hold of Jim's hand when he moved to withdraw it. He smiled to himself. The tyres hummed as the car surfed across the corrugations. If they were to get back in time for tea, they would have to use the old crossing. Jim picked up speed. A plume of fine dust rose in their wake.

Jim shifted his weight on the bench seat. Normally he could drive eight hours straight without batting an eyelid. But today he couldn't get comfortable; if he held his driving arm straight, gripping the top of the wheel, it got tired. If he let his elbow lie on the door rest and steered from the bottom of the wheel, he didn't feel he had proper control of the car. He just wanted a breeze on his face and to feel the sun on his forearm.

Jim stole a glance at his wife. The mostly white dress, with a print of large, open red roses, was one of his favourites and though it had faded over the years, the way Felicity wore it, you would think it was still the height of fashion. It was like Trudy Palmer said: 'If it's presented well, even the most average work can look impressive', not that his wife was 'average' by any means, Jim thought to himself, annoyed that he was so poor with words.

Trudy Palmer taught Prep to Year 10 in Kimbanyon's one large hall. She had grown up in the town before leaving for teachers' college and had returned to save the community from countless young educators who dutifully did their time in the outback to win approval for placements in city schools. For staying, she had won the support of local parents, though not all of them backed her attempts to help their children 'go on'. Traditionally, many parents in the area preferred their children stay close to home, with sons taking railway jobs at fifteen, and daughters marrying when they were not much older or got pregnant, whichever came first.

At the end of last year, there were three girls enrolled in the tenth grade with Helen. One of them was now engaged and saw that as reason enough to leave, another was waitressing full time in the pub dining room and the other was finishing her schooling in Adelaide, living with a relative.

I guess Helen could live with Katherine. She's probably still there. She's probably still a right cow of course. We should try and fix that, for Helen's sake!

Jim tightened his grip on the wheel as the car slipped in and out of a shallow rut.

They never did do this bloody road properly. And that bloody eyesore…

'Look out!'

Felicity's scream rose with the car and was instantly silenced by the penetration of a steel rod through her larynx. The man she had loved since childhood dropped back into his seat as planks snapped over the bonnet and pushed the engine toward his legs. As sometimes happens when catastrophe is unfolding, the world reshaped in front of Jim distinctly and in slow motion. He saw an eyeball roll into the kaleidoscopic valley of glass bowing toward his face. In snatches, he saw teeth, ribs, nothing, then blinding light punching through elaborate crimson spiderwebs. The couple were engulfed in a grotesque maelstrom of flesh, metal and wood. And then they weren't.

It took just seconds for the Muldoon's car to become airborne, plough through the livestock carriage of the Tea and Sugar train and nosedive to a crumpled halt on the other side. From that point on, everything Felicity and Jim had achieved with their lives would be lost in local memory and their names synonymous with the worst single car rail accident the country had ever seen.

[4pm, Thursday, March 17, 1949.]

Helen burst into the store, not so much late as feeling like she couldn't afford to be. She was uncomfortably anxious, as if she had something important to remember but just couldn't. It wasn't that her employers were ogres or that the customers were overly demanding; it was just that she had trouble reading people and often misinterpreted what was being asked of her and anticipating difficult interactions put her on edge most of the time she was in company.

Bert and Mabel Johns had employed Helen for two years now in the only general store for 350 miles. She was punctual, honest and a hard worker and they trusted her with money and customers. But despite her worth as a storehand, they hadn't warmed to the girl. It was an odd thing; when she stood in front of him, fidgeting as he spoke to her, Bert felt like he was seeing twigs in her hair or a smear of mud on her face – remnants of some misadventure that no civilized young woman would have been a part of – and yet in reality those things hadn't happened and weren't there.

Bert was sitting on a stool doing his paperwork at the far end of a counter which divided the family home from the shop, when Helen appeared – her arrival announced by a familiar slap of the door and the consequent tumble of the bell from its wire perch above.

'Sorry Mr Johns; I'll get the stool and rig it back up,' Helen blurted out.

The commotion brought Mabel into the shop from the rear residence, directing her irascibility at her husband, rather than Helen, for whom her words seemed to have little effect.

'I don't know how many times I've asked you to fix that bell; one day it's going to clock someone and that, you lazy oaf, will be on your head.'

Bert had learned to keep his thoughts to himself when being admonished by his wife but that didn't stop them appearing on his face.

More likely the customer's head than mine!

With the sound of Mabel's voice, Helen ducked below a flour shelf, strands of her hair lighting up in the glare of sunlight through the window behind her and fading again as she dropped below it. Mabel shook her head, sighed loud enough for Helen to hear and then stole the accounts book from under Bert's pen to disappear back into the residence, where she had a single cup of tea waiting. Bert watched as Helen climbed onto the footstool. Predictably, she became entangled in the plastic ribbons of the new curtain and began fending them off with disproportionate vigor, the bell ringing wildly in her hand as she did so.

Helen reminded Bert of a rabbit he had seen last year while walking on his cousin's property. It had been chased out of its burrow by a ferret. Instead of high tailing it out of there, it had turned and faced the ferret, defying its genes in some misguided attempt to regain its home. In that split second, the rabbit had sealed its fate. Bert had never seen anything like it; the ferret had torn it to shreds. He could still see the whiskers twitching on the rabbit's severed head, though his memory of the ferret dragging its bloodied body back into the burrow had faded. This girl, Helen, was a twitcher, he thought. She would flit between her chores, filling shelves, packing orders, forgetting something, flitting back, ticking it off. But sometimes, without apparent provocation, her face would storm over with such an intensity it looked like she would come out of it covered in bruises.

Heaven help that one if she ever turns and faces her demons.

'Helen, you onto that order? Mrs Simmins is due in this afternoon.'

Mabel was back, spinning around on her low pumps and heading for the storeroom to the right of the shop entrance when the phone rang from the small table just inside it. Helen would not be able to fill the order now until Mrs Johns had finished talking; her calls were 'private matters'.

'I'll take this,' Mabel called over her shoulder, drawing aside the olive curtain that served as a door and disappearing as its folds fell heavily back into place behind her.

She needn't have bothered calling out; neither Bert nor Helen would have dreamt of answering the phone when she was there. The likelihood that it was for either of them was much slimmer than it being one of Mabel's girlfriends setting up an early pub dinner before the men got in, a night of bridge, or even a trip to Port Augusta or Adelaide when the sales were on.

Mabel was popular in town, partly because she held the power to give credit and partly because she made frequent trips beyond Kimbanyon and could be asked to bring back personal items. The fortnightly Tea and Sugar served the community well for groceries, fresh meat and standard clothing items, but there were other things such as gifts and dress clothes that could not be got via the rail. For the right compliments (and price) they could be got from Mabel.

Generally, she would only pass on calls to do with the business, leaving the phone on the table, pulling the curtain back to leave and dropping it again usually all before Bert had crossed the shop floor. So when the usual happy banter, the sounds of gossip and arrangements being made didn't come muffled through the curtain and Mabel didn't emerge calling for Bert, he called out to her: 'Everything all right love?'

[2.10pm, Thursday, March 17, 1949.]

Jim could not isolate a particular injury that might be responsible. He just felt death was upon him and was struggling to comprehend why. Nor could he explain the glittering clusters of light surrounding him.

Are they diamonds? There's something floating in them — roses. Roses from Felicity's dress … .

'Flick?'

Jim tried to move his head but it was held firm, shunted by the compressed roof into his collarbone. His neck was all pain. His ribs were squeezing his lungs. The steering wheel was embedded in his chest.

'Felicity?'

Unable to see them, Jim attempted to raise the fingers individually on his left hand. He could not tell which rose and fell on the request. They were jittery, sparking at the end of an overwhelmingly heavy limb. He reached out an inch or two across the seat, his fingertips forging short paths through the film of blood and glass on the vinyl. He closed his eyes against the throbbing. He fancied he touched Felicity's hand. A hoof toppled to the floor.

[3.15pm, Thursday, March 17, 1949.]

The ambulance had been pelting down the centre of the road for about half an hour. The younger of the officers, Hank, was on his first run and had chatted nervously as they left Port Augusta on the new highway. It was smooth and he was keen. It wasn't until they had been driving for another half an hour on the old highway, which aligned more closely with the railway line, and he had accidentally bitten his tongue as the tyres bounced over rough repairs, that he fell quiet.

Ewen, a career paramedic who was never happy about taking a rig out past Port Augusta had been hoping for a recall before they had got this far. He looked over his right shoulder, somewhat mesmerised as he watched the steel lines jump into the silver gaze of the sun, until the divergence meant he could no longer safely keep an eye on the road at the same time.

When the new highway to the west had bypassed Kimbanyon, there were those who thought it would become a ghost town. Lobbying by the railways and a subsequent government decision to build a line through the town to central Australia had saved it from that fate, but construction on both projects had been marred by delays and poor planning. Connecting Kimbanyon to the new highway had seemed an afterthought, one many suspected had not even been budgeted for.

Townsfolk were ultimately directed to a section of the old highway from which a grading had been developed for trucks on their way to the construction site. Not only was the grading a poor ramp to the new highway but those heading to Adelaide from Kimbanyon were expected to travel around half an hour in the opposite direction to access it.

It wasn't surprising then, with a journey of hours ahead of them, that many locals still chose to use the old highway until they were closer to Adelaide. For those who drove alert to the hazards, there were only gains to be made by taking this route. But the risks were high for those who failed to drive cautiously as they approached the rail crossing, flanked as it was by an abandoned mine shaft and a failed tourist attraction that could leave drivers blindsided to the Tea and Sugar supply train on its way through to Kalgoorlie in the west.

On the premise that the dilapidated buildings fell on a route no longer in use, there had been no rush to demolish them or even to upgrade the crossing. If a poor government decision had approved an enterprise that restricted vision of the crossing, it was indifference that failed to tear its remains down before the Muldoons tempted fate that day.

Hank looked at his partner who was slowing down for no apparent reason. His gaze was fixed on the massive sign they were approaching – a wind-washed, cockatoo-chewed, giant miner grinning from under his Akubra and holding the 'biggest gold nugget ever found in Australia' against his drizabone – frozen in time as a prospector of both good and bad fortune. At his boots were several large rocks that once glittered with metallic paint. As Ewen turned the rig to round them, he was forced to swerve wildly to avoid a larger boulder that was inexplicably in the centre of the highway.

What the hell?

'Lucky we weren't going any faster; that'd kill you for sure,' Hank predicted, turning to look back at the obstacle over his shoulder.

In front of them, Ewen was discovering a scene of plunderous mayhem.

'It just might have. I hope you're ready for this, mate.'

Train carriages were splayed across the tracks like limbs rolling free from a broken spine. The engine of the Tea and Sugar remarkably was still standing. The smell of a butcher shop gulley trap hit the medics before they pulled to a stop.

'Jesus Christ.' Hank's whole demeanour carried an offensive hint of excitement – an unfortunate result of the profusion of naivety and adrenalin that afflicts earnest young people the first time they sense their dreams of being useful might be coming to fruition.

About a dozen people were wandering dazed through the debris. Six large sheep were trotting aimlessly through the spinifex, their legs choppy underneath them. Their bleats were undirected and disconnected. They vacated their bowels in voluminous muddy streams. A torso of beef – its blue and purple veins rising underneath a white film of skin as if a heart was still pumping inside it – had been thrown up to a dozen feet from the train. It had the appearance of being sun dappled as flies landed, lifted and resettled on its ribs.

A young girl, who may have been similarly thrown on impact, was squatting beside it. She had a gash to her forehead that extended through her left brow. Blood had congealed over her eyelid and was making it droop. A fly disappeared partially into a deep cut on her chin. She sat mute while people around her sifted through wreckage, her eyes fixed and glazed.

'Bloody hell,' Hank added, speaking more slowly this time, as he stepped down from the cabin.

Ewen was already at the back of the unit gathering his kit. A face, pale and pitted with bloodshot eyes, appeared suddenly at his shoulder with several other passengers behind him.

'Come with me,' the driver said.

'You go,' Ewen told Hank. 'I'll check the carriages and you men see if you can get that boulder off the road, will you?'

Hank followed the limping run of the driver, who stopped at the engine and pointed past it.

'Over there.'

The chaos on the other side of the tracks was mirrored, except for the anomaly of the partially crushed vehicle in the centre of it.

I got this.

'What have you got Hank? Ewen's voice carried from inside one of the rolled carriages.

The car had no bonnet. The roof was depressed, concertinaed and strewn with entrails. Hank gagged, involuntarily turning to look at the train driver to see if he had noticed. He had followed and was now squinting to see into the front of the vehicle. Hank forced himself to follow the line of sight and note each forensic detail, knowing he would have to write it up when they got back.

No-one could survive this.

'Hank, what've you got?' Ewen's voice was more insistent.

'I'm on it,' Hank called back.

He peered through the gap where the windscreen had been and tried to collect himself. His voice broke like a teenager's as he called to his partner.

'Two inside, checking for signs of life.'

[5pm, Thursday, March 17, 1949.]

Mabel put down the phone, heavy in her hand. She blinked, frowned, looked at her shoes for a moment, then, as if composing herself to sing an opera, drew in enough breath to slightly stretch the pale peach machine knit of her stylish twin set across her breasts. And looked up. Despite knowing it was Helen she had to face, she searched the shop first for Bert, feeling an unfamiliar compulsion to draw on the strength of the man her father had called 'Mr Reliability'. He was sitting behind the counter, his bifocals resting on the end of his nose, bills and lists spread out in front of him, chewing on the end of his pencil, a habit which on any other day she would have found disgusting and chided him for.

She tried to imagine their Edward, or Sissy, as they tended to call Cecilia when she was little, hearing the devastating news that she was about to give Helen, and winced with the pain of it. Both their children had been a handful growing up but both were now finding their way in the world. Edward was at university in Adelaide, in some bachelor pad with friends she'd rather not know about, and Cecilia was married to a nice young chemist whose pharmaceutical company paid him well enough for them to travel overseas frequently, just not well enough to come visit them in Kimbanyon.

She saw her children in Bert's face, their strawberry blonde hair still visible in his grey. She breathed deeply and turned abruptly from her husband to Helen, fearing the sentiment would wane and she would falter. The girl was taking calico bags of flour out of a box and stacking them on shelves on the west wall of the shop, stopping every now and then to check for weevils.

Mabel felt an oiliness travel up her oesophagus.

'Helen, dear, I have something to tell you,' she blurted out with uncharacteristic affection.

Bert should be doing this. She listens to him. All I can think of is 'your parents are dead'.

Before she had time to strangle the thought, the words had gambolled off Mabel's tongue as loudly and eagerly as children racing for a swing. Mabel desperately hoped it had only happened in her head, her eyes sweeping the store for confirmation that everything was as it had been before the call, but it was not. Everything bent had straightened up and was looking directly at her. She forced her eyes back to Helen.

'There was a terrible accident. The Tea and Sugar ...'

What is Mabel on about?

'I'm so sorry Helen.'

A chill began to crawl across Helen's skull. It stopped, it started – and as Helen composed herself enough to register the look on Mabel's face – it found a crevasse to slink into.

Her toes tingled in her shoes as if they were about to drop off. Her ears were popping with bubbles of silence. She made out a word here and there: 'Did everything they could, ... sheep had to be destroyed, ... Mr Grimsley's nephew was there.'

Helen directed what little focus she had to Mabel's lips. It was a technique she used when she was going through the motions, or 'sleeptalking', as her mother called it. It allowed her to remain in the sickly sweet world of the vague while garnering just enough information to function. With her sight locked in, the feelers of her subconscious forayed to collect the elements of the message. When they were corralled in her head, Helen tried to force the random, wounded syllables into a friendlier combination. But they would not cooperate, stubbornly gathering instead in the poisonous combination in which they were uttered, forcing the lens of her mind to pull back and refocus.

She stared through Mabel, looking for an explanation in the heavy folds of the stockroom curtain behind her. The unsettled woman took an awkward step back as if to avoid a collision with some imagined stranger pushing past.

Bert, please, make her understand.

Responding as much to his wife's imploring look as Helen's confusion, Bert came to the girl's side, startling her by putting his arm around her shoulders. Helen pulled away – a shocking thought occurring to her simultaneously that no parent would ever comfort her like that again. It was clearer to her now that she had nowhere to turn. There was no boyfriend, no best friend. There had never been a need for anyone 'extra'. She had company if she chose it at school, and sometimes took her sandwiches in the classroom with Miss Palmer. But at the end of each day, she would go home for tea … for teasing conversations with her father, for crosswords with her mother at the kitchen table into the wee hours after Jim had gone to bed. They were a family that breathed collectively, opening and closing according to a comfortable routine, like sea life catching lesser organisms as they passed by them on the ocean floor. With her bumbling words, that hateful woman had just taken it all away from her, sucking the oxygen from the water and leaving her to drown.

The mouth was moving again: 'Just for the time being … stay with us. … it's not right … empty house.'

Helen did not hear the insufferable merriment of the bell tinkling as she stumbled from the shop, clutching a bag of flour crawling with weevils. Stepping into the burnished flush of evening light, the colour rose in her hair the way the juice of an over-ripened peach bloats under its skin. The warmth of the sun touched her face and then burnt it. She dropped the bag, sending a puff of white powder up around her legs.

Unconsciously she pinched a roll of her inside cheek between her teeth and clenched. As she made her way through town, blood-laced saliva pooled around her gums. With each step, her mind lurched wildly between two thoughts. She postured, with the endorphic excitement of denial, whether her parents might yet be waiting for her. Or, if this was real, she might well be experiencing the most devastating loss of her life. She would be wrong on both accounts.

3.

Nothing but white noise.

[Friday, March 18, 1949. Kimbanyon.]

Friday the trees stood still. The sky was pale and indifferent. Helen watched the crows walking around the yard from the loungeroom window. She pondered the angled lines their feet left in the dirt, creating patterns akin to a slew of matches. Her grief congealed slowly within her; filling her chest, her ears, the pathways between thought and physical function so that even the most trivial of intentions were easily thwarted. She could not remember how she got home yesterday. She recalled Mr Grimsley calling to her from the station – something lost in white noise and then, with great clarity, 'I'm so sorry dear' – but she could not recall his face or looking at him when he said it.

She recalled it was dark out when Miss Palmer had knocked on the door and then tapped on the window, just a step or two along the verandah. At first it had been a rap on the pane, then silence. Then a tentative scratching began, like a tree twig being slapped against the house in a storm. Helen wasn't sure if Miss Palmer had stopped first or night had fallen, driving her away. It wasn't that Helen was being rude, she was just unable to move from the lounge, her body resting in the cushions concaved by years of her parents' companionship. She had heard their voices in the silence last night – the light hearted teasings of her father:

'D'you teach Trudy Palmer anything she didn't know today, sweetheart? You get all your smarts from me you know. In fact,' he whispered, 'it would be a kindness to your mother to give her a hand with the crossword.'

On cue, the dramatic lament of her mother came from the kitchen: 'Goodness it's a tough one tonight. I could do with some help in here.'

It was harder in the daylight to hear their voices. Harder not to be exhausted by the listening. She had left the couch only a couple of times today. The first time she had pulled her underwear up while still urinating. The thought of cleaning herself up had given her such a headache, she sat back down on the seat in her soiled clothing until the pungency of it became distracting and her thighs became numb. The second time, she had followed a compulsion to enter her parents' bedroom, approaching it in the same manner a parent might approach a door closed on a suicidal teenager. She had sat tentatively on the end of the bed, picturing her mother plumping up the pillows, then drawing the spread over them and patting them down again. More than once her father had remarked on the pointlessness of fluffing them up if she was only going to flatten them, but she had just grinned at him.

Helen felt guilty being in their room. Then foolish for feeling guilty. Then embarrassed to be talking out loud, mimicking familiar conversations. The emotions had immobilised her and she had sat there too, until she was numb. Until she could make the effort to return to the entertainment of the crows.

Several days passed, with Helen ignoring a procession of people who felt some need to atone for their cruel words of the past or to uphold the reputation of remote folk pulling together in a crisis, by coming to her door. Most seemed relieved to share the news that Helen had 'gone to ground' and, 'as expected', foolishly rejected their help, even though they had not gone anywhere near close to offering any.

Bert and Mabel Johns brought their compassion in a small, deep cardboard box covered by a white linen tea towel. Helen recognised the throaty rumble of Bert's diesel truck and took herself off the couch to stand perfectly still in the kitchen, out of sight from the loungeroom window. After a few minutes, she heard her employers discussing their next move.

'If she's not home, there's no point leaving it Bert,' Mabel pointed out, emphasising each word as if her husband was hard of hearing. Helen knew Mrs Johns' hand would be on Bert's arm, a gentle intimidation reinforcing her tone.

'We may as well leave it; she can't be far away,' Bert replied, adding conspiratorially, 'What if she's inside and just doesn't want to see anyone?'

He was always closer to the mark than Mabel, Helen thought with some affection. His wife on the other hand, probably didn't care where Helen was; she was probably just being cheap, not wanting to give away her groceries if she didn't have to.

'Well, what about the funeral arrangements, the message from the aunt? We can't leave everything up to Reverend Holbrook, as willing as the dear man is, and it's not our responsibility,' Mabel asserted with an agitated tone.

'Just leave it in the box, love; there's not much else we can do. The kid's gonna have to grow up real fast, may as well give her a couple a days to get used to the idea, and then Holbrook can deal with the rest.'

Their voices began to fade as they turned to leave, with Helen just making out Bert's reassurance to his wife that 'the Reverend's quite capable of getting things moving – it's what the Muldoons wanted anyway'.

Helen's first real conversation with anyone since that day in the shop was with the Reverend. The box she had recovered when Bert and Mabel had left had been his ticket in. Apart from a casserole and some other groceries, it had contained a letter from her aunt – a Katherine Westcott. It set out the Muldoons' hopes for their daughter, including that she live with Miss Westcott and attend school in Adelaide, and Miss Westcott said she was giving consideration to those wishes. In the meantime, the aunt had written, Helen was to look to Reverend Holbrook for guidance and practical support; she should put her trust in him as it was her parents' wish that he be her guardian in the event that she was unable to take on the role.

Do I get a say in this? I've never even met the woman!

With the letter folded and slipped underneath her thigh after its fifth read, Helen fell asleep on the couch and failed to hear the last arrival until the snap of the screen door. Jim had likened it to a farmer's dog, saying those who wished to avoid a bite, should always treat it with a firm hand. Yet, despite the weighty sounds of the steps on the porch, some trepidation must have crept up on the visitor because the door turned on its hinges and slapped back suddenly on the unsuspecting hand. Immediately the injury occurred, the victim responded with an unseemly and loudly enunciated 'Christ'. Helen found herself curious, and looked up. From behind the door, the profanity was followed by a pointlessly remorseful and softly uttered 'Damn'.

She got off the couch, ducked below the window to avoid being seen, and searched for an identity in the kaliedoscopic shapes and colours of the face behind the dimpled glass panel. A flutter of a grin swept over her as she realised it was the Reverend. Had she been Mabel Johns she would have dined out mischievously on the profanity for days. Thankfully she was not Mabel Johns, but that did not prevent her from making a poor judgment call that day. In inviting Avery Holbrook in and shunning the genuine kindness of Trudy Palmer, Helen would encourage the attentions of a man as oblivious as she was to the porous nature of his convictions and mental distortions that would engulf them both when crossing the threshold at Eyre Street in years to come.

Families are strange animals.

[Monday, March 21, 1949. Adelaide.]

Twenty three Prunus Avenue was a small bluestone residence behind a low red brick fence above which bobbed the cheery lilac constellations and broad green leaves of a row of Agapanthus.

Avery Holbrook parked on the opposite side of the road in front of number ten and walked past several historic sandstone homes with evenly spaced white and red rose bushes and upright post boxes before crossing the street. A tricycle was parked beside the front door of the house to the left of number 23 and a bicycle leant against the house of the neighbour to the right, a little way down its narrow driveway.

A central path of crushed white stones divided the impeccably manicured lawn of his destination, ending at a brown and white tiled entrance to a heavy green door. Avery lifted a bronze lionhead knocker and rapped it several times.

From the corner of his eye he saw a lace curtain that had been drawn aside fall back across the window. A few moments later, the door opened.

'Katherine Westcott?'

'Yes?' She lifted glasses on a chain around her neck to the bridge of her nose.

'Miss Westcott, I'm Reverend Holbrook from the Presbyterian Church. I called you last week. I'm very sorry about your loss.'

'Oh, yes, Reverend Holbrook; I've been expecting you, though I don't really know how I can help.'

Miss Westcott's pinched smile softened with her summing up of the Reverend as being much younger than he had sounded on the phone. She turned away when he noticed her inquisitive gaze and stepped back to let him in, then pushed a little rudely past him in the narrow hallway to gesture the way into the living room. It was light-filled with creamy carpet and a glass-topped coffee table on a circular, fringed rug with a weave of pale pink and blue flowers. A cherry wood piano, with European-style candle holders stood to one side of a bricked up fireplace encompassing a small gas heater.

Miss Westcott made herself comfortable in a large wing-backed armchair, crowded with small embroided cushions. Avery deposited a few more of them onto a two-seater couch under the window in order to make room for himself on a smaller armchair. He sat clasping his hands.

'Katherine … May I call you Katherine?'

'I'd prefer Miss Westcott, if you don't mind Reverend.'

'You have a lovely home, Miss Westcott; it must seem quite large at times for one person.'

Miss Westcott raised one eyebrow slightly at the perceived inference but Avery continued undeterred.

'I won't beat around the bush. I'm sure you understand how difficult it is for a girl of Helen's age to lose her parents – both her parents – at the same time.'

Miss Westcott smoothed her dark, pine green skirt over her knees, setting the pleats straight.

'Yes, it's a dreadful business. As you are aware, I have also lost a loved one, Reverend; my sister was my only living relative.'

'Apart from your niece,' Avery offered gently.

'Yes, of course … apart from my niece.'

A shallow sigh escaped Avery and, to mask it, he drew Miss Westcott's attention with feigned admiration for a doily on the coffee table in front of him. It featured a red flower with a dark centre.

'I see you share the same talent as your sister. Such small stitches; it's quite a skill. Is this the desert pea?'

'Will this take long, Reverend? I thought I made my position clear over the phone.'

Avery stopped fingering the doily, which he knew full well depicted South Australia's emblematic flower, and stared blankly at it for a moment, apparently planning his next move. He looked up at Miss Westcott, who sat poker faced until he looked as if he might speak himself, and then moved to cut him off.

'Reverend, can I just say before we go any further that I'm aware of the will. Felicity rang me at the time she and Jim were drawing it up, soon after the girl was born. Of course, she never expected that we would be in this position; she would never have named me as a guardian otherwise I assure you. We haven't spoken since our mother's funeral when the girl was about five.'

Avery looked surprised. The Muldoons had struck him as being very generous in nature.

But then families are strange animals.

'I don't suppose you know anything about our mother, do you Reverend?'

'I never met her, no. I met Felicity through the congregation of the Inland Mission. She was a very religious and giving person.'

Miss Westcott smiled, the same tight smile he had seen at the door. She breathed in deeply, and released it laboriously, her patience apparently wearing thin.

'And you think I'm not a good person, Reverend,' she said, with such a slight lilt in her voice that Avery was unsure of whether she was challenging him to account for his unchristian presumption or amusing herself by determining him a fool for getting it so wrong. She fixed her eyes defiantly on his.

'I don't suppose Felicity told you either that it was me who cared for our mother for years to spare her from a nursing home?'

Avery sensed it prudent to hold his tongue.

Miss Westcott rose from her armchair, smoothed her hands over her skirt, which appeared to be a habit of hers, and went to the window, staring out beyond the front lawn. The sky was pale but glowing, a mask of milky grey and lemon-white clouds with the glare of the afternoon sun behind them. Distracted by something not yet seen, she looked at her watch.

'It's almost three thirty,' she said in a more gentle voice, her back still to Avery.

'The children get out of school soon. The boys like to rip the heads of my Agapanthus but I put a stop to that. Now they run sticks along my fence and strike them off if the mood takes them.'

There was no agitation in her voice; she was perhaps even a little whimsical despite the obvious care taken to maintain her garden and the perceived threat to its order.

'I'm sure they don't mean anything by it,' Avery offered in the children's defence. Her silence made him wish he had a hip flask of whiskey in his pocket, and a cup of tea to sneak it into.

'Does it surprise you Reverend Holbrook that I am not married? That I still live in the home I grew up in? That I will never have children?'

Avery hoped these were rhetorical questions and was disappointed when Miss Westcott turned from the window and looked at him expectantly.

'When father had his heart attack, mother was left to raise us by herself. She took in washing and ironing. We got by. We became very close – Felicity, mother and I – much closer than we had been when father was alive.

'Reverend, would you like a cup of tea or something to eat?'

Miss Westcott seemed to have decided that her story would take some time and that it would be rude to let the Reverend sit without condiments. Avery shook his head, unwilling to disturb her train of thought though he would have loved a cuppa.

'Thank you, I'm fine.'

'As the older sister, I helped out more than Felicity; mother always said she should be left to do her homework first and then it was always too late after that for her to be involved in chores. It didn't seem to bother her that I was in senior year and elbow deep in dishes and laundry while my prospects slipped away from me.'

'They sound like very tough years,' Avery offered.

'Yes, but no tougher than for other families who lost fathers and breadwinners,' Miss Westcott replied, matter-of-factly.

She arranged the cushions Avery had deposited on the couch so that an even number was at each end and then sat between them. Her back to the window now, she missed a few schoolboys running past the Agapanthus. Avery was keen that they not distract her.

'Your mother must have been a strong woman.'

'I suppose so, yes, until her memory started to go. It wasn't bad at first, just forgetting whose ironing was whose and where clients lived, which was confusing for me because I used to run it back to them in our old pram, sometimes across town, and a wrong address meant I had to cart it all the way home again, by which time it was generally creased up again and then stay in until the client rang up to complain so I could get the right address.

'That was my job for years, Reverend, and all while Felicity did her homework and went out on dates.'

A boy older and taller than those who had previously passed by had just come into Avery's view on the right side of the window. He was waving a stick around casually as he walked past. Avery turned back to Miss Westcott.

'Your mother must still have been a young woman.'

'Young but not strong of mind, Reverend. She nearly burnt the house down once. She left the iron on when she went to collect the mail and got distracted squeezing aphids on the roses. She called us girls out to help. Thank goodness, it probably saved our lives.'

Miss Westcott looked wistfully down at her hands, the lines on her brow lifting as if she were surprised to see them looking so old or maybe she was imagining them stained by insect green. Avery prompted her gently.

'What happened?'

Miss Westcott clasped her hands and looked towards a scene that only she could see.

'Felicity and I were having a competition, counting each aphid as we killed it and calling the number out over the top of one another. We didn't see mum wander off. The fire took hold very quickly. We smelt the smoke at the same time as we saw it. I remember it pouring down the front stairs like a river of stretched cotton. I told Felicity to go next door to Hanley's and ring for the fire department. Then I ran into the house looking for mum.

'I fainted before I even made it to the ironing room. I don't know whether it was because I was coughing so hard in the smoke, or I just panicked.

'I'm not good in a crisis, Reverend,' Miss Westcott said, looking directly at Avery.

'I tend to hyperventilate, which of course didn't help.'

Avery smiled encouragingly.

'The fireman who carried me out went back in to get mum. He left me on the footpath with Mrs Hanley. Felicity was squealing and kicking another fireman who was holding her to stop her running into the house too.'

'They did a good job to get your mother out of there.'

'They didn't actually. Another neighbour found mum three blocks away, posting our mail in someone else's letterbox. She didn't know anything about the fire.'

Miss Westcott sniffed and visibly dispelled any emotion attempting to settle on her face. She informed Avery that she would be needing a cup of tea now and promptly left the room to put the kettle on.

Avery was drawn back to the steady line of school children passing the window, with one boy about to disappear from the view on the left side. On his last visible step, the boy took a vigorous and athletic sweep with his stick, slicing off several stems of the Agapanthus in one blow and sending the blooms flying. His actions seemed to sanction the violation for those behind him; more boys appeared on the right side of the window, running and taking their own improvised swords to the helpless plants.

Avery thought about knocking on the pane to get their attention when Miss Westcott returned with a tray carrying two teacups and a small plate of store-bought biscuits. He noted how generously she had buttered them, despite rationing still being in force as the country recovered from its war efforts, and made a mental note to be particularly gracious about her hospitality when he left.

She gingerly put the afternoon tea down on the table between them and resumed her place on the couch.

'It's tragic don't you think, Reverend, that the last time the women in my family were all together was at my mother's funeral. And now I will see my sister after all these years in her own coffin.'

Avery couldn't help but bristle at Miss Westcott's attempt to garner sympathy.

I'll tell you what's tragic – being an orphan with no one to look out for you …

The Reverend paused before responding, wanting the tone of his voice to be less abrasive than that of his thoughts. He picked up the cup closest to him and added a biscuit to his plate before taking a sip. His host did the same.

'But about Helen, Miss Westcott. Her parents had intended her to go to a school here in Adelaide. The money is already in trust and could be paid directly to the school with no fuss for you.

'My only concern,' Avery mentioned with reluctance, 'is that the amount in trust is unlikely to be enough to cover the boarding school.

'So your assistance in giving Helen a home could mean the difference between her going to school in Adelaide or potentially dropping out of school in Kimbanyon.

'It would have meant a great deal to Flick … Felicity … to know that you might do this for her – and of course, for Helen.'

'I've been trying to tell you, Reverend, if you'd just listen to me for a second. I believe senile people have no business being responsible for others. In all likelihood, I'm genetically disposed to the affliction that voided my mother, so you can see why I have not made plans that include having children of my own.

'I expect to end my days with nothing to love but perhaps a few hundred stray cats to fend off nosy neighbours trying to force me into a nursing home. Have I made it a little clearer for you now, Reverend Holbrook?'

Avery had lifted his cooling cup of tea to sup from, but found himself putting it back down again. He could not manage a smile, despite Miss Westcott's effort at humour. Acerbic as it was.

'If you don't mind me saying, Miss Westcott, you appear to be progressing in years much like many other women in their early sixties, perhaps even a little better. Don't you think it a bit premature and foolish, the way you're thinking?'

Totally tactless, Avery. Well done.

Miss Westcott simultaneously straightened her back and her face, then put her teacup and saucer down on the table with a clink of china that might have chipped a less sturdy set.

'Reverend, I have lived my life believing it to be a foregone conclusion. Whether that is foolish or prudent, I don't know. No doubt you have formed a view on that, but either way I am unlikely to change my thinking now.'

'Surely, Miss Westcott …'

She took a last gulp from her cup to finish off the cold, leafy dregs, and stood up.

A subtle change of colour occurred in Avery's eyes (to a more intense blue). He moved to speak, but Miss Westcott preempted him and raised her voice over his.

'I wouldn't wish it on my worst enemy, Reverend, and I will not impose it on my niece. I only wish I'd had a choice. The truth is Felicity got off lightly in this life. And I'm sure Helen will find her way in this world without my help, or indeed my hindrance.'

Miss Westcott's whole body seemed gripped with the discomfort of voicing her greatest fears. She gestured again – this time for Avery to leave. Reluctantly he allowed himself to be shepherded out the front door, turning on the threshold to address his host one more time.

'I will post you details of the school and the trust in case you …'

'That is kind of you, but don't expect a response.'

The Reverend walked down the central path, the small stones crackling against his soles, the door already closed behind him, wondering at the aunt's total lack of compassion. He was irritated that he could not return to Kimbanyon – and his wife – with the news that Helen would soon be living with her rightful guardian and going to the school her parents intended her to. And he was more than a little annoyed that Miss Westcott had not freed him of his obligation in the matter there and then.

How can two sisters be so different? Is it possible she's already as mad as a cut snake and making all this up?

As he reached the footpath, Avery briefly lost his footing, his boot slipping unexpectedly on the stem of a severed Agapanthus.

He tossed it with vigour back into the yard, instantly falling victim, as the schoolboys had, to the transfer of a generous smear of vegemite to his hand and cuffs.

5.

A sense of place and path

[Summer of 1941 – '42]

L ike her father, Gwen had a keen mind, one that could identify the tenets of any philosophy and the interplays of any mechanical thing. If she could separate the logical parts, she could also combine them into their greater sum – a talent that would serve her well for the better part of her life.

And yet if not for the war, it would have been likely that Gwen's particular skills would have gone unrecognised in her working life, given the limitations on what was considered a good career option for a woman at the time.

With no brothers and a father who, at 65, was unlikely to be called to service, Gwen's interest in the war in its first years had been largely peripheral, her curiosity limited to those she knew who might have joined up or who had married unexpectedly (foolishly in Gwen's view), perhaps looking for certainty in uncertain times.

Though her parents listened religiously to the radio at night, Gwen preferred her *Reader's Digest* paperbacks or the 'Mere Male' stories in her mother's *New Idea* magazines. Whenever she did sit by the radio, she generally tuned out to anything other than the big bands, nodding or smiling blithely when the folks gave her knowing looks or were amused by snappy lines in a play.

In November of 1941, the news that a German cruiser had reached the coast off Western Australia introduced a tension in the family's interaction with the air waves that would not ease for another four years. Challenged by the HMAS Sydney, both ships had been sunk, leaving Mr and Mrs Dalana on the edge of their seats night after night waiting for reports of rescues. It filtered in that more than 300 German sailors had been picked up by passing tankers and warships and a number of boats had made it to shore. Over the course of two weeks, Mr Dalana adopted an uncharacteristic sternness that had not yet left him and Gwen's mother's usually robust colouring turned to blancmange. All hope was gone for the 645 crew from the Sydney, and also for the tread of any conversation in the Dalana household to be light or trivial.

Several weeks later, 17 days before Christmas, Gwen ventured into the solemn space that the room had become, looking for company. She had brought her Pitman's textbook in, kicked off her shoes and tucked her legs underneath her on the old two seater, forming an awkward desk on which to practice her shorthand phrases. She would complete just three exercises by the time Advance Australia Fair was on its last note and John Curtin, prime minister then for just two months, began his address to the nation.

The Japanese had bombed America's Pacific fleet in Pearl Harbour on the island of Oahu, Hawaii, around 5,358 miles north of Darwin. Thousands were dead.

The speech delivered into Gwen's loungeroom and millions more like them that night left its audience in no doubt that Australians would now be fighting the war on two fronts – against Germany and Italy in Europe and North Africa, and against their ally Japan in South-East Asia and the West Pacific.

The man who went to jail briefly for protesting against conscription when it was touted in the First World War would come full circle within a year of this speech, extending conscription for overseas service. Within three and a half years of the broadcast – six weeks before the Japanese would surrender – he would be dead from a heart attack.

Her pencil flicking in her fingers, Gwen found herself drawn in by the urgency in the prime minister's voice as he described how

150 years of peace and security 'in this spacious land' was coming to an end.

Japan was 'set on aggression and lusting for power' and had chosen 'the Hitler method', ignoring the conventions of war to strike 'like an assassin in the night' in Britain and America.

'These wanton killings will be followed by attacks … on … the Commonwealth of Australia … if Japan can get its brutal way …

'The stern truth is that war has been forced upon us …'

Gwen watched as her father dropped back into the depths of his armchair, his face falling out of the lamplight and his thumbs looking all the whiter for remaining in, pressed into the clasp of his hands.

Gwen's mother sought out her husband's touch across the bridge of their armrests but was left hanging.

'I say then to the people of Australia,' the prime minister continued, intakes of air loudly punctuating his words, 'give of your best in the service of the nation. There is a place and path for all of us … for the nation itself is in peril. This is our darkest hour. Let that be fully realised. Our efforts in the past two years must be as nothing compared to the efforts we must now put forward.'

Gwen's parents turned to her simultaneously, as if youth were both the cause of – and the answer to – everything they were feeling. Mr Dalana finally took his wife's hand. Perhaps it was the look of foreboding they gave each other in that moment that made them seem to Gwen suddenly very old and frail – part of a generation no longer capable of sorting out their own mess.

It's up to us now.

Though telling her parents was hard, leaving secretarial school was the easiest thing Gwen had ever done. She began training with the Australian Army Nursing Service but quickly found that it was not a good fit.

She thought the lessons on anatomy and identifying surgical implements were relevant and important but was surprised to find that tuition on cleaning bedpans and keeping castors on beds and trolleys straight was given equal time.

While studying the textbooks was enjoyable for Gwen, who had never had a problem with rote learning, she was confused by the messages coming from experienced instructors; trainees were told the medical knowledge they were receiving would be critical in supporting doctors but they could also expect to farewell soldiers back to war despite thinking them unfit. It would never be their call. They were told their duties might include writing patients' letters home to their parents, girlfriends and wives, but also to avoid 'getting personal' with injured soldiers. They were summarily warned not to get 'caught up' even when offering comfort might seem to be the most natural thing in the world but on the other hand, to be aware that compassion went a long way on the road to recovery.

Gwen could see herself frustrated by trying to get a doctor's attention for minor procedures when she felt capable of doing them herself. Having to deal with the emotional baggage that no doubt would come in on every stretcher would, in her mind, only make things worse. When she expressed her concerns, the Sister in Charge reassured Gwen that almost anyone taking her place in the nursing service would likely do a better job and congratulated her on her choice to move to the Australian Women's Army Service (AWAS).

So, as the war was getting louder, with the Japanese having taken Singapore and reports of Australians being chained in POW work gangs, Gwen found herself on a train with dozens of other recruits to begin instruction in Victoria. She would live for the next few months among hundreds of women of all ages in barracks converted from sheep stalls, cattle and horse pavilions at the Melbourne Showgrounds.

On Gwen's second day there, the Japanese bombed Darwin. At his desk, John Curtin reportedly sobbed. 'It's come; the honeymoon's over. We're in for it now,' he would later be recorded as saying. His government banned media coverage after the news first broke, intending to prevent panic. The numbers – more than 240 killed, 400 wounded, 30 aircraft destroyed and 11 ships sunk – would not be known for years. At the showgrounds at least, the censoring of information seemed to pay off, with both the knowing and the not-knowing heightening the trainees' resolve and naïve eagerness to get to their own fronts of the war.

Despite being away from home for the first time, Gwen was thriving. She loved the routine of repetitive drills and found the atmosphere of nervous energy envigorating. She surprised herself by how quickly she excelled at vehicle maintenance and how little she cared about her skin taking on the smells, grease and wear associated with working on engines.

From her initial training with AWAS, Gwen progressed to the first base workshops in Bandiana, a north-eastern military township near the border town of Wodonga. There she honed her skills as a Craftswoman with the Australian Electrical and Mechanical Engineers and was soon on her way along with a dozen others, to service internment camps in the Victorian countryside.

Their destination was the Tatura district in the Goulburn Valley, a place where (according to a bureaucrat's report to the Crown Lands office) interactions between 'the lower classes' were 'tending to the destruction of the Aboriginal race' a century before. Like many of her colleagues she was travelling with that day, Gwen was oblivious to the misery and resilience of that time. What she knew of the area tended more toward stories of gold rushes, bushrangers and pioneering squatters.

So while the tug and drag of humanity in this place was firmly embedded in the soil, there would be no further reflection on it until the POW camps were nothing but broken foundations in grassy paddocks and descendants of Italian and German inmates were able to visit them in their own local cemeteries – because while it is in its throes, war is a business. Military bureaucrats in the early 1940s were concerned only with the area's ability to sustain a substantial food and water supply (from the Waranga Reservoir) and its considerable distance from any seaport to discourage escape. The focus for Gwen over the next few years would be even narrower, happily limited to practical applications and repairs to achieve that sense of contribution and fulfillment.

The journey over the two and a half hour drive north of Melbourne was a fairly uncomfortable affair along the Murray Valley Highway, with a dozen women in army greens seated six to a bench on opposite sides of the truck, crowded by their kits underfoot and the canvas canopy trapping the warm breath of unspoken anticipation above their heads.

Apart from a passing note of the architecture as they drove through the town of Murchison (it had three impressive churches), the talk among the women was mostly about how well they would be eating, with fresh produce from local orchards and dairy farms giving them far better options than they had enjoyed as civilians subject to rationing.

By the time they arrived at Camp 13 – where they would be stationed along with other support staff and guards from the various garrisons – Gwen was tired but elated. She felt in her bones that this was a place where she would not only experience the collegiate spirit Curtin had promised her, but that soon she would be able to take it forgranted.

Accommodation was a mix of galvanized iron barracks and tents that the Army would constantly assure its inhabitants would soon be replaced. Gwen was among a handful of those who would benefit from this largely unfulfilled intention, finding herself moved within weeks to a farmhouse nearby. While the arrangement did not fit with Gwen's desire to be mucking in with the masses, she would quickly come to cherish her luck, along with every other resident who found it hard to believe the house had not been made the private domain of Camp Commanders or other senior officers.

Bought from a family of five, the property would house up to ten craftswomen at a time during Gwen's stay there. They would create a vegetable garden out the back and make the place, with its three fireplaces, large central kitchen, and mosquito-proofed sleepouts, remarkably homely.

As all the living and dining areas had been converted into bedrooms, much of the womens' down time was spent relaxing among a mixture of cane furniture, old armchairs and couches on the enclosed return verandah. Gwen put her own orderly stamp on this relaxed section of the house, designating one side a place to smoke and have the occasional beer, while the other three could be used for 'quieter' pursuits such as reading letters or games of checkers and chess. It was flexible of course, but as one of the first residents in and as someone increasingly fond of order, those were the rules she established, attempted to enforce and continued to adhere to.

At 21, Gwen had found herself somewhere to fit in. The greater sum was a hierarchical organisation saturated with a purpose strong enough to make even the minutia of it seem worthwhile. Among the logical parts of that greater sum, perhaps the west verandah of her new accommodation was the most significant. Not only did it draw the glow of the sunset onto its boards of an evening in a way that was perpetually revitalizing, but it would also be the place where Gwen would find herself some years later, pressed against a rail, softening into a life changing kiss.

6.

Adrift in vanilla.

[August, 1949.]

T he bell over the shop door tinkled and held firm as Avery parted the vertical drop of colourful plastic strips that was intended to stop the flies accompanying customers through the open door.

Upon seeing him, Mrs Johns skirted around the counter, making a dramatic welcoming gesture that bordered on a curtsy. Bert and Helen exchanged looks, a raised eyebrow and mild surprise that they were sharing a comical moment at Mabel's expense.

'Thank you for coming Reverend,' Mrs Johns said, adding in a subversive, woolly tone, 'We've had a difficult week.'

Helen did not take offence. The woman was right, except that their 'difficulties' were not confined to the past week, rather the past couple of months, since the deal had been struck whereby Helen had moved in with them and her family home had been rented out to pay for her keep and board.

As if I would have made that choice for myself.

Helen watched Mabel shepherd the Reverend through the shop and into the passage that led to the kitchen behind it, shielded from prying eyes by the back of a broad staircase which led to the bedrooms and small lounge upstairs.

'I've made scones especially and the kettle's just boiled so we can have a lovely chat while we're waiting for Helen to finish her chores.' The last words trailed off as they moved away from the shop and towards afternoon tea.

Bert looked directly at Helen and called after Mabel: 'I wouldn't mind a cuppa an' all – if you've got the time, love. Not too much sugar, though; I'm cutting down. Oh, and don't you worry about the shop; Helen and I have got that covered.'

The grin Helen returned was the most genuinely affectionate Bert had seen since she'd come to live with them. It almost chased the shadows out from under her eyes.

We won't have her forever, Mabs. And it's not like she costs us anything; there's more than enough coming from the rent on Jim's house to feed and clothe her. And it's not like our own kids visit us. Is it really so bad having her around?

As Bert distracted himself with his thoughts, Helen returned to the mundane task of stacking shelves. When he looked up he could see only her fractious hair appearing above the rows of stock and disappearing again as she stooped to draw packets out of a box at her feet. He tipped himself back into the books.

Mabel's laughter, a little higher pitched than usual, soared out occasionally from the kitchen as they worked, and while it was not possible from the shop to make out the conversation, Mabel barely seemed to draw breath.

When the first cup of tea had been drunk, she summonsed Helen with an overly modulated call to the shop. She was directed to the bench stool which she had taken to since moving in and, with bemusing formality, was offered her own cup of tea and scones neatly placed on crisp white crocheted doilies that Helen had not seen before.

What, no curtsy?

The red formica-topped table swirled with white and trimmed with silver painted tin was also new. It had come in on the Tea and Sugar just three weeks ago, on Bert's insistence that the small table he and Mabel had shared since the kids had left was now more suited to card games than 'family meals'. Both Mabel and Helen had bristled at his use of the word 'family' and he had quickly added that it would be easier for him to spread out his newspaper without knocking things over if he had a larger surface.

The Reverend waved away Mrs Johns's offer of more scones. He thanked her for providing such a wonderful afternoon tea, effectively signalling she was no longer needed in the kitchen, and watched her all the way back into the shop before turning his attention to Helen.

'They're good you know,' he told her, licking his finger and using the moisture to pick up a few extra crumbs off the plate. Helen looked over her shoulder to see if Mrs Johns had witnessed the display of bad manners that would have won her a slap had she tried it.

'Now, Helen,' the Reverend said, with his back to her as he turned to the refrigerator, 'How've you been settling in here?'

Ah, there's the milk; yep, lid still intact.

Helen was considering her response when the Reverend turned back to her, shaking a bottle vigorously. 'Fine, I guess, Reverend.'

'Please, call me Avery.'

You're not a child anymore. Now, is there a pantry?

'I don't suppose there is any vanilla in that pantry, is there?'

'I could ask Mrs Johns,' Helen offered, getting slightly anxious at the thought she could be blamed for using something Mrs Johns treated as a luxury item, refusing to stock it in the shop and buying it in for customers only on a 'special order'.

'No, no, I'm sure if I rummage around I could find some, just a little for my milkshake. You want one?'

Helen found herself grinning again, a small one this time. *I'm not a child anymore, you know.* She shrugged in an offhand way.

'Sure.'

There were many more meetings with the Reverend over the next few months, always in the Johns' kitchen, and, despite Mabel's best efforts to skirt around the fringes, mostly out of earshot. The woman always had a chat with the Reverend first, and for a long time afterwards as well. Despite her fawning ways, Helen was aware that Mabel was genuinely looking for the Reverend to take some of the pressure off her in dealing with the fallout from Helen's volatile emotions.

On more than one occasion Mabel had told him at a less-than-discrete volume that she was simply vexed beyond belief and was not up to dealing with another teenager at her age. Once she had even inquired about the aunt in Adelaide and when the woman might take on 'the burden' that was rightly hers in the first place.

Helen picked up bits of conversations Mabel had had with others over the shop counter, hearing second or sometimes third hand how Ms Palmer had tried to get Helen into a school in Adelaide. She resented Mabel asking anyone who would listen in an almost shrill tone: 'Who's going to pay for that, I ask you?'

Helen knew the Reverend was married, but he must not have kids, because they would have played him for a fool for sure. His approach to moulding her into an easier house guest, which it seemed obvious he had been commissioned to do, was to ply her with milkshakes and chatter which purposefully avoided any sore spots or sensitive topics. Helen played along, amusing herself with the knowledge that, while Mabel put so much stock in the visits, they were completely pointless and simply an excuse for her to get out of chores.

She and the Reverend talked mostly about life in Kimbanyon, as if both were visitors making casual observations. They spoke of unusual items that had been brought in on the train and speculated on who had spread the latest rumour of a seam being discovered nearby. They wondered at how often mining conglomerates could be wooed to the town looking for 'the big one' only to find themselves significantly out of pocket for 'fool's gold'. They laughed at the often crude pageantry the residents united in to maintain the illusion for the sake of sharing in the spoils.

As a result of being in close proximity to one of Kimbanyon's most chatty gossips, Helen was usually pretty well informed. Whereas previously she had taken little interest in Mabel's phone conversations, these days she hovered somewhat closer, choosing to stack shelves or do chores that would position her close to the olive curtain so she could pick up snippets that might interest the Reverend.

Occasionally, the Reverend would quote to her from the bible or find parables that he obviously felt would benefit her in some way. These too, Helen played along with, unaware that her sense of wanting to please the Reverend was becoming something more than just a frivolous pastime.

Sometimes, during these conversations, they would blithely observe each other. Helen would notice that Avery's sideburns had been trimmed and, when her gaze traced the line of them up to his forehead, how strong and intelligent his brow looked. To prevent him catching her, she never allowed her gaze to settle too long. And she never looked into his eyes, but if she crossed their path, she softened her focus so that her thoughts might not be so easily discernible.

Avery's initial impressions of Helen were always coloured by Mabel's bleatings about her moody walkouts and her insistence on reading novels in the stockroom – a habit that played havoc with the inventory. Sometimes Mabel complained about the girl's poor attention to hygiene.

The Reverend put little stock in any of it. He had never found Helen to be unclean and, in moments of generosity, would even consider her attractive. Though her freckles collected in smears unevenly spread on either side of her nose, her jawline was slightly more angular than a woman's should be and her hair was often unkempt, she was smooth with youth and it appealed to him.

One afternoon when Mabel had accused the girl of being conceited, stubborn and not worthy of charity, Avery decided he had had enough. He informed Mabel he would be giving her a break from the girl and getting himself some fresh air at the same time, by ministering while they strolled.

The change suited Helen; she felt liberated, happier talking to the Reverend by her side, rather than having to defend herself across a table, and free from the distress of hearing Mabel shuffling around the edges.

Over many weeks, the conversation expanded with the surroundings, from how to live harmoniously with Bert and Mabel to her plans – for further study, for moving back home, and naturally, the benefits of keeping God in her life.

Some topics were left firmly in the kitchen. She no longer wanted to hear of Trudy Palmer's offers to coach her for scholarships to private boarding schools despite accepting a regular rotation of books from her extensive library. She no longer asked after her aunt or whether her aunt had asked after her. The woman had not even introduced herself at the funeral. Helen had already tossed her from the family tree.

So I'm a tree of one now.

There were ideas that germinated in Helen's head as she walked and at times seemed all consuming, yet foolish if she tried to communicate them. The thought of being alone was one that becalmed her on a raft in the middle of the ocean. To be orphaned, without siblings, without the comfort of another human being who shared her memories.

She had trouble discounting the thought that if her parents no longer existed, then she no longer existed – a soul adrift with no ability to connect with the world. She felt like she was in one of those movies where people sit by the bedside of their recently deceased loved one, clasping their hand and urging them to walk towards the light. But she couldn't work out if she was supposed to be the one by the bed or the one being expected to move on.

Despite the amount of time they would spend in each other's company and the depth of her anxiety, Helen would continue to find the Reverend a little distant. She was never sure he would take her feelings seriously if she was brave enough to reveal them to him. She knew it wasn't his job to make life easier for Mabel, although Mabel certainly thought it was, but still, she wasn't really sure why he kept coming.

When they were in the Johns' kitchen, he just raided the fridge and pantry. When they were on their walks, after long periods of silence during which he presumed to know what she was thinking, often the most he could offer was a passage or two from the bible. It seemed to make **him** feel better.

Perhaps if she was honest with him, it would be different. But Helen didn't know how to say that she hated herself because she couldn't recall whether her father's split thumbnail was on his left or right hand. She didn't know how to say that she felt angry almost all of the time because it was galling to live in a town that did not collectively shudder when the Tea and Sugar swept past – its rhythmic clacking suggesting not the slightest remorse for breaking her parents over its back. He might think her mad if she admitted that she had called out to her mother one night and half expected to feel her cool palm pressing on her forehead to stop her thrashing her head from side to side. And how could she tell him that, as she lay in the former bed of a boy who would flirt with her at school and then ignore her when others were around, she questioned the sincerity of everyone around her.

So, because Helen didn't know how to say those things, to describe how she tormented herself regularly and regretted it deeply, she hid them from the Reverend and Bert and Mabel and Trudy Palmer and other well intentioned townsfolk who ventured a pitying look at her across the shop floor.

Had her response to those who paid her any attention at this moment in her troubled life taken on the appearance of anger – of the defensive kick of an animal caught in a net that subdues with the realisation that it is being freed – Helen may have been forgiven. Instead, because she could not bring herself to trust, she belittled kind offers with a nervous hostility and earned herself a reputation for being ungrateful and cruel.

Helen may have forseen a time when she would no longer be captive to her fears and when a stranger might see her disposition as nothing worse than aloof. But as she struggled to deal with her loss, she could not have foreseen how her community would cast her in that moment. She could not have anticipated how, decades later, many of those same townsfolk would be gathered in a hall for the sole purpose of deciding whether she was eccentric or dangerous or how their prejudices would swing the pendulum.

The Wily Rooster.

[Spring, 1950]

The Wily Rooster Hotel, or 'Brooster' as it is called by the locals, is a homely outback pub built by a retired ganger named Riley Brewster. Brewster was a nuggetty, wifeless man who wore the dirt of his day so comfortably it couldn't be distinguished from the rich ochre tan that comes from years working under the sun.

The pain of a very physical life had been a factor for Brewster for so long that it did not occur to him that he might be carrying cancer. The paper bag found in his hand, that many suspected at the time was actually penned by the patron who found him collapsed behind the bar, made Brewster a local legend. Handwritten and to-the-point, it gave ownership of the Brooster to the town, declared it should never be sold and that all profits be fed back into the town, bar the wages of staff who should be descended from his chief bar maid or appointed by said person.

The Brooster in 1950 was a squat, mud brick 'watering hole', with a rust streaked tin roof, a broad timber bar, an eclectic décor and more importantly – being the last petrol stop before heading into the parched expanse of central Australia – a long standing reputation for generous servings of decent tucker and beer that was never watered down.

Men had a choice of two toilet areas. The outside one, behind corrugated iron walls, was no wider than a phone booth. Travellers were directed there, though few enjoyed the experience as it was also the last port of call for those leaving late at night who were so accustomed to leaning forward against trees that containment was a vain hope.

The women's toilet was to the left of the bar and was kept meticulously clean by Dot, owner and chief barmaid, three generations post. The only thing known to put Dot in a bad mood was the pervasive smell of the septic tank. For many years she tried valiantly to maintain a flower vase beside the hand sink in the women's toilet – there being no point in the men's – but flowers in enough abundance for that task were not easy to come by, so she stapled a large plastic sprig of lavender to the back of the door and sprayed it liberally with perfume – at times so liberally that it was almost as overwhelming as the tank.

The wall behind the bar of the Brooster was a collage of number plates, some with the obvious attraction of amusingly conjoined letters, such as SXE or DUM, and others with no apparent justification for their hanging, but a story for the asking. Many of those in the last category were bent from a collision with an unfortunate marsupial frozen in the wrong place at the wrong time by oncoming headlights.

Edward Johns had his own plate that he had scored for the bar soon after his 18th birthday. He had been making his first licensed ride to a cricket match for the Adelaide club that had invited him to play in their top division. It had been a big deal and he hadn't wanted to be late for the warm up.

The plate – EDD 588 – had been on a city car, navy blue with silver trim around the doors and nicely polished underneath the light spray of the day's dust. The driver had been overtaking him and lost control on the loose crust of the untarred surface, forcing Edward off the road and into a skid that separated him from his motorbike and saw them both scuttled over a number of metres.

The driver of the car stopped well ahead of him but did not leave the vehicle, watching with unseen emotion as the fallout settled in the rear view mirror. After about five minutes, Edward had pulled himself awkwardly to his feet, amazed he was still in one piece. As the driver shamefully chose to speed away from his victim, Edward reached into his backpack, withdrew a cricket ball, aimed and struck the number plate of the absconding car with such force it buckled, snapped its screws and fell to the road, skipping along it like a stone on a pond almost to Edward's feet.

When Edward read that number plate, now nailed between one a policeman donated from the truck of a tourist gone missing in Cooper Pedy and widely thought to be down a mine shaft ('SNK-666'), and one that spelt 'OOB', he knew he had been born lucky. When he looked at that plate, he saw himself by the side of the road, shaky but standing, saved by his leather pants and jacket from being smeared all over it. He read 588 as 'fate'. Ed's fate. And what a good shot, eh? So the plate came straight to the bar and the ball took pride of place in his bedroom, adorning a bookshelf beside the fielding trophy he had taken out that same season.

Edward didn't replace that motorbike, much to Mabel and Bert's relief; he drove a new car now and was pretty particular about avoiding chips in the paintwork when he came home, which wasn't that often. In fact, Mabel and Bert had seen so little of their children over the past year that they hadn't felt any urgent need to write to them and tell them that a young woman was living with them now. Actually, Bert didn't know whether to describe Helen as a tenant or a foster child, or whether they should be discussing adoption. As he couldn't explain the relationship to himself, he felt poorly equipped to explain it to others, particularly not his own children, and Mabel seemed equally inept, hoping it (meaning Helen) would all just go away before any explanation was necessary.

So when one of Edward's former school mates, George Munt, called Edward home for his birthday, Edward wasn't expecting to see his childhood room had been dispersed into labelled cardboard boxes at the back of the shop storeroom. Disgusted, he left his bags in his car and rang George, whose original invitation to Edward had been little more than an enthusiastic rendition of a rooster crowing over the phone, to pick him up for a few schooners and a feed.

It was well into the evening when George was called on to commiserate the fact that Edward's legendary cricket ball and trophy were now in boxes alongside the Cornflakes and washing powder.

'It's odd her staying there, don't you think?' Edward asked him, already beginning to slur his words.

'I mean it's my home; she's in my bedroom. I'd be well within my rights to just crawl in alongside her don't you reckon? I'm pretty sure she fancied me at school. Probably happy enough sharing for a night don't you reckon?'

'Hold on a minute, Romeo!'

'Well, where'm I s'posed to stay? In the pub with you all night?'

Edward threw George a look of repugnance and then braced for the onslaught.

On cue, George grabbed him in a headlock with one arm and started pummelling him in his stomach with the other. A ganger for five years now, with a generous coat of muscle and beer fat over most of his body, he went in harder than he had intended and Ed, whose lean muscles were the result of a university gym rather than hard labour, found himself winded and sliding from his bar stool onto his knees the second George released him.

The scuffle didn't phase Dot, a leathery grandmother with a penchant for pink lipstick, who had five sons of her own. 'Last drinks, boys,' she called in her smoker's rasp.

It was a big crowd tonight, with five miles of track expected to be laid in the morning, and almost as one, patrons headed for the bar.

Ed found himself being shoved into the legs of stools and unable to get off his hands and knees. He shouted out from between hairy skin and oily shorts: 'Oi, get off me; George get me up, ya bastard.'

A large hand came down and hoisted him back onto his feet.

'Ya may as well stay at mine tonight mate,' George offered. 'You can 'ave the couch, if you don't mind sharing with the dog. 'Course if he minds sharin' with you, you'll have to sleep on the floor.'

This time Ed lashed out, but it was more of a loose swipe than a punch; George's couch sounded like a good option, even if the pillow was going to be Max, his blue heeler. George caught him as Ed's body followed through on the punch that was never going to land and tossed his arm around his mate's shoulders to hold him up on the walk back to the truck.

As soon as Max, who'd been sleeping in the tray, saw George he went into a frenzy of wagging and barking. As soon as he saw Ed, he leapt down and squirmed nimbly up under the passenger side door which George had sprung ajar for Ed to get in.

To Ed's irritation, George didn't boot the dog out, he just sank into the driver's seat, staring straight ahead with the engine running, until Ed gave up and hauled himself into the back where the dog had been seconds before.

'Where the hell's your place anyway,' he called through the dusty back windscreen.

'A ways out a town,' George yelled back, pulling away from the pub. 'Have a snooze, mate; it's all good.'

Ed felt the chassis bounce up into his tailbone and slid across the tray on the hessian chaff bags underneath him. It was hopeless trying to prop himself up and once they crossed the rail line, he lay down and watched the lights of the town dwindle into pinheads.

The repetitive drum of the suspension skimming over the ripples in the road reverberated through the hessian Ed had swept into a pillow. He imagined himself riding a motorbike over a giant ribcage, which may be why he was dreaming about barbecued ribs when George shook him awake some time later.

'Wha? George, where's the sauce?'

'Think you've had enough of the sauce tonight, mate. I'm gonna help you into the house, but after that you'll have to settle the sleeping thing with Max, an' he's a bit sharper on his feet than you right now, so I'll hold him for a minnie and you go for it, alright?'

It was a clear night, with a fullish moon and the couch with its featherdown mint and white plaid cushions could be seen clearly through the window from the verandah.

George was struggling to hold Max. 'On yer marks, get set ....'

Pushing himself past, Ed tumbled in first. Max lunged forward to jump over him and George, still attached to the collar, was pulled in on top of them both.

The dog broke free and Ed pushed George off of him, the smell of his large exposed armpit sitting rank in his nostrils and their laughter leaving them breathless.

'Whose place is this anyway?' Ed asked, clawing himself into a sitting position and noticing with disdain that Max was already settling himself on the couch.

George had disappeared into the hallway and came back with a grey army blanket. He tossed it at Ed.

'I'm renting it from your dad, ya silly bastard.'

A significant interloper.

[Summer, 1950]

As time passed, Helen sharpened the edges of her routines with the stoicism of someone who feels in their bones that they have no choice. Deliveries were picked up from the station and boxes unloaded. Stock was recorded and lists tallied. Shelves were cleaned. Money saved, put aside for who knew what. Time was served without ambition or expectation.

She grew less interested in the gossip that sashayed across the counter daily, generated and served up by the same people. If the Johns children came to visit or Mabel had a dinner party, she took herself off for a walk up to the old miner's cottage with a book, or beyond it to the windmill.

Sometimes Helen would take her meal at the pub. She would read until it was brought to her, and then push aside her book to make room for the plate, nodding her thanks. Left in peace, she would sometimes raise her knife and fork and leave them slightly aloft, hovering briefly over her chicken parmigiana as she closed her eyes and took in the ambience – the clink of glasses on taps, the interplay of bodies moving in and out of each other's hearing, the odours of working men and the soft thud of darts finding their way into a cork board or balls rebounding off the felt edges of the pool table into others with a wholesome clack.

On the odd occasion, Helen would emerge from her momentary trance to hear a snigger too close to her to be directed at anyone else. She never acknowledged it or the fact that she knew the women, tilting their heads into each other's faces and giggling, from her school days. Like someone else's memories, she assigned them a remoteness that made her less vulnerable to the mockery.

As with many who suffer a significant loss, it was the routine of Helen's days and periodic escapes from them that kept her feet on the ground and persuaded her to participate in the minutia of her reasonably comfortable life. The Reverend Holbrook had become a significant interloper over the past year – his fortnightly visits as predictable as the Tea and Sugar, his idiosyncrasies and the line of his profile in various lights and locations growing in familiarity.

With unseen bravery, Helen had allowed the Reverend to share the special place inside her where her parents remained. She had let his knowing look stretch around her and his breath warm her until, eventually, he smelt of family.

As she worked through the maths problems and essays dropped off by Miss Palmer who was insisting she get through the eleventh grade (even if she had to do it in her own time), she found herself doodling the Reverend's face in her workbook.

She would place the sketches between the pages of a favourite novel, destroying the last at the end of each visit so she could replace it with a new one, taking in any changes she might notice in his appearance or mood with a fluid stroke of her pencil. The Reverend was not striking, but he had an intensity that appealed to her and was growing in her thoughts daily.

It was Mabel who interfered with her ability to perfect the image. Some eight months after that first visit, Helen's employer could no longer hide her resentment at the Reverend taking her away from her tasks and had dissuaded Avery from visiting during work hours, while insinuating that 'after hours' walks might encourage 'the gossips'. She had offended them both and in doing so, put a chink in the relationship.

Avery's visits became irregular and Helen found herself in a cycle of anticipation, disappointment, then grateful surprise or anxiousness. When he did come, he seemed distracted, concerned with other issues or people in the region, and seemingly intent on sticking to a schedule. Helen's insular mind, not yet able to wander far from its own wounds and frightened of being shunned by a broader intellect, had responded defensively.

Instead of showing her pleasure in seeing him, she would defy him, tease him, flirt with him, chide him. In trying to impress him with her wide reading and knowledge of philosophy, she also provocatively challenged the teachings of the church. If Avery appeared calm or distracted throughout her antics, it would send her searching for a sharper weapon to draw on him, to stop him in the tracks of his retreat.

Though he'd never said it out loud, Helen knew Avery relished the idea of saving souls – the more injured, the more estranged from God, the better. He was always saying, 'Wait on the Lord. Be of good courage, and he shall strengthen your heart,' because, in Helen's view, it was weak hearts he wanted to nurture, to take to God, to make strong and feel like he had a hand in reviving.

I've been doing better; that's why he's losing interest.

So Helen resolved to give him her weakened heart, tragically at almost the exact time that Avery had determined that his work with the girl was done. He had agreed with Mabel Johns that Helen had made good progress since the death of her parents – that her community and the church had rallied around her and brought her to the next juncture of her young adult life. The time was right to suggest to Helen that the walks come to an end; that she could come see him in future at the church, as did many other residents of Kimbanyon, when, or if, she had anything to talk about. He agreed with Mabel and Bert that they would continue to manage the Muldoon house as a rental property while she was living with them and to hand over the trust to Helen when she reached an appropriate age or married. He would give the girl the news on one last visit.

When Avery finally returned, he found Helen all smiles and eager to leave the shop in his company. The afternoon was clouded over, easing itself into the end of the day without a breeze, no prospect of rain but no significant humidity either.

Avery took off his suit jacket as soon as they were past the immediate township and slung it over his right shoulder. He felt Helen's warmth through his sleeve as she slipped her hand through the crook of his arm. Their steady pace, locked into the unspoken destination of the windmill and unmarred by conversation, connected each of them in their thinking to very different destinies. For Avery, this chapter – this weaning of an orphaned, irreligious child from her grief – would soon be in his past. It was not that he had run dry of charitable sentiment but it was, as Mabel had said, time to move on.

For everyone's sake.

Helen tried hard not to smile to herself, pleased as she was to be out in the open and by Avery's side. She would show him today that she was still in need of his care, that she was a willing, but challenging (and time consuming) candidate for salvation. She leant into the Reverend a little more, watching her feet and willing them not to rush him toward this revelation by reaching their destination too soon. They weaved deftly in between the blue-bush mounds along a familiar path.

'Helen, I've enjoyed our walks,' Avery said suddenly in a strangely bombastic tone, disconnecting Helen from her attempts to set her face in profound misery.

'But all good things come to an end.' As soon as he said it, Avery regretted his glib tone; it wasn't even something he had meant to say. So he blustered on, leaving no room for interpretation.

'Helen, you are a confident, capable young woman and I don't believe there is much more I can offer you through these personal visits.'

Avery ploughed on, surprised that Helen had not prickled, turning every pore on her body inside out with indignation as he had seen her do many times when she perceived she had been wronged. He feared she might stop dead and demand that he look her in the eye and repeat his words as if they meant something to him. So he strode on determinedly, dragging Helen with him, her grip now pincered painfully in the crook of his elbow.

A flush rose in Helen's cheeks as she clenched her jaw. She felt the sting of tears. They came silently, glazing her face like a slow drizzle set to fall weightlessly for days. Helen was as sure that she could conceal them from the Reverend, as she was that she could not stop them.

Avery pushed on with his agenda, offering no solace or chance for his words to sink in.

'You know you can always see me at the church. I come on the third Sunday of the month and I will always make time for you.'

The panic beating in her ears was too loud for Helen to think clearly. She tried to scoff, to show Avery she considered his words to be insincere and trite, but it came out wrong and she coughed, and then hiccupped. She withdrew her hand from his arm and turned her ashen face back toward town, the tears rolling unrestrained now and forcing her to stride away to keep the skin on her composure.

Avery followed her lead, a little startled at the girl's resolute step. The soft crush of rock underfoot seemed magnified by Helen's silence and Avery struggled to fend off an irritating sense that he might never be free of the girl – that the moment could linger in them unresolved unless kinder, more considered words were said. And yet, if those kinder, more considered words were said, it would be even harder to sever the tie. *And also to forget about her.*

With a longer stride, he came almost parallel with Helen at one point and extended his hand to her shoulder to encourage her to face him and acknowledge what he had said. At his touch, Helen had stopped but did not look at him. She ducked out from under his hand as if it were diseased, and then resumed walking. Avery simply followed, not wanting to provoke her further or deliver her back to the shop in a temper.

The railway line rose under their feet before either of them had realised they had walked that far and Helen slowed instinctively, noticing the shimmer of the lowering sun snaking along the metal.

She felt like she had stopped crying, though her skin was irritated and crusted as if by salt from ocean spray.

Suddenly her feet were standing at the spot where she had last waved goodbye to her parents. Abruptly, she turned to face the only person she felt a connection with to confirm that he was choosing now, at this place, to leave her. It was too much. Her breath chilled on her ribs and evaporated within the cavity.

'If it's done, it's done,' she said in a voice as steady as she could make it and extended a rigid hand. Avery accepted her gesture – almost comical in his eagerness – and shook vigorously on the deal.

The affront of his obvious relief stuck Helen in the guts, but she straightened herself and looked him in the eye: 'Your train leaves in ten minutes; I don't need to be walked back.'

Buoyed by the thought his headache may not turn into a migraine, Avery watched her walk away from him, all outline. She was taller than he remembered, the appearance accentuated by the trail of hair that fell between her shoulder blades. From behind, her constrained demeanour made it easy for Avery to convince himself that she would be fine, that any tears would be gone by the time she saw Mabel and Bert, and that she would get on with her life perfectly well without him.

As his mind emptied itself of a burden it no longer wanted to carry, he allowed himself a last visual indulgence. His gaze travelled a direct line down to her buttocks, curled around them and floated in the light, summer skirt that hung over her thighs. He remained mesmerised until he feared the heat of his stare might cause her to turn around. The Reverend patted down his waistcoat pocket and confirmed that there was a freshly ironed handkerchief in it, not because he was becoming emotional, but because he wanted to feel his wife's presence at that moment.

He felt the rumble of the train in his legs before the sound of its whistle registered its approach. He had never been more grateful to hear it.

Time to go home.

9.

Your ten minutes starts now ...

[January 15, 1943.]

'**I** aint goin' out there,' Mary said, retrieving her boots from under the kitchen table, having wrenched them off to let her swollen feet breathe during a sit down lunch.

'That place gives me the creeps. Send The Engineer; she'll do a better job anyway.'

Mary's last words were thrown back at Ruth from the front step as she swung away from the request and into her afternoon's work without so much as a look over her shoulder.

Ruth frowned. 'Well, you go tell her she's got the job, because there's no way I'm going anywhere near those Nazi bastards,' she called after her disinterested room mate.

As if on cue, Gwen strode into the kitchen fixing a bobby pin into her hair and retrieving another from between her teeth to secure the last wayward curl behind her ear. Most of the AWAS mechanics who shared accommodation at the farmhouse managed to slip in at midday for a clean-up and sometimes a sandwich and a cup of coffee in the kitchen before returning to the workshop to complete their jobs. This day Gwen had whipped in to splash some water over her face and grab clean overalls. She leant on the fridge door like a hungry teenager, looking for the sandwich she had made up for lunch the night before. Spying it behind the egg carton, she grabbed the greaseproof wrapping and bumped into Ruth as she stepped backwards to shut the door.

'Just who I was looking for. I need you to get on over to Dhurringile and pick up an officer, a Captain Holbrook, whose jeep broke down. You're to fix the vehicle on the spot if possible and, if not, bring him back to barracks and then retrieve the jeep.'

Gwen rolled her eyes at being assigned chauffer duty for the morning but wasn't entirely put out by the job; it was a pleasant enough drive to Dhurringile and as long as the officer wasn't a complete twat, it would be a change from her normal routine. Much to Ruth's surprise, Gwen shrugged and agreed, snatching an apple from a bowl on the table in case it turned into a long day – and accepting the job without opposition.

She stepped outside, scanned the few number plates remaining in the yard for the one with the chipped V, checked no-one had pilfered her tool kit from the back of the jeep, and headed for the old mansion, north of Murchison.

Given the workload that would be waiting for her when she got back, Gwen was keen to make sure she enjoyed everything about this short break, and paid particular attention to enjoying her surroundings.

Offshoots of the Goulburn and Murchison rivers couldn't be seen from the road, but the presence of water seemed to make the smells of the fauna she was passing more pungent. As she scanned the sides of the road for unpredictable wildlife, she noted with surprise the captivating nature of the shrubbery, with its brittle, leafless branches seeming to have been teased upwards, like an elderly woman's hair alive with static.

A spray of fine stones came up from under the wheels as Gwen's vehicle slipped over the edge of the broken bitumen on the old highway and back up again as she pulled her gaze back to the road.

Giant pine trees became more frequent, giving the impression that those who planted them many years before had intended to make an impression of grandeur on guests long before they reached the property. But the closer she got to Dhurringile, the more the pines began to look less like a guard of honour and more like wounded soldiers, staggering but not yet fallen. Substantial limbs had been ruthlessly hacked off and for the most part, left to rot on the ground. Chainsaws had chewed into the sides of trunks but not finished the job and new growth was spurting from stumps like the twisted mange of an unkempt dog.

Closer to the mansion the trees disappeared altogether. Growing taller on the gentle rise, and far more entrancing than the roadside foliage, was the Dhurringile's grand central tower, housing its most notorious prisoner – Theodor Detmers.

Gwen turned into the long driveway surrounded on both sides by a dry, open expanse that continued on the other side of the high wire fencing adjoining the checkpoint entry.

Flush from the battering of fresh air and time to herself, Gwen addressed the guards with unusual informality.

'When are you fellas gonna sort those trees out back there? One strong wind and they'll come down, block the road and maybe even kill someone.'

The guard on the driver's side had the bulk and proportions of a high school football player, and the confidence too it seemed. He took the liberty of letting his gaze travel all over Gwen before he answered.

'Yeah, yeah. You know the army: why do anything properly when you can do it by halves?'

The other guard lost interest at this point and began investigating something fascinating that he had retrieved from his ear. His colleague however was on a different wavelength and was now resting his forearm along the top of Gwen's windscreen and leaning down toward her in an openly flirtatious manner.

As a rule, Gwen believed most people were unremarkable. It was, however, a conviction that she was prepared to test out in the field, and doing so provided her with an infallible source of entertainment. Ironically, it also imbued her with a positive outlook, because challenging her low expectations forced her to look for the good in people.

When meeting someone for the first time, Gwen stayed alert to distinguishing traits that might elevate his or her character into the mildly interesting category; it could be in the steering of a conversation, the telling of a half-truth, or even the suggestion of being a deep thinker brought on by a quirk of appearance or mannerism.

According to the rules Gwen created for the pastime, the existence of any of these traits had to be revealed to her within the first ten minutes (although a little extra time might be allowed for those who didn't speak English). The game had become such a favourite that, even when she didn't engage her private protocol, Gwen was inclined to tune out after the allotted time and had rarely given anyone who failed within it a second thought.

He has amazing eyes, but I'm still predicting the clock'll run out on this one!

'Warms me heart to see a pretty girl smile,' the Corporal said with a wink, foolishly believing Gwen was being charmed rather than amusing herself at his expense.

The young man had a chance of getting over the line with Gwen based on his looks alone if not for the fact that he seemed incapable of collecting his facial features in any other formation than a leer.

So, after just a few minutes, and despite having begun the informal conversation, Gwen found herself irritated. She checked his shirt for a name.

'I'm here to see to a jeep and pick up a Captain Holbrook. Is there something else you need Corporal Bates?'

Being diminutive, with light brown curly hair that bleached brassy in the sun, Gwen had often been likened in looks, if not temperament, to the singing, tap dancing child movie star, Shirley Temple, when she was younger. As an adult, her urchin-like appearance seemed to strip her of any bearing and meant she had to work harder to be taken seriously, particularly by men.

It made being in the AWAS, and having the ability to achieve rank, that much more satisfying. By the time she was in her second year in uniform, she had gone from Craftsman to Corporal and, as her training and skills had progressed, she had been promoted to Sergeant.

Gwen was one of the more senior women in the house, but it was foolish to pull rank there. Once a Craftswoman had attempted to draw up a shower list according to seniority, failing to recognise the shifting hours that everyone worked and how impossible it was to keep track of your own shampoos, let alone the rank of someone clad only in a towel who may, or may not, be needed urgently elsewhere. In the end, the routine reverted to the less stressful mayhem of first in, best dressed, and last in, quickest out – generally because the water was cold by then.

When it came to the outside world however, having the rank of Sergeant had its benefits, and today's squirming of this Corporal rated as one of them.

'Your papers seem in order. Straight up to the main entrance, Sergeant.'

You're all business now, aren't you, Corporal? How's that warmin' your heart?

The officer Gwen had been sent to collect made her wait for more than two hours beyond the time it had taken her to ascertain that his abandoned jeep would need to be towed. She hadn't been able to arrange it in that time, so it meant her day was now going to be impossibly long and the screeching of cockatoos that seemed to have followed her back along the highway just added to her frustration and restlessness.

Finally, as she was dozing off, her head on the steering wheel, she heard voices and looked up to see two men step out from under the arches. Gwen recognised the shorter, rounder one as the Camp Commander, Major Burns and saw that the other man was a Captain, a Captain and a Padre. Major Burns shielded his eyes as he turned to the other man, whose kit bag was so full the straps barely contained it, and extended his hand. He spoke clearly but at a level indicating it was a private conversation.

'Thank you Padre; your assistance is much appreciated. We'll take care of the paperwork at this end, but if you could see your way clear to coming back over the next few days, it would really help us out.'

The Padre shook the Major's hand, then pulled a handkerchief from his pocket, dabbed his forehead and nodded. Gwen was curious to see more of the Padre's face but he dropped his gaze and his eyes disappeared into the shadows beneath them.

The Major turned back toward the alcove. 'Excellent,' he noted to himself, his thoughts moving on to other things as he was blanketed in shade.

The Padre stood for a minute or two, oblivious to Gwen's salute, then picked up his kit and walked toward the jeep.

'You must be my driver?'

Gwen tightened up her wiltering arm.

He's quite young. You don't think of padres as young. Or handsome.

'Yes, sir.'

Gwen expected him to either return the salute or wave away the formality but neither happened.

'Well, I'd like to get wherever it is we're going as soon as possible.'

There was a business to the man that wasn't there seconds before and Gwen found herself bristling.

'I understand there's a vehicle …'

'Never mind that now; just get me somewhere I can clean up, would you?'

Unbelievably rude for a padre! Your ten minutes starts now.

The ride back to base was uneventful – no rabbits running across the road, no cockatoos to startle them in the open cabin of the jeep, and disappointingly, very little conversation. Usually drivers found their pickups, no matter what the rank, were full of questions when they first arrived. Perhaps they saw it as a chance to casually quiz someone they were unlikely to have much to do with once safely delivered, about innocuous things like the quality of rations and regularity of leave. *To get a sense of the garrison,*

I guess. In return the drivers could expect to learn the purpose of their passenger's visit or posting and both parties would enjoy a conversation they would be unlikely to have with the other in a more formal setting.

Despite the fact that the padre had not followed this expected pattern, Gwen was intrigued by him. She began filling the silence with an imagined conversation of questions she thought he might have asked her and found her answers came remarkably easily.

She asked herself: *'So, tell me Sergeant Dalana, when was the last time you attended church?*

(And answered) 'I've never felt a need for it, padre; I believe that people are responsible for everything that happens to them and therefore not answerable to the whims of God.'

Gwen veered around a pothole she had dropped into sharply on the way in, having made a mental note to avoid it on the way back. The padre was still staring straight ahead, the point of his focus unchanged.

'I see,' was the ineffectual response Gwen gave on his behalf, conveniently opening the way for her to further explain her position.

'Relying on God to make plans for us, or blaming God's plan for everything bad that happens to us – like there's nothing we could have done to prevent it or should do to change it – seems like a complete cop out to me.'

Gwen sat more upright in her seat, quietly congratulating herself on how well she had articulated her views (and how well they had been noted by the Reverend). She relaxed her grip on the wheel and steered with one hand from the bottom, occasionally checking the sides of the road for random wildlife that might cross their path.

To relieve the boredom of a steadfastly silent passenger, she continued her imaginary conversation.

'I'm sorry to hear that you are missing out on everything God and the church have to offer,' she told herself on the padre's behalf, heightening her own entertainment by allowing him a mildly sarcastic tone.

One of her eyebrows wandered up her forehead in a theatrical manner reminiscent of the young guard she had brought down a peg some time earlier and a cockiness took hold of her.

*'That's not to say I believe you have **nothing** to offer me, padre!'*

Despite being the architect of the dialogue, the flirtatious turn embarrassed Gwen. She blushed, and returned her left hand to the wheel only to realise they were already upon the barracks. She turned sharply, sending up a spray of gravel and causing the Reverend to grab onto the windscreen of the doorless jeep.

'Thank you, Corporal … , I think,' Avery said, when they had pulled up, patting both hands on his thighs a couple of times the way an old person does when they're nervous about tackling something physically challenging.

'Right, let's get this day done and dusted,' he said more to himself than anyone else, and reached for his kit bag.

The back of the jeep was empty, the bag having slid off and skidded along the drive when Gwen had swerved. They spotted it at the same time, about about ten paces behind them. The padre jumped out, strode over and scooped it up, surprisingly without a word.

Gwen winced just a little as she watched him turn his kit over to satisfy himself that the straps had held and nothing had been lost.

As Avery strode towards his lodgings, keen now to put some distance between them, Gwen called after him from the jeep, 'It's Sergeant actually, Padre.'

Avery turned abruptly at the door to see the face of the driver who had the temerity to take that tone after letting his kit fly out the back.

Looks like Shirley Temple, thinks she's Sugar Ray Robinson!

'I might see you at dinner Padre. You'll find we all muck in together here,' Gwen continued, wondering herself why she couldn't just let it go.

Avery was desperate to end the small talk, get clean, comfortable and have a drink.

'Sergeant, I'd like to unpack whatever's not broken in my kit, have a quick shave and end my first day here with a glass of something smooth in my hand, so all I need from you right this minute is directions to the officers' mess.'

Gwen wouldn't see Avery in the mess that night. It was near five o'clock when she had delivered him to the camp and almost seven by the time she had got his jeep back from Dhurringile. And she still had to clear her day sheet.

The last item on the list was a crankshaft check, an unpleasant job for three reasons. Firstly, the damn thing weighed at least 68 pounds. Secondly, establishing how to proceed was a tedious process; if the circular or tapered dimensions of the main bearing journal and connecting rod journals were more than .001 of an inch out of specification, the shaft would have to be replaced. Thirdly, installing a new crankshaft involved cleaning all oil passages by blowing them with compressed air. The manual actually suggested 'placing the fingers on the oil hole in three of the bearings while the nozzle of the air gun is placed in the oil inlet of the cylinder block'. Not only did it mean black fingers and nails for days, short of a gravelly scrub, but also the slightest shift could mean a spray of oil in the face, which is what happened to Gwen that evening.

By the time she got back to the house all she wanted to do was take a long, pounding shower. She ditched her boots, grabbed the shampoo she kept in a small suitcase under her bed and stared momentarily at the last fresh razor in her hidden supplies.

If I shave my legs tonight, I could probably slip away for a swim in the river tomorrow after work. If I could be bothered.

If not for dinner, Gwen's timing for a shower was perfect. It was late enough for the water to have reheated in the tank and for no-one to be pressuring her to get out. She turned up the flow so it was torrential and lifted her face to it. Then she let her head fall onto her chest and rotated her shoulders so every tensed muscle had the chance to be battered by the warmth. Her arms limp, she watched for a few minutes as the dark streams of oily water cascading from her fingertips found their way in rivulets to her toes. Then she closed her eyes and allowed everything to drain away.

10.

Now the devil can polish his own boots.

[Earlier that day, January 15, 1943.]

'Ah, Padre, thank you for coming.'

Camp Commander Tom Burns swung from behind his desk with the air of an executive welcoming the person who would spare him the job of firing most of his workforce.

A bombastic man of healthy proportions, he greeted the Padre with an enthusiastic 'Excellent' and pumped Avery's hand until it grew sweaty.

'Before we get started Major,' the Padre jumped in, 'Would you mind sending someone to get my jeep? It broke down a few miles out. I managed to hitch a ride here but I'll need a lift to the barracks when we're done if that can be arranged.'

'Of course,' the Major replied, needing only to catch the eye of the Corporal who had escorted Avery to his office to know that it would be done.

When they were alone, the Major moved to the front of his desk and perched on the edge. Avery had the impression that the Commander liked to be on the move but he also exuded a settled competency – a combination that immediately put him at ease.

'It's an interesting posting this one Padre. Have you spent much time at the camps?'

'Not yet. I'm not long back from overseas, so I'm still catching up I'm afraid.'

'Of course. You'll find your way around in no time I'm sure, but I'll give you a brief overview before we get to the business at hand,' the Major said, handing a glass of water to a grateful Avery.

'There are four civilian camps for mostly Germans and Italians, and to a lesser extent, Japanese. Camps 1 and 2, near Tatura, are for single men and we've put the families at Camps 3 and 4, near Rushworth. There's around about a thousand interned in each of those camps and they fare pretty well, with a decent hospital and school, and even the opportunity to go work on the local farms and orchards.

'Then there's three POW camps, including Dhurringile, and we can take up to 150 German officers and around 50 other ranks here.

'You'll be garrisoned outside one of Camp 13's compounds I'd imagine. They're pretty rudimentary barracks – the usual gal iron I'm afraid – but the tucker is always fresh and in good supply.'

The slight frown on the Padre's face caused the Major to pause.

'Well, I imagine that's all you need to know for now on that score,' he offered.

'Why don't you have a read of the file. Then I'll show you around and you can ask me what you like before you meet the Sergeant.'

The Major pulled open a deep drawer of the filing cabinet behind him and flicked through a number of manila folders, choosing one marked only with a date, and presented it to Avery across the green leather inlay of his rather fine desk.

'I'd like to handle this matter internally,' he told the padre in a more serious tone.

'One more dead German is just collateral damage as far as I'm concerned. But Land HQ don't want Sergeant Tenterfield returning to barracks until special investigations have spoken to him and I want him to be in good nick when they get here. That's where you come in Padre.'

The last sentence would linger in Avery's mind like the press of their first handshake.

The Major poured himself a glass of water, set himself up with his own reading then dropped into a round-backed, leather-seated chair that squeaked as he rocked it back on its coil.

Avery picked the pertinent elements from the file he'd been handed and repeated them silently to himself in the hope of retaining the detail.

Tenterfield followed his son Albert into the services, despite being excused from duty to continue farming. Was stationed at Dhurringile in 1940, guarding internees and supervising work release. Stationed at Camp 1 following transfer of internees. Returned to Dhurringile when it reopened as a POW camp. Currently serving at the rank of Sergeant. Reprimanded for drunkenness on duty following news of the sinking of HMAS Sydney by the German Raider HSK Kormoran off Western Australia in November, 1941. Albert Tenterfield was among those presumed drowned. Several further incidents of drunkeness in 1942 requiring discipline. On 12/01/43 Sgt. Tenterfield discharged his weapon in the German quarters with the result that the prisoner Gunter Merkle died of a head wound. Gave himself up to Sgt James Hollis who was first to the scene. Relieved of arms. Confined on site. Under guard awaiting investigation by Land HQ.

The Major nodded at the file in Avery's hands when the Padre finally looked up.

'It's lucky Tenterfield missed his target, really. If he hadn't, I'm fairly certain we'd have a mutiny on our hands.'

Avery could only raise his eyebrows, exhausted as he was by the morning thus far and wishing he had settled in at the barracks first and attended Dhurringile the next day.

'Right, let's get some air,' the Major said enthusiastically.

Avery gladly followed him back through the enormous entrance hall and into the Italianate portico of the mansion. He shielded his eyes from the glare of sunlight that was bouncing off everything it seemed.

The Major preempted the Padre's questions by continuing his briefing.

'You might think that because we're a small camp with mostly officers that we might have less trouble, but don't make that mistake Padre. We have some pretty serious Nazis here and it means our boys have to stomach things up close and personal.'

'Such as …?'

'One of the Reich's favourite sons – Theo Detmers. The Germans awarded him the Knights Cross for torpedoing the Sydney and then promoted him to Captain last year. Some of the guards found the presentations pretty galling.'

The Major now stepped out of the portico onto the driveway, far away enough to admire the breadth of the mansion in front of them.

'Impressive, isn't she?'

Avery looked up.

'That tower block's a statement alright,' the Padre agreed.

'There's a second mansion south of here across the river, built by the brother of the fellow who built this place. When they wanted to get in touch, they'd light a signal from their towers and one or the other would come over.'

'Major, do you mind if we get out of the glare for a bit? I've got a corker of a headache.'

'Of course.'

The men moved back under the tall brick columns that ascended to white archways that framed a tunnel of shade traversing the building's northern and western frontages. The clip of their soles on tiles echoed as they walked.

As they turned the corner, they simultaneously stepped into the adjoining shade provided by a giant gum tree. Avery was seduced by the fall of its broad trunk – like milk pouring from the sky. He felt compelled to look up to see how far it stretched and was struck again, this time by the way the light weaved through the drizzled canopy – colouring the thin leaves olive green where the shade fell and apple green where it struck.

'How do they get on generally – the guards and prisoners?'

'Generally? Not much trouble. But it has to be managed. We had some maps stolen from a truck once and Detmers turned up bold as brass and handed them over to me the next day, no doubt having already copied and memorised them. There was a push by the guards to do daily searches of the rooms after that and some of them didn't like my call, I'm sure.'

The men strolled past prisoners in the exercise yard, individual garden plots and long lines of washing before stopping near the eastern end of the mansion.

Avery took the opportunity to pose a question he had been mulling over for some time.

'Is Tenterfield the only guard to have lost a son to a German now held in the camp?'

'That would be a difficult thing to find out, Padre. But I'll tell you this, most of these prisoners aren't trying to make things worse for themselves.

'I'll give you an example of something I found quite astounding. A while back we had a fundraiser here for the families of The Sydney. Most of the garrison came and a good many townsfolk. Some of the prisoners heard the garrison orchestra was going to play and offered to join in.

'It's not always that convivial, of course. We have our moments,' the Major continued with a wry smile. 'But, as you can see, we're well set up to deal with those.'

As the men continued to walk along the eastern end side of the former mansion, Avery looked down the wall to the left of his feet and saw several basement rooms. A lightwell just wide enough to pace in bordered them and was connected to ground level by a ceiling of barbed wire.

'You had this built, Major?'

'Didn't need to! There's four rooms down there, built by the original owners as a kind of summer home to get away from the heat. They've been modified of course, but they're perfect for solitary confinement.'

The men walked on in a clammy heat, the coolness that seemed to have followed them from the alcove long gone. Avery waved at the back of his neck, mistaking the solar fusing of his skin and collar with the sting of an insect. He wondered whether his hair was beginning to thin on top and whether in fact those underground cells were a blessing rather than a punishment for those interned.

The Major, despite wearing a slouch hat, seemed similarly uncomfortable. 'Let's get out of this heat, shall we?'

Once back in the office, Avery turned his attention to the file he'd left there.

'How did the shooting come about, Major? There's not a lot of detail here.'

'Tenterfield was in charge of escorting the officers to their rooms from the yard,' the Major explained, pouring them both another glass of water, 'and this Eisenheimer got under his skin about something. Never shuts up that one – thinks he's running his own personal Reich.

'It seems Tenterfield was walking back along the hall, checking the rooms, heard Eisenheimer giving his batman an order and shot off his weapon. No provocation as far as I can tell, but you might be able to tell me something more after you've spoken to him.'

'Is there any chance it was an accident?'
'We think it was spontaneous, but that Eisenheimer was the target. It's a bit confusing but his batman – Gunter Merkle – might have tried to stop it by stepping between them. Alternately, I wouldn't put it past Eisenheimer to have pulled Merkle in front of him.' Avery nodded, trying to picture it.

The Major laid his empty glass to rest on the desktop.

Avery checked a date in the file.

'Just one more question, Major. This man's been a guard here for years, so what set him off last week?'

'Ah, now that's something I think I **have** worked out. The day of the shooting would have been his son's 22nd birthday.'

***

T he Vagabond, a columnist for *The Argus*, climbed the tower of Dhurringile in September, 1884, and described the view for the newspaper's readers as follows.

'The ranges afar off, the long tract of level country, park like where it has been cleared, but dismal to the eye where there is nought but mile after mile of dead gum, the woolshed close at hand where fleeces are transmuted into gold – all this must be a pleasing sight to the owner of these broad acres, and with a bottle of choice Falerian and a two dollar cigar, I think I could even find life endurable under such circumstances.'

The view from the second storey room where Edward Percival Tenterfield was detained some sixty years later was just as infinite, but perhaps less endurable. After years of being turned over for wheat, lucerne, and grazing, the paddocks now lay fallow – no doubt a frustrating sight for a farmer who had walked off his land to serve his country. A dirt road in the distance may have given the Sergeant a subliminal impression that there was direction in his life – a future beyond his predicament – but, as it ran parallel to the horizon and without intersection, it added no sense of purpose to the landscape. The one consistently pleasurable aspect of the room was that it looked out over a balcony to an immense eucalypt that offered a prism of filtered light, greenery and – when the wind or rain tussled its leaves – a pungent aroma through which everything else could be taken in.

The Padre made his way to Sergeant Tenterfield via a central staircase with an ornately carved bannister. A broad landing, marking its change in direction half way up, was floodlit through six stained glass windows of differing sizes, depicting rural scenes, animals and a coat of arms. If Avery appreciated any of the features, it was only in the context of how surreal such grandeur seemed – rising as it was in the centre of a prison camp.

Under guard by the military police, Tenterfield was revealed to be sitting at a simple desk, his posture erect and his feet squared flat on the floor. A piece of paper lay before him, several pencils on its blank face.

'Sergeant Tenterfield,' Avery ventured after nodding for the guard to close the door, 'mind if I chat with you a while?'

When no reply came, he prodded again without raising his voice: 'Sergeant Tenterfield?'

The tone of the response was as flat and thin as the wretched soul delivering it: 'If you like.'

Avery sat on one of the two beds on either side of the desk, not close enough to crowd the man, but not so far away as to suggest they were on anything but the same side.

Tenterfield turned his head slowly to see what new level of military menace had come to draw him out. He saw a man about ten years younger than him, though it was often hard to be certain about the age of people during war.

'You should know you're wasting your time: I'm saving it for the court martial,' he mumbled.

Avery adopted a casual tone.

'I'm Captain Holbrook, the new district chaplain, and I'm not here for any of that, Sergeant. This is more of an informal visit.'

Tenterfield shrugged and turned back to the blank sheet of paper and began a flowing, directionless sketch of the ghost gum outside the window. It was the same giant eucalyptus that Avery had admired earlier.

It was probably a result of extreme tiredness, but something about the way the light accentuated the side of Tenterfield's head as he drew, his back to Avery, reminded him of his father. He recalled how the fresh growth from his crew cut had been scratchy on his face when hung over his father's shoulder in a sleepy carriage to bed. For a shiver of a moment, Avery forgot where he was.

'Feel free to leave anytime, Padre,' Tenterfield offered rudely, without turning around.

The words brought Avery back to the confines of the room and with some effort, he redirected his mind to the case file.

'You're not needed here you know,' the Sergeant repeated slowly, somewhat annoyed that Padre was still hovering with nothing to say.

'You might be right,' Avery replied, 'but what if there's a chance that I can help you and you don't take it?

Tenterfield came back at him with vigour.

'Look Padre, if I tell you anything about what happened in that room, I go down. Right now, it's my word against a Nazi officer and I reckon I'll take my chances explainin' myself to the big brass the way I want to, not the way you want – with me sobbin' and you threat'n'n me with God 'til I confess.'

'I'd hate to think I've ever threatened anyone with God, Sergeant,' Avery replied with feigned indignation, 'and I'm certainly not here to put you under any more stress.'

'But you would like my confession …'

Given Tenterfield's reported silence over the past three days, Avery was both taken aback and pleased at his willingness now to be so vocal.

It didn't mean his job would be easy. Tenterfield's eyes were furtive and he was quick to vitriol. Avery felt that the man still had the twitch of the shooting about him.

'Cigarette?' the padre offered, standing up to withdraw the packet from his pocket and eyeing Tenterfield's drawing across his shoulder.

It captured a sweeping canopy but had little tonal depth. Perhaps sensitive to the critical gaze, Tenterfield switched pencils and began shading one side of the branches.

'No thanks Padre – I don't smoke. Don't drink either. Doesn't make me a popular guy around here.'

Avery smiled, remembering the case notes. He withdrew a cigarette, tapped it a few times on the packet, then flipped it to the other end and tapped again.

A bright square sharpened on the carpet as the sun reached across the balcony. The Sergeant suddenly screwed up the sketch and moved to one of the beds, looking a lot like he might lie down and go to sleep.

'I never smoked 'til I came here,' Avery revealed, hoping to attract Tenterfield back to the conversation.

He gripped the cigarette in the corner of his mouth and patted his pockets down to find his matches.

Damn, I've left them on the bonnet of the jeep.

He returned the cigarette reluctantly to the pack and left it on the edge of the desk. Tenterfield was eyeing him halfheartedly.

'You never smoked 'til you came to the camps?'

Avery laughed and sat down on the bed opposite.

'No, 'til I came to Australia.'

'Where you from originally?'

'Birmingham.'

'So how'd you end up here?'

'Guess the folks just thought I'd be a better farmer than a dustman.'

Absent mindedly, Avery reached for his cigarettes. Tenterfield watched the Padre go through his routine, relieved to be outside his own story for a while. Avery patted his empty pockets again before returning the unlit cigarette to the pack with some disgust in himself for the repetition.

Tenterfield smiled.

'D'you go to one of them farm schools then?'

'Yep. I was a happy, impoverished teenager getting on with life in the motherland, when someone over here dreamt up a scheme to buy a Dreadnought for the British Navy to show how much they cared.

'When that didn't happen, some other bright spark decided the money raised for the ship could be spent bringing British boys out to train up for farming. Odd swap, but there you go!'

Tenterfield seemed to be mulling it over. Avery, who knew from experience that sharing something personal often relaxed a person who was slow to trust, gave him a little extra.

He got up, closed the door on the guard and leant against it to resume his story.

'I spent a couple of months at Scheyville, just outside Sydney, learning that I was never going to be any good on the land, then a couple of years getting a hiding from unhappy farmers. Soon as I could, I joined the army and here I am.'

'But why a chaplain?'

'There was a man who used to visit Scheyville – a priest. He brought me cigarettes and books, extra food sometimes. Anyway, I hated farming and the army seemed a good way out, but I couldn't see myself firing a weapon …'

Tenterfield looked at Avery like he was being judged anew, prompting the Padre to quickly qualify his comment.

'Don't get me wrong – I was glad to be surrounded by great marksmen in Malaya – but it wasn't a good fit for me, so I asked Father Lucas for advice and he convinced me I knew the teachings well enough to be a an army chaplain and that the training would be pretty straightforward.'

Not that I can do the job without making it up as I go along most of the time!

Tenterfield cut back into the story, bemused by what he'd just heard.

'So you never wanted to fire a weapon but you've been in Malaya? I always thought you guys stayed away from the action – you know, the chairbourne division.'

It was the second time Tenterfield had made Avery smile. He'd heard of padres being called the 'paragraph' division because of the letters they would write home for the injured or dead, but not that.

Avery, who had been looking out the window onto the silent branches, now moved back to sit on the bed facing the Sergeant.

'We're all doing our bit, Edward, and the fact is, most of it you could live without.'

Tenterfield could feel himself letting go. Implausibly, he felt like he was talking to an old friend, as if they were sitting on a bench under a tree near the tyre swing at his old farmhouse, and perhaps any minute now, his wife might bring them a cold beer and a plate of pikelets.

'So that's my story anyway,' Avery said after a short silence, and waited. When Tenterfield didn't look like he might fill the void, the

Padre searched his mind for another way in, but it would not be necessary.

'He wasn't even supposed to be there – my boy,' Tenterfield offered.

'He never even swum anywhere but a dam fulla yabbies. What kind of army puts a boy like that on a gunship? You sign up for the airforce and they put you on a boat. What'd they mix the forms up or something?'

A swell was building under the Sergeant's face, and he gave the Padre such a look of vulnerability that Avery had to resist an urge to put a hand on his shoulder.

Tenterfield dropped his head into his hands, his oversized knuckles jutting out of his greying, cropped hair like boulders in a hazed cornfield.

'I'm a churchgoing man, Padre,' he said softly, 'but this – what's going on here – it's just wrong.'

'Tell me more about Albert,' Avery said gently. Tenterfield looked up, his eyes glowing with an impossible heat.

'My boy was a gift, Padre. He was my whole life. When my wife died, that was hard, but we did alright. He set his sights on the Royal Show and practiced his wood chopping 'til that axe was like an extention of his hand. An' he could ride like a mountain man. Sometimes he would cut through the herd and send 'em everywhere just to round 'em up again. Used to drive me nuts!'

'He sounds like a wonderful lad,' Avery offered, immediately regretting using the present tense.

It did not jar with Tenterfield; now that he'd started talking, he didn't seem able to stop.

'We never fought like we did 'bout him joining the airforce. He wanted to go so bad but he never went 'til he got my permission. Convinced me that bein' up in the air was gonna be safer than in some jungle getting a bayonet in the guts.'

Tenterfield's face had been alternately lively and sunken as his love brought his son back to life and the memory of his death drained them both.

He took to his feet, too agitated to remain seated but limited in his ability to pace by the constraints of the room. He put his back to the door, and periodically chewed at his thumbnail as he spoke.

'They put him in 9 Squadron to fly these things called Seagulls, except him and his mates called them walruses. He wrote me about how they'd catapult these things off the ship, with him in them, and they'd fly around on their missions, and when they get back, they just land on the water and wait to be picked up by a crane that drops them back on board.

'He was scared witless of drowning but he was havin' a real adventure, Padre; that's how he saw it.'

Tenterfield's tongue flicked to the floor the sliver of a nail that he had finally dislodged from between his teeth. The distraction dissolved, he turned to the desk and a fresh piece of paper.

Avery reached to the side of him for the cigarettes. He knew full well he had no matches, but felt the ritual would help him think.

'Edward, can you tell me about Albert's birthday?'

Tenterfield hesitated, then turned to the padre with narrowed eyes. He shook his head as if he should have known that's where the conversation was headed all along.

The Sergeant shunted his desk chair so that it partially faced the Padre and spoke to him in a conspiratorial tone.

'We all know the numbers don't add up: both ships go down, but 300 Germans survive, and every one of our boys dies. That's 600 and more of our boys dead.

'You know what they're saying about why the Germans survived? They're saying they strangled our boys in the water.'

Tenterfield lent closer to the Padre. His words came out like the growl of a threatened dog: 'And then they bring the German bastards here.'

He shifted to the bed and scratched his skull, back and forth with both hands, until he caught a thin tuft of hair. He dislodged it from under a fingernail with a shake that did not seem to completely leave his hand.

'They're just rumours, Edward,' Avery began, but Tenterfield cut him off, his leg acquiring its own shiver.

'The crew of the Kormoran, they put most of them out at Camp 6. You know what we call that? The holiday camp. They've got their quota of wood to chop and when that's done they can nick off for a swim in the river.'

'But the officers are here,' Avery reminded the Sergeant. 'They'll see the war out in this camp.'

'And what have I got to look forward to, Padre? For the rest of the war I get to listen to those officers barking at their lap dogs to remind everyone that they're something special in Nazi land. That's what.'

Tenterfield's whole face was now dripping off the bone. His nose ran. He spat with every second word and his eyes screamed out as if they had been washed in lime.

'How can they expect me to be part of this?'

Avery reached out to him, smothering the shiver of the man's fingers inside his hands and feeling, finally, the strength of the 'right' words rising within him.

'Bertie wasn't forsaken, Edward. He is with God now. And you will not be forsaken either. God will put strength in your heart.'

Tenterfield roughly withdrew his hands.

'Respectfully, Padre, you know that's bullshit; I shot a man who did nothing but salute.'

'Corinthians tells us that anyone who lives again in Christ is a new creation – that their former self is gone,' the Padre responded. 'It's true that you sinned in killing an unarmed man Edward, but you should think of that as an act of your former self.

'It's up to you to be the man you want to be. The Lord is most forgiving of those who accept their wrongdoing. Through his forgiveness you can become your new self, and He will be with you on that journey.'

A clench took hold of Tenterfield that would bring him pain in his jaw and the tendons of his hands into the last few hours of his life. He looked Avery directly in the eye.

'I won't be forgiven Padre, because I don't regret it. It's just wrong that Albert is dead and that these Germans are alive. It's wrong that these officers get to bunk in with their batmen and have their boots and bloody egos polished for them every night.

'And I'll tell you this for free Padre. When I saw that lap dog saluting that officer, like this guy was still in charge, I lost it; I told him to lower his arm but he wouldn't do it. So I did it for him. I put a hole in that salute. I splayed his fingers all over his face – put a big spray o' blood on Eisenhower's smug face too.'

Tenterfield's offensive grin waned almost as quickly as it had appeared.

'It doesn't matter whether I meant to kill Gruber or not. He's dead. So you see, I'm screwed. No regret, no repentance, no forgiveness, no redemption. No seeing my son in Heaven. Screwed. Royally.

'But don't worry Padre, it won't be on your head. You see, I've made my peace with God already. We already see eye to eye on this, according to the book of John.'

Avery was both disappointed and intrigued – emotions that Tenterfield found hard to read on his face.

'You're surprised I know my bible, aren't you? You can thank my mother for that. In the book of John, you see, we're told not to love the world or anything in the world. "Do not love the world" – that's John right there. "For everything in the world – the cravings of sinful man, his lust, his boasting" –and maybe even the murder of a Gerry officer, Padre – "these things don't come from God, but from the world". And the bible tells us that if anyone loves this world – our world, Padre, with its bombs and Gerry bastards – well he doesn't have the love of the Father in him.

'Well, I was guilty of loving two things in this world – my wonderful wife and my boy. And He took them both. We'll never win against Him, so we may as well see it His way. So, now I love nothing about this world, specially not those Nazi officers or their suckup handmaids.'

Avery wanted Tenterfield to feel heard. He wanted him to get it all off his chest and not to be seen as the one who beat him down. When there seemed to be enough of a pause, he attempted an explanation of the passage from John. But Tenterfield rallied and would have none of it.

'That's what it says, Padre. Look it up if you like. I don't need to; I know it by heart. Bottom line is I've had the chat with God, we've come to an understanding, and we don't need any middle man to confuse the matter.

'But I can see that that's not good enough for you, so seeing as I'm all talked out, how about you come back tomorrow and we'll thrash it out then. Maybe bring some lunch.'

With that, an indolent Tenterfield swung his legs up onto the bed and lay down. He rolled into the wall and shunned all behind him.

As Avery moved to the door, happy enough to let the man sleep and return the next day, Tenterfield gave him a last muffled thought.

'You know scriptures wasn't the only thing my mother taught me. She used to say "the Devil finds work for idle hands". Well, now the Devil can polish his own boots.'

11.

A rare moment of internal sunshine.

[January 16, 1943.]

The trucks were always the hardest worked of the vehicles used by the army. They often carried far more than they should and were the least well maintained. The trucks were picked up and signed for but rarely were they in the 'care' of their drivers. Any concern over the consequences of thrashing the motor or generally treating the vehicle with contempt didn't seem to apply to the trucks because they were rarely in the company of a driver for more than a few hours at a time, or at most, a day. This was particularly true of the 1½ tonners – not big enough for carting machinery around but useful for transporting people, soldiers, prisoners, building materials, office equipment, furniture and anything else that could conceivably be scaled up from a medium to large sized job with little more than an eyeball assessment and an 'I reckon it'll be right'.

Small jobs rarely came Gwen's way. Because she had a reputation for being able to get vehicles back on the road quickly, they were usually in need of a total overhaul, and for the most part this was the way she liked it.

The weather on the day following Gwen's first meeting with Avery was spectacular: open, blue, cloudless, crisp in the morning, softening into a breezy butterfly's caress in the midday shade and bordering on sultry in the early evening.

Several mechanics were already at work in the large galvanised iron hangar when Gwen arrived at 6.30am. The doors were already retracted to their furthest point, allowing the allure of the morning and the bush, with its tang of warming gum leaves, to waft in briefly, not to be overpowered in her nostrils by the heavy smells of diesel and oil for at least half an hour while she prepared her workspace.

Like her, Gwen's colleagues were aiming for an early finish, but her job sheet was the only one which included an overhaul, diminishing both her mood and the prospects for a swim significantly. She spotted the Chevrolet truck, parked alongside the other four vehicles she had been assigned for the week, in the eastern corner of the workshop – her usual station. The familiar number plate only caused her more grief. The model came with an engine that should rise to 90 horsepower at 3300 revolutions per minute, but, according to the scrawled note marked for Sgt Dalana under the windscreen wiper, this truck could 'easily be overtaken by a cyclist on any rise bigger than an anthill'.

It should be retired, not overhauled.

Not to be defeated, Gwen determined it would be a straightforward job done in record time. She set herself up on the mobile tool caddy she had fashioned from a tea trolley, laying out the tools she would need in the general order that she would need them. She spread a drop sheet, lined up the sturdiest of the engine stands, a cylinder hone, dial gauge and ridge reamer and greased the tops and palms of her hands with a thin smear of vaseline which she found saved her significant scrubbing at the end of the day.

Normally after set up, Gwen would have got herself a mug of weak, black tea, but today she didn't want to interrupt her own rhythm so she jumped straight in, draining the ochre-coloured liquid from the radiator before removing it along with the cylinder block. She detached the hood and side panels, leaning them up against the hangar wall. Disassembling the engine was not without its hitches; all three of the cap screws which mounted the clutch and brake pedals to the housing had rusted solidly and wouldn't be shifted, slowing Gwen down before she felt she had even started. But by lunch, The Engineer had made pretty good progress and allowed herself a short break for that cup of tea.

The kitchen had been set up in the corner of the workshop through some inventive plumbing which utilised the existing pipes associated with the one toilet and handsink which was poorly separated from the workshop by a cubicle of asbestos sheeting and a poorly hung laundry door removed from the womens' quarters. An extra power point had been installed on the wall adjacent to the cubicle which served both the bar fridge and a kettle which featured a 'do not remove' sign sticky taped to the handle but which failed to prevent its frequent disappearance.

There were no benches or cupboards, so most of the mechanics brought their own cups and sat them alongside the kettle, toaster, tin of tea bags and jar of coffee which crowded the top of the fridge.

Gwen begrudgingly added a splash of milk to her tea to cool it down quickly and looked for a spot along the warm walls of the hanger's exterior to lean on. She slotted herself into the casual lineup of her colleagues who were caressing mugs and cigarettes in their blackened fingers, closing their eyes and lifting their faces to the sun.

Despite wanting to avoid the delay of social interaction, she slotted herself between two other members of her household and found herself tuning into the banter of their familiar voices.

Corporal Mary O'Hanlon had been asked to work on the jeep deserted by the Padre near Dhurringile; it was a standard G503, of fairly new vintage, and was going to be an easy job, she was telling her commanding officer, Ruth. Likely an alternator.

Well done, Mary; I'm sure Ruth is impressed by your diagnosis. And if it's not the alternator, it's going to take all your brainpower to come up with an alternative. I'll be finished my overhaul before your slack arse gets that jeep back on the road.

Mary took a sip of her tea and then turned the conversation in the flick of a cat's tail.

'I hear the special investigators are in town, Sarge,' she began, in her strong Irish accent which twisted itself around Gwen and held her just as she was about to move away to find a quieter spot in the shade.

'Do you now, Corporal,' Ruth came back in her familiar laconic drawl, drawing on her cigarette and releasing the smoke around the words, 'why would that be?'

'The Engineer can tell you; she's right in the thick of it. Aren't you Sergeant Dalana?'

This girl was always taking liberties with Gwen. She was the only one who ever used her nickname in front of a superior officer and certainly had none of the humility her very average mechanical skills should have endowed her with.

Gwen had generally been conservative when it came to taking risks, yet she was harbouring some guilt, and talk of special investigators had the immediate affect of prickling her palms with sweat and imagining a flutter in her chest to be instantly unbearable.

Why would I be at the centre of anything to do with special investigators? Nobody knows about my parts supplier and if they did, they'd never complain about a sweet turnaround. That's what they all want. They want the job done yesterday. It's their own fault.

'You drove the Padre back from Dhurringile yesterday, didn't you?' Mary persisted. 'Did he get the guard to confess?'

Ruth also spoke in a lowered voice, but hers was tempered with the responsibilities of rank as she stretched the sentence over Gwen's confusion like a bandaid: 'Do you know anything about this Gwen?'

'About what?'

Mary was only too happy to help out.

'There was a shooting, a murder really, of a German prisoner. It's been hushed up but this Sergeant, the shooter, he's not coping very well and it's all coming undone. The prisoners want him punished and they're …'

The conversation paused abruptly and the women waited in silence until another mechanic had passed them down the line to find her own wall lean.

'What do you mean coming undone?' Gwen asked, genuinely interested now.

'Oh for God's sake Sergeant,' Ruth interjected before Mary got nasty, 'You drove him back to base. What did he tell you?'

The Padre? Right. Not the parts. Him? He just sat like a lump beside me, staring at the road ahead with those intense grey eyes ... or were they blue?

'Well?' her colleagues asked in unison.

'The Padre? Nothing, actually. Not a damn thing. He's an odd one, that one,' Gwen replied cavalierly.

'Are you holding out on us, Dalana? Because this is big. HQ is going to be all over this; it's that serious.'

Mary scanned Gwen's face, the tight bun she had tied her dark hair back in and her inquisitorial squint making her own seem severe despite her youth. Without shifting her gaze, she snapped out of detective mode and went straight to snide.

'Nah, she's not holding out; she doesn't know anything. The Engineer missed the most exciting thing that's happened around here for a long time, with the real story right under her nose.'

Gwen took a deliberately long sip of her now luke warm tea, trying hard to make its consumption look deeply satisfying.

'If the WO or the provosts want to question me,' she told her colleagues teasingly when she'd drained all but the last swill of the cup, 'I'll make myself available to tell them what I know. But right now, you seem to know more than me, so I'd appreciate it if you'd stop giving me a hard time and let me get back to work.'

She flung the remains of her mug out into the dirt, forcing Mary to jump back to avoid it splashing against her legs.

As she strode back to her station, Gwen offered one more quip: 'As for you, O'Hanlon, if you'd taken the pickup like you were asked, you wouldn't have to rely on me for your gossip.'

The rest of the afternoon passed in snatches – irritable, tedious, snatches. Gwen could feel the progressive steps of the task in front of her detaching themselves from her memory as she was trying to retrieve them.

That rude man didn't even have the decency to tell me what was going on … What am I saying? He didn't do anything outrageous. He just didn't talk to me. I was his driver. It wouldn't have hurt him to be civil. Where's the dial guage?

The tendons of her thoughts variously drew tight and then flung loose as her mind churned over the events of the previous day and struggled to commit to the job at hand. She recalled that she had been having a repartee with herself in the absence of any other conversation on the drive back and realised now with some guilt that the Padre may have had bigger things on his mind.

I was pretty flippant; it's hard stuck in this shed to remember there are people in this war who need fixing too. Can't imagine why I'm not a nurse!

Gwen leant on the trolley, looking despondently at the black trim around her fingernails and spotted the dial gauge. She inserted it into the cylinder bore, and moved it up and down its full length. Normally Gwen would have been able to remember the variations in the cylinder wall but this afternoon she knew it would be advisable to write the readings down. She continued with the gauge rotations, still so distracted she was forced to repeat some calculations.

Did I check the pistons? Maybe. Do it again.

She remembered with some pain how fast she had been driving on the way home, with the Padre not saying a word about it. She flinched at the memory of his kitbag being flung from the vehicle.

What a disgrace. I can't believe I did that. I should be in the brink for insubordination.

By sunset, Gwen was way behind where she would normally be for a three-day job, but it was pointless continuing with her head skipping around the way it was. She decided to leave the truck in orderly disassembly and commit to a super early start tomorrow.

She could see dusk dusting the shrubbery and saplings beyond the workshop with fine spatters of azure and cornflower. She separated her own tools from the army issue ones on the trolley and rolled them up in the leather skin wrap stamped with her initials.

Coming from her father, it was one of her few treasured possessions here.

As she drove along the narrow dirt road running parallel to the river, the number of parked vehicles still waiting for occupants to return was dwindling the closer she got to her favourite spot.

Confident she was alone and eager to wash the day's grease from her, she stripped off the minute she pulled up. She had her swimsuit on in seconds and headed down the steep and darkening track to the water.

The milky brown surface was smooth, apart from a few patches dimpled by the breeze – a gravel rash on the river's skin.

Gwen slowed her descent down the steep bank by putting her hands up against the slim trunks of gums on either side of her at intervals where it seemed she might lose her footing.

On the edge of the water, her feet, stinging a little from the stab of twigs and stones, sighed in the cool, slimy mud. She stood for a minute, no longer desperate to be immersed, but enjoying what she loved about the Australian bush, like only a city girl who believes her experience of it to be fleeting, could.

Her toes curled into the wet brown and she breathed deeply the pungency of her eucalypt-drenched surroundings.

Motionless, she consciously channelled the echo of bird cries which leapt from tree to tree around her. She drew up through her feet the pulse of throaty frog calls and allowed the frenetic trill of unseen cicadas to rise and fall through her system as if she were in sync with the rhythmic whirrs of a bullroarer.

Only when she had satiated herself of the life force around her, did Gwen venture into the water to allow the cathartic peace of it all to envelope her and relieve her overtired body.

Just metres along the riverbank from where Gwen was swimming, the Padre had ventured out from the barracks for a change of scenery. It had been suggested to him by a casual lunch companion in the mess that the river was a pleasant place to unwind but not to consider swimming until he learned where the hazards were from someone more familiar.

So he had walked along the edge of the river until he had arrived at this spot where a bank of sand upstream and a giant gum, which had fallen downstream and lay outstretched like an enormous cylindrical bridge, had formed an idyllic oasis. As it was his first visit and dusk had stolen his confidence, he chose not to swim but to kick off his boots and perch himself on a broad rock.

Finding himself dozy, he lay down. The hard edges and any remaining tension melted as his back drew in the stored heat from the stone and his face was brushed lightly by a gentle breeze.

When Avery heard a vehicle pull up, he found himself too lethargic to sit up and check it out. He assumed he would have a little while before he needed to seek out the driver to ensure he could get a lift back to barracks and allowed himself to drift into sleep.

It was getting on for night when a cry of pain brought him abruptly to his feet and sent him staggering drowsily to the water's edge.

'Are you alright?' he called out in the direction of the voice.

'Oh, thank goodness. Over here! I have a cramp. Cold water pocket; I should know better. Would you mind?'

Avery stepped cautiously into the water, barely able to see the woman's outstretched hand. He gasped at the chill himself as it reached his crutch and wished the victim had been in shallower water when she got into difficulties. Once he had connected with her fingertips, he was able to judge her form and moved to bring his arm around her back but she disappeared again, doubling over and gripping her calf.

'I've never had one this bad before,' she moaned.

'I'll carry you if you like,' Avery offered, instinctively bending down to scoop her up behind the knees.

'No. No, thankyou,' the woman said quickly as if to prevent a second misadventure and pulled away from him.

'I'll be fine if you just walk me in. Slowly. And thankyou.'

After some hesitation, she began to hobble up the steep embankment with Avery's assistance, every now and then pausing to grab her lower leg.

As they neared the roadside, Avery connected the voice he had thought familiar with a face.

'Sergeant Dalana?'

'Yes?' Gwen had been so caught up with her leg that she hadn't, to this point, been curious about the man who was supporting her despite being in her bathing suit.

'Padre?'

'I guess I'll have the pleasure of driving you back to base this time, Sergeant Dalana. Any luggage?'

'My uniform!'

Peering into the half light, Gwen made out the bundle she was looking for in a tumbled grey knot on top of a tree stump where she had left it, halfway up the embankment. Still leaning on Avery, with the memory of pain raking lightly across her calf, she turned them both towards it, taking tentative steps and keeping her arm in front of her face to ward off flicking twigs and spider webs fading in and out of the dusk. She reached for the bundle, not completely convinced it would not bite or take flight, and was relieved to find that it was her towel.

'Would you mind waiting by the jeep?'

Avery agreed, despite his concern at leaving her behind in the dark.

When the crunch underfoot softened and Gwen assumed Avery to be a reasonable distance away, she unfurled her towel only to spill her underwear onto the dirt. *Damn it.*

'I'll get you some light,' Avery called out, blinding Gwen momentarily with the jeep's high beams as they bore a luminous path through the scrub, bleaching an enormous red gum behind her and throwing an elongated silhouette up against the trunk.

Annoyed, Gwen abandoned the search for her underwear and stepped briskly into each leg of her shorts. She quickly buttoned up her shirt over her wet swimsuit, finishing it just as the Padre called out with more unwanted assistance.

'Need any help down there?'

'No thanks, I'm fine. Just drop the high beams if you would,' Gwen called from the centre of the spotlight.

Reluctantly, the Padre, who now looked like a man who had stumbled on a bush nymph after a year in solitary confinement, dropped the lights to low beam. However he must not have been entirely able to flush the colour of whimsy from his expression because Gwen felt compelled to check that the ends of the towel she had draped around her neck were still spread wide across her breasts to cover the wet patches which had bled from her swimsuit through her shirt.

Avery fiddled pointlessly with the stickshift, checking it was in the right gear, and then stared straight ahead over the steering wheel, his back upright, as if he were a chauffer awaiting an expectant client. The passenger door was open. Gwen couldn't make up her mind whether the gesture qualified as gentlemanly, was intended to be a joke, or whether it simply displayed more of the arrogance she remembered from their first meeting.

As soon as she was seated, Avery reversed back, swung the rear wheels to the left, straightened the jeep up and headed back to the dirt road he had walked in on, trying hard to remember landmarks in the dark.

'Lookout!'

Avery saw the rabbit in time to veer slightly out of its way. He smiled at Gwen's concern for the vermin, grabbing a glance at her before picking up speed again. Her hair seemed to be lifting as the ends dried, curling up into loose ringlets on her collarbone.

'Do you come here a lot?

'When I finish early enough. A swim helps me unwind.'

'Left or right at the intersection? I walked in you know, took me hours to find that water hole.'

'Left, then it's a few miles on the bitumen and back onto the dirt again. I'll let you know.'

Avery waited at the juncture for a considerable period despite there being no approaching lights, thinking of something interesting to say to distract himself from the way Gwen's dampened shorts were clinging to her thighs.

'They say a French vigneron set up a punt service here in the 1850s to ferry miners between the goldfields,' he finally blurted out as he turned onto the narrow highway.

'And I thought I was the only one who knew how to find this spot!'

'You don't have to worry about me. Padres know how to keep secrets.'

'Is that right?'

'Nobody would believe our stories anyway. Imagine if I told someone how I went for a swim and found a bush nymph flailing around in the mud instead.'

'Funny, I don't remember it that way at all!'

Avery could barely believe how enchanted he was with his companion. It seemed like years since he had felt this way and his appetite for it was rapidly stripping away at his normally guarded nature.

'So how does a nice girl like you come to be in a war like this anyway?'

The question caught Gwen off guard. It should have offended her feminist leanings, and it would have if they were strong enough, but instead they were overwhelmed by the hint of flattery.

'Turns out there's a shortage of men to do everything around here,' she replied, making a good fist of ignoring her initial reaction.

'Also turns out that I'm a damn fine mechanic – so good in fact, the other girls call me the Engineer!'

Gwen blushed at the boast that had escaped her in a juvenile rush to impress Avery, and was grateful for Avery's distraction with a poorly lit bend in the road. With it safely navigated, he returned to the conversation.

'Was your father a mechanic? Is that why you joined the corps?'

Now Gwen bristled.

'Why does a man have to be at the heart of everything a woman does? Honestly, what's wrong with plain old fashioned patriotism? I joined because it was the right thing to do.'

'If only everyone saw things as simply as you do,' Avery said, responding with his customary condescension. 'It would make my job a lot easier.'

Sarcasm.

'Yep. It's all very clear to me. War is all about good and evil. Didn't you know that? Isn't that what you guys preach?'

'Touche. So why don't you tell me why you really joined up?'

'Is this your standard ice breaker? Because I have to tell you a couple of years into the war, it sounds a bit lame!'

'You think that's a pick up line?'

This time Gwen's blush was easy to guess at as she shifted uncomfortably in her seat.

'It's okay, I was just stirring you,' Avery said to put her out of her misery.

'Actually I have a theory I'm working on,' he ventured, dipping into a large pothole Gwen habitually avoided when taking this route.

'I met this soldier in the Pacific who carried a poster from the Great War in his duffle bag.'

'What was on the poster?'

'Conscription propaganda – a kind of reverse psychology describing those against conscription as "worm enough" to vote "no".'

'I don't get it.'

'The poster listed things a "no" campaigner might think, like saying desertion is a noble act, or that people who get shot for helping the allies get their just desserts.'

'That's horrible! Why would he carry something like that around?'

'That's what makes it interesting! It was his dad's and even though his old man had come home from the Great War half blind from mustard gas and begged his son not to enlist because war is hell and so forth, the boy didn't listen to him.'

'Why not?'

'Because of that poster. He said he wasn't "worm enough" to let others fight the war for him.'

In the silence that followed, Avery eased his foot slightly off the accelerator so as not to arrive at the camp too soon.

After a while Gwen chipped back in.

'So, you're telling me he enlisted because of a keepsake and it had nothing to do with his father being a war hero.'

'Now you're catching on,' Avery responded to her mockery. 'People will tell you they joined up because of what the Japs did to our nurses or because they bombed Darwin, but my theory is there's generally something more tangible involved, like that poster.'

Gwen couldn't help thinking of Curtin's speech that still hung in her head like an echo, finding its voice particularly when she felt homesick.

It occurred to her that she clung to that broadcast in the same way that the soldier was attached to his poster.

'People just want to do the right thing, Padre,' she reasserted. 'It really is that simple. They'll stand up time and time again if the cause is right, even if the odds are against them.

'Take Jimmy Stewart. He had it all – good looks, Hollywood at his feet … .'

'So that's your type is it? Nothing but Hollywood for Sergeant Dalana,' Avery teased.

'I'm making a point here! He turns up with his draft papers and they reject him because he's too skinny … .'

'A runt of a man,' Avery goaded, straightening up in his seat to pull in a stomach that was hardly oversized.

'Instead,' Gwen continued with an overt pronunciation on the first word, 'he goes home, fattens up and now he's flying combat missions over Europe – because, like the rest of us, he has a sense of duty to his country.

'Here, turn now,' Gwen suddenly advised. Avery swept off the highway and back onto the dirt road leading to the camp, grinning all the while.

'And he'll come home and play the role of the returned soldier in another brilliant film and a whole new generation of girls will swoon over him,' the Padre said in a sing song voice.

'You're impossible!'

'Perhaps he's leaning out of his aircraft as we speak, laying 'em in the aisles and crushing the enemy with pure talent and big screen integrity.'

'You're not honestly … yes you are … you're jealous. I don't believe it!'

'So, do you want to know how my theory works here?'

'Sure, this oughtta be good!'

'Jimmy Stewart enlisted because he got an award he didn't deserve and he had to prove himself to the world. The Oscar was his reason.'

'Which one?'

'"Philadelphia Story". It should have gone to Henry Fonda for "Grapes of Wrath".'

'Stop right there; now you're just making a fool of yourself.'

They pulled into the camp driveway with the moon bright above them, bumping in their seats as the tyres bounced over a cattle grill, their minds alive with the mischief of their talk and their hearts languishing in a rare moment of internal sunshine.

12.

cat not far behind.

[November, 1979.]

Helen sat, her legs outstretched, one silk sock stocking around her ankle, the other pulled up over her shin. Drenched in stale air, she appeared to be melting into the curdled cream of the wall behind her.

Helen was one of the youngest residents of the Tarcoola Nursing Home, among a handful of those inappropriately housed there and forgotten by the Health Department. She did not have the untamed profusions of white hair in places youth would never allow or the thin, mottled flesh of a life loosened by age but she moved like an old woman. Perhaps it was mimickery. Perhaps it was the early onset of dementia that made her appear well beyond her forty three years. Certainly dementia was the likely cause of her carrying her regrets around like a heavy duffle bag on occasion, and, on the next, having no idea of what could be in it.

For weeks now Helen had come to this spot in the hallway, sitting midway between the bedrooms of a man who never recognised his family despite weekly visits, and a woman who had not managed to make it to the toilet once since she arrived without her dignity leaking down her leg.

A poor choice of resting place, from that point of view.

Outside the home, the day was rippling, basting. The few pot plants at either side of the entrance were slapped limp and the resident dog looked all but dead, foolishly taking refuge under the shade of a battered four-wheel drive instead of the nearby trees. Cat had not made an appearance.

Helen could find little relief from the heat. Her memories were jostling against each other, adding to her discomfort. Some days they were fulsome; people had names, places, belongings, even agendas. Today they were fragments of unrelated images threatening to breach.

She stared at the linoleum – its pattern resembling a green vegemite smeared through cottage cheese. It was a ghost catcher, the swirls forming themselves into strangers professing to know her and throwing back accusations like a wicked stepmother's mirror. It was like this most days now. Helen would sit mesmerised, appearing almost catatonic, until the nurses carted her to a chair in the television room or woke her to ease her into the mouth of her bed.

The only thing Helen seemed to know for certain was that she would not find peace without the imprimatur of Cat. It was widely suspected that being stalked by Cat was the kiss of death. In fact had his coat been black and not marmalade, he may not have survived the odd scream of 'devil spawn' thrown at him by residents fearing their countdowns had begun.

She had watched Cat over the past year, padding behind the unsuspecting – silently, persistently – until they gave in to him. He would slip under their frail hands and they would stroke him and tell him of their glory days and dark hours. The sensation of his pelt triggered in each of them a different reaction. In some, it was an urge to urinate, as if their fingers had dropped into a bowl of warm water set beside their armchairs while they slept. Others attempted to draw the feline closer, only to be rewarded with a hiss or a swipe of his paw.

Rather than be afraid of Cat's attention, Helen craved it. She believed him to be a guide capable of crossing soft-footed between this world and the next. As she watched his habits anew – the failings of her short term memory offering endless opportunities to refresh the entertainment – she determined that Cat was benevolence itself.

If it was love and tenderness the dying craved, he gave it to them, purring as his fur rose under their stroke, its silkiness reminding them of the touch of a child's cheek or that of a lover long gone. If it was a reconciliation of their life, he had the staying power to sit by his charges while they worked through their issues, mumbling to themselves until they could pass away unburdened at last.

It had not been easy to bring Cat to her heels, so instead, Helen began to follow him. On some days she did it because she wanted to trade her story for safe passage to a happier place and on other days it was because her feet told her to. She became a shadow inept at staying connected to its own lifeforce, but remarkable in its determination to cling to another.

It was only when Helen had given up on convincing Cat that she was worth his time that the feline had shown an interest. He still would not come to her on request, but deigned to slip in under her hand if she were slumped in the corridor, apathetic about his presence, mumbling 'All those years, wasted' as she had become wont to do, sometimes out loud, sometimes bouncing the phrase like a squash ball repeatedly against the walls of her mind. Her hand would dissolve into his coat and his heartbeat would rise up through her arm into her own. When her body succumbed to sleep, Cat would slink away, leaving her fingers to curl up again like drying leaves.

On this hot November day, Faye spotted Helen asleep and adrift in the corridor. Cat was nowhere to be seen. An ample, good-humoured British girl who had emigrated in search of warmer weather, she had a fondness for Helen that derived from her being of similar appearance to her much missed mother.

'Lend a hand will you Carmel?'

Faye squatted down beside Helen.

'Yah poor old girl. Can't keep droppin' off like this in the middle o' the hall, you know. If Cat catches you napping, you'll be done for.'

She crudely but gently bent one of Helen's legs into a position where she could support herself once she was up. Helen was startled, but had awoken more lucid than she had fallen asleep and, recognising the blaze of frizzy red hair as Faye's, did not resist. Together the nurses helped Helen to her feet, visibly relieved that she had recognised them and that there would not be a fight.

Each of the nurses took an elbow and began to guide Helen to her room. Carmel winked at Faye as she spoke to her charge: 'Why don't you have a nap now and maybe we'll wake you when Wheel of Fortune comes on, alright?'

The trio trod a familiar path down the hallway. Cat not far behind.

A proposal.

[VJ Day, August 15, 1945.]

When the allies declared victory in Europe, the excitement in Australia had to be swallowed down while the fight in the Pacific continued to take lives for another three months. When news came that the Japanese had surrendered, Gwen found herself joyfully caught up in a celebration that was all the more rowdy and overwhelming for it having been put on hold.

Along with everyone else who could leave their posts, the women mechanics descended on the garrison mess to pour as much celebration down their throats as their personal stashes and constraints allowed.

A teary and unsteady Mary O'Hanlon threw her arms around Gwen's neck, declaring her the best mechanic she'd ever worked with and offering her a job on her family farm, which, it turned out, had just one old tractor in the shed.

'Mary, you're slobbering on me,' Gwen told her. 'And I've never worked on a tractor, but I'm sure you'll get it up and running in no time.'

Mary seemed quite pleased to get a compliment from the Engineer and loosened her grip to concentrate on the facial muscles she was attempting to manipulate into a beaming smile.

'Anyway I've got plans of my own,' Gwen informed her.

Ruth, who had been drinking with guards from the internment camps propped up at the bar, eyed her best mechanic with something that looked fleetingly like pity.

Despite being enmeshed in the bustle and energy of the room, shoulders nudging through to their friends with drinks from the bar, scores being settled and seductions growing less discreet by the minute, Gwen felt Ruth's gaze and turned to her. Her superior officer took up the challenge and made her way over to call above the ruckus: 'Sooo Dalana, what now for you?'

'I might start up my own engine shop. I've got a good set of hands, or so people tell me,' Gwen said, looking disdainfully at her roughened fingers and nails.

Ruth called her close with an exaggerated curl of her finger, the breath of cold throat spirits blunting against Gwen's cheek.

'Sspeaking of people who might appresshyate those skilled handzofyours, here comes your Padre,' she informed Gwen in a smoky, conspiratorial tone barely audible over the throng.

'What?' Gwen raised her eyebrows but Ruth merely tipped her head in the direction of a man whose eyes fired her own from the other side of the room. Ruth grinned to herself as she sashayed back into the push of bodies.

Avery was hooked several times in exuberant hand shakes, shoulder and back slapping and the odd knowing wink from those who had sought counselling from him over the past two years as he weaved his way through the swathe of sweat, tears and exhilaration to the only person he genuinely wanted to celebrate with.

Just as he reached Gwen, a succession of lightbulbs popped above them, throwing the mess into darkness and bringing a collective cheer and more clinking of bottles. In a moment of boldness, Avery slid his arms around Gwen, settling his hands in a clasp at the small of her back and leaning down to find her lips.

As his rounded shoulders encapsulated her, Gwen succumbed to a dizzy warmth, closing her eyes and erasing her entire surroundings but for this one man. As their mouths connected, Avery was pushed forward by a drunken member of the military police who was making it his mission to end his duty on a good note and going about it in the most blustery, bombastic fashion that he could.

A number of hurricane lamps were being lit around the mess, though they did little more than reveal everyone's increasingly messy profiles to each other.

'Do you want to get out of here?' Gwen asked hopefully, her eyes repeating the words overridden by despondent groans protesting the appearance of light.

'Let's get out of here,' Avery suggested, his words also going unheard. To Gwen's quizzical look, he extended his hand and led her through various entwinings of gregarious, maudlin and flirtatious men and women, sharing their plans for the future – the most fantastic of them being made up on the spot.

For some, it was a long awaited night with their wife, shoes off at the front door, backyard cricket, babies grown to toddlers in their absence. Elderly mothers were being lionised in anticipation of gravy soaked welcomes and soft sheet sleep ins. For others it was Saturday nights with the mates, Sunday hangovers, barbecues, fishing, footy. For a few it was travel to the remotest of locations where they hoped to put the war behind them and find some quiet in their lives. Their hopes were etched on their faces, their stories bumbling from their mouths bearing only a slight resemblance to what they were thinking and completely unnecessary in fulfilling the moment. Everyone understood.

It was a night of exceptions typified by the normally reliable and commanding Ruth who had shocked everyone by producing a bottle of fire-engine red polish and streaking her fingernails one by one in between shots of whiskey. By the end of the night she had also managed to do her toenails and those of a young guard she had fancied for the entire time she had been posted to Murchison.

But the most surprising thing, to everyone but Ruth it seemed, was what happened shortly after midnight on the deserted western verandah of the mechanics' homestead. With the boozy cacophony they had left behind still faintly in earshot and a perfect crescent of a moon overhead, Avery and Gwen attempted a conversation that didn't reveal to the other how desperate they were to keep each other in their lives beyond their wartime service.

'I'm leaving the army,' Avery told her, more loudly at first than he needed to, given the din was no longer a challenge.

'I'm going to work with the Australian Inland Mission as a patrol padre; I'll be ministering through most of the south, and up into central Australia.'

Gwen, who was not a regular drinker and was losing her inhibitions rapidly to the effects of her earlier consumption, had simply wanted her kiss and was a little annoyed at first that she was not getting it.

'I'm not sure what that's got to do with me,' she said, leaning back against the railing and pushing her moderately endowed chest forward in a less-than-subtle manner.

'I've bought a truck from Army surplus and I'll be needing a mechanic to keep it in order across some pretty rough terrain,' Avery continued, teasing Gwen with a mock formality while moving closer to her evolving frown.

'Just think Sergeant Dalana, you would be one of the few women leaving here who'll be able to keep working in your chosen profession, if you accompany me that is.'

Gwen now moved forward off the railing and took a step toward Avery, her hands on her hips.

'I'll have you know, Captain Padre sir,' she said, taking another step that forced him to take one backwards along the verandah, 'that I expect to work in any outfit I choose.'

She took another step forward, and he, another back.

'And I won't be taking a man's job because, as it turns out, no man is as good as I am under the bonnet.'

Avery now stood his ground and pulled her close to him, whispering in her ear: 'I think I'd like to test you out under the bonnet, Sergeant Dalana.'

Gwen blushed and pulled away, a little excited, and a little ashamed that Avery could think she was like many of the other women on base.

'I'm shocked Padre,' Gwen said in a mocking voice that carried a hint of haughty. 'You know you haven't said a single thing that makes your proposition even slightly attractive to me.'

With some trepidation, Avery reached into his pocket and withdrew a small burgundy velvet box. He went down on one knee, popping it open in front of her as he did, to reveal a white gold ring with a small diamond at its centre.

'Gweneth Dalana, would you do me the honour of …'

His words were smothered by the sudden intrusion of Gwen's lips.

14.

The day of the transgression.

[May, 1950.]

The day of the unthinkable transgression was a Monday, a pleasant one towards the end of autumn. Gwen stepped outside to look for the newspaper and took it all in: the sky was a milky blue and what few leaves were left to fall from the Adelaide trees rode a soft breeze to mottle green lawns in turner's yellow, burgundy and chestnut. A cool dew envigorated her bare feet as she stepped lightly across it.

Avery had caught the Trans Australia the night before, catching up on some reading as the city petered out into the suburbs and the fences turned from palings into wire. He was asleep when the train stopped at Port Augusta and remained so for four of the next five hours it took him to get to Kimbanyon.

When he poked his head from the train at much the same time Gwen was sitting down with her newspaper and a cup of tea, Avery was pleased to feel a mild, rather than confronting, heat waft over him. Having already smoothed his hair down with a sparing amount of Brylcreem, he had gone to the carriage stairs facing away from the platform to clean his teeth, using water from a bottle he always brought with him to swish away the paste and spit onto the track. He looked up onto a broad, endless expanse of ochre-coloured soil bathed in a lively light, saw a roo bound away to no particular destination in the distance and smiled contentedly.

He had arranged to meet Gillian Brown, who was running a mobile library service from a converted school bus with the barest of government funding, and found her already waiting for him when he alighted, refreshed, on the other side. A former librarian who had retired when she moved to Kimbanyon with her prospecting husband, Gillian was a good Christian with boundless energy and fun for Avery to be around because of it. Her thick greying hair tied in a simple pony tail, she stood in front of the bus to greet him while several children remained inside perusing old titles that were new to them and unloading their returns from drawstring bags.

Avery pulled down on the edges of his waistcoat to straighten any carriage creases, and walked briskly toward her. After a fond greeting, Gillian slid behind the enormous steering wheel and Avery took up his usual post, perched on the nearest passenger seat from which he could lean forward and converse.

They drove to camps and homesteads between Kimbanyon and Tarcoola in what was a mutually beneficial arrangement, giving Avery a chance to make contact with the people who didn't make it to church and Gillian a chance to lobby him for funding. Avery enjoyed the morning and made promises of return visits to several homesteaders before accepting Gillian's generous offering of lunch (she had made twice her normal selection of sandwiches) before dropping him at his appointment.

His 'business' was at the Van de Velts – a troubled home he had visited many times before to see James who had lost his ear on the world and whose view of life was distorted because of it. He had fought alongside his younger cousin Henry in Libya, and had been waiting with their troops outside Tobruk for an expected German and Italian attack. They had been armed with Italian field guns captured just two weeks before and James, particularly, had had little confidence in his ability to use them.

When an enemy tank had stopped almost directly in front of their bunker, Henry had signalled James to cover him with the field gun while he scrambled onto the tank with the intention of dropping a grenade into it. James had raised it to fire well above the manhole once Henry was in position. But James had misjudged the low angle at which the gun operated. The first volley had shot Henry's legs out from under him. Aghast, James had leapt from the bunker to retrieve his cousin who was still clinging to the tank, but it was now on the move and Henry dropped the grenade. Pieces of him had been scattered among the debris – projectiles spliced by fragments. James had kept his limbs, but he would never fully recover his hearing or his ability to sleep.

Avery had pieced together the story over more than a year of visiting and walking with James. It had come to him in snatches and garble, involuntarily it seemed, fuelled by a nervous energy peculiar to insomniacs, and the echo of Henry's screams.

But it was not James the Reverend was coming to see this day; it was his mother, Mrs Van de Velt, whose elderly husband had joined her in welcoming their son back to Kimbanyon only to be taken by a heart attack 18 months later.

In that first year or so of being home, James had mostly stayed indoors, mentally opening and closing his own wounds, contributing his pension to the family's wellbeing and keeping nothing for himself. When Derk died, his son had responded with a soldier's pragmatism, appointing himself head of the family and reinventing himself as a man fit for work. Veteran's Affairs had convinced the railways to give him his old job back and equipped him with a hearing aid.

The other fettlers in his crew got into the habit of looking directly at him when they spoke and did their best to keep both themselves and him safe on the job. James returned the favour by joining them at the bar after work – a pastime he initially hated because the silence was more pronounced when it was animated by a raucous crowd.

Over time he found he could get by and even enjoy himself by guessing at their stories, pouring down beers and mimicking their laughter when he saw it light up their faces.

It was Mrs Van de Velt now who was suffering, home alone and only seeing her son when he was drunk or woke her in the early hours to unwittingly draw her into his nightmares. A stoic and once respectful woman unused to asking for help, she had grown bitter and resentful at her lot.

The Van de Velts lived in a modest timber cottage. It was a busy house without appearing cluttered, but on the day the Reverend went to see Mrs Van de Velt, every item in it seemed to her somehow unfit for its purpose. She tipped an ironing board back into its concealed cupboard in the loungeroom wall as she directed Avery to one of two lounge chairs with broad wooden arm rests. He wondered absent-mindedly whether they had removed a chair when James Senior had died or whether James Junior had not spent time in there with his parents. Plastic covers squeaked underneath them both as they settled.

The verbal assault began as soon as Mrs Van de Velt sat down. She told Avery she needed help talking to God. She didn't know how to ask Him – 'in a way so as he might listen to me this time' – to find a way for her and her son to live together like they used to. Avery spoke to her in biblical parables, in metaphors that just seemed to annoy her, and finally asking her to understand that a lot of men had come home changed by the war. He struggled to find the words to suggest her son was unlikely to 'improve'. He spoke of tolerance and it being God's will that his people now rejoice in peace time and accept each other for who they were. Revelations, he said, described Jesus as both a lion and an innocent lamb – dwelling together …

But Avery was not given the space to explain what he meant by that. An impatient Mrs Van de Velt demanded to know whether her son was the lion or the lamb in the scenario and assured the Reverend that neither she nor her son were of a constitution that would lie down.

'I would have thought that an army chaplain would have more to offer,' she said in a tart and condescending tone that would ring in Avery's ears at his lowest ebbs over many years to come.

Avery felt sure Mrs Van de Velt was looking for a way for the church to take her son off her hands, to provide him with support elsewhere. But while she alluded to it, she could not bring herself to make the request. Knotting her fingers over and over again in her lap, she seemed desperate for someone to recognise the hardships she had faced holding together a family that bore no resemblance to the one she and her husband had nurtured and enjoyed before the war.

Once they both understood that the widow was not ready to forgive God for what he had allegedly done to her life but that Avery was ready to hear her out, a torrent of vitriol was unleashed on the Church. The Reverend told himself that it was cathartic for the widow and that, as long as the Church withstood the abuse graciously, she would not abandon her faith.

He was thoroughly exhausted when he received the call from Mrs Johns at the Van de Velt home. Mabel had tracked him down through her network and wanted him to 'come sort Helen out once and for all'. With her words tumbling over each other in a melodramatic rush, all Avery really took in was that whatever it was that had got Mabel's goat, it was 'the last straw'.

Petulant woman. I thought you didn't need my help anymore Mabel. That didn't last long.

Despite his history with Mrs Johns, Avery was relieved to have an excuse to leave the Van de Velt's, with there seeming to be no easy exit otherwise. Huffily, the widow walked him to the door and then, as he was wondering what last words to offer her, the wind of her temperament changed.

'I'm sorry your tea went cold, Reverend,' his host said, as if he had just dropped in to borrow a book and they'd got caught up chatting about nothing more intense than the weather. An incredulous Avery managed a smile, cushioned the sinewy hand extended to him between his with practiced warmth, and left.

On his walk to the grocery shop, a short one unfortunately by Kimbanyon standards, the widow's volatility sat salty in his wounds. He wondered at her ability to make him feel that the war had ended only months ago, rather than five years, and how she could rattle him. He had had more affinity with James than he did with his mother – even in the silences – and yet her thinly veiled attacks on the value of Faith kept him coming back time and again to try and win her over.

As he walked toward another emotional crisis, he found himself questioning whether he really needed to be in Kimbanyon as often as he still was. He wished Gillian would swing by in her bus and sweep him up and that this elongating and emotionally strenuous day would be over. Knowing the likelihood of that was getting slimmer by the minute, he deviated slightly to the station, to check on the possibility of a later train than the one he usually caught home.

By the time Avery finally arrived at the shop, it took all his willpower just to walk across the threshold. It was Bert, not Mabel, who was in his face the second he emerged from under the plastic strips, that damned bell collapsing as he passed through the doorway.

'I swear, they're going to kill each other, Father.'

Bert had been raised a Catholic and despite being a lapsed one, had never bothered to address any member of the cloth of any denomination anything other than 'Father'.

'What the hell happened here, Bert?' Avery halfheartedly kicked aside a number of potatoes scattered on the floor.

'Mabel found Helen's book in the storeroom and threatened to tear it up. As you can see, Helen thought otherwise. And I can tell you, she's got a good arm!'

'Mabel or Helen?' Avery asked, with a warm smile and a hand on Bert's shoulder. His frame seemed to soften under his touch.

'Where is Mrs Johns?'

'She's driven to her friend's place in Tarcoola. She says she won't come back until Helen's gone. I'm sorry to put this on you Father, but I don't think we can be this girl's parents any more. It wasn't this tough when our own kids were teenagers and, well, we just don't need the stress at our age!'

I don't think you know the half of what your Edward got up to Bert.

'Any idea where she went?'

'She went to Tarcoola … .'

'Not Mrs Johns, Bert. Helen.'

'She said she was going home.'

Bert looked beaten, the two women in his life gone in opposite directions, leaving him to broker the deal which would see them all back working the shop – their good memories intact and not sullied by the ugly ones now running riot.

'She's a young woman now Father, and a real handful,' he said apologetically. 'We didn't want to say anything. Not like this at least, but we gave that ganger notice last month. The house is hers if she wants it.

'And Father,' Bert called after Avery as the Reverend disappeared in slices through the plastic curtain on his way back into the street, 'I'll make sure she can keep her job. We'll work something out.'

Avery shunted the bell to one side as he left.

***

The Muldoon house, vacated just days ago, was empty. Avery had expected to see Helen sitting on the verandah, her gangly legs flowing from her work tunic in a graceless splay, her hand twirling a stick through the powdery red dirt she had dragged out from under the steps because it had been spared the crusty glare of constant sunshine and was more malleable for her distracted scribblings. He had come to find her like this several times before – when the ganger was away, it calmed her down to be here.

Today, there was no Helen, but there was a note, protruding from under a small rock on the top step: 'I knew they'd send for you. Come to the old miner's house.'

I'm the plaything of a teenage girl! I should just leave her there and send Bert back to pick her up on my way to the train. It's half an hour's walk to the miner's cottage, or 50 minutes back to Bert. This day just gets longer and longer.

Avery suddenly wondered if the ganger had left his truck parked behind the house. It was possible that the Johns's had allowed him to leave it there while he was away down the line with no pressing need to sort new accommodation.

He walked down the deteriorating concrete driveway that had been Jim Muldoon's pride and joy, spinifex tufts now appearing through the gaps, and found, with some gratification, a truck parked under the Hills Hoist.

Emboldened by the success of his intuition, he backed himself again to find a key gummed to the back of the sunshade over the driver's side windscreen. He grinned.

Perhaps it was the war years, where innovation was so often necessary or perhaps it was just the way outback people never hesitated in helping out if they could, but Avery didn't give borrowing the truck a second thought.

It kicked over with a hoarse cough and didn't clear its throat until Avery had almost flooded the engine, but there was half a tank of petrol and he was soon swinging onto the track around the outskirts of town to the stone cottage on the rise. At least this way he'd be able to sort Helen out and get back in plenty of time for the 6.30pm run, rather than wait for the freight train at eight.

Bumping along, the springs in the seat buoyant despite the age of the truck, Avery's mood began to lift. He hadn't realised before now how much he'd missed having his own vehicle. Enjoying the freedom of it, he undid the buttons on his waistcoat and collar and thumbed the shirt apart to allow the sun to spread over his chest. Though it was a short drive, Avery felt largely relieved of the anxiety that permeated the Van de Velt household by the time he pulled up at the stone cottage.

Several sheets of tin roofing had blown off the verandah since he had been here last, leaving the aged sapling posts exposed and split. As he rounded the corner to check for Helen, the girl leant forward through a window at the far end.

Her grey tunic seemed to melt into the silver timber frame and dark recess of the interior, leaving the impression that her tawny shoulders and tanned face were floating within the space. Seeing Helen this way added somehow to Avery's growing peace, despite his earlier expectation that his day would continue to writhe in unwanted angst. Perhaps it was his desperate need to unwind or the fact that he was unwinding too quickly that opened the door for what was to happen between them. Either way, it began with a fleeting thought that acted as a kind of release valve on the pressure that builds inside anyone who attempts to maintain goodness against a barrage of human nature.

No Mabel. No Bert. No eyes.

'Go back and come to the door properly,' Helen ordered audaciously. 'And this time, call out: "Hi honey, I'm home!" '

Helen showed no sign of having been the tornado which had flung Mabel to Tarcoola and Bert to the nethermost regions of his tolerance. She was animated and cocky – hardly able to contain herself. Avery found himself smiling.

I've got the truck. She's in a playful mood and there's nothing waiting for us back in town but a kitchen confessional. I may as well relax up here for a bit and take her back to Bert when the dust's settled.

'Fancy yourself as a good homemaker, do you Helen?' Avery approached her from the outside of the window, the wry smile still on his lips. 'Now what the bloody hell's going on?'

Helen enjoyed the fact that the Reverend blasphemed regularly in her presence; it made her feel like he was different with her and that theirs was a secret relationship to be encouraged whenever she could.

'Well, don't expect me to ask how your day has been and get you a cup of tea then, if you're not going to announce you're home like a good husband.'

She sashayed away from the window, hoping Avery hadn't seen the blush which arose hotly in her face the moment she had uttered the last word. Avery followed her in, intrigued by this clumsy parody of confidence and vulnerability.

'There's not much left of the old place now,' he said, surveying the litter of animal faeces on the rammed earth floor and the dangle of nests, new and old, in the supporting beams of the tin roof. Random tin sheets had lifted in the corners, allowing floods of dust-glittered light to fall in angular patterns at their feet. Their intrusion unsettled the neglect, and Helen sneezed.

Avery pulled a handkerchief out of his waistcoat pocket and handed it to her, realising at the same time that he was still unbuttoned. Helen noticed it too and was surprised to see a light spray of dark brown chest hair.

'Why you're quite the average Joe today aren't you? I knew it would be impossible to dress so stuffy all the time.'

She found herself wondering what the Reverend would look like completely undressed, but recoiled from the thought of his bare, middle-aged girth. Avery saw the withdrawal and felt an involuntary sensation of regret that he had not kept himself in better shape. Slightly embarrassed that he cared, he walked back outside into the softening sunshine, doing his buttons up as the girl followed.

'Seriously, Helen, what's going on with you and Mabel?'

Helen cocked her head to one side and pursed her lips, like a child trying to decide which of two hands closed in front of her holds a sweet. When she straightened her gaze, she held his directly.

'Walk with me,' she replied, mimicking the Reverend's voice and hooking her arm through his.

The pair strolled in silence for a while, with Helen leading Avery towards the open plain that flowed from the rear of the cottage to the lilac-washed mound of Mount Arah and, further beyond, The Lions (because the twin peaks resembled them), rising from the range on the northern horizon. The desert plain that went as far as the eye could see, and then stretched out across the belly of Australia, licked at every other corner of their view.

Avery drew in the breadth of the mountains, the fall of the colours as they travelled from the peaks to his feet and felt his rattled constitution breathe.

His stride grew longer, forcing Helen to extend her own. Her arm sat comfortably in the crook of his, and he looked down on it, marvelling at how happy he was.

I love the drape of her wrist, the freckles on her forearm. And her smell – like warm lemongrass.

Avery knew before long he would need to address the issues Bert had raised with him, but for now he would enjoy this small respite. The watery copper of the afternoon had evolved into a dirty dusk before Helen broke the rhythm with conversation.

'Have you ever felt totally alone?'

The sound of her voice startled Avery, so in tune was he with walking to no destination in particular.

'I can't honestly say I ever have,' he responded without giving any thought to the motivation behind the question. 'That's one of the benefits of having God in your life.'

It was a practiced response he had used often in his ministering and anything but honest, given his experiences when he first came to Australia, for all intents and purposes as an orphan.

'Well I envy your ability to have faith in the unfathomable,' Helen responded.

Avery conceded to himself that he had missed these walks and the banter he had with Helen.

Helen dropped her elbow a little and let her fingers sit lightly in the crook of the Reverend's bare arm. Avery felt every one of them.

'When you asked me before what was going on, well, it's complicated.'

'Try me.'

'It worries me that I'm alone – that I don't have any family apart from Aunty Katherine who doesn't give a damn whether I live or die. She doesn't count. It's not that I'm not surviving well enough without my folks. It's just that it's just me. I never hear their names anymore. It's like they were never here and then I think about what it would mean if they were never here and I was never born. And then I wonder would anyone miss me. So I have to ask myself, what the hell difference does it make whether I'm here or not?'

Avery said nothing, allowing Helen to say the things he was aware had been troubling her for some time. Her gait had become a little erratic as she grew agitated, making it difficult to maintain a comfortable pace together, so he slowed himself down and took shorter strides to steady her.

'The whole thing with Mabel is about me crawling into the storeroom to see if I can see my own hand in front of me in the dark.'

'But potatoes Helen? Do you have to throw them at her?'

Helen continued, enjoying the smirk in his voice.

'Sometimes I see myself on a raft. It's a bed of twigs in a great big swill that could be sucked under at any time and I'm like a leaf on top, with no hope of holding on.'

Avery gently took control of the walk and redirected them into an arc that would take them back to the truck before nightfall. He had not previously considered Helen to be a very deep vessel despite the amount of time they had spent together and stole a few glances at her face to validate the idea.

'Just when I think I'm going to drown, when I'm completely exhausted, my raft washes up onto the shore of this island. I get up and stagger onto the sand, but when I look back to the raft, it's gone. I walk around the whole island looking for something, I don't even know what, and then I realise, I haven't left a single footprint in the sand. Not one. There is nothing on that island to say I've ever been there.

'I know it's a daydream. Mum used to say I was a daytime sleepwalker; I could sleepwalk through the boring bit of my day and no one would ever know. But there are times now, when I think I don't even know I'm doing it.

'The other day, I was walking by myself and I just froze. I was so convinced that my next step would be invisible to everyone except me that I was too scared to take it, in case I was right. Just like on the island. I got stuck, halfway between the shop and my house. My heart was beating really fast. I don't know how long I was there before I realised it was just a stupid idea. Sometimes I think I'm just losing the plot.'

Avery took his bearings, spotted the rise with the miner's cottage on its crest still a fair way off to their right and adjusted his step, picking the broadest gaps between the blue bush as the light continued to fall.

Helen's head had dropped a little, she was no longer the cocky young woman who had commandeered the attentions of an older man and taken him out of his way by having a tantrum at home.

She's a thoughtful, troubled soul and right now I wouldn't give up her arm for all the sunsets of the outback.

'Let me pose a question for you.'

Helen looked up.

'Will my answer get me locked up?' She asked only half jokingly.

'It's not that kind of question. But you do have to think about it. It's one that philosophers and scientists both have a view on and neither can be said categorically to be right or wrong.'

Though Helen had no desire to get back to the miner's cottage just yet, her step quickened with the intrigue. 'Well, go on then, what is this amazing question?'

'Imagine for a minute that you are in a forest ...'

'Anywhere but on that island works for me ...'

'You are surrounded by trees – tall, skyscraping trees – but you are alone in this forest, surrounded by trees.'

'I may as well be on the island.'

'Now say one of those trees falls, comes crashing down. You would hear it, wouldn't you?'

'Of course.'

'Now picture the same forest, but this time without you in it. The same tree falls, crashes to the ground. If you are not there – if no other living soul is there to hear it, has it made a sound?'

'Of course it has; just because someone doesn't acknowledge something doesn't mean it hasn't happened. What kind of a question is that?'

'Think about it a little more. The bigger question is about perception. In our world, the things we think, are just as important as the things we do. It's about influence and changing realities and I guess, putting ourselves at the centre of our universe.'

'I thought God was at the centre of our universe. Reverend Holbrook, are you challenging the teachings of the Church?'

Avery feigned a look of rebuke and continued.

'The Buddhists describe it this way. Three men are watching a flag blowing in the wind. The first man sees the flag moving, the second man sees the wind moving, but the third man tells them that it is neither the flag nor the wind that is moving. It is …'

Helen interrupted him.

'It's their minds that are moving, right?'

Avery was impressed, and Helen felt a tinge of pride and gratefulness to Miss Palmer for lending her such a wide variety of books.

The cottage was in full view now, and the sun a blotted orange yolk languidly leaking into the crest of the rise.

'Do you understand what I'm saying?' Avery asked Helen.

'You're telling me that the trees in my forest can all stand tall and strong if I believe they are tall and strong, which is a good thing. And that knowing that could stop me falling over.

'On the other hand you could be saying that if I sit on a sack of potatoes in a dark storeroom with my hand up in front of my face and I can't see it, then perhaps my hand isn't in front of my face at all – that it's all in my imagination. And if I'm left with my own imagination running the show, that's a bad thing, and I'm likely to fall over anyway.'

'You've got a mind like a twisted sandshoe, you know that? What I'm saying is that you don't need to sit in the dark, that whether or not you let the light in, growing strong and making something of your life is up to you.'

Helen squeezed a little tighter into the crook of Avery's arm.

'You know you're my only friend, right?'

As they walked along again in silence, Helen realised that she did not want the walk to end. Why was the Reverend the only person she wanted to spend time with? She felt real when he came to see her. She left footprints when they walked because he was beside her.

Avery dropped Helen's arm as they approached the rear of the cottage, conscious that the solitary landscape was falling behind them and that beyond the truck and this extraordinary fillip of peace, the township lay in front of them.

She skipped ahead like the schoolgirl she still should have been and leant against the driver's side door of the truck, her face turned toward the sunset, her eyelids closed to meld the moment to her memory.

He stood beside her, his back to the tray of the truck and sighed deeply.

After a minute or so in which neither of them spoke, Avery rolled away from the reflected warmth of the vehicle and began rummaging in his pocket for the keys. Helen remained where she was, blocking access to the driver's seat. Avery attempted to shift her aside, without success. She looked up at him, earnestly holding his eyes with the poignancy of a first time dissolute soul about to wander too far and the rebellious flicker of what that might entail.

'C'mon Helen. Out of the way please.'

She slowly brought her arms up to wrap them around his neck and Avery's restraint began to fray at the edges. He gingerly moved his hands onto each of her slim hips and held her there in a feeble attempt to keep their bodies apart, but with every shift of her weight he found himself desperate to draw her closer. Her face had stolen the sunset and her eyelashes were florid brushstrokes of liquid white. He knew that she would allow him to feel the soft down of her skin on his lips if he were to put them on her neck right now.

She sucked her bottom lip in and then let it pop out, moistened. Avery could resist no longer and pulled her hips toward him as he leant down slightly to take those lips into his own. She pulled one of his arms around her waist and left her other hand tussling the hair at the nape of his neck. His skin was tingling as she twisted her head from one side to the other, sucking his lips in a tantalising mimic …

Avery gasped. And shuddered. And exhaled with a whimper. The inevitability of his ejaculation had been assured way back when Helen was still steeling her nerves to the deed.

Confused at his noises, Helen looked at their feet, thinking Avery may have been bitten and was in pain. Then she saw the darkening patch on the Reverend's trousers. The realisation came to her more slowly than it should have, given her intentions, but when it did, she felt a tumult of pride, fear and a little disgust.

A crow landed noisily on the remnants of the cottage roof, turned its head jauntily in her direction and distracted her with its cool yellow eye. She took a step back, screwed her nose up like a toddler covered in fingerpaint and taunted the shrinking figure in front of her in a sing song voice: 'So you do want me, Reverend Holbrook!'

'I need somewhere to clean up. Now. Right now.'

Avery was barking defensively, but Helen was unphased, heady at the thought of her influence on the Reverend and her mind racing ahead to what it might mean. Almost roughly now, Avery pushed her aside from the door, waved her away to the passenger seat and turned the key in the ignition. He was grateful it started first time.

After they had driven down the slope without a word, Avery addressed her with a slightly too loud clip in his voice, his eyes unmoved from the road.

'Are there any of your father's clothes still at the old house?'

'I packed up most things. I gave them to you, remember, for the Church?'

They drove on in silence, Avery heading for the Muldoon home anyway. His heart racing.

15.

A souring gaze.

[May, 1950.]

'There is a camphorwood chest in the main bedroom,' Helen offered. 'There might be something in there you can change into.'

Night was creeping into the desert and would soon be blanketing the township of Kimbanyon. The Reverend Holbrook and his young companion were on the verandah of her former family home, opening the door with a key Helen had not used for more than a year now. She had some trepidation about seeing inside, about how the displacement of furniture since its rental might shuffle her memories. Like deck chairs on the Titanic, she thought, borrowing a phrase her father had been fond of.

As she jiggled the key in the lock, Avery was mentally sizing up the late Jim Muldoon and holding tightly to his recollection of them being a similar height.

This is Gwen's fault. All that talk about the optimum time for sperm delivery. I can't do it anymore. Don't I deserve to have good old fashioned sex with my wife?

Helen found her way to the nearest light switch as Avery forced himself to think about something else. She seemed oblivious to his discomfort, even mischievously happy about it, laughing to herself as he swept the loungeroom curtains swiftly across their rods to shield their presence from the street, despite there being no neighbours for at least three miles.

The guilt inside Avery was on the move, shifting again, sharp and anxious, pushing threateningly against soft tissue. He followed Helen into her parents' bedroom. An old newspaper was spread out on top of the camphorwood chest, with a bottle opener on top of that. The ganger, it appeared, had not felt the need to clean up before he left. When the newspaper was removed, it revealed a lid of a deep ebony hue, elaborately carved with the horizontal branches of Chinese trees and snow- capped mountains of varying sizes. Another key was needed to open the box, but it was already in the lock. Helen held the heavy lid up with some difficulty while Avery lifted those contents at the top out onto the carpet beside them.

Helen tightened a corner brace to secure the lid while she too removed items. With each extraction she looked toward the bedroom door, half expecting to see her mother, her father's shirts ironed and folded flat in her hands, standing stiff at the sight of her daughter going through her things. There were letters, bound together by rubber bands, yellowing at the edges. There were crocheted doilies and fine white linen table cloths with scalloped edges.

A parcel wrapped in brown paper and tied with string looked like it might contain clothes, but turned out to be a set of sheets. A note included in it was marked simply 'For Helen's Hope Chest'. It was written in her mother's hand, with its small neat letters and long, leaning loop on the 'l' and tail on the 'p', the strokes looking like they had grown into the unnatural position in the way new branches on tea trees by the beach point in the direction blown by the prevailing wind. Helen sunk to her knees, and rested on her calves. She lay the sheets now on her thighs and the note on top of them, patting it with spread fingers, lightly as if it might turn to dust.

Avery had left the room to search through the rest of the house and had been relieved to find exactly what he was looking for – a pair of navy blue suit pants which had fallen from a lone hangar to the bottom of a cupboard in the sunroom, overlooked when it was cleaned out. They were a little musty and crushed, but the material was fine enough that most creases would soon fall out once he wore them for a while, and everything else could be explained by the discomfort of a train journey. They were almost a perfect match in colour for his waistcoat and jacket. The length could be a little shorter and the girth a little larger but they would get him home and out of trouble.

He walked back into the bedroom, freshly attired and consulting his watch. Helen had put everything back in the chest and was locking it as he entered, pocketing the key.

'I'm staying here,' she announced with steadfast eyes, defying Avery to suggest otherwise and continuing to talk in case he did.

'I'll drive you to the station. Leave your pants; I'll soak them. Tell the Johns's I'll be at work on Monday and I won't bother them after hours.'

She drives?

Avery moved to speak and was abruptly cut off: 'This is my home Avery. I'm staying.'

The Reverend saw the girl was not going to take an argument but didn't want to leave matters unresolved with Bert.

'If you drop me over to the shop, I'll explain things to Bert – tell him you wish to move back home. But you should talk to them both as well, Helen; I think you may owe them an apology.'

Avery stopped mid-sentence, the validity and value of his ministering, so fulsomely evolved over the last 18 months, now impossibly thin.

'Mabel will live,' Helen said curtly. 'Do you have the keys?'

Avery had already transferred the keys from his soiled trousers to the new pair and he jiggled them in his pocket in confirmation and turned to the laundry to hang his washing over the copper tub. He would rather they be burnt but did not want to compound the sin with the ceremony of a fiery annihilation, or raise attention with the smoke.

They really should be drycleaned. Helen can throw them out when she realises the washing has ruined them.

'Helen, we should talk about this.'

She's so stubborn. And totally shameless. If she thinks this is going to happen again, or that I am in any way to blame …

'Reverend, the keys?'

'I'm driving,' he asserted, pulling himself together. 'You will drive the truck home where it must be left for the ganger and not driven again. The key should be put back under the sunshade.'

Helen looked bemused; she had taught herself to drive the deserted truck weeks ago and had laughed out loud when she had seen Avery pull up in it that afternoon.

Was that really today? It seems such a long time ago. And he seems so much less attractive now. What did I see in him?

Avery gathered his wits under the girl's souring gaze. He took in the corners of the room they were standing in and tried to imagine her a child in her home. A tall reading lamp stood beside an armchair to the left of the window. Its wooden stem was carved like twisted rope and its broad canopy was edged with fawn cotton bobbles. It would have been a comforting light to doze off by. Safe.

'Reverend, did you hear me? The keys?'

'You'll have to drive it back and I'll have that on my conscience the whole trip home. Now get in!'

She was on the point of giggling now.

'As if that's the worst thing you will have on your conscience!'

'Listen to me Helen. You are young and attractive and have obviously suffered from being without a mother. I want you to think about your behaviour this afternoon and how you are going to act around men in the future. Promiscuity is as much a sin of the mind as it is the body. You were lucky, I would say, that your target was me and not someone who might have taken advantage of you.'

Somehow Avery's assuredness in what he was saying helped him to deny the hypocrisy of it all, despite Helen rolling her eyes at his use of the word 'sin'.

'There are things about you that only your husband should know, Helen. These are not things we should share. What I want to share with you is the ability to be at peace with yourself, to breathe calmly in God's world and not so heatedly within yourself. You'll expire living that way.'

Helen was affronted. She wanted to say that she was not the one that soiled herself – not the one who had 'expired' or should she say, 'expelled'. She had been enjoying a nice sunset while he was obviously having sinful thoughts about her. She blinked back the hot pricks of moisture rising under her lashes.

He tells me to apologise to Mabel, but he has no apology for me. What have I done? Looked for a kiss. How is that as bad as his 'sin'. He should burn those pants. Or perhaps I should send them home to his wife.

'Helen?' Avery drew himself up against the hurt and indignation radiating from the girl. He stepped outside, heading for the truck, the keys still in his pocket.

Expecting her to follow.

16.

Dry Creek Station.

[Summer of 1947.]

Duggarie was born to a Pitjantjatjara woman following the Spring rains of 1912 when wildflowers peppered the plains west of Lake Eyre with vivid scarlet petals and rambling protrusions of green.

Yanyi's two previous children had been stillborn and her recovery from birth drawn out, so when her contractions began she set off by herself, determined to suppress her labour until she found a place where she felt at ease. After an hour the pain became more severe and frequent and she found relief only by walking on her toes.

Finally she settled beneath a red mulga coursing with honeydew. Her waters broke within minutes of her camping underneath it.

After several hours of labour, Yanyi felt the baby's head breach and his legs slip through. She was elated to hear her baby cry. Her aunties who had followed her and were hovering nearby came over quickly to retrieve the placenta.

They lifted Duggarie onto his mother's leaking breasts and severed the umbilical chord with a sharp stone. As Yanyi looked up at the stars twinkling through the branches, she felt overwhelmed with gratitude to her ancestors for this gift. But in the light of the partial moon, her aunties could tell something was wrong. Before the baby could suckle at his mother's breast, he would feel in his own chest the violent convulsions of her heart attack.

As Duggarie's spirit settled him into his country, Yanyi's would be torn from it.

***

Thirty five years later on Dry Creek Station, some 100 miles or so west of Yanyi's mulga tree, Duggarie was awaiting the birth of his own child.

He had confined himself to a stable block that was no more than seven strides across in order to pace unseen. He had been here for hours now and the light was beginning to withdraw from the yards. Shadows curled around random clumps of bluegrass and streaked behind the poles of stock fences like a charred reflection in the inflamed dirt.

Duggarie crouched, his brow threaded. When he stood up, he wiped his sweaty palms down his thighs but the dusty moleskins only made them feel greasy. He leant back against the mud bricks of the stable wall rolling his head to the side and closing his eyes against the memories of how he had swelled inside Elsa here. He could almost feel her nails pulling the skin of his neck into her mouth to muffle her gasps and her teeth bite him gently when he came. Immediately afterwards, she had buttoned up, donned her Akubra work hat and led her horse out without looking back.

That woman, so clawing, so fierce.

The other Aboriginal stockmen – those who could still buy beer out the back of the local pub at least – had cleared off to it. Duggarie was rumoured to be 'the boyfriend', 'the lover', the stockman who 'did' the boss's wife, and he had confirmed it for them by deserting the roundup when news came that she had gone into labour.

Duggarie tried to clear his head. The sun had dropped almost to the horizon, giving the dirt floor beneath his feet a golden glow. His gelding stirred, the girth of its saddle swinging loose under its belly in the nearest open stall. There was a wet snort and a stomping of its hoof, before a torrent of urine bore through the dust, baking the air with a virile odour.

Duggarie had galloped all the way to the homestead, without a thought for what he would do when he arrived. So he was hiding here, less than twenty feet away from Elsa's cries and guilt ridden for being so close and so far from her at the same time.

Women's business happened away from the men. It was how it should be. But Elsa had no aunties around her either. The boss's suspicions had led him to deny his wife their 'black hands' – and Duggarie feared for his child because of their absence.

A noise like a stirrup being dragged across a car wreck burst from the house, propelling a flurry of white cockatoos into the air.

From a ventilation gap in the brickwork, Duggarie saw the boss jump up from where he'd been sitting on the verandah steps. His brother Marty came from inside the house to update him, as he did several times over the next hour while the contractions and howls continued. To Duggarie both men seemed harassed and out of place. He hated to think of Elsa in their ignorant care.

Wrongway business.

After a while, whether it was because Elsa's contractions had eased, or simply that her labour had quieted and Duggarie was unable to hear it, the next hour produced nothing to either frighten or calm him.

He waited patiently, sitting without movement on the stable floor, until the gelding came to him having discovered its feed tin empty. It nudged Duggarie's shoulder forcefully and when no response came, Duggarie felt its whiskery muzzle brush his cheek and its warm, moist breath fooffing him. So it was that Duggarie thought the low growl that began softly some time later was emanating from his horse's stomach. But the growl rolled on, cutting through the still night air like an undercurrent and gnawing at the weathered bricks around him. Duggarie rose to look through the ventilation gap. Bossman was pacing up and down the verandah but had not gone inside. A watery scream hurled itself down the front steps, followed by a whimpering as persistent as the growl had been.

The boss called to his brother: 'What's going on in there?'

He got no response. The house was silent.

Marty came to the door and put a hand on his brother's shoulder. 'It's not yours mate.'

The boss jumped up and tripped over himself in his haste to see for himself. His brother attempted to help him up but was violently brushed off.

'Take it easy in there Nate,' Marty called after him, 'She doesn't look too good.'

Dugarrie dragged the back of his hand across his mouth to wipe away a salty tear that had dropped there in the instant of those words. He took himself back into the stables and crouched down – self loathing a clench in his chest. Suddenly he stood, punched his fist into the wall and turned to his horse, now restless and shaking its head as if a thousand flies had landed there at once.

Duggarie tightened the girth a notch higher than he should have, roughly redid it to relieve the pinch and lifted himself into the saddle.

He would ride that gelding until it was lathered and heaving and the idea of returning was a fright in his mind. It would be a decade before that fright became regret, and more than twenty years before that regret became someone else's problem.

17.

Dug over coals.

[Summer of 1947.]

Several weeks after he had gone on the road as a patrol padre, Avery had bought a small round mirror with a wire hoop on it from a hawker. As he sharpened his razor, sweeping it back and forth on a leather strap, it gave him a quiet satisfaction to look up and know that he hadn't yet failed to find a branch or protrusion on which to hang it at the perfect height.

A tumble of noises reverberated in the leafy canopy above the Holbrooks' campsite. Sounding both near and far were currawongs, curlews and kookaburras. Sometimes there was a loud crack followed by the boom of a gum branch falling, or a quiet but persistent rustle of dry leaves and sticks, suggesting wildlife nearby.

Tipping out the last of her tea onto the dug over coals of an earlier fire, Gwen delayed packing up the truck to draw the ambient smells and sounds deep into her core. She took particular pleasure in immersing herself in the sharp, dank scent of the eucalypts surrounding their campsite. It always managed to revive in her a sense of belonging and adventure, for the first few hours of every day anyway.

As they cruised along the mostly dirt roads in the Chevrolet, Gwen took comfort in knowing that she and Avery and their material belongings – the vehicle, the wireless, the cooking utensils, the tent and everything that kept them connected with Avery's patrol – were inconsequential to the timeless environment they were passing through. Nothing they did would have an impact on the way the sandy soil was picked up by a tussle of wind and spun wildly in the whirly whirlies, the way mysterious narrow and curly paths were gouged into the trunks of giant scribbly gums, the way the sky fair burst from its skin with a blue so pure and unbroken the colour should not be demeaned by being assigned a name.

Avery, she knew, thrived on ministering at the stations. He took a warm pride in baptising young children who had grown from babies waiting for such a visit, and performing weddings and even memorial services that brought families together once every couple of years. For Gwen, a deep wellbeing was sustained by the moments in between the visits where she and Avery shared a mateship that deepened with every solitary mile they travelled together.

It had taken the best part of a year for Mr and Mrs Holbrook to become the expert travellers they now were, needing for so little and so comfortable with compromise it scarcely rated a mention. Gwen had become so good at it that her mechanical improvisations – which once notoriously included getting a car with a broken fan belt back on the road by splicing a leather belt and sewing its ends together using a needle of bone and shoe laces – were beginning to follow them around as the stuff of legend.

Initially when she and Avery had first gone on the road, the landscape had all looked the same. Now Gwen knew how to identify the mulga, woollybutt, pearl and bladder saltbush when they were driving through sandplains and woodlands, and to expect cottonbush, coolibahs, Broughton willows, hopbush and tea trees when they came across floodplains and creekbeds. She had become knowledgeable enough to argue the beauty of the orange and purple clusters of summer flowering emu bushes and the wild yellow flourish of cassias in the uplands with any suburban gardner.

Her tolerance for being a passenger (Avery rarely ceded the wheel) for hours on end had also improved as her appreciation for the bush and bush folk grew. She came to understand that the job was characterised by independence, unpredictability and often drawn out days where it was hard to recall anything of note actually happening in the hours before or after you noticed your window arm showing signs of sunburn.

Often their only directions came from a hand-drawn map. Flat, crevassed or crutched roads all seemed to lead to more of the same, for miles and miles and hours and hours. Gwen's buttocks and thighs would be numb on the seat and her bladder fit to burst before Avery would agree to a stop 'to stretch the legs'. And then she would have to squat behind a tree, far away enough to be discreet and yet not so far that if she were bit by a snake he could not find her. Just when she thought she could not take the sticky flies or dust anymore and found herself alternating between winding the window up against them and winding it down again to let out the stuffy air, he would point to a light from a window and they would soon be washing up with strangers, welcoming for the most part.

Today, it felt quite wicked to be driving just for them – not for Avery to conduct a wedding or a funeral, not in response to a call from the Flying Doctor Service or an obligation of another kind. They were headed toward the base of the Eyre Peninsula on the last leg of the drive to Silver Flats sheep station where they were to stay with friends of Avery's who were managing the property.

The couple had been the first and only war-time marriage service Avery had conducted. It had been hastily arranged by Jack, then an injured serviceman hospitalised in Johor Bahru. They were among the few friends Avery had wanted at his own wedding to Gwen, but he hadn't been able to track Jack down. Now, as he left the mining town of Iron Knob behind with another 60 miles to go to Silver Flats, he was surprised at just how much he was looking forward to seeing them again.

With wide corrugations, Avery settled on a fast rather than slow speed that kept the discomfort to a minimum, and maintained it from the broadest part of the road. Choosing heat over dust, Gwen wound her window up and found the cabin quiet enough for conversation when Avery followed suit.

'How did Jack and Betty meet?'

'Betty was with the AGH in Malaya. She nursed Jack there,' Avery replied, leaning forward pointlessly as another dust cloud fogged the windscreen. 'But don't talk about the war with her, Gwen; best to leave it alone. She had a rough time of it.'

'She didn't end up on Banka, did she?'

'I'll tell you what I know and then I don't want you to mention it again, at least not in front of Jack and Betty, OK?'

Gwen sat in silent agreement.

'Jack and I were shipped out separately, within days of me marrying them. Betty and some other nurses were escaping Singapore but a Japanese air raid sunk their boat off the coast of Sumatra. She ended up in a POW camp at Palembang. But I'm guessing a few of those nurses executed on Bangka Island would have been friends of hers.'

'How did …?'

'She was liberated from a rubber plantation after the war ended. The Japs had hidden them there to feed them up, thinking they'd be treated better themselves if their prisoners weren't near dead when they found them. Unbelievable really.'

'Jack must have been out of his mind with worry,' Gwen said, gripping onto the dashboard as they rolled into and lurched out of another depression. Avery fell silent again.

Gwen mulled his words over for a while. She had heard stories of torture and starvation in the Japanese camps and made a pact with herself not to mention anything to do with the war while she was at Silver Flats.

But we're not there yet.

'Did you know Jack before the war?'

Avery steered the truck to the side of a deep fissure and did not answer Gwen until it narrowed into a flat surface again.

'Jack and I met on the boat from England.'

Something else we don't need to talk about right now.

'I thought I could detect a British accent creeping in every now and then, particularly when you're making a point that no-one understands, or sprouting latin to explain a concept – where did you learn that anyway? Surely not as a farm hand!

Gwen asked her question tentatively, aware how wrong it was that she felt like a stranger prying into her husband's past because of his reluctance to talk about it.

'I was trained as a farm hand, but my "trade" has always been as a Reverend,' Avery responded tritely, 'just as you were trained as a mechanic and are now a Reverend's wife 'by trade'.'

'And with a job like that you can see why I'm so keen to have some fun, now can't you?'

Gwen took the hint and decided to focus on their brief holiday instead.

'Betty probably hasn't spoken to another woman for months, so she'll be pretty starved for intelligent conversation. I can't wait to meet her.'

Finally, several cattle grids and a few gates later, they arrived at Silver Flats Station, parched and desperate for a wash.

On hearing the dogs bark, Jack fair bowled out of the homestead at the rear, where the truck had pulled up and grabbed Avery's hand, shaking it effusively, every muscle in his forearm lifting to the surface and a broad smile on his tanned face.

'Great to see you Ave! Been looking forward to this for a long time. And where's this new wife of yours?'

Jack stepped forward and kissed Gwen lightly on the cheek.

'Gwen, I presume. The brains of the outfit from what I hear. You've done well old man!'

Gwen blushed, barely having gathered herself for the greeting before it was upon her.

'Here, let me get you a cold drink,' Jack offered 'and come meet Betty. We've got enough supplies to feed a hundred shearers, and only sixty coming, so I hope you've got an appetite.'

'Thanks Jack, but would you mind if we unpacked first, then I don't have to worry about it later,' Gwen asked, catching Avery's eye in the hope he'd swing back to the Chevvy and grab their gear.

Jack caught the look with amusement.

'What are you looking at him for? I've got a beer waiting for him and it's not getting any colder.' The tired glare which met his joke had Jack scrambling to appease Gwen.

''Course you can unpack: let me give you a hand.'

'Actually, I was thinking I might quickly wash up while you men unpack the truck. Would Betty mind if I used the bathroom?'

'She'd probably prefer it if you didn't do your business in the yard,' Jack laughed, unwittingly offending the tired Gwen for a second time with his offhand humour.

Gwen opened the screen door onto a large, stone-floored kitchen, to find Betty, who had overheard the commotion and was waiting with a neatly folded towel and a cake of soap.

'I don't welcome everyone this way you know, although almost everyone who walks through this door could do with a wash.'

Gwen looked ready to weep, misconstruing Betty's comments for more of Jack's unwelcome humour.

'Well, it's hard to stay fresh on the road,' Gwen said curtly, whipping the towel and soap from Betty and hoping to make a quick dash for the bathroom. But it was hard to be indignant and make a decisive exit when she had no idea where the bathroom was. She looked to Betty for assistance, a forlorn figure with nowhere else to turn. Betty also looked distressed that she'd offended her guest within seconds of meeting her. Simultaneously, they offered, 'I'm sorry'.

Gwen was about to continue, to explain how tired she was, but Betty cut her off.

'Down the hall and to your left. I'll have a drink waiting for you when you come out.'

'Not that I need one!'

Much.

Jack, shorter than Avery by almost a foot, nudged his friend in the ribs with his shoulder in a mock football gesture as they walked to the truck.

'She did that nicely mate. Not even in the house yet, and she's in the shower, and we're unloading the truck. How do they do it, eh? They've got us completely outfoxed!'

Avery grinned, watching Jack release the tarp like he had done it a hundred times already that day and catching his enthusiasm. Truth was, it had been a long drive and right now he was just as happy to let Gwen take charge as he was to listen to Jack kidding him about it.

Jack had stacked several suitcases on the tray of the truck, edged them a third of the way over the edge and slid in backwards underneath them, pulling them onto his back as if it were an extension of the tray. He took a few steps forward, his back and neck rigidly horizontal, his arms tucked by his sides and his hands cupping the rear of his load.

With visibility confined to his feet and a few paces in front of him, he dropped his knees and began staggering on buckled legs like a drunk in a silent movie.

'What the hell have you got packed in here?'

Gwen reappeared in a fresh lilac blouse and tan shorts, having had the quick shower that those accustomed to drought and water tanks have. She was so relaxed she had left her shoulder length hair twisted in a towel to dry in order to take the shandy that had been offered to her.

Heading to the back door to see Jack labouring with the luggage, she chastised her husband: 'Avery, help the poor man; he's not a camel!'

'He's doing just fine,' Avery called back. 'Is that my glass you're holding because you know a bottle would do!'

Betty came to the broad open doorway and stood beside Gwen, having exchanged the safari-style shirt and jeans she had been wearing for a teal blouse and knee-length skirt and tied her thin black hair into a short single plait. Her shandy was already half drunk and she leant on the frame finishing it off like cordial while shaking her head with amusement at her husband's antics and Avery's unwillingness to help him.

She spoke loudly enough to startle Gwen, who had been watching the show oblivious to the company beside her.

'Men drink when the chores are done around here and not a minute before,' she said in such a sharp voice that no one except Jack knew she was joking.

Avery looked exceedingly put out and turned to his wife, rather than Jack. 'Well it wasn't my idea to unpack just yet,' he complained. 'Gwen you'd better get over here and give Jack a hand; this whole situation is your fault.'

Jack lifted his head to catch Avery's expression and caused the smallest of the three suitcases to slide from the top of the stack on his back, landing in the dirt behind him.

A cattle dog on a long chain pegged under a tree some twelve feet away started barking lazily, the level of action now too much to ignore.

'Oh for heaven's sake,' Betty scolded, striding towards Jack and the cases. 'Can we just get these two in from the heat and stop letting the flies in?'

Gwen suddenly felt embarrassed that at her first meeting with this couple she had left them to unpack the truck while she showered and pampered herself. She whipped the towel off her head and hastily flung it over the wooden rail she assumed was there to tie horses to and rushed to help Betty.

Avery had taken charge of the remaining cases which looked set to follow the first in a topple off Jack's back and was standing with them beside each leg as his wife charged toward him, taking a sip that inadvertently became a gulp because of her haste.

'Hold this,' she told him, handing him the near empty glass and bending down to grab the luggage. Avery could not help but notice the way her youthful breasts rolled forward to fill her bra, and his senses dissolved with the smell of scented soap.

Oblivious, Gwen turned on her heels and walked toward the house with the case, Avery watching the muscles in her smooth calves tighten with each step. With Jack bemused by seeing the

Padre leering at his wife and Avery bemused by the mock fear Jack was displaying at her ferocity, both men erupted in laughter. Jack tilted his beer bottle towards the glass Avery had been left holding and toasted the ingenuity shown in turning the tables on the women who had become the porters after all.

'Now that's how it's done, old man!'

The evening settled around a large wooden table, with Betty ladling out her 'famous' kangaroo stew. It was a little gamey for Gwen though she had learned over years on the road to finish whatever was served to her to avoid offending people who generally didn't have a lot to spare.

The Holbrooks filled Jack and Betty in on their exploits, with Avery proudly telling of Gwen's famous fanbelt fix and ensuring it would continue to do the rounds of the outback for a few more months.

Gwen thought she saw genuine admiration in the glint in Jack's eye as he proposed yet another toast, this time to a woman's ingenuity, 'essential in helping man reach his potential'. He even offered a story of his own about Betty, who had apparently gone out on horseback looking for him when he had been late to return from a sheep muster and turned up with two camels in tow.

'If you've ever tried herding camels, you'd be seriously impressed,' Jack informed his friends, before adding with a grin, 'I have no idea what she thought we'd do with them!'

The following day the friends drove out to explore a fraction of the 195,000 acres of the station, with Avery and Gwen learning that Jack and Betty had retraced the journey originally made by John Eyre in 1839 from Streaky Bay on the western side of the Eyre Peninsula through the Gawler Rangers to the head of the Spencer Gulf. Apparently this is how Betty got the idea that a few camels might be useful to have around.

The Spinifex was particularly high and Jack stopped several times to clear the vehicle's radiator screen and slash and bundle the grass onto the roof rack of the four-wheel drive. An Aboriginal stockman had once shown him how to extract resin from the stalks after they burnt and he had found hundreds of uses for it in repairs around the station and shearing sheds.

When they reached the northern boundary of the property, the vast salt pan of Lake Gairdner spread before them in glaring splendour. They left the vehicle to take in the silvery plain, with Gwen cottoning on, much to everyone's amusement, to why the property was named as it was and how it had nothing to do with mineral wealth! She wondered how such a place could ever be called a lake.

As impressive as it was when it was dry, Jack asserted, it didn't compare with how it looked after the big rains. He and Betty had seen it only once but had been lucky enough to view it from the air when the owner of the station had returned by light aircraft and taken his party up for a 'joy ride'.

'Normally the lake is this great white, crusty plain with pink sands around it,' Betty said, interrupting Jack's story.

'But when it filled this time, it was like a giant water world with rocky outcrops and green islands that broke through the waters like the backs of whales. And so many birds; I've never seen so much wildlife come out of something that was so barren.'

Betty, who hadn't strung so many words together in a conversation since the Holbrooks had arrived, laughed with undue embarrassment at waxing lyrical about her extraordinary backyard.

'C'mon,' Jack urged them after a while. 'I want to show you something closer to the house.'

Not far from the shearers' quarters, columns of rhyolite, like clay organ pipes, sprung from the earth for no apparent purpose in the natural order – 'other than God showing off', Avery concluded.

The sightseeing had taken the better part of the day and while it was not oppressively hot, the group was happy to be close to the homestead and wander and chat with it in sight. Betty suggested to Gwen that they might see if the wildflowers that usually appeared at this time of year were out yet.

Out of earshot of the women, Jack produced a pouch of tobacco and some papers and sat down on the flat of a large, low rock, spreading his feet wide apart. Avery kicked at a fallen tree trunk to make sure he wouldn't be disturbing anything in the hollow that could bite him and took a seat near his friend.

When Jack had had a few puffs of his cigarette, blowing a few smoke rings to the sky for his own entertainment, Avery shared his thoughts.

'Jack, do you think if you hadn't ended up at Scheyville, you would have been happy to work in the city?'

'You know I've never been one for the big smoke, mate. What's on your mind?'

'I'm thinking Gwen and I might settle in Adelaide soon – maybe start a family – and I'm not sure it's going to be a good fit for me; I've been in the outback pretty much my whole adult life.'

'You old dog … you want to be a dad?'

'It's the next logical step right?'

Jack shunted some dirt over a large bull ant hole he had been keeping an eye on at his feet and watched it disappear into the centre and re-open again. When he didn't respond, Avery came back to him.

'Does Betty ever talk about having kids?'

Jack looked up from the ant hole that had finally had its fill of dirt, and slung his gaze across the open expanse, preferring to look at the landscape rather than Avery when he responded.

'We're happy enough as we are.'

The men sat in silence for a while before Jack finally changed the subject.

'You know Scheyville was turned into a training camp during the war; Bunter ended up back there with the Parachute Battalion. Never actually made it through the course though, stupid bastard.'

'I heard.'

'All he had to do was get to the front and then he'd be so busy thinking about getting back safely, that he'd forget about all that stuff.'

Bunter had been popular with the boys when he first arrived as a fourteen year old at the Scheyville training farm. He had stringy red hair, freckles and an unfortunate red birthmark that covered one eye and part of his right cheek, but he was also quick with a joke and never complained about the eczema that seemed to flare on his hands and arms whenever he had anything to do with the livestock. Because of the rashes, and perhaps his unfortunate appearance, the instructors targeted Bunter and he was often given latrine duties that made his skin even worse.

Despite his former life in Liverpool sounding less than glorious, homesickness had set in him like a rot and it seemed at first that the only thing that gave him some relief was the visits by Brother Lucas, who posted letters to his parents for him. Bunter received none back but he was not surprised; if he was barely literate, they were even less capable in that area.

As the time came closer to be sent to work on a farm, Bunter had become more withdrawn. Brother Lucas had offered to make arrangements for him, but it was Brother Francis, known to the boys as Feely Francis, who had taken him on numerous 'excursions' to properties. Bunter usually returned from these field trips more depressed than ever until finally he took a position. Avery had lost track of so many of the Dreadnought boys, that he had not given Bunter a second thought until he had heard of his death.

Can't believe he shot himself.

Jack had been rolling a second cigarette and passed it to Avery, looking up to see where the women were and concluding they must have headed back to the house.

'I counselled a man once who killed himself the next day – my most spectacular failure,' Avery said dispassionately, looking at the cigarette he hadn't expected to find in his hand as if it had hidden properties of interest.

Jack looked over at his friend. Squinting against the sun lowering behind Avery's head and unable to see his expression, he said nothing.

'He was a guard at a POW camp. His son went down with The Sydney. Must have been stewing on it for years, then he just snapped and shot off his gun in this prisoner's room and killed his batman.'

'What the hell was the batman doing there?'

'Yeah, I know,' Avery said, 'they were interning them with their officers.'

'So you talked to this fellow?'

Avery took his first drag of the cigarette that had been burning down in his hand and let it sit inside him for a while, the smoke wafting from his nostrils like plumes from the windows of a burning house.

'The day after I went to see him, he opened his window, walked out onto a tree branch and hung himself. Nothing I said to him was worth a damn.'

Jack put his hand out, drew deeply on the cigarette passed to him and handed it back.

'Shit mate. You can't be expected to save everyone; it's not always up to you.'

'Yeah, well. Maybe it should have been. I can't help feeling some other padre might have done it better.'

'Look Ave. If there were guidelines about this stuff, we'd all be doing God's work.'

'There are actually ..'

'What?'

'Guidelines.'

Avery paused, wondering why he had even begun this conversation but Jack encouraged him.

'Well don't leave me hanging! Oh, sorry mate, I didn't mean ...'

'You really want to know?'

'I really wanna know. Tell me the secrets of the padres.'

'Ius ad bello and ius in bello.'

'Ah, the secret language of the church – designed to stop the ordinary bloke getting his hands on salvation!'

'Do you want to know or not?'

Jack was a stirrer who was rarely deterred once he got going, but even he understood from the tone in Avery's voice that his friend needed to be serious and say out loud things that had been noisy in his head for some time.

'Sure. Sorry mate. You were saying?'

'Loosely translated from the Latin, it means that governments are morally culpable for the decision to go to war and soldiers are responsible for their actions when they encounter the enemy,' Avery explained.

'The thing is, there's a lot of grey area in interpreting that kind of thing when you're a guard in a prisoner of war camp and your boy's potentially been slaughtered at sea waiting for a pickup after his ship's gone down.

'A Principal Chaplain once told me that I'd constantly be doing the sums as a padre – moral and ethical sums – and these principles would help. I've never been good at sums, Jack. In fact I have a suspicion,' Avery said, drawing his gaze up from his boots to his friend's face with a rather weak smile, 'that I'm totally crap at the whole religious thing.'

'Yeah, well, I wouldn't be too hard on yourself, mate. He wouldn't be the first grieving father to tell everyone to go fuck themselves, now would he?'

'Did he have a family?'

'A sister in Adelaide apparently – a nurse, Sally. That's the other thing – I'm carrying around this bundle of letters they found under his bed. They're all to her but he never sent them.

'I should just throw them out.'

'You know you can't do that.'

Avery nodded. Jack was right.

'Why don't you try the Nursing Service? This Sally's got to be registered somewhere.'

Avery nodded again, wondering why he hadn't thought to leave the case of correspondence in their hands earlier.

'That's exactly what I'll do,' he said more to himself than Jack.

His mate rose from his rock and the two men started back, falling into an easy lope. They were no more than twenty paces from the house when Jack suddenly broke the silence with an apology he asserted was long overdue.

'I'm sorry I couldn't be at your wedding, Ave. When I saw Betty stumble out of that Dakota in Darwin … I just wanted to take her home and stay there.'

Avery was relieved beyond measure to feel he had somewhere to leave Sergeant Tenterfield's baggage and would have forgiven Jack anything at that moment.

'Tell you what Jack, you can make up for it by coming to the christening. If I know Gwen, she's going to pop one out as soon as we land in Adelaide. Play your cards right, and you and Betty could be godparents – at least the closest thing to it any kid of mine could have!'

A baby enclaved.

[Summer of 1947.]

Gwen headed for the rear of the Chevy. Normally she would step up onto the running boards, hitch up her skirt, steady herself on the spare tyre above the mudguard and then hoist herself into the tray, but as Mr Normanby was in the front seat and had turned around to watch her, she felt self-conscious. A hand in this matter from Avery would have helped but they had been on the road so long it didn't occur to either of them that he would leave the driver's wheel to assist his wife.

Both Gwen and Avery knew of Normanby by reputation. As the only funeral director in the region, he was privy to a lot of personal information about the families who needed his services and he wasn't known for his discretion.

Gwen was already embarrassed in his company and did not want her clumsiness to be added to a story of her mechanical incompetence. She had only hubris to blame for that. When they had come upon Normanby broken down by the side of the road, she had guaranteed him that she could get him moving again but his station wagon – a poor excuse for a hearse – had defeated her. What makeshift refrigeration existed at the start was near ineffectual by the time Gwen had declared the engine repair a lost cause almost two hours later. There was no choice but to transfer Normanby's grim cargo and eight large blocks of dwindling ice – into the Chevy.

Everything the Holbrooks owned, apart from the pedal wireless, had to be unloaded in the exchange. Their clothes and cooking equipment was piled now under a tree, like an unmanned garage sale, and Avery was keen on a quick turnaround to prevent them going walkabout.

He called out from the front seat, with one eye in the rear view mirror: 'Everything alright there? We really should be making tracks.'

'Fine,' Gwen called back, slightly irritated by his impatience.

She turned back to the shoes in front of her on the tray of the truck. They were made from caramel-coloured leather – petite and protruding from a canvas cocoon. A shoelace was tied around both, keeping the feet together and pointing rigidly skyward.

Avery watched his wife disappear from his view in the side mirror with some discomfort. Somehow Gwen's insistence that she accompany the deceased woman made him feel he lacked chivalry.

She'll regret it soon enough but then she'll be too stubborn to do anything about it and she'll be stuck there.

Avery pulled the stick shift into first gear. The familiar jolt felt more violent to Gwen in the back than it did from the passenger seat as she stepped around the body and the wireless. The truck was already in motion when she got to the parcel shelf abutting the rear window of the cabin and she landed with a thud, scowling at how cavalier her husband had been with her safety.

'I've been meaning to get to Dry Creek Station for some time,' Avery told Normanby once he had settled into top gear.

'Bit late now, Reverend,' Normanby said with no indication he had ever employed tact in his conversations.

'What happened out there?'

Normanby as it turned out, knew it all; he had been a friend of the Timmins brothers – Nathan and Martin – and had watched the relationships sour in the years after Nathan had married.

'It all went wrong when Elsa came,' Normanby began with relish. 'Right bitch as far as I could tell.'

Avery frowned but decided not to rebuke the man for his unchristian language. They would be in each other's company for some hours and he would be coming back, afterall, to offer counsel to Mr Timmins, so context could only help.

Normanby, a wiry fellow with a long thin neck, a lazy eye and whispy strands of hair that gave him the look of a skittish emu, seemed entirely comfortable telling the tale.

'Nate was in love with that woman but his brother could take her or leave 'er.

'She came from a big station on The Downs. Thought she knew it all. Was gonna help them make it big – big runs, big profits.

'The only thing she didn't know was how to pay for it. Marty and Nate ended up having to go cap in hand to her father. Elsa had no idea how hard that was for them; they never borrowed a cent until she came.'

With the wind racing past her ears, Gwen could only imagine what Normanby was saying. The idea that this woman who had obviously suffered could be the subject of gossip by two men who could never know what women truly went through, made her feel queasy.

'Elsa was calling all the shots,' Normanby told Avery. 'Daddy was the bank and she was the one in charge of it all. In the end, Marty told Nate he'd have to choose – her or him.

'Nate was so riled he wasn't thinking properly. He picked her. Borrowed more money and bought Marty out. Marty's got a small holding now – nothing like Dry Creek – and Nate might think he owns somethin' but Dry Creek will be part of The Downs before I put Elsa in the ground – you wait and see.'

After travelling in the back for the better part of an hour, Gwen had a sudden urge to peel the canvas back. She had been staring at it, watching the stiffness wilt over the contours of Elsa's brow and settle in the hollows beneath her cheekbones before falling away around her neck. Gwen's emotions fooled her into sharp but brief moments of panic, usually coinciding with poor performance by the suspension, in which she almost convinced herself Elsa was suffocating.

She became fixated on imagining Elsa's last expression, using the shadows and highlights to reconstruct her features.

At the wheel, Avery turned to Mr Normanby, who was picking tobacco from a pouch, his fingers discoloured from years of the habit.

'How exactly did she die?'

Normanby licked the edge of a cigarette paper with slow deliberation and began carefully lining up small wads of leaf in it.

'Childbirth,' he said finally. 'Should 'a' known better. It's like with shearing sheds, or boats – there are some places women shouldn't be.

'Marty and Nate's own mother left them when they was pups, for crissake. She hated the place. They loved it. Go figure.'

Avery was getting a little frustrated now.

'Were they happy – Elsa and Nathan?'

'Nah, turns out Elsa was a cheatin' whore an' all. Baby came out black as the ace of spades.'

Avery clenched his jaw at the crassness of the man beside him and felt something like pity for Elsa at having had this man's hands on her after her death. When he remembered to breathe in again, the powdery dust from the road attached itself to the sides of his throat and brought on a small coughing fit. Tobacco leapt from the unrolled paper on Normanby's thigh as his side of the vehicle dipped into a rut and he swore under his breath, reaching for his pouch before it fell to the floor. Avery turned his attention back to the road but needed to clarify what he had just heard.

'So, Timmins wasn't the father?'

'Look, I never seen the kid, but I knows.'

Normanby sighed, the volume of air leaving him seeming to settle his restless eye, and resumed twisting his freshly rolled cigarette until it was the preferred thickness.

Drawing deeply as he lit it, he set his gaze on nothing in particular tracking past his window, settling on silence and moving only to picking a loose strand of tobacco out from between his teeth every now and then.

The trip to Mundine's Pub was 312 miles from where Avery and Gwen had taken on custodianship of Elsa Timmins – nothing much in outback terms. But during the afternoon the temperature had risen sharply. The gums were listless, the birds were quiet and roos moved languidly or flopped down under trees with shade.

The ice around the body had long since melted, creating a brackish moat that seemed now to be cooking it. Welts of dark green were blooming and combining along the canvas roll and seemed, in those spots, to have thinned the barrier between the cadaver and the sickening pungency emanating from it. For the most part, the smell was whipped away but when Avery slowed down on the rougher roads for Gwen's safety, it was impossible for her to avoid it.

Leaning out the window just as Gwen gagged over the side of the tray, Avery called out to her.

'You alright there Gwen? There's room to squeeze in here if you want. I can pull over.'

'I'll be right. Is it far to go?'

'Not too far now.'

So stubborn.

The Reverend had slowed down so much he caught a whiff of his wife's deteriorating companion and felt compelled to spit. Normanby chose to do the same, though it seemed he was merely mimicking the Reverend's action because he hadn't had a spit in a while. Both men wound their windows up, choosing the heat over the odour, though it would have been lost to them on picking up speed.

'I was the first person Nate called that day, drunk as a skunk,' Normanby resumed, startling Avery who thought he'd heard the last of the story.

The funeral director pulled another thread of tobacco through a gap in his teeth with a loud sucking noise, then retrieved it and wiped it on his trousers, refusing to open the window to flick it out.

'Had one of the Abo kids on the pedal wireless. I could barely hear him for the swearing. Made out just enough to know Elsa was dead and he wanted me at Dry Creek.

'It took me a couple of hours to get there but Nate was nowhere around; there was only the house girl, all hysterical.

'Kept sayin' it wasn't her fault. Said Marty had gone to the blackfellas camp all worked up an' she wanted to go home.'

'What about the baby?'

'Nate took it from her and walked into the bush she reckons.'

'Did you find Timmins?'

Normanby didn't seem to have heard Avery.

'I never held anything against that woman and no one could say I did, even though she always said such shit about me. Cleaning her up was the biggest job I ever done. Never knew so much blood could be in one woman.

'I dressed her up real nice for Nate. Got the housegirl to clean the floors and burn the bedding. Nate didn't have to do nothing.'

Both men fell silent again, with Normanby absent mindedly stubbing out his cigarette on the arm rest of the door. Avery frowned at him and Normanby swept up the ash into his hand, leaving a light grey smear. He looked around the cabin for somewhere to put it and settled on depositing the stub and its detritus in his pocket. Avery urged Normanby to go on.

'There's not much more to it. I put Elsa in her Sunday best, like I said. She could 'a' been an angel sleeping but Nate never thanks me nor nothin' when he comes in. He just goes 'n' get hisself a drink. I could 'a' done with one an' all but ...'

'And the baby?'

'I asks if he wants them buried together an' he says it was born dead and no-one need worry about it. Then he gives me this look and I knows the rumours about his wife's cheating ways were right and that she's had a creamy.

'Nate's a good man, Reverend. He doesn't deserve any more bad luck. Best just leave be.'

In the heat behind the men, Gwen was swinging between stupor and stoicism in enduring the journey. Her body was still propped on the parcel shelf but her mind was wandering in all manner of strange directions. In the last hour, Elsa's face had seemed clearly visible to Gwen; she fancied the woman had a high brow, a fine nose, sculpted cheekbones and, limp, flaxen hair. She had convinced herself that no amount of professional manipulation by Mr Normanby could ever hide the contortions of searing pain and fear that would have shaped Elsa's expression in the moments before her death.

But this hour – the third hour that she had been alone with the deteriorating body – Gwen could take the illusion no further. She could not picture Elsa's eyes.

She shook her head, pulled her gaze away from the tarp and looked out. She skimmed across the familiar and found herself drifting out into the changing hues signalling that time was moving on. She tried to lock onto the horizon, now marked by ridges of gums, but the purple haze of the vaporous oils that emanate from eucalypts had left nothing distinctive to hold her attention.

She looked for wildlife but found none. She looked for rock formations, telephone poles or windmills, but found none. There was nothing to attract the eye or make this stretch more memorable than the last or the one to come. There was only a gaping, unfathomable sky.

Gwen began to feel maudlin, even foolish for choosing to sit so uncomfortably in the back as a sign of respect for a woman she didn't even know.

***

When they finally got to Mundine's Pub, Avery decided to reclaim the tarpaulin Elsa had been wrapped in. She was slowly unravelled onto a sheet that had been laid out on the incongruously plush lawn, nurtured by an extensive groundwater system. Her shoes remained together and her arms remained crossed on her chest, the way Normanby had arranged them.

Gwen had been right in thinking Elsa's hair was flaxen, though the dusk and an increasingly overcast sky made it look more grey than blonde. The skin on her face had drained thin over her cheekbones. Her eyelids were closed but the visible thread of veins running across them gave the impression that the featherless bodies of newborn birds had been rolled into the sockets.

The smell was so ripe when the body lay fully exposed to dry out the dampened clothes, that even the funeral director gagged, masking his shame by forcing a cough. Gwen felt sure the ghastly odour had gone all the way into her lungs and that she would be breathing it for weeks. It would linger much longer, it turns out, in her memory – dormant for more than thirty years, when it would rise to warn her she was about to stumble on death by mishap once more.

Whether it was to distance himself from a stench that reminded him of field hospitals, or because his nature was to be both practical and thrifty, Avery roughly bundled up the tarpaulin and went in search of a hose. Gwen and Normanby took either end of the swaddled body and followed a portly and aggrieved Frank Mundine down broad concrete steps into a shallow basement. They laid their load to rest on the concrete floor while Mundine jiggled a key into the padlock on the door of his generously proportioned coolstore, hissing barely suppressed expletives at the 'unnatural and unhealthy' nature of what he was being forced to do.

Normanby was called upon to help Mundine stack various cartons of beer to one side of the storage room, leaving Gwen once again staring at the face exposed when a corner of the sheet had come untucked on the way down. The harsh yellow light of the single bulb above them only partially subdued the anemic horror of it. Normanby, who had negotiated a good price on a carton which had been displaced by the new arrangement, followed Gwen's eyes to Elsa's face – and the open mouth – and scowled.

From above them came the sound of high-pressure water drilling onto the tarp, spattering the air with the pelt of a rainstorm and causing Gwen to lean toward the noise, distracted by thirst. When she turned back, she was affronted by the sight of Normanby straddling the body. He had one hand cupping the top of the woman's skull, and before Gwen would protest, shunted the butt of the other up sharply under Elsa's chin. The crack flicked off the basement walls like the end of a bullock dray whip and was followed crassly by a release of flatulence.

Avery reached the bottom of the stairs just in time to break the fall of his fainting wife.

***

In the next few weeks that Avery and Gwen were on the road, Gwen barely participated – in anything. She smiled distractedly at a baptism, politely refused numerous afternoon teas on welcoming stations and chose instead to help out a mutual friend with a flying doctor fundraiser rather than accompany Avery to Dry Creek station – an arrangement Avery thought prudent under the circumstances.

She felt acutely the tragedy of this woman who was loved by two men and yet so very alone and vulnerable when she died. She wasted road hours of every day wondering how Elsa had managed to keep her secret from her husband for so long and how distracted she must have been during the birth by her fear of being forced to give up her baby. As the month drew to a close, the sense of loss that had been planted in Gwen began to settle in her womb as if she herself had suffered a miscarriage. It keened with the ferocity of an abscess.

Did the baby really die or did Nathan Timmins dispose of his shame so it would not follow him around for the rest of his days?

Gwen did not immediately translate her obsession and ache as a longing to start a family of her own. Though she loved Avery, she had not previously thought about anything more than the seemingly perfect equation of the two of them and their Chevrolet. Their life on the road was, for all its physical discomforts, an easy one. You couldn't ask for a better way to get to know your spouse, with all their idiosyncrasies, or yourself as one half of a couple, than be in their company 24 hours a day. And yet, she had to admit now, in all their hours of conversation and easy silence, they had not broached the subject of children.

The thought crystallised in Gwen's head after speaking to her mother. She had called her from the landline at Mundine's pub, quietly desperate to hear the voice of another woman, especially one who loved her unconditionally. She did not tell her parents why she was calling, allowing her father first to prattle on about politics and then her mother to mention again how much she would love her daughter to settle in Adelaide. The desire for a baby drifted innocently into Gwen's psyche on the questioning lilt of her mother's voice when she had noted how much easier a move to Adelaide would make it for her to help out with grandchildren, if any were to 'come along'.

The more Gwen tried to push the thought of having a baby aside, the more it filled her. At first, Avery was surprised to hear the woman he often called his 'attractive travelling companion' talk of settling down. But he came to think of it as proper that a woman might assess the worth of her marriage by a yardstick greater than the sum total of what she could pack on the back of a truck. It was his duty to give her a home and a family, if that was what she wanted, despite his own reservations about the kind of parent he could be.

As it turned out, the crossroads in the Holbrooks' lives were all but built, with a new direction planned for Avery by his church elders. The railways were connecting more towns in Avery's expansive parish and there was less need to be on the road as often as they had been, according to 'head office'. Of course there would always be a need to visit outlying stations, but there was also a need for experienced religious practitioners like himself to bring an ambivalent public back into suburban houses of worship. Head office would be happy to find Avery a church and rectory, along with a small increase in his stipend, if he wanted to pursue that path.

So Avery and Gwen would make the move to Adelaide, much to the delight of Gwen's parents, with Gwen's mother eagerly helping out with a makeover of the rather neglected rectory they had been given in Walkerville and her father eager to point out the interesting history of Avery's new parish to his son-in-law. But the rectory, with its windows painted shut and various insects nesting in every corner, would be a short stop for the couple. Perhaps if they'd stayed there longer, closer to the church, Avery would later think, he might not have let himself stray so far from Gwen and from God.

19.

Apparitions of shared moments.

[July, 1950.]

Moving home had been Helen's ambition for months. She had initially resisted the gravitational pull of those broad streets she had walked along from school and from the shop, to avoid the gutting she knew she would feel on that first step, knowing the house was empty. After a while, resistance became avoidance and an ache had developed in her gut anyway.

When the ganger had moved in, he dislodged for her the apparitions of shared moments that settle in rooms inhabited by the same folk for a long period. They floated in bubbles pushed in front of him, dissolved as he moved through them, and were left underfoot like the remnants of last Autumn's leaves. The soul of the house, the curator of those intimate memories, died in her reckoning when the ability was lost to keep them whole.

And then, somewhere along the line, perhaps as Helen hardened to her new life, she came to think of the house as a refuge – not because of its history or a longing to be enveloped in the ambience of a place where she was loved, but because she saw it as her only option. She could no longer bear to live where she was and, rented or not, the house on Eyre Street, the only one in Eyre Street because the growth of the town had not followed it out there, belonged to her and it was time she reclaimed it, and her life.

She forced herself to take evening walks, circling closer to the darkened windows and the moonlit silvery hue of the old wooden verandah, its grain so familiar under her fingertips. A truck parked outside did not always mean the ganger was home. She learned to distinguish the bark of his overweight dog, a husky hairball that jumped from its throat with great gusto only to land heavily at its feet, as if half of it had been swallowed on the way out.

If the dog was around, it meant the ganger was inside and she would divert away from the house and continue instead to the windmill or the old miner's cottage. If all was silent and the ganger elsewhere, she would approach the house and sit on the verandah with a book, as if it were the most natural thing, as if she still lived there and could go inside if she wanted a cold drink, nudging open the screen door with her shoulder while continuing to read, and navigating the fridge in much the same way.

Yet even in her dreams she could not cross that threshold; it did not even exist. In her dreams, the house was nought but a single wall and she, a ghost-like figure staring at it as if building it might somehow bring her back to life. She would walk around it and become entranced by the stormy swirls of the wallpaper on the other side, until, from seemingly innocent patterns, mangled cars and train carriages would emerge. As soon as they revealed themselves, they would be gone again, wiped in the paper as it peeled away in front of her, layer after layer revealing underneath it another ugly thought. Eventually the wall would be stripped away to nothing, leaving her breathing noisily, alone in the void of the street.

So when she actually did take the steps to the front door, with Avery and his soiled trousers, she found herself enormously relieved. The walls in the loungeroom were a little more neglected than she remembered them, the paper dogeared at intervals around the ceiling, but its patterns were resolute and the effect solid. Entering her parents' bedroom was also not as confronting as she thought it might be. The mattress had been bare. The smell of cigarettes had permeated the carpets, or was it the butts still left in an ashtray on the table by her father's side? Either way, there was not the faintest perfume lingering from her mother's favourite hand cream and nothing to remind her that it was a private space that a child should not visit when her parents were not there. Except for the camphorwood box.

The events of that day had changed everything for Helen – the fight with Mabel, the afternoon with Avery at the miner's cottage, crossing that threshold into her family home for the first time in more than a year. She had decided then and there that she was not going back to live at the shop and she was not going to be lectured by the Reverend anymore. Her anticipation of his arrival at the miner's cottage had been so sweet and when he had appeared, from around the corner of those sandstone blocks glowing gold in the sunset, she wanted with all the world to think of him as her sweetheart, the older man who would take care of her, forever. As it turned out, he was more like a sad old sugar daddy and all she wanted to do was take charge of her life without being lectured to about what that might entail. It was enough.

Bert had been good about things. Mabel had gone on from Tarcoola to Adelaide for the rest of the week in order to catch up with Edward and Cecilia, so he set about 'making the best of things' while she was gone. That had meant closing the shop the following morning, and helping Helen move back into her old home. He had even packed her some complimentary groceries, adding a small bottle of vanilla 'for the milkshakes' and dropping in a handful of potatoes 'to keep your arm in'.

Bert must have been a good dad.

When he had left, Helen had sat in the loungeroom, shoes off, legs crossed underneath her on the couch – waiting to feel like she was home, but falling asleep first.

20.

An incompetent cervix.

[August, 1950.]

To Gwen, the word 'fecund' sounded like it should describe something gutted and ailing – like a uterus too weak to hang on to the first cells of a child. So when Doctor Bettinger told her she would never be fecund, she heard 'you will never be barren' and smiled, a cautious smile that would have broadened in the bask of other smiles around her, if only they'd come.

'Do you understand what I mean by that, Mrs Holbrook?' Dr Bettinger's voice was milky.

She felt herself blush. She turned her attention to the metal clasp on the bag she held on her lap. It was reflecting the movement of a ceiling fan in the suburban surgery, like a golden spinning daisy. She waited for the doctor to continue with the explanation.

'A fecund woman will fall pregnant easily, sometimes produce multiple births and be responsible for a large brood over her lifetime. You are not that woman, I'm afraid.'

She remained fixed on the clasp.

Why didn't he say fertile – 'you're not fertile Gwen' – that would have done the job.

Dr Bettinger waited for his patient to look up, and then for her to look directly at him, pulling her gaze up with his.

'I'm not saying it's impossible for you to fall pregnant, just that it is unlikely that you will conceive easily and, if you do, it is even more unlikely that you would be able to carry to term.

"

'You have what is called an incompetent cervix, which is basically a situation where during pregnancy your cervix will dilate and efface, or thin, to the point that it isn't strong enough to hold onto a foetus.'

He paused to allow Gwen to take it in. She noticed his hair was greying at the temples and sideburns but that his eyebrows were still a deep brown.

'And I suspect you also have endometriosis, which could explain the pain you've been experiencing,' he went on.

'If you like we can have a good look at the pelvic cavity; it's an invasive procedure but the only real way to confirm the condition.'

Gwen still had eye contact with Dr Bettinger, but was not registering his expression. She had always respected the doctor for his willingness to give plenty of detail, but right now, she felt a growing animosity towards him, not entirely separated from the discomfort he had caused her during the earlier examination.

More invasive than what you just did? How is that possible?

A small part of Gwen was still holding out hope that the doctor had misused the word 'fecund'. She knew she had to ask, but instinctively felt the answer would come like a slap in the face.

'So you're saying I'm unable to have children?'

The doctor removed his thin-rimmed glasses and cleaned them vigorously with a white handkerchief. He did not respond before returning them to the bridge of his rather large nose.

'In your situation, I'd never say never, but you could waste a lot of years trying, without success, and find yourselves blaming each other and forgetting what you already have; I've seen it ruin a lot of marriages, Gwen.'

Dr Bettinger searched his patient's face with the calm of a chess player who has made just one move and already knows his next three. She seemed ready to crawl into her handbag.

'If you don't mind me saying so, I think it would be more positive to assume that children probably won't happen for you and your husband and then if you do conceive, think of it as a gift and we'll see if we can get you to term, one way or another. If, in a few years' time, that hasn't happened for you, you may like to look at the alternatives, like adoption.'

At this point, another doctor might have handed Gwen the slip of paper that would translate into a bill, risen from his own seat as an indication that the appointment was over and gently ushered her from the room into the reception area, his hand a light guide in the small of her back. But Dr Bettinger was always running late because his patients were allowed to take their time.

Gwen was offered a cup of tea with the intention that she let it all soak in while supping it in the waiting room. This she declined, remaining seated opposite him, but now scanning his bookshelves.

Dr Bettinger tried again. 'Like I said, we can investigate surgically, just to be sure. And if you'd like me to explain things to your husband, I'm happy for him to make an appointment. Just let me know on both counts.' Now he stood up.

'Can I borrow some books on fertility?' Gwen asked him directly.

'I'm happy to give you a list of titles you might find in the library,' he offered, taking a notepad from a drawer in his desk.

Gwen noticed the photograph of three children in school uniform on the windowsill of the bay window behind the doctor – a girl with long plaited pigtails and two smaller boys, one with his front teeth missing – and the colourful crayon drawings taped to the walls.

'Yes, thankyou, that would be helpful.'

Gwen put the piece of paper into her handbag. The fan seemed to be spinning furiously though she hadn't seen Dr Bettinger turn it up. She strode through the waiting room, conscious of walking 'tall' but not realising she was clenching her teeth. A part of her felt like a girl being paraded in front of a class after wetting her pants.

Do they know, those busybodies pretending to bury their faces in their stupid magazines? Did they hear anything? Will they all be talking about it when I'm gone? 'It's not the Reverend who can't have children; it's his wife.' … It's me.

21.

Lapping waters and slippery souls.

[Thursday evening, November 23, 1950.]

Avery had been at the church. Waiting. Outside, the paint sat up brittle on the edges of horizontal boards and grass seeds ingratiated themselves in the dirty cracks of the window frames. Inside, the walls breathed heavily and the air slumped sullen. A tired string of silver tinsel was draped along the edge of the stage in anticipation of Christmas. It took a fanciful countenance to believe this place was held dear by its community and, for want of possessing one, Avery felt weary almost immediately he had entered it.

Some days the reverend saw value in entertaining the overquick talk of lonely or captious women who had been deprived of interested company for weeks at a time – their husbands working down the line or simply too tired to do anything but socialise at the pub basking in the easy familiarity of their mates rather than prickling against what they saw as the arduous expectations of their wives. Some days the chatter brought some cheer to the church and just by listening, even peripherally, Avery could tell he brought some relief to those who were spilling over.

But in the past few years, Avery had had to accept that Kimbanyon was no longer a town that saw fit to maintain or clean up the church in preparation for his visits and, on some days, he could not help but feel slighted. On those days, the tumbling banter rang in his ears with the tinny clang of gossip. On those days, he felt denigrated as a minister, denied his role of offering guidance and the support of the church, and denigrated as a man, feeling that he was seen himself as little more than trivia's company rather than a man prepared to do an 'honest day's work'.

Leaning against an old table, he restlessly turned his bible over and over in his hands, watching the worn gold lettering on its cover disappear from view and then return again. The motion relaxed his mind so that he became mesmerised by the hand on top – its clarity falling away with the daydream – and the irrational idea that as he turned the book, the words within might slide to the edge and be absorbed into the flesh of his palm. Lulled by the intimacy of the moment, Avery pressed his hand flat against the thinning leather.

Anyone looking on might imagine the Reverend felt a need to validate the book's worth, or his allegiance to it through the act of swearing on it, as if in court. But there was no such deliberation; Avery was instead now drifting into the past, losing himself to a sea of faces scarred by the collusions war put in their path. In the twilight between dozing and falling asleep, he began a climb across them, pushing down bodies with more fight in them after death than they ever had before it, beginning a familiar search for one young man.

He closed his eyes to the present and allowed a midnight ocean to rush silently around his thighs with a familiar yet unsettling warmth known best to children in the moment before they wake to find they have wet the bed. A pulse other than his own took hold of Avery's heart, imbuing it with a beat so bloated it reverberated in his ears. The water grabbed at his clothing, pushed in a wrestle of directions by the wake from silent amphibious troop carriers. An overwhelming smell of diesel and burning oil stung his nostrils and flooded him with nausea, forcing him to brace himself against the table to stop himself sliding into the churn and sludge.

Avery willed his eyes to open but had to blink against the setting sun glaring through the stained glass window and closed them again. He realised that he knew this place – the place where the sky was smeared with charcoal and wildfire and every horizon was spattered with striking eruptions from oil wells set on fire. Now the allies were landing, in the hundreds, confronted not by the enemy but by the carnage the enemy had left behind and the task of holding the coast against them.

Avery felt his face bloat in the thick air. The moon was a bruise. The water a weeping wound. If the New Testament described Hell as a 'lake that burns with fire and brimstone' this was surely it, but Avery sensed it was also Tartarus, a place below hell, where feet found quicksand and a pervading cold reached up for unsure souls.

Noise seeped into Avery's consciousness slowly but it was building with the tenacity of a migraine. He and the ocean were pulsing together now, competing to be heard over the mechanical throng of the amphibious carriers landing along the breadth of the shoreline, spewing an endless, dishevelled line of hapless men into the next misadventure of their war. They ploughed through, following the pointed white light of lanterns set up every couple of metres on the beach to direct them in.

Avery was not moving. The water was now high around his waist. He was still focussed on the beach lanterns that meant relative safety, but he had no control over his feet. He felt he had not jumped out of a landing craft but he must have been drawn into the water for a reason. His arms were aching as if he had been marching with a bren gun for a week. Avery realised in the dark that he was bearing the weight of another human being, and that he had allowed that person to slump into the water, submerged to his chest.

The man was slight – a young man, a boy really. His sharp shoulder blades, barely contained by the shirt sticking to him like a second skin, were pushing into Avery's forearm. Loose strands of hair floating in the water were entwining themselves around his fingers cradling the boy's head. He must have been lost from his regiment for quite some time for his hair to have grown this long. The Reverend had the uneasy feeling that he had had this inane thought at least once before and perhaps many times before that. Inky waters were lapping around the boy's jawline, changing Avery's perception of its shape. Torrents of fire from the oil wells threw sporadic washes of tangerine across the boy's face, pooling around his features before being absorbed by the night. White flashes from the beach lanterns darted between the legs of men staggering onshore, reaching Avery and the boy as broken spears of light but dissolving before either was able to make out the other's features.

Avery heard the boy gulp and spew the ocean out. His hands were briefly immersed and warmed with the blood they had swept up. He lifted the boy's head out of the water as a random ray of light shot toward them. His eyes were glassy, shattered by panic.

'Tell my folks I was baptised, Padre,' he wheezed.

The Reverend did not need to make out the words, or even be able to identify the dying boy's face. This 'soldier' had taunted his subconscious in many forms since the end of the war – feeding on his insecurities as a chameleon, yet as familiar to him as the Lord's Prayer. Avery knew instinctively that he had failed the boy, that he had made a critical error of judgement that had put them in the tumult of the ocean now, being shouted at by the war and barely heard by God. Perhaps Avery had believed the boy would pull through and that he would appreciate a proper ceremony. He had probably encouraged the boy to believe he would live and that the baptism could be done when he could truly take part in it.

Today, with his mind wandering unchallenged, Avery's subconscious would drag his nightmare into his current realm, bringing the young soldier and his request into the Kimbanyon church, creating a cruel backstory from an amalgam of experiences with extraordinary clarity. The soldier stood before him in silence, his face that of a teenager, fresh, clean, thin but ruddy with life, every tear of flesh healed, the shifting line of his jaw stilled. Then he spoke, with the voice of a much older man, the tone of one who has known what it is like to be powerless but is now sustained by a consuming resolve.

'I don't want just a sprinkling of holy water, father; I want it done properly. Like John the Baptist,' he told Avery.

All too quickly, the sunny colouring in his face began to fade and ashen blooms swirled under cheeks that were chalking as he spoke.

'My mum, she really wanted that for me before I left. The whole family was being done – my little sister and my dad, even though he always said his praying was best done at home.'

His lips were fraying, thin peels of skin lifting white.

'They did it so she felt we was all protected – so we wouldn't have any trouble with St Peter!

'But I refused 'cause I didn't want to jinx myself thinking about dying before I even left. It really upset her.'

A mottle of mucus and dirt was clouding his eyes.

'Please help me, Padre. I should 'a' done it before.'

Avery gripped the table but the sensation of it was not enough to dislodge the dream. Suddenly, they were back in the sea, both of them wanting so badly to make it right. Cradling the crumpling body in his arms, Avery pressed his hand against the boy's clammy forehead. But before he could utter the first words for his salvation, the boy's tentative grip on the Reverend's forearm slipped into the lapping waters, along with his soul.

***

'Reverend Holbrook, sir?' Luke had entered the church tentatively, not wanting to disturb the Reverend if he was giving counsel to someone, but thinking more likely the poor fellow had dozed off waiting to be asked for it. There had been a wedding in Kimbanyon last year and a funeral earlier this year, but mostly these things happened closer to the city and the only ones looking to keep it local were the oldies not yet in nursing homes, and others wanting to keep in God's good books by paying their respects more regularly than the six times a year the Reverend travelled to hold services there. The third generation miner couldn't work out why the guy kept coming. It wasn't like Kimbanyon was isolated anymore. The road was good and the rail was getting more regular all the time.

But there the Reverend was. Alone. Against a table, staring at nothing, as if someone had suddenly drawn the blinds on him. White as a ghost.

Jesus, has he had a heart attack?

'Reverend Holbrook, are you alright?'

After a moment long enough to frighten Luke even further, the Reverend drew in a deep breath, his nostrils and rib cage the only parts of his body expanding. He became conscious of his surroundings with the sluggishness of a three-legged dog rising from sleep having forgotten its missing limb. He pulled his gaze from the picture rail on the opposing wall of the church where it had been fixed for the past quarter of an hour, and turned himself to the insistent young man who had wrenched him from the South China Sea.

Relieved to see movement, Luke let go of his own breath, a little surprised to find he had been holding it.

'You scared me Reverend! Sorry to rattle you; it's just that I gotta set up for the bingo.'

Avery collected himself: 'Fine. Fine. Yes. I'm fine. You go ahead. I was just leaving.'

But before he had convinced himself it was safe to lift his weight from the table, the breath of a thought, uttered as if from a jealous older sibling wanting to both protect and hurt, formed a smoking whisper inside his head. He heard himself utter the words: 'My work here is done.'

Without the self flagellating quip, as stinging in its sarcasm as its honesty, Avery may simply have returned to Adelaide feeling a little flat and spent the better part of the evening in his study 'sulking' as Gwen would say, before emerging for a strong cuppa and an evening sitting alongside his wife in their respective lounge chairs devouring recent newspapers and swapping items of interest.

Without the quip, Avery's life might have travelled along a far more comfortable course, but its mischief – conceived as it was from within – turned it into a personal affront. And, being both a military man and of an arrogant intellect, Avery's mind chose to gather his wits, maneuver through the minefield and respond. He stared into the open, slightly panicked face of the young miner who would not release his gaze, and presumptuously determined the boy's concerns – all of them – to be petty.

How could someone so young have any real worries? It's peace time for Chrissake. Bingo?

Avery genuinely missed the raw intensity of ministering to soldiers who desperately wanted to enter an afterlife cleansed of the brutality they had seen, and been variously a reluctant or eager part of. The thought that his own life – the fulfilment of his calling – had paled significantly since the end of the war began to take form.

And then a second feral dog emerged from the dark alley of Avery's subconscious – a beast that would give him cause to act this day like he had never done before, and that would continue to lope restlessly, menacing his thoughts for the rest of his life.

He turned his face to the windows, where the coming sunset was forcing its way through the leadlight, splintering at the breach and sprinkling itself on a flotilla of unsettled dust. He reached out with his right hand to weave his fingers through the glitter, his body amusing itself while his mind conceived a plan.

To Luke, the older man appeared to be wanting to shake his hand, or to be helped up from his perch and steadied on his feet. But as the confused boy moved to respond, the Reverend withdrew from the gesture, straightened up, pushed past him and walked directly out of the hall.

With purpose, Avery strode past the overgrown bramble enmeshed in the wire fencing that sagged between long-split and silvered wooden posts, past the grocer shop, where Bert Johns was unloading boxes from his truck, past the station and over the rails.

He walked until the dirty pink light blotted the shadows, the shadows had dissolved into each other and the town was flush with an eagerness for the cool of evening. As he charted a course towards a particular part of town, it dawned on Avery, with mild astonishment, that he was not being drawn by a street or a house, but by a particular person, and that his desire to be with that person was becoming more consuming with each step.

He stumbled slightly with the realisation, but quickly regained his gait and purpose. The Reverend spoke to himself along the walk, building a scaffold of justification, a fort with which to contain the intensity of his desire.

Helen is becoming a woman; she is at risk of falling prey to others without intervention. She's already shown herself capable of seduction. She has refused to see me for guidance and will not come to the Church. It is my duty to ensure she does not stray any further from God's house. Or into the arms of another man.

The rippling thread of a windmill churning on a strengthening breeze spurred his pace. He recalled vividly the softness of her kiss.

Despite his resolute steps, doubts about Helen's reaction to him when he arrived began creeping into his mind. It was possible that she hadn't come to the church because she had no need of his services. It was possible also that she no longer desired him. The thought gave him a strange sensation – part anger, part fear. His vest felt tight against his chest; he undid a second button to ease the constraint.

She ambushes me, like the daydreams. If I could just shut her out.

It was true his mind's meanderings around Helen were becoming more frequent, and increasingly visceral. They had become so distracting as to nullify his gaze for minutes at a time, often in company. In them, he saw himself as a fit man in his thirties (at least 10 years younger than he was) with a healthy cover of dark brown hair, just now beginning to fleck grey through his sideburns, wearing the light khaki shirts from his days on the road, his sleeves rolled up, his forearms tanned.

Despite his widening paunch and lack of breath following his walk, Avery was convinced this was how he appeared to Helen. In a truly narcissistic way, he saw more of himself when he looked at Helen than he did of her. Her hazel green eyes, blotted brown around the pupil, spliced by tangerine lashes and buried in a sandy smear of freckles which darkened as they collided on the bridge of her nose, registered in his sight as a whole image, indistinguishable and unbroken by its features. Unremarkable.

But the interchange of visage and perception proved intoxicating: this was the face of the girl who wanted him.

And she does want me. Remember the cottage. Remember?

Everything about her, lingered about him. He had not been able to forget that kiss no matter how hard he tried. When he denied his feelings to himself, they nevertheless remained an inclination of his mind, thickening like treacle on a hot pudding at random moments…

My hand on her breast.

Avery drew on his watery reserves to fight his urges, juggling words from the scriptures to find a voice that would speak to him with meaning.

What causes fights and quarrels among you? Don't they come from your desires that battle within you? You want something but don't get it…. You do not have, because you do not ask God. When you ask, you do not receive because you ask with wrong motives, that you may spend what you get on your pleasures.

Avery clenched and unclenched his now sweaty palms and took the first step onto Helen's verandah. He had sifted all the words in the passage from the Book of James, and all that remained were the words 'desire' and 'pleasures'.

Why use the plural for pleasure? Does it occur over and over again, multiples of an original pleasure, or an original sin … ?

Avery mulled it over until he no longer remembered why he had chosen that passage as a means of slowing his heartrate when it was in fact having the opposite effect. Why was was he here, when his thoughts were as impure as those of a soldier given leave for the first time in months? Why was he still on Helen's doorstep with 'wrong motives'? Could he hide his thoughts once she appeared in front of him? Wasn't it already too late for that?

Matthew says: 'Anyone who looks at a woman lustfully has already committed adultery with her in his heart.' Haven't I already been banished from entering God's house? Have I anything left to lose?

As he took the last step, Avery gave himself one more chance, asking again: *Why am I still on this doorstep, knowing what might happen on the other side?* The answer came to him in a soft but emboldened whisper: *Because you hope against hope that it will happen.*

With both feet at the edge of the precipice, Avery turned the handle to find the door unlocked.

22.

Out cold.

[Thursday night, November 23, 1950.]

It was a balmy Thursday evening in Kimbanyon. Trucks, utes and cars were parked irregularly around The Brooster and Dot was run off her feet keeping up with the jugs being ordered and slapped down on tables as quick as others were emptied.

Her new wingman, Gerard, a young British tourist who was heading to Alice Springs on his motorbike, had agreed to stay on for a while to cope with the influx of men making the Brooster their home away from home every night in waves from six 'til nearly close.

The hotel's fortunes rose and fell on the thirst of a mobile workforce and Dot had stocked up to meet the needs of yet another exploratory drill being set up a dozen or so miles to the west of Kimbanyon.

Don't they ever learn?

At the same time the Commonwealth Railways Department was building a longer siding to make changeovers of goods and passengers from one train to another easier when the narrow track changed to a standard gauge. It was boom times for The Brooster for the next few months at least. Dozens of men had come from Port Augusta, a railway town overlooking the Spencer Gulf. Many of these men – track layers, gangers, fettlers – were accustomed to leaving their families behind for weeks at a time as they worked down the line but lived together as a family of sorts while they were away, Dot had told Gerard, with some affection for her patrons.

As for the miners, they were a different mob altogether, she had asserted – a mixture of company men and drillers who had no thought for returning beyond their time in the area and had no interest in the mateship shared by the rail workers who would inevitably run into each other time and time again.

The rail workers had collected their pay from the Tea and Sugar earlier in the day and were doing their best to blow the top off their packets at the bar. The miners had been settled in for a while, with meals already consumed and second and third rounds being shouted.

'Bloody hell, Gerry, this mob can put it away, eh?' Dot laughed, with a smoker's cough cutting her breath short as she swept back behind the bar to refill another jug. 'You got the back table's steak and mash?'

'Right on it, maam.'

'The name's Dot, Gerry; I'm not running a brothel here!'

The thin, fair haired Englishman backed himself into the kitchen with dirty plates to replace them with the back table's order. Wearing the 'waiter's uniform' of black shirt and pleated pants, his appearance gave the bar a more formal look than it had seen before.

'An' watch yerself; them miners are looking for trouble tonight,' Dot tossed at him by way of a warning, her raspy voice just loud enough to be heard over the din and her gaze pointedly dipping towards a group of blustery and over-indulged drinkers to the far left of the room.

A ruddy, bloated, bullock of a man in a check flannel shirt screwed his face up at the young barman as Gerard approached the table, deftly weaving his narrow hips through patrons, carrying three plates of steak and chips with the middle one stacked gingerly across the other two.

'Jesus, what happened to the waitress? What's the bush coming to when all ya get to look at is some poofter or mutton dressed up as lamb over there?'

His mates rolled back on their chairs, scoffing in agreement.

'Show us yer boobs, ya pommie bastard!'

A near-empty jug was knocked over as the men fell about with the sport of it all. Gerard put the plates in front of them without a word, collected the jug and walked away to calls of: 'Hey, we haven't finished with that, yet. Oi, that was full, mate; you'll need to bring us another one on the house!'

Dot passed him with her own meals, as he headed back behind the bar where the regulars were looking quite put out at the delay.

'You doing alright?' she asked him.

'They don't bother me,' he said good naturedly, moving straight to the beer tap and cupping a glass underneath it, asking rhetorically 'What'll it be chaps?'

George Munt, in his cleanest blue singlet, muscled his bare, hairy shoulders in between a couple of other patrons as Dot took up station next to Gerard, the last of the meals delivered.

'Hey Dot, you seen Ed Johns tonight?' The ganger threw his words deftly over the heads of a molten crowd gelling with the bar.

'Playing darts, love.'

'Give us a jug to go will ya? An' two pint glasses as well?' Having successfully convinced Dot to serve him first, George lifted the jug above the crowd with one arm, and the two glasses overhead with the other and gave a blistering whistle through his teeth to alert Ed to his arrival.

The jug safely deposited at a surprisingly empty table nearby, George immediately set about pouring a glass for himself.

'How ya been, anyway, city boy?'

'Rubbish, mate. I'm down about five quid. Fix that bloke up for me will you?'

George took a swig of his beer, put it down on the table and looked at Ed as if he'd spoken complete gibberish.

'Let me help you out with that,' he said, spilling beer from the top of his glass as he dug into the back pocket of his friend's jeans to relieve him of his worn sandwich of a wallet.

Over at the far table, Robbo, the Great Southern Mine Company's head driller on the Kimbanyon exploration, was elbowing his mate, Jonesy, jeering at the two men who had been interlocked by the dart board.

'Jesus, what'd I tell ya? They're all bloody poofters!' Rob licked his thumb, using the spit to re-glue a strand of black hair that had fallen out of his comb over despite a heavy paste of brill cream.

Jonesy recognised the pre-emptory preening that usually meant Rob was about to get messy, and intervened.

'Leave it be mate, those gangers are a feral lot an' I don't fancy leaving this jug to get you out of a scrape on account of yer big mouth.'

Robbo sniffed by way of considering his options, did a quick scan of the pub to see how outnumbered the miners were and looked back at his mate.

'Settle down Jonesy I was just thinkin' we should take some money off these dickheads with a little wager,' he said with a wink that suggested otherwise. 'You boys up for that?'

Perhaps considering the head driller's love for a brawl and the size of his target, just one other man besides Jonesy got to his feet. They both took a couple of seconds to skull the last of their beer and then fell in behind Robbo, whose large frame was already dodging table corners on its way across the floor, confident at least a few of the team would follow.

Jonesy parked himself on a bench next to Ed, gave him a friendly nod and then as a safeguard, warned him: 'Don't get any ideas, princess; you're not my type.'

Robbo glared just long enough at the only other contender that Ed snatched back his own five pound note from George and deserted the game for the bar. George was happy enough to negotiate the stakes with Robbo for a new game, while Al, a wiry older man who generally tagged along with Robbo and Jonesy as part of his long term plan not to lose his job to a younger man, hung back until agreement was reached and then produced a pencil out of nowhere and pronounced himself scorer.

The game was 501. The men would play in teams of two, with the winner being the first to zero and the loser shouting the next two jugs for the opposition. 'And a pack a smokes,' Al chipped in, putting his tobacco pouch away for want of papers.

'Fair enough,' said George, standing up first, rolling the shafts of several darts between the palms of his hands for luck. He handed two to Ed and took aim with the third.

It lilted lightly, its brass tip just catching the cork in the outer rim at the top of the board as it came down.

'You beauty. Twenty points off for the home team, Al,' Ed directed, thankful that George, who threw a punch straighter than a dart, had kicked them off well.

The big man's next two shots were not as impressive, but did bring the score down eight and 15 respectively.

'You're up Jonesy,' Robbo said, puffing up in a way that suggested he didn't think a starter of 43 was going to be tough to match.

Jonesy got to the required spot – a scuffed line of black paint some 12 feet from the board which was hung from a railway dog spike in an exposed vertical beam in the wall.

Steadying himself to fire off a dart was another matter. Every now and then he would look at his impatient audience, raise his eyebrows, sway a little and then turn back to the task at hand, squinting at the board like it was a boxing opponent falling victim to his psyche out.

Missing the board was always a costly mistake. Mudbrick buildings don't take kindly to being knocked about and what should have been no more than a pinhole in a surrounding cork board could easily become a chunk of dirt on the floor if struck hard enough and at the wrong angle. The wall already looked like a flock of cockatoos had had an afternoon's entertainment taking it apart and if anyone cared to look over their shoulder they would have seen Dot cursing under her breath at the state of the player rocking in front of it, 'spear' in hand.

Remarkably, Jonesy let one fly straight as a die, and Al was instructed to strip 12 off the miners' score. His next shot clipped the metal rim on the board and fell to the ground impotent. Robbo was given leave to steady the man, line him up and step back for the final shot, which stripped another five off.

'Righto Ed, you're up,' George said, slapping him on the shoulder blade as he rose from his seat next to Al, keeping an eye on the scoring. 'Dead eye Dick, that's you mate,' George coached. 'Easier than taking a number plate from a hit 'n' run; just aim and throw!'

Ed did his job, scoring a 20 first up with his cricket arm returning to form on the memory, followed by an 18 and a 13. The game continued, with only a few clumps of dried earth being dislodged, until a heated examination of Al's rough pencil scrawls revealed Robbo and Jonesy as the winners.

With Dot ordering them to 'stomp the divots' back into the wall, George bristling and Jonesy's wobbly legs refusing to walk back to their original table, Robbo surprisingly offered to share the winner's jug. The men stayed where they were, drinking with long-night rhythm. George and Ed played the part that locals had played for years, giving the long history of the goldfields, how they were named after a Melbourne Cup winner in the 1890s, how there was still plenty left, and talking up the prospect of 'hitting the big one'.

'So you guys must know all good spots, having lived here all your lives, eh?' Jonesy could hear the windup in Robbo's voice.

'You must be pretty dumb cunts then not to have made it rich by now.'

Robbo was looking from George to Ed, so as not to miss a sign between them that he could launch an offensive on. George sighed and downed the last of his beer. Ed leaned forward, appearing to be fixated on the extraordinary protrusion of Robbo's nose hair that came from just one nostril and extended into the curl of an emerging snarl.

'We do alright,' he responded, in the laconic drawl of someone who believes he is in the company of less educated men and lets them know it through understatement.

'As long as you subterranean types keep coming back fossicking around and finding nothing, we'll keep doing just fine,' Ed patronised them.

'We'll feed you, we'll rent you our houses, we'll take your money – the only thing we can't do for you is bring up the gold. So I guess that makes you the dumb cunts now doesn't it?'

Robbo leapt from his seat, but George was already in between them, holding the miner at bay with an extended arm. Backing down wasn't usually George's thing, but he was pretty sure he'd be nursemaiding Ed for the next week when the first blow landed and that didn't thrill him at all.

'Just siddown, mate, he doesn't mean nuthin' by it,' he told Robbo. 'He doesn't even live here so what would he know, eh?'

'Gerry,' George called out by way of moving on, 'another jug over here mate?'

Robbo surprisingly sat back down and moved the conversation in a new direction.

'So, what's property worth around here anyway? Maybe you guys need a middle man – someone to hook you up with miners who need digs. For a fee of course. Whaddaya say?'

'I got a spare house in town,' Ed came back. 'Should have two houses really. George used to live in my rental, didn't ya mate?'

Al, who didn't want to be left out of any potential business opportunity, wanted some clarification.

'So you got one house or two – which is it?'

'I got a rental and it's in a good spot too – the only one on Eyre Street. There's a woman in it but I'm about to renegotiate her lease.'

Jonesy was drawing with some disgust on a cigarette from the packet George had been obliged to buy Al. He nodded knowingly: 'Good luck with that mate. Women always make stuff complicated.'

A smudge of resentment seemed to cement Ed's expression so that, for a moment, it looked like he might just let the story swill around in his beer, spiral to the bottom and drown, but the men were interested now.

'You're the landlord,' Robbo spelt out slowly. 'She's the tenant. What's the problem? Boot 'er out. I'll get you good rent, take my cut and guarantee you'll still end up ahead.'

Ed took another swig from his glass.

'He's got a thing for her, I'm guessing,' Jonesy posited. 'Getting a bit on the side are we boss?'

'It's complicated.'

'Sounds like something a woman would say,' Al said, 'just before she dumps ya.'

'She owes me, but it's gonna take some working out,' Ed responded defensively. 'My folks took her in and now she thinks she's family or something and we can't get rid of her.'

'That's a bit rough mate,' George put to his friend, his gratefulness at being taken in briefly by Bert and Mabel when he was in a tight spot not far from his mind.

'Not true Munt. She was 16; she could 'a' gone out on her own instead of leaching off us. You joined the railways younger than that. Now she's like this rich spinster. My folks give over the shop to the Railways, move to Adelaide, leave her in charge; I've got them on my case about everything now. Mum turns up on my doorstep every week for Chrissake.'

'Yeah but your folks get the lease money and your mum likes Adelaide anyway. It's better this way and you know it. Anyway, what've you got to complain about? You get a Sunday roast. You love her roasts. Shit, I love her roasts.'

Ed turned on his friend, forgetting momentarily that others were listening with great amusement.

"Snot the point. She trashed my home and she's living in the other house rent free. The minute my folks became her folks, that house became a Johns house – my inheritance.'

Ed downed the last of his beer, losing a fair bit of it from the side of his mouth, and slammed it down on the table. Everyone but Al stood up.

Robbo lifted an eyebrow at Jonesy, with a look that suggested his night was about to get a whole heap more interesting. He turned back to Ed, spat lightly on the palms of his hands and smoothed his loose strands of greasy hair back over his skull.

'Now ladies, seems to me this bickering is getting you nowhere. This girl obviously owes you something, and seein' as you're a mumma's boy, I reckon we oughta go along to give you a hand collectin' on that. Only house in Eyre Street, that right?'

'Now hang on, Ed, this is bullshit,' George interrupted. 'You need to sort this out with yer folks, not her.'

Robbo looked like all his Christmases had come at once.

'What'd I tellya! These boys couldn't sort their way out of a paper bag without checking with mum first!'

For the second time that night, George extended his hand to Robbo's chest, but when Robbo winked at him, it could be argued that it was instinctive that George's other fist would swing around to break the miner's nose. Ed would swear later that, even as the blood poured from Robbo's face and he'd staggered back to fall into a chair that had been rapidly vacated behind him, he was grinning like a crazy fool when he turned to pick it up, raise it above his head and bring it down on George.

The ganger hadn't seen it coming, distracted as he was by trying to shake Al off his back, the old guy having sprung there immediately Robbo got struck due to his habit of being seen to get in early (in a manner that didn't injure his arthritic hands) and getting out early if he could manage it.

The melee of fists that had erupted near the dart board spread quickly across the Brooster, with surprisingly little demarcation between the two groups. Perhaps it was moving too fast for the largely drunken crowd to make the distinction or perhaps, in some cases, it translated as an opportune way to relieve the tension of the working week and so it didn't particularly matter to those individuals whowas on the receiving end.

Either way, one of the more capable brawlers in the room – George – came out of it more injured than most, having taken a steel-capped boot to the head more than a few times after the chair felled him. Concussed, he spent most of the next 10 raucous minutes being randomly stood on or kicked while he was down. It wasn't until Dot fired her shotgun off into the ceiling, causing several weeks of dried mud divots to fall from the roof and walls, that George came to.

A minute or so later, he dragged himself to his feet and looked around. Dot was picking up chairs, Gerard was sweeping up broken glass and the last of the patrons were a straggle on the way to the door.

He followed them out to see a ganger he knew urinating against the toilet wall.

'Hey Jim, you seen Ed Johns?'

'The skinny fella? Yeah, he was looking for a ride. Mighta got a lift with one a them miners.'

Coz 'e hasn't caused enough trouble for one night!

George smiled to see his dog asleep in the back of his truck. He opened the passenger door and whistled loudly, prompting unexpected pain and a spray of vomit that only just missed Max as he leapt into the cabin. Unperturbed, George roused up a cleansing spit, settled himself in the driver's seat and headed for Eyre Street.

23.

[Friday morning. November 24, 1950.]

When Trudy Wentworth opened her front door to George Munt early on Friday morning, she only did so because he was a former student and had always seemed a decent fellow.

He had arrived long after she had switched off her bedside lamp, and stood on her porch, the top of his head and shoulders illuminated by the dim overhead light, recognisable more by his distinctive shape than any facial features. Trudy could see through the screen door that his singlet had been torn from one shoulder. He smelt of beer and sweat.

'I know who you are George Munt but it's the middle of the night; what do you want?'

'Sorry Miss Palmer, it's 'bout Eyre Street; there's been some trouble an' I just reckon you outta bring her back to your place for the night. Miss Palmer?'

'You've been drinking George. I'm not sure what you want, but I'm just going to get my husband, alright?'

'You got married Miss Palmer? That's great,' George said effusively. 'I always said it would be a lucky bloke who got you. I never believed you was gonna be a spinster.'

Trudy was irritated – not being awake enough yet to be offended. She opened the screen door a little more, without stepping out or letting her visitor in.

'For heaven's sake, George, what's happened?'

'There's been some trouble and I think maybe Helen might want to be with you tonight.'

Trudy unconsciously grabbed together the sides of her thin dressing gown around her neck and frowned at George.

'Don't look at me like that. I'm not on the prowl or nothin'.'

Trudy pushed open the door fully to look at George, who was now shifting his weight impatiently and looking even unsteadier on his feet because of the random way the porch light was shooting out between the bodies of fluttering moths that had gathered on it.

She could see now that he had a cut above his left eye and a broad graze, or perhaps dirt smear, on the shoulder where the singlet strap was torn.

'Focus George: why would Helen be in danger?'

'Yeah …'

'At Eyre Street?'

'Eyre. Yeah, Eyre.'

Though George had sobered a little with the concussion, he was still drunk enough to find the rhyme amusing and rock just a little too far onto his back foot, causing him to slip off the porch into the darkness.

A man in his sixties, with a canopy of thick white hair that protruded from a natural cowlick, appeared behind Trudy in the doorway.

'I'll go check this out, Trudy,' Gill, said, pushing gently past her, tucking in half of his shirt with a hand jiggling keys. 'You stay here.'

'I'm coming with you. I'll get dressed.' Trudy went back into the house, shedding her dressing gown and kicking her slippers off as she headed for the bedroom.

Gill waited for her on the porch, straining to see who had woken them in the middle of the night. George looked up to see a slighter man, the light revealing a scuff of hair protruding from the neck of his shirt and a face in shadow.

Gill extended a hand down to George and pulled him up onto his feet.

'Looks like you've been in the wars son; you want to tell me what you've been up to?'

'I roughed up a few miners, but nothin' serious,' George responded.

'What's this got to do with Trudy's friend?'

'They was gone when I got there. I think Ed seen 'em off but the door was jammed an she was yelling at us to get lost, so I figured she might want a woman to help an' I came here for Miss Palmer.'

A moan drained from the bundled figure in the back of the truck, followed by a low growl.

'Don't worry 'bout that – I tied 'im up an' e's good to go,' George responded. 'But you need to get to Eyre Street 'cos strange things happen at that place. My truck used to go walkabout an' all!'

As Gill headed toward the back of the truck to investigate, Max brought his growl to the edge of the tray.

'C'mon Maxxie,' George called softly so as not to hurt his head any further. The dog leapt past Gill's face to the ground and in one extraordinary spring, launched himself upward through the passenger side window to sit beside his owner. Gill had seen a number of working dogs perform the same feat, but he was somewhat gob smacked to see it from a dog of Max's age. He was still distracted by it when Trudy emerged dressed in a t-shirt and jeans, drawing her hair into a ponytail.

The truck spun a rut in the Wentworth's driveway as it turned for Tarcoola, the noise muffling Ed's demands to be untied.

'Pipe down mate, it's sorted,' George muttered to himself, barely noticing that Max had begun to lick his forearm, as the dog was wont to do when his owner was sweating alcohol.

Gill headed for the couple's four wheel drive.

'Did you know he's got someone tied up in the back?' he asked his wife as he turned the key.

'Wouldn't surprise me. Right now I just want to get to Helen.'

Trudy pulled herself forward in the seat and put her hands on the dashboard as if she were bracing herself for a crash. Gill responded by pushing the accelerator to the floor.

24.

A proxy for a friend.

[January, 1951.]

More than one child had rudely told Trudy Palmer to go away in her time as a teacher. But she had never thought it would be Helen.

But then again, I never expected Flick and Jim to die either.

After the accident, Trudy had taken it for granted that if Helen was going to turn to anyone as a proxy for a friend, a sister, even a mother, it would be her. Yet she had spent hours on Helen's doorstep that night, her hand numbed from being leant on, curled up, knocking gently on that steadfast door, one long tear on either side of her face that would not finish its descent. The girl had rejected her then and was still fending her off, despite her obvious need.

So why am I still trying?

It was the weekend and Trudy needed some space to think. She had come to sit in the empty schoolhouse, piling some neglected paperwork in front of her as if to justify why she was there. Her pen had been knocked accidentally onto the floor some ten minutes before and Trudy had not yet moved to pick it up. Instead, she scanned the shadows of the faces that had been there that day – the day Flick and Jim Muldoon had ploughed through the Tea and Sugar.

Next to the window, the one that had been sealed shut with careless painting years ago, was James Brown, a kid without a musical bone in his body, and luckily no chance of sinking into a life of drugs either despite his namesake. James would complain that it was too hot where he was sitting and ask to be moved. But James was the stinky kid – bladder problems – and no one else wanted to be near him.

At the centre of the back of just five rows of desks were the twins Maddie and Ruby Paton who were bright as buttons – working at grade six level despite being young enough to be doing grade four work – and easily bored, so they regularly sought amusement distracting the others around them.

I remember I had a pounding headache that day and I wasn't putting up with any mucking around. But I shouldn't have yelled at Helen.

Trudy moved back to the papers on her desk. That day, Lillian would score a perfect 100 on both her spelling and maths tests. There hadn't been a mark in the class like that since. She was the twins' older sister, the same age as Helen – an affable and capable girl, but her parents had no intention of her continuing school. She already had a job lined up as a waitress in the pub. Trudy had at least talked Lillian's family into letting her stay at school until she was 16 – one year past the age she could legally be pulled out.

She had taught Helen since she was eight and over the years had witnessed her tendency to be either aloof or strangely suffocating with her friends. New cliques would form but she never seemed to be welcome in any of them for very long. Only once had she seen Helen smile at a boy in a way that suggested a joke or something friendly had passed between them. *Was that Edward Johns?*

But because she had thought Helen, who was also one of her brightest students, might influence Lillian in valuing her education, Trudy had sat the two girls together for the first time that day. Helen wasn't the sort of kid who was distracted by what others said or did. She was more likely to follow her imagination than a classmate's banter in wandering from a lesson. But that day, the girls were chatty and it seemed in fact, that Lillian might have been having a negative influence on Helen.

Whether Trudy admitted it to herself of not, when it came to Helen, she had always had an agenda. She had been keeping her teacher company after school since the age of 13, when both Helen's parents and Trudy herself had deemed it beneficial that she spend an hour or so before she started work at the grocery shop doing additional schoolwork that might potentially lead to a scholarship, not that they had shared that ambition with her at the time.

Having brought in a kettle, Trudy was happy to pour an extra cup for Helen and watch with satisfaction as she supped and read whatever novel or text she had recommended. Sometimes they talked – about life in Adelaide and beyond, as Trudy had experienced it, and often Trudy would toss Helen the juicy bits and leave the dry ones out in order to make life outside of Kimbanyon sound more attractive to the girl. Sometimes they just got on with their work as if the other were simply a loyal dog at their feet by a fireside, in no need of attention but happy to have a pat if the moment arose.

All these years later, Trudy still regretted her part in how that day would play out in Helen's memory.

I shouldn't have yelled at her. It was madly hot in the afternoon. The fan had come loose from the ceiling and was too dangerous to use. James was bashing at the window with his fist, swearing that the bloody thing wouldn't open. It was going to break for sure. Evelyn was accusing Maddie of copying her work and wouldn't pipe down. Lillian wouldn't stop talking about how she was going to leave us all behind when she had enough money from her waitressing to mix with 'classier' people and then Helen …. Helen wanted to leave early because she had a long night ahead of her at the grocery shop unpacking the monthly delivery from the Tea and Sugar.

Trudy could barely dredge the words up from that part of her memory where she had interned her response.

'For God's sake Helen, do you want to be unpacking boxes the rest of your life? It isn't important. You have no idea how much your parents are willing to sacrifice to get you into a good school – and all you can think about is stacking shelves. You may as well be serving up the slops with Lillian. For God's sake, forget the Tea and Sugar.'

There was no chance of Helen ever forgetting the Tea and Sugar after that day. She had barely spoken to Trudy since – accepting only polite chat at the grocery shop and the odd loan of a special book, mostly without comment on their return, though she knew Helen had enjoyed them from the dog eared pages and the odd dirty smear from whatever place she had taken it to read.

Years later, her contact with her favourite former student would be equally as traumatic as the day that stole her parents.

When Trudy and Gill arrived at Eyre Street that night she could not have predicted what she would find. Even now, she wasn't sure what had happened. The whole episode, beginning with George Munt on her doorstep, had been surreal. She hadn't seen George, an ordinary student and generally predictable boy who never got into too much trouble unless he was led into it, since he had left school to join the railways at 15. He was a few years ahead of Helen and though Kimbanyon's only school combined primary and secondary students in the one classroom, she didn't think there had been much crossover, with George attending school haphazardly due to his father's working life until the last six months when he lived with the Johns's because his father, a sole parent, had found work in Western Australia and chosen not to take his son. George had been inseparable from the Johns boy until Mabel and Bert sent him to boarding school in Adelaide to stop him joining the railways with his best friend. Edward and Helen had shared a year or two of school, but Edward was drawn to the chatty, flirty girls, so Helen was unlikely to have been on his radar.

How those boys were involved that night at Eyre Street, Trudy didn't know, but the police had questioned them both. Their statements revealed that they had gone to the property on a 'hunch' following a drunken conversation with unidentifiable patrons at the Wily Rooster on the night of the brawl, and found Helen alone and distressed but unwilling to talk. George's explanation for hogtieing his friend related back somehow to the pub brawl and Ed wanting to continue it with his dog. In defence of the police, Trudy had to admit that the statements she and Gill were able to make would have been equally unenlightening.

When they had arrived at Eyre Street at around 1.30am, there was only one light on. A panel on the front door had been split and a chair had been wedged underneath the door handle on the inside, preventing it opening.

Gill had gone around to the back of the house, stood on a water tank and taken the louvres out of the toilet window. Being too big for the opening, Trudy had ditched her sandals, accepted his leg up and clambered in, her feet only just reaching the sticky enamel of the cistern once inside.

She had found Helen in a corner of the loungeroom, folded in on herself, her arms around her knees, pressing her stomach to her thighs as if trying to suffocate a cramp. An old bedspread or rug was draped around her shoulders. Trudy had moved to stroke the girl's hair and had found it wet.

'Helen? It's me: Trudy. Are you alright? 'Sweetie? I think maybe we should go to my place and talk about it there, okay?'

25.

[March, 1951.]

It pained and infuriated Trudy to think that someone was going unpunished for what they had done to Helen, so she set out to learn exactly what that might have been. Her inquisition hung over every sip of tea, every laundry basket, every passing in the hallway. It had even put a damper on Christmas, which came with the gift of a lush dressing gown from Trudy to Helen, accompanied by the usual aside that anytime she wanted to talk, Trudy would be there for her. Gill's gift to Helen was a tactless argument with his wife in which Helen's name was raised and muffled more than once, reaching her ears in snatches between swings of the kitchen door.

Over the three months that Helen lived with the Wentworths, she began to feel persecuted, inadequate and unworthy. The more Trudy tried to penetrate Helen's protective shell, the more the girl receded into it and the less capable she seemed of ever moving home.

Now standing outside the door to their ensuite bathroom, the usually easy going Gill was losing his patience. Trudy knocked gently.

'Helen? I think you should sell the Eyre Street house and live above the shop; it's safer in the centre of town.'

The glutinous sound of vomit plopping in the toilet water and splashing up the sides of the bowl cut Trudy off.

Gill threw up his hands and strode dramatically from the bedroom, his growing disenchantment with his wife's charitable nature making him grumpier by the day. The girl was obviously a nut case and Gill, who had come to the marriage already retired and with an agreement from Trudy that they not embark on a family, failed to see how she was their problem.

'It might help to talk to Reverend Holbrook about all this. He's going to be in town next week,' Trudy persisted.

The sound of another heave of vomit and a thin moan from a tired chest seeped under the bathroom door. Gill was suddenly back beside his wife, having given up his attempt at discretion in favour of being Mr Fixit.

'Listen Helen,' he said abrasively to the door, 'you're obviously not coping with things right now. Stress is something you've got to deal with and if you won't let Trudy help you, it has to be the Reverend or someone else you're close to. Is there anyone you'd like us to call? Do you have family somewhere?'

Helen did not respond. His last words had fallen to the floor and crawled under the door to her like maggots from roadkill. Trudy glared at Gill.

'Look,' he explained to his wife in an aggressive whisper, 'you tell me you've always been close to this girl but we've never had her over for dinner, caught up with her for a drink or even mentioned her before that ganger turned up on our doorstep.'

'That's not true,' Trudy began, punching the words out defensively but failing to stem Gill's tirade.

'Suddenly I've got the grocery shop girl in my bathroom – throwing up – and you're supposed to be her best friend but she won't talk to you. From what I hear she's a serial house guest and I'm telling you, Mrs Wentworth, this is not going to be her next stop, so you'd better get her head straight, or get someone in who can.'

With that he left his wife sitting on the floor, her back to the bathroom door, and Helen on the other side, rinsing her mouth out with a hand cupped under the sink tap, trying to work out her next move.

She had been with the Wentworths for too long, she knew that. Gill had replaced the door at Eyre Street and fitted a new lock.

Though he had initially made her feel welcome here, it was obvious he hadn't expected her to stay as long as she had.

Helen had not missed a day of work, opening the shop every morning at 6am and locking up every night at seven. It was Sunday today and she was at a loss for where to go. When she imagined herself going home, she also imagined tortured faces looking out from the windows – her own included – and hands with curled fingers lightly dragging across the glass. *Heathcliff. Cathy.*

She finally opened the door to Trudy, who looked at her so pityingly, she thought for a moment her stories might simply flood from her. But Trudy spoke first: 'You're pregnant, aren't you?'

26.

[March, 1951.]

Helen had begged Trudy not to call Avery, despite waiting for him to return every moment since she had seen him last. Trudy had assumed it was shame.

She had never known Helen to have a boyfriend while she was at school and was sure Mabel Johns would have let it be known if a young man had been hanging around the shop calling on her. She rarely went to the local hotel and then only stayed for dinner. As far as she knew, Helen had no girlfriends.

'There are places where you can go in your situation,' she had told Helen. 'Reverend Holbrook has looked out for you in the past; let him organise this for you. I can make the call. You don't have to be involved.'

I don't have to be involved? Who is carrying this baby?

Helen had expected Avery would have returned to visit her and found her gone from Eyre Street. She had imagined him worried, and to come in search of her. But he had stayed away. There was no call, no inquiry. Nothing to let her know he knew or cared. So it was with a sense of humiliation that she learned he had been speaking to Trudy for months.

He visits that Van de Velt woman, rides that bus around with Gillian Brown to hand out propaganda, he'll even sit in that stupid church for hours waiting for strangers to tell him their pitiful problems, but me? He'd rather talk behind my back.

'He doesn't care about me. He has a wife,' Helen blurted at Trudy, in the same embittered tone the words had erupted in her thoughts.

Trudy raised her eyebrows. She examined Helen's face and saw a crumpled indignation.

Oh no! She's got a crush on the Reverend!

Trudy decided to ignore it.

'The church has many married men in its service, Helen; it is only the Catholics who don't allow their priests to marry. Sweetie, Reverend Holbrook is a compassionate man. He won't judge you. He has shown you a particular kindness over the years and he will know how to deal with this, discreetly.'

A particular kindness. Helen felt like she'd been punched.

When Avery appeared on Trudy's doorstep, he looked every bit the resident Reverend of a suburban church. He no longer wore the deep blue suit and waistcoat with its satin-covered buttons, donning instead a black shirt with a stiff, white, round collar and neatly pressed black trousers. His manner was upright, confident and unequivocal. He did not want to hear what had happened. He was not a policeman or a social worker, he said, and he certainly did not intend to pass judgement. Trudy smiled at Helen, but wished, having heard it said by another, that she had not used the phrase herself.

When Helen sought out Avery's eyes, he averted them. Once, when they inadvertently connected, Helen thought she saw an apology, but when he next spoke she sensed nothing but indifference.

'I'm not here to give counsel today, Mrs Wentworth,' the Reverend advised Trudy as if Helen were not in the room.

'There are others more skilled with this kind of thing – kind Christian women who run a retreat in Adelaide and find good homes for unwanted babies.'

Who are you to tell me my baby is unwanted?

Seated in narrow cane chairs in Trudy's unusually cool sunroom, across a tiled coffee table on which several cups of tea grew cold and homemade cornflake biscuits remained untouched, the two women sat in silence, thinking their own weighty thoughts while the Reverend directed the conversation.

Helen concluded very quickly that she was on her own. She noticed a thinning of Avery's hair as he leant forward to pull his tea closer to him. He continued speaking as he stirred it, his eyes downcast, seemingly intent on a thorough infusion of the milk.

'So you can see that this is a good option for us … for you, Helen.'

Disturbingly for Helen, as she sat marmoreally, Avery grew more dispassionate. When he spoke of the Benevolent Shelter for Women and its good Christian ethos, it sounded like propaganda from a newsreel. Hundreds of babies had been endowed with a positive future at the shelter, he said, 'relieved of the burden of their sinful conception'.

As Trudy stole a glance at the face of the young woman she had heard muffling cries in her room more nights than not, she felt herself a Judas.

Suddenly Avery rose from his chair and went to Helen. Dropping on one knee, he took her hands in his. Surprised, she flinched but then held herself perfectly still, anxious that the intimacy be real and for the slightest of moments, wondering whether he was about to propose. Avery closed his eyes and spoke as if in prayer.

'Be of good courage and the Lord shall strengthen your heart and set you upon rock. Under his wings you will find trust again.'

When the Reverend opened his eyes briefly to see how Helen was receiving his words, he was forced to close them against a fearful glare.

'Let this truth be your shield and comfort,' he concluded.

Helen abruptly withdrew her hands, a contempt in her eyes that would have scorched a less audacious man. But instead of the Reverend responding with greater sincerity, all Helen saw was the look he solicited from Trudy – one that aligned them as adults in a task beyond her comprehension.

'You must understand Helen, there is only one choice for a woman in your situation,' the Reverend put to her, with renewed composure.

'You are not showing very much at this stage, but your pregnancy will soon be beyond doubt. It's best if you let Sister Michaels care for you and reside with her for the rest of your term.

'I have already alerted Bert and Mabel …'

Words of protest leapt instantly from both Helen and Trudy's mouths, with Trudy despairing of Mabel as the world's 'worst gossip' and Helen rising to the slap of another perceived wrong having been done to her.

'I was discreet,' Avery assured them, settling Helen back into her seat with a Moses-like downward flutter of his extended arms and broad hands. Trudy regretted for a second time her choice of words in describing the Reverend earlier.

'They believe Helen to be taking a long vacation and have no problem with her returning to her job if she wishes to when this is all over,' he explained, 'if, of course, the Railways hasn't made a permanent change by then.'

Helen would later listen with quiet anxiety to the conspirators walking down the hallway to the front door, talking in hushed voices.

'I suppose that went as well as it could have,' Trudy would say as she accompanied the Reverend to his car.

For whom did it go well, Miss Palmer? For you? For Gill? I guess it did. You get to be rid of me. And so do you Avery. No scandal for a failed guardian. And me?

She imagined what she was feeling might look like tapeworms stretching under her skin and the thought of it made her gag. She rushed to the bathroom with her hand to her mouth, expecting to vomit. Leaning over the sink with the tap turned on, she looked down to confirm the dirty pooling of an aggressive nosebleed.

27.

House of new beginnings.

[March 1951.]

The Benevolent Shelter for Women in Islington Road, Walkerville, Adelaide, opened in 1881 in response to reports of 'baby farmers' taking on the offspring of impoverished unmarried mothers for a fee and then allowing them to die from neglect.

A local historian, Geoffrey Manning, would describe the ugly prelude this way:

'In the hills which nearly surround our city, there was more than one neat little cottage, which from its situation and surroundings, the passing traveller would suppose to be the abode of innocence and domestic happiness, but which in reality was a veritable Golgotha – a den where many a helpless baby was made to suffer a torturing and lingering death. Into these retreats children were taken by their unnatural mothers, ostensibly to be nursed, but in reality to be made away with by starvation or slow poisoning.'

The matter was discussed by colonial politicians over many years but perhaps no one challenged them to open their eyes as articulately as a Mr Geoffrey Crabthorn, writing for South Australia's first newspaper, The Register in 1873:

'You know as well as I, my public, that this is an everyday occurrence, which nobody ever dreams of regarding with anything but horror and dismay. And therein lies the depth of its significance. For who is responsible for this wanton rejection of one of God Almighty's most precious gifts? Who has to answer for this heedless profanation of the sacredness of human life?

'Is it the unhappy mother, who, hoping against hope, is too often driven by sheer necessity to abandon her foremost duty as the only alternative against starvation? Or is it society who refuses her the means of earning a pittance, however hard, while her babe is still clinging to her breast, who tacitly gives her to understand that her only chance of winning back a position of respectability is to get rid of such an objectionable encumbrance and who, when its ruthless scorn on the one hand and its indirect encouragement on the other, have led to the destruction of a life, complacently folds its hands in gratulation over so happy a release, and impiously commends the decrees to beneficient Providence that "orders all things for the best"?'

The Benevolent Shelter for Women would operate in various guises under various names and be run by various charitable institutions for just six years shy of a century (with the exception of three years during which it was a boarding house for homeless or itinerant men).

Church records would show that it provided care for unmarried expectant mothers 'who previously led a respectable life' and married expectant mothers who had been deserted and left in precarious circumstances.

Its purpose was to 'restore penitent unmarried mothers to paths of virtue and to train inmates to support themselves by some respectable occupation'.

Lengths of stay and treatment at homes such as these across the country varied over the years, most likely reflecting attitudes, funding and demand. Those admitted might have vastly different experiences, ranging from being tricked into consenting to adoption, having their baby whipped away immediately at birth while lactation suppressing drugs were administered, to being supported to stay with their newborn for a year and then offered a placement as a domestic servant in a wealthy home prepared to allow the child to accompany its mother.

Six years after World War II, waiting lists for babies around the country were growing. Hospitals in Victoria, where more than

400 couples wanted to adopt, and New South Wales would be investigated for alleged racketeering. Doctors delivering the babies of unmarried mothers would be accused of selling them for an average of fifty pounds each.

In 1950, more than 350 couples in South Australia were waiting to adopt a girl, and 121 were looking to adopt a boy. Demand was far outstripping supply.

Helen was aware of none of this as she unwittingly entered the market. At the time the Benevolent Shelter for Women was presented as her only option, she thought her situation entirely peculiar to herself.

On the day she was frog marched to the Shelter, time stretched itself around a bubble. Sometimes she was inside it, entranced by the filmy images swimming around her. Then, abruptly, she would find herself outside it, bracing against a hostile reality – her longing for love and family encapsulated in a fantasy that was denied her.

When she didn't think about what was happening – leaving her mind vacant to avoid the injury she sensed was coming – she became nauseas and clumsy. If she did think about what was happening, she became anxious and panic stricken, her breath caught in an icy wind weaving rapidly in and around her ribcage.

The first time fate had changed her life, Helen had been oblivious to its creep. She had skipped over the railway line and meandered to school without looking back. If she had known it would be the last time she would see her parents, who had dropped her off together, she would have paid more attention to her father's arm stretched lazily across the top of the bench seat, his fingers resting lightly on his wife's shoulder, the light catching the ginger hair on his forearm. She would have wondered at how her mother could still look so elegant, and why she had taken particular care with her hair that morning.

Today, fate was making Helen an accomplice to her own downfall. She was about to lose her independence and herself all at once – being led into the abyss one child-like step at a time. This time she could anticipate the sick sense of wanting with every fibre of her being to be able to change this day. But for that to happen, she would need to eradicate a lot of things – particularly her relationship with the man leading her up this particular garden path, dressed once more in his familiar navy jacket and waistcoat.

'This is all for the best, Helen. They're good people – part of our church family,' Avery said gently but firmly, sensing Helen's wilting resolve. He took her small suitcase from her as if lightening her load might quicken the pace.

Helen's stomach felt like it was filling with melted butter and grass seed. Her throat was swelling with stifled words, and her head was buzzing. She saw the street in flashes of colour, blinking nervously as if a rash of locusts was blowing into her face. Heritage green trim on a yellow weatherboard house. A rolled up blockout blind left on a verandah. A letterbox stuffed with mail. A rampant bougainvillea spotting purple over a rusting wire fence. Was that a woman bent over, pulling up weeds? She blinked again and saw instead a Labrador, lying down, its paw resting on a dead bird, its head pulling back, teeth enmeshed in flimsy grey skin, the feathers long ago lost, tearing away the wing. She closed her eyes, opening them again to the pavement.

Avery's smooth-soled shoes made a relentless rap on the cement; his clip was now so determined and steady, it was almost military. Helen would have preferred to walk alone rather than be marched in by this man whose heat she had experienced now growing colder and more remote by the minute. Even Trudy would have been better.

Every time Helen brushed against Avery, he seemed to pull back until it felt as if he was striding on one side of the broad suburban street and she was bumbling along the other, moving in sync but miles apart. Every time she put her foot down, the path seemed to shift. The edge doubled in her vision and again she stumbled, grabbing instinctively for Avery to support her. He clasped a clammy hand over hers on his arm but removed it as soon as she had steadied.

How Helen wished she could turn into any of the homes along the way – sidestep the whole affair, visit for a cup of tea to update friendly neighbours on how the family was going. How she wished that was her life. The houses were probably full of married women sniggering, married men judging her.

Do they all know?

She fell a step or two behind, reaching her fingers to the leafy tips of a dense hedge. She tracked along it, her skin alternately brushing softly against plush growth and being scratched by barren twigs until she was forced to stop just behind Avery, who had turned to open a gate.

She followed him in, her hands moving protectively now to her swollen abdomen, which was threatening to reveal itself through the split in her mauve wrap dress. At her feet, weeds had pushed their way through gaps in the brickwork. The edge of the path had collapsed, the bricks fallen away, sunken lazily into the earth like the blanket of soil dried out and fragmented over her parents' graves.

She stopped; her feet would not go another step, her eyelids would not hold still and her ears heard nothing but a drone of wings rising with such shrill she hoped fancifully that they would somehow carry her away and put her back beside the rail line, on her way to school, the day before **that** one.

'For God's sake Helen,' Avery snapped, uncharacteristically profaning in public and grabbing her by her elbow. She drew in a pouch of air then imagined it full of tiny insects and spat it out, the last of the phlegm dribbling appallingly from her chin.

'What is this nonsense, Helen?'

Avery turned to her and firmly gripped each of her upper arms. He stood there briefly, looking directly into her eyes.

'I know you are anxious, but dawdling won't change the destination and spitting like a camel won't win you any friends in your new home. And that is what this must be Helen, your home – until this business is done. And then we will see.'

And then we will see.

Helen felt an urge to hold Avery's hand, but did not seek it.

Beyond the hedge, the house occupied a double frontage bordered by a neglected lawn and framed on either side by giant gum trees. Dried twigs and leaves protruded from the gutters, giving it a kind of malevolence when it was silhouetted, while the shadows thrown from the wide eaves over the top storey windows looked to Helen, who had squinted up into the sun to see them, like dark shadows under watchful eyes.

As they took the stairs between two columns into the sheltered doorway, Avery's hand brushed up against Helen's. It was fat with warmth. At first she thought the contact had been an accident, but then his little finger hooked around hers. Just for a moment. She thought to respond but Avery withdrew his caress before she had a chance to curl into it.

Though her heartbeat was racing, Helen stood dazed and mute; she didn't hear the knock, didn't hear the door answered, didn't hear Avery's voice and couldn't even be sure he had spoken first. She registered the sarcastic drawl of a woman who was obviously familiar with Avery but not the form of her words.

'Ah, Reverend. You have brought us another young soul to save. How thoughtful.'

Despite the matron's comforting endowment of flesh, any hope Helen had of falling into the care of a motherly figure was quickly dispelled. The woman stood fixed to the step, giving the impression that an offering of some kind might be required before anyone entered. Helen tried not to 'sleepwalk' through this, and set her mind on making a good first impression. The effort so consumed her attention that she lost control over her gaze and became entranced by the woman's enormous breasts which were squeezed into submission with some difficulty by an almost blindingly white apron.

As Helen's gaze travelled, so did her thoughts, or maybe it was the other way around. Either way, when she settled her attention, it was on the pocket of the apron. The stitching at the edges had come away, giving it a dog-eared appearance which probably only escaped repair because it also escaped the matron's line of vision. The fabric around it was just a little creamier in colour than the rest of the apron and it was fattened by a bundle of unopened letters.

The matron's ankles were so thick as to make preposterous the idea that they could bend enough for her to climb stairs and Helen found herself wondering if she was permanently stationed at the door like an umbrella stand that came to life in an Alice-in-Wonderland way when someone came knocking. After imagining the woman this way, Helen felt brave enough to draw her eyes up from the ankles to her face and to imagine it painted with the gaudy colours of a Mad Hatter – a much less frightening prospect than the complete stranger in front of her now.

The woman's chin was plumped softly into her neck yet her skin was stretched tightly over her broad cheeks so that they appeared hard. They were spotted red by tiny blood vessels and her lips had disappeared into a tight short line by an ingenuous attempt at a smile. Her eyes …

'Helen,' Avery snapped again. 'This is Sister Michaels.'

Helen jumped a little in her skin. The matron responded in a sandy drawl that was a little lighter this time, as if she was bemused.

'Yes, yes Reverend, by all means, make the introductions, though I don't need to be so rude as to look her up and down to get the measure of her. What's your name lass?'

'This is Helen,' the Reverend replied, in a protective tone which instantly lifted Helen's spirits. 'I'm asking the girl, if you don't mind Reverend.'

'It's Helen, ma'am.'

'You can call me Sister, or matron, I don't mind which. Now take your suitcase up the stairs to the room on the left. We've had a young woman leave this morning and you can take that bed for now.

'If you still remember your name when you get there, introduce yourself to Susan who has the bed next to yours. She has drain duty today and you can help her with that until we can get you on a rostered day of your own.'

She turned to Avery expectantly and said in a teasing voice: 'Unless the Reverend has brought with him a cheque or a plumber to assist us?'

Avery remained silent, simply frowning at the matron, who showed no signs of withdrawing from the question.

'I see from his face the expansive pockets of the church are empty today. Maybe on your next visit, Reverend.'

Helen found herself smirking, just a little; she had never heard Avery spoken to that way. The authority and confidence in the woman's voice made it easier to make the transition from being directed by Avery to being directed by the matron and though she still felt largely powerless in her fate, the burden felt a little lighter as she climbed toward the bedrooms.

Helen's room for the next few months was small, spartanly furnished, filled with light and the smell of antiseptic. Susan was actually Sybil.

'Both start with "s", so I it doesn't really matter,' Helen's new roommate said matter-of-factly.

'It's not like the mullet – matron to you – is going to remember if I tell her again, so she can keep calling me Susan, but if you're gonna share my room, it's Sybil – Miss Sybil until I know you're alright and gonna pull your weight because I'm not doin' your drain duty just 'cause you're feeling sick or sumthn'; everyone around here feels sick so it doesn't make you special and if there's no bed and we get told to bunch up, I'm not gonna be the one that has to sleep in the bath. It's gonna be you – so long as we're clear on that, we'll get along just fine.'

Despite the whiney tirade, Sybil hadn't moved or looked at Helen for more than a second or two before returning to stacking her magazines on the left side of the chest of drawers between the two beds, closer to her own, and refolding what appeared to be an already folded nightie and retucking it under her pillow. The girl was at least three years younger than Helen, with pale blue eyes and hair so fair it looked as if she had no eyebrows, giving her a ghostly appearance which some might think pallid and not at all forceful, yet she had Helen riveted to the floor as if being barked at by an army commandant known to have eyes in the back of his head and given to horrendous punishments for the slightest deviation.

She was wondering how to respond to Sybil when Sister Michaels lurched up the final steps and occupied the entire narrow landing as a stage for the next few uninterrupted minutes.

Had Helen not been so distracted by Sybil reading her her rights, or more accurately, her lack of rights in the new relationship, she might have heard the matron's advance. The wooden stairs were far too narrow to be used regularly by pregnant women and as the matron was for the most part bigger than even those reaching full term, they barely contained her, so her passage was both laboured and noisy. Not that that stopped her pitting her varicose veins against the hike several times a day to keep the house running smoothly.

Sybil and Helen's room was the first of seven bedrooms off a long corridor. Despite its proximity to the bathroom on its right, bedroom number one was the least popular room in the house. In an unfortunate reflection of circumstance, the carpet secured by the church as a charitable donation from a local business for the hallway had been cut about three feet too short, meaning entrance to bedroom number one was across exposed and uneven floorboards, and, to the rest of the sleeping quarters, up a lip of dirt-infused threads.

Invariably, the girls had to put up with various residents cursing as they stumbled or stubbed their toes on the raised carpet lip, mostly because they couldn't judge where it began from the viewpoint across their enlarged bellies, and the ensuing chastisement from the matron, bellowing from downstairs every time the girls swore.

The bathroom also had its problems. Brittle turquoise tiles had come away from the base of the yellow porcelain sink, leaving only a corrugated film of old grouting cement and frighteningly rotting floorboards through which the light from the downstairs dining room shone. It seemed an inevitability that the sink would crash through the boards sooner rather than later and in all likelihood kill some unsuspecting diner below, if they had not already been forewarned by droplets of water from the ceiling diluting their meal as they ate and prudently shifted to a safer seat.

As none of the girls wanted to be held responsible for such a disaster, or to have the bill for the long overdue repairs sent to their already put upon families, they tended to wash their hands over the bath. The enormous bath had not been used for almost 18 months now, because it exacerbated the drainage problems and because it had turned out to be a useful, if uncomfortable, spare bed.

At times when the shelter was overcrowded, the bath could be bridged with adjoining wooden palettes and foam rubber cushions retained from the couch that went out with the rubbish when the Islington Road boarding house turned its ministrations of benevolence from homeless men to unwed mothers. Those girls unfortunate enough to be directed to bedroom number 1B (B for bathroom), rarely got a good night's sleep, were restless and loud and protested strongly every time any of the other girls woke them to use the toilet, and even more strongly if they had remained asleep while the toilet was being used but were then rudely awoken by the toilet user forgetting the bath was occupied and attempting to wash their hands over it as they had been accustomed to doing to avoid the possibility of killing unsuspecting diners by overburdening the sink.

All of this Helen was yet to learn. In the meantime, having already taken on Sybil's instructions, she was obliged to hear the matron out with hers.

'I expect you to settle in well and be grateful for the care you'll receive here, Helen,' she said between wheezes from the considerable effort it took to get herself up the stairs.

'We all help each other out and we don't like tears.' The matron paused for more air.

'This is not a house of sadness, it is a house of new beginnings … for you and the families who will be offering your child a better life than you are able to.'

By this stage, the matron's lungs had recovered and she was able to look Helen directly in the eye. 'I don't care what miscreant behaviour has got you into this mess,' she began with new vigour.

'And I don't care what your last name is or whose family it is you're hiding from while you're here. I do care that you keep yourself and your room clean, that there's no whingeing about this girl or that girl or what's for dinner, that my toilet doesn't back up because you've skived off drain duty and that I'm not woken in the middle of the night unless waters have broken or there's blood involved. Are we clear?'

Apparently the final question didn't require an answer because the matron had already swivelled to begin her descent and the thud of her shoes on each step confirmed she had no intention of waiting for one.

Helen had not uttered a word since entering the bedroom. Now she moved over to her bed and lay her small suitcase on the faded lime green towelling spread to unpack. That done, she found she didn't have the strength to go through with it; her shoulders collapsed and she suddenly felt desperate to be walking away with Avery.

Through the window between the beds she could see the almost oval shape of his back, becoming smaller as it receded into the thin end of Islington Road. It disappeared and reappeared in disjointed navy blue blobs through the blur of smears on the glass, until his image became as intangible as heat rising from train tracks. She watched him all the way to the end of the street and around the corner, without seeing his face.

Helen took one step back from the window, squinting to prevent a tear escaping. The smudges on the pane now seemed to her to be the shape of finger tips. She saw, in the clouding, the form of a hand pressed against the glass. She followed four smears in tracks down to the frame as if the hand had slid upon the realisation that it was not needed to wave goodbye because the shape they were connected to had not looked over his shoulder, to elicit a farewell and give the promise of a return.

He didn't look back, not even once.

'She's not so bad; says the same thing to everyone,' Sybil offered in a conciliatory tone, now resting on her bed, flipping through an old copy of Women's Weekly.

'I bin here three weeks now – never heard a different speech. Not once. If you're lucky, the mullet'll never speak to you again. Until it's time. Now the religious nuts – that's another matter. They never shut up. Until they think you're good 'n saved anyways!'

As unlikely as it seemed, Helen had momentarily forgotten why she was being left behind.

Until it's time.

Her eyes were still pinned to the empty space where Avery had last been but her hands were now pressed to her growing belly, drawing the warmth of her baby up to fill her cavernous chest.

28.

Earth to Kate.

[1967.]

Kate's pale green eyes followed the sparrow under the table, over her friends' shoes, tail up and down as it shook a stale crumb to break it into a smaller portion, eyes always on the lookout for softer offerings sprinkling the Adelaide sidewalk.

Sparrows never miss out.

Kate flew through her days – confident, popular, on top of her studies, always on a mission of some kind. She had just put an exam behind her and was rewarding herself with a strong coffee in the outdoor section of one of her favourite cafes. But already she had the next exam in mind. Every high score was one step closer to her moving out of home, financed by her proud dad, only he didn't quite know it yet.

'Kate, Kate …. Earth to Kate? Don't tell me that exam rattled you?'

Her friend since primary school was just as wise to life as Kate, perhaps a little more so since her parents divorced, leaving herself and her younger brother playing emotional ping pong and distributing their wardrobes between two households. Generally Melinda and Kate got on pretty well, more when Melinda did the 'can I have a sleep over with a real family' thing and being sweet as pie to her parents, than when she let her jealousy of Kate and her 'perfect' life get the better of her and she would lead Kate into the kind of fun that would ordinarily have serious consequences, if only the girls weren't so good at the deception.

Kate enjoyed their sleepovers as much as Melinda did. It was the one chance she got to shut her door on her parents, whose only real moments of intimacy seemed to be when they put themselves in the same space to listen to great church choirs of the world, their feet up on the olive green vinyl poofs, mother with a lap rug of brightly coloured crocheted squares and Avery with his hands resting on his favourite bible, a pencil and his partially written sermon on a small coffee table beside him in case he became inspired while relaxing.

Behind her bedroom door, Kate could cut loose with Melinda, try new makeup, talk about music and boys and gossip late into the night and bring some of the real world inside No. 7 Irving Street, Walkerville.

'It was shit easy,' Kate responded to Mel's rhetorical question, talking around the rubber band she had clasped between her teeth while using both her hands to pull her auburn hair away from her face and into a ponytail.

'But I've really got to get ready for Politics; I've got a sneeking suspicion the referendum will be a late inclusion and I haven't read all the analysis yet.

'I wish I'd been able to vote on that one,' she added, looking with disappointment at her empty mug. 'It's only right Aboriginal people should be included in the census, don't you think?'

'Sure, sure.'

Mel didn't care much for politics and she certainly didn't believe Kate when she said she was unprepared for an exam. Even when tests were sprung on them, Kate did better than everyone else. She squirmed like she had sand under her skin if she wasn't in control of every situation. Actually it was more like a twitch; you could see her mind ticking over, working out how to manipulate things so that they worked out her way. Unconsciously irritated, Mel kicked away a sparrow that had hopped close to her feet after some minutes' of tipping its head from side to side in consideration of the consequences of going for a large stale crumb which may have been there since the lunch crowd. But Kate was no angel. As far as Mel was concerned, her friend worked her parents like a pro – better than she or her brother had ever worked theirs.

The waitress brought more coffees, a little spilling over onto the saucer as she put Mel's in front of her. Both girls looked relieved, having now justified their spots in the café where they had already sat without buying anything for the better part of half an hour, the afternoon crowd circling keenly for their seats, and availed themselves of the second cups they had wanted for most of that time.

In Mel's assessment, Kate's father was strict, though he obviously adored her, and her mother spoiled her rotten – she always had something new to wear. Neither of them knew what Kate got up to behind their backs.

The suckers buy every story she gives them.

For herself, Mel did not want university, she just wanted out. Out of school, out of home. Out. Period. And Kate was kidding herself if she thought she would graduate if she did go to university. It wasn't that Kate wouldn't get her way, it was just that Mel doubted if deep down Kate really wanted it. She wanted to show herself good enough for it, but it just didn't seem to lead anywhere for girls, and one thing Kate hated more than her overbearing father was wasting time.

If truth be known, Kate was quietly anxious about her future. She had always said uni shouldn't just be a way for men to secure good incomes while women became nurses, teachers or worse, housewives; she wanted her share. But she was studying such a diverse range of subjects – combining humanities with science – that it was hard to see the job at the end of it.

While the sciences could lead a woman into nursing, medical research or even life as a doctor if they were good enough, they were Kate's weaker subjects. Maybe she could use her understanding of how society worked to change it for the better, but how many years at university was that going to take?

Mel and Kate both wondered sometimes if Mel would end up paying the lion's share of their rent if Kate went to uni and she took a job.

That fantasy will never happen.

For now, Kate was just concentrating on getting the marks that would encourage her father's weekly contributions to a bank account set up primarily to pay for a car to get her to uni. If Mel got to uni as well and they were forced to remain at home, the car would be fantastic, but if she took a job and they could move out, then surely rent was a legitimate way to spend the money – it would mean Kate could study without the pressure of having to earn it herself. Either way, she had no intention of rocking the boat at the Holbrook house. Not yet, anyway.

29.

Fat paper.

[1968]

'Kate, you home?' She heard the key turn against the old brass casing of the front door lock, the other keys on the ring jangling against each other as her father forcefully angled the appointed one to the side of the barrel where it didn't stick.

Lying on her bed, in a room two doors down the hallway, her textbook resting on her stomach, Kate mischievously decided not to answer. Her ears reached for her father's movements, trying to determine whether he was listening for hers. The door, swollen by the heat, grazed the floorboards in a well-defined arc.

Kate heard the heels of his boots swivel as her father moved to close the door, and then nothing. It was those boots that had led her to give him the nickname of Hilbilly at six years old, after seeing a comical figure in a book wearing a check shirt, chewing on a piece of straw and kicking his heels up at a dance in boots just like her father's. Avery had whipped her onto his lap after she pointed it out and told her that hilbillies were Yankies and that *his* boots were 'R.M. Williams', but she had stuck to the name anyway. She still used it when he seemed in a good mood and willing to be teased. For a few seconds, Kate waited, wondering if he was contemplating sneaking up on her and bursting through the door with a monster roar, like he used to when she was little. Silence for a few moments longer, then she heard the familiar sound of paper, fat with mystery, rubbing up against itself. She found herself embarrassed that, at 16, she could think they could go back to that playful time, and that she even wanted to. More fat paper.

He's sorting through the day's mail, shuffling the envelopes one in front of the other until he gets back to the most important one, to put on top. What's more important Dad? Today's bills or whether or not your daughter bothered to come home from school today?

More silence. Kate flipped the volume of photocopied poems and articles, which she had let rest on her chest, so she could finish the passage on William Blake. She barely registered her father's footsteps proceeding down the hall, past her bedroom, too mesmerised by his mail to pop his head in the door, too caught up in the tide of a routine that would sweep him into his study until dinner time.

'Was that your father?' Gwen called from the other end of the house.

'Yes, mum,' Kate called back from her bed, her voice capably wafting out the door, and back down the hall to the kitchen where her mother was folding washing on a large table.

'Did he say hello?'

'Yes mum,' Kate called back without hesitation.

Lying was easier than having that conversation all over again, or even hearing her mother deflate after setting free one of her voluminous, judgemental sighs. Her loud disappointments never achieved anything; as far as Kate could tell, they were intended to let everyone know they had behaved badly. Not everyone received the message of course; her mother's notorious sighs rarely drew a response from Avery.

'Dinner in half an hour everyone.' Gwen sent the words down the hallway like forward scouts, with no interest in whether or not they connected with their targets. It was more like a warning shot – signifying that should anyone try to delay attending dinner because whatever they were doing was more important to them than the two hours she had spent in preparation and the hour or so she would spend cleaning up afterwards there would be justifiable hell to pay.

Gwen was already testy about the contempt Avery was showing to his family when he got home: no acknowledgment, no token words like 'how was your day?' He had simply continued his day from the peace and quiet of his rectory office, perhaps only directing his thoughts to his wife when he became hungry and then probably only wondering how he could get her to bring his meal into the study without a fight. She wondered whether he really did say hello to their daughter, let alone asked after her exam.

Kate listened to the clanging in the kitchen and realised dinner would be a testy affair.

Cutlery for three people can't possibly make that much noise. It must have been scooped up at least five times, dropped in the sink at least half a dozen times and 'sorted' another three or four. It's actually going to drive her mad if Dad doesn't get the hint.

'Dinner in five,' came the next call, the voice as sweet as Gwen could manage given the highly irritable state she had worked herself into.

Kate folded the notes she had been taking while reading, dropped them on her desk, grinned to herself and headed into the fray. As she walked down the hall, the rhythm of her father's typewriter, which had neither sped up nor slowed down as a result of the last warning, suggested he had either not heard the call or had no intention of being 'on time'.

Gwen strode down the hall, barely slowing down to edge past Kate in order to make sure the recalcitrant typist was able to hear her.

'Dinner Avery. Don't let it go cold, please.' The anticipation of his usual response sharpened the polite end of her request like a knife whittling a stick into a spear.

'Be there in a minute Gwen,' Avery replied in a tone glazed with disinterest. 'Perhaps you and Kate might like to start without me?'

It was painfully obvious that Avery's attention had not shifted from his page or his thoughts from his own undertakings even for the length of time it took to convey the message that he would not be joining them for dinner.

'Right,' Gwen quipped, lightly biting her bottom lip and glaring at her shoes as if they were somehow responsible for the events at hand. She took a deep breath, solely through her nostrils, and then released it as if she was the wolf at the home of the three little pigs and would get some satisfaction out of seeing the house of Avery crumble in a heap around him.

She collected herself, walked towards her daughter and brought her close with a less than gentle arm around the shoulders, swivelling her towards the kitchen.

'C'mon Kate, I've got an apple and rhubarb pie for afterwards, so I guess your father will just have to make do with whatever we leave him.'

Gwen spoke loudly, only half kidding. If she thought he wouldn't screw with the grocery money, she would probably tip his dinner in the bin long before the heat had left it.

Kate watched Gwen serve up a gravy-soaked casserole so hearty she could see the muscle in her mother's forearm rise under the skin as she manoeuvred the serving ladle to her plate. A well-whipped dollop of mashed potato collided with the rest of her meal, and a roughly broken, buttered bread roll landed on the smaller plate beside it. A tumble of peas made a splash as a side order. A glass of milk spilled a little as it was set down unceremoniously on the table. A fulsome glass of red wine went to the right corner of each of her mother and father's place settings, despite Avery's absence.

She'll drink hers while we eat and then half of dad's while she's doing the washing up. If I'm lucky I'll get to polish it off when they both go to bed. God, I'm going to have to eat double rations to compensate for his empty plate, aren't I?

'Thanks mum, that's enough. I'll need to save room for dessert too.'

Gwen looked up and realised that she had given her daughter two giant scoops of everything.

'C'mon Kate, you need your energy for tomorrow; you've got swimming in the morning, two exams and a riding lesson after school don't forget,' she said lamely to hide the fact she had been on auto-pilot.

I don't know why I said there was apple pie; I'll tell her when she's finished her dinner that there's no dessert. Maybe she'll be happy with just a bowl of icecream. Damn that man.

Mother and daughter ate in silence, not uncomfortably. The sound of Gwen's fork became less pronounced on her plate as she settled into the rhythm of the meal, subconsciously slowing her own eating to make sure she finished at the same time as her daughter. In case she wanted to talk.

Unexpectedly, Avery arrived in the kitchen doorway. He had removed his waistcoat and was undoing his top button as he looked pointedly at the setting without a meal. Gwen put her fork down and left the table to get it from the oven, where it had been returned for warming. She rolled the tea towel she had grabbed over the edge of the plate to withdraw it.

'This is nice,' Avery said scanning the spread of dinner on the table and washing baskets still full of clean clothes stacked in the corner for sorting on the table after tea.

'And did I hear something about dessert?' he asked, winking at Kate.

'For God's sake, we can't have sweets every night,' Gwen retorted, putting his plate on the far side of the table and shaking her hand to dislodge the heat which had come through the towel.

Avery surveyed the room again. His dinner was now on the table, warm and wholesome, with more meat than vegetables and plenty of salt he was sure, just the way he liked it. Kate had almost finished hers and Gwen had only a bird size portion left and seemed so prickly tonight that she probably wasn't going to be good company anyway.

He stepped to the side of the table and grabbed a bag of bread, slipping a slice into the toaster on the bench, and taking an exaggerated sniff, despite the fact his back was to the table.

'You've outdone yourself, Gwen; it smells fantastic.'

Gwen removed the bread roll that was waiting for Avery beside his casserole, put it in a plastic bag and tossed it into the freezer.

'It was good,' his wife responded. 'I can't vouch for yours; there's only so long you can keep a meal warm before it dries out and it seems you're still not ready to eat, so it could well end up dried out and luke warm. You do this so often, I can only assume that's the way you like it.'

'I'm just getting some toast, Gwen,' Avery said in a tone that suggested he'd reached his level of tolerance.

Kate had picked up the pace as the tension built between her parents and skulled her milk so quickly she felt it coat her top lip.

If mum got blood noses like I do every time I boil over, she'd be anemic.

'Can I leave the table now?' she asked. 'I really do have to get back to my books.'

She took the scowl from her mother and the slight look of disappointment on her father's face as approval and fled the room.

Her exit was enough of a reason for Avery to turn his back on a family dinner, rationalising that without Kate there, it was no longer a family affair.

'I'm snowed under in paperwork myself, I'm afraid Gwen. Sorry to desert you but I really need to see to the parish tonight.'

He forced his unbuttered toast underneath his casserole, dragging the meat and potatoes on top with his cutlery. Grabbing a second piece of bread, he then took his plate and headed back down the hallway.

The evacuations left Gwen with little heart for indignation. She scraped the remnants of her own meal into the bin, stacked the remaining dishes and pots in the sink, wiped the table with a sponge, dried it with a tea towel that was still warm from being draped over the oven door handle, and tipped the washing basket back over the surface, losing a few socks and underpants onto the floor. She stooped down to pick up one of Kate's school socks and was surprised to taste the salt of a tear on her lip.

At least Avery left me his wine.

30.

Sex, of course.

[Thursday, November 14, 1968.]

'**I**'m glad you decided to come with me, Kate. It gives us a chance to talk.'

''Bout what?'

'Your mother and I have been noticing changes in you Kate; you're growing up and she worries that we've been putting off having a talk with you about how that all works.'

In his usual tactless fashion, Avery had just jumped straight in. It was a style he had developed early in the teenage years and while Gwen often accused him of using Army tactics – get in, get out quick – in order to speed up his 'fathering' so he could get on with things that were more important to him, there was a good rationale behind it. His approach was in fact calculated to get to the core of the issue without diversion or manipulation of the facts – in other words, without his daughter becoming so emotional that the lesson was lost. Once he had thrown the pre-emptive grenade, there could be no hesitation.

'Dad, I'm seventeen. I think I know how it all works.'

'I'm sure you think you know how it all works, Kate, but you simply haven't seen enough of life to see things as clearly as your mother and I.'

As usual with her father, Kate felt completely ambushed.

Could he be more patronising?

'If I'd known I was going to be trapped with you lecturing me for hours I never would have come. I should have known better; you haven't taken me on one of your parish runs for years.'

'Don't be like that,' Avery said in a soft and all too reasonable tone despite Kate's defensiveness.

'We're just chatting. It's no big deal. Just has to be said once, that's all.'

'So, why couldn't mum have done it?' Kate asked, anxious not to appear to be fighting off the back foot.

'She tells me she's tried a few times but you just fob her off, so now it's my turn.'

'Well, you don't have to bother, Dad. I know everything. OK?'

'What do you mean by everything, Katherine? What is it you think I'm talking about?'

Kate's buttons were far too easy to push and Avery's use of her full name had done the deed. Though she didn't lick her lips, she enunciated the reply with such visceral clarity she may as well have declared herself a prostitute in her father's ears.

'Sex of course, Hilbilly.'

Avery, feeling the weight of the kilometres ahead of him and not wanting to be trapped with a defensive, angry teenager, wondered now at his own stupidity in jumping in so early in the journey to Kimbanyon.

'Well, yes, sex of course, but more importantly, how you handle yourself so sex doesn't ruin your life,' he said in the voice of someone narrating an educational coming-of-age film.

'What makes you think sex is going to ruin my life?'

'What I think is that sex is for marriage and I worry that you don't share that view and that you haven't thought about the consequences of behaving the way you've been behaving.'

'And how have I been behaving?'

'You could dress more modestly for starters.'

'So it's the way I dress that's bothering you, not the way I behave…'

'Katherine, the way you dress says something about the way you're willing to behave.'

'You can't crucify me for something that's not real. Your opinion's got nothing to do with reality as far as I can see.'

'Please don't use words like "crucify" so frivolously, Kate. And please calm down; we've got a long drive ahead of us and I don't fancy sitting next to you in a near-hysterical state.'

'Again with the imagination … it's not me being melodramatic. You're the one who's saying I dress like I'm asking for it. The fact that you're even looking at me and deciding what men might think is creeping me out.'

'I'm only going to say this once Katherine and I expect you to remember it. Girls of your age have to take care that they are not misunderstood by young men, who generally have one thing on their mind.'

'Dad, it's not like that.'

'It's exactly like that – I've seen you when you come home from a night out looking like everyone's party girl.'

'A party girl? What is that a euphemism for?'

'Look Kate, I know you understand there are certain truisms in this world and one of them is that nice girls are the only ones that get taken home to meet the parents. The others get left on the heap.'

Kate was taken aback.

Now what's he suggesting?

Avery continued.

'No other sin affects the body like sexual sin.'

'You're going to preach to me now? Just pull over. I need to get out.' Kate turned to the car door, feigning interest in a rolling escape.

'All I'm saying is there are consequences for every action and I would hate for you to suffer them for the sake of being careless with your sexuality.'

For one of the few times in her life, Kate could not find the words to respond. She stared wide eyed through the windscreen as Avery pressed the end of the indicator arm to squirt water onto the glass now hazy with a film of red dust. Finally, the best she could come up with was to repeat her father's words in an exaggerated and offended tone.

'Careless with my sexuality. Wow. What does that even mean?'

'C'mon Katie,' Avery said in an almost imploring tone, 'you're a bright girl. You know exactly what it means.'

The dust was gathering in wet, curved lines where it had been dragged by the wipers and was smearing across their vision, making it harder to see than before. Avery chose to concentrate on his driving, giving the windscreen another squirt, staring straight ahead and ignoring Kate for the next couple of hundred kilometres.

At least I can tell Gwen we've had the talk.

31.

The drafts of memory.

[December, 1968.]

At night before she went to bed, in the kitchen of the childhood home she had moved back to, Helen saw him sitting at the table waiting for a cup of tea. It was the way she thought it would be when she was young and naive. His broad brow in shadow, falling outside of the dim cone of yellow light from the ceiling lamp, his mouth a thin line neither curved upwards or down, his generous torso straining against the navy blue silk covered buttons of his waistcoat, his legs comfortably lolling each side of a chair leg, his boots polished and feet splayed. It was a contradiction she had crafted in her mind and grown accustomed to – from the waist up a stern, judgmental man capable of compassion and cruelty in equal measure, from the waist down a man overfamiliar with his surroundings and as relaxed as any might be when alone in the company of his wife.

Sitting opposite her vision at her kitchen table, under the jaundiced glow of the overhead light, Helen saw in the face an inflammation of the hypocrisy and righteousness Avery had displayed in Trudy Palmer's sunroom all those years ago.

With an accompanying shudder, as violent as those that follow quick births, she tried to dispel him, consciously unclenching the folds of her face, talking herself out of a headache and getting up to put the kettle on.

As she turned to the sink, she smelt his musk and imagined him dripping into himself behind her – his face seeping into his collar, the collar into his waistcoat. And the blue from the waistcoat would lead it all to the floor, curling cat-like around the table legs and skulking into the corners of the room where the shadows gather and melt into one.

Helen had become adept at conjuring Avery's presence through imitation; if she tidied a strand of hair from her face, drawing it behind her ear, she could feel Avery stroking the side of her forehead lightly with his forefinger and tracing the curve of her earlobe, squeezing it gently between two fingers and pulling it down slightly before releasing it with a smile that curled with the warmth of a teasing parent at one end and the lust of man confident of seduction at the other. If a stranger urged her along in a queue at the Brooster to order dinner, touching her peripherally, she could summon the feel of Avery's hand reaching for her waist and drawing her to him.

But these were the drafts of memory, built on the promise of an intimate moment, with nothing to sustain them. Inevitably Helen was left with longing. Guilt over the longing. Anger over the guilt. Impossible hurt and self-loathing. The ache Helen felt over the loss of her daughter was dull, ever present, and corrosive – like a grub at the core of a lettuce, boring and spoiling from within. Memories came by stealth. She had no defence against them, even encouraging them with a longing to relive that time and have it end another way.

Helen watched the water swirl around the plug hole. From the depths of the pipes, a stagnancy wafted upward, as it had done at the Benevolent Shelter for Women. A coagulation of hair and soap was burping noisily from the constricted snakes of plumbing. How Helen hated drain duty – the pumping of those giant plungers into every sink in the house and the stench of the trap at the back door where the kitchen drained. She rubbed her hands vigorously over each other again and again in the hot water until the red rawness made her feel safe from infection.

Helen's mind climbed the stairs of the Benevolent Shelter. The door of Room 1 opened slowly to her, revealing two single beds with terry toweling bedcovers. Both of them were made up, but only one had pyjamas folded neatly on the end of it; Sybil had moved on and no new mothers or expectant mothers had yet been assigned to her room.

Unexpectedly, Sister Michaels brought her baby to her. With a clarity that defied the years in between, Helen saw her daughter's face again. She had expected a plump, white, feathery being with ruby lips, but the first time she was handed her daughter, her skin seemed to be nothing more than a scald stretched across bones.

Helen saw again the surprising streaks of russet hair, the deep skirmishes of purple bruising above the ears. She felt the unbelievably soft down on the child's upper arms, as her fingertips traced over them, loosed from the swaddling. Helen cradled the infant in the crook of her left arm and used the fingers of her right hand to direct a nipple into the baby's puckering mouth. The faded outlines of bunnies on the cotton blanket and a nightie that Helen had washed countless times for others, seemed a little more colourful and lively now that they were adorning her daughter. But she was listless.

Helen pushed the flesh of her breast against the baby's check, inadvertently forcing milk to squirt over the baby's face. The little one's nostrils flared again and she latched on once more, this time taking the whole areole into her mouth. Helen slid her hand under the swaddling to feel the baby's stomach extend as she fed her. She felt the pegged stump of the umbilical cord. Over the back of her hand, the swaddling could not contain the incredible heat of the human life beneath it. She slipped her little finger into the hollowed curl of the baby's fist, feeling the grip tighten just a little around it as her daughter suckled.

In her dimly-lit kitchen, Helen was Miss Havisham clinging to a world beneath cobwebs. It was cruel how clear her memories were despite the passing years. She only found the willpower to withdraw from them when her grip on the tap had tightened to the point it was threatening to meld with the metal, and water was gushing unabated. Helen loosened her fingers and let the voluminous flow swallow every other night sound until she had shaken off the cramp.

As her fingers relaxed, she realized the smell had gone, the water was running clear and flowing without hindrance. Slowly, she closed the faucet.

Helen headed back to her chair, leaving the kettle beside the sink, empty. A tea towel inexplicably draped over the crook of her arm fell to the floor. She sat down and chose a space of air over the table to stare at. One of her stocking socks slid down to her ankle, the elasticity long gone. She felt it lightly on the surface of her skin but remained inert. An hour would pass before Helen's eyelids would droop and her head would roll forward to her collarbone. Another half an hour would pass before she would leave the house and walk out into the night.

32.

Follow me.

[Thursday, November 14, 1968.]

A slap of a wind blasted the pair the minute they stepped out of the car. Avery turned his head just as it changed direction. The dirty gust that sprayed his face also coated the back of his throat and had him coughing for several minutes, with Kate patting him on the back.

Anyone else would spit, Nick thought casually, waiting for Kate to notice him.

No doubt the Reverend will wait for a glass of rusty tank water from the church, and then look utterly surprised that it's warm and brown.

Nick studied the Reverend – his greying temples, broad brow, pale but piercing blue eyes that seemed somewhat less luminous when conversations turned to the menial despite the rest of him appearing attentive. He was not particularly tall but his broad shoulders and preference for standing rigidly upright, and sometimes a little too close to people, gave him an imposing bearing. Some thought him arrogant, perhaps even a little haughty, but Nick was not intimidated – his own father, Ron, had a similar distaste for compromise and an innate belief in his own views.

It's just a matter of choosing when to stand your ground and when to stand down with men like that.

Nick had serious doubts about whether the Reverend would agree to him marrying Kate. Not that he'd ever raised the idea with him, or even Kate for that matter.

Never do anything big without having a strategy first, as Dad would say.

His workmates thought Nick's obsession with 'the preacher's girl' a great joke, warning him that she 'may as well be a nun' and that her father would shoot him if he laid a hand on her. But as puffed up as Avery Holbrook could sometimes seem, Nick thought he had the man's measure.

The way he watches over that girl – pulls her away when I'm around – he's got bigger plans for his princess. And they definitely don't include me.

Nick's preoccupation, not only with Kate, but with the differences between father and daughter, kept him amused in the long months between her visits. It wasn't that he denied himself the chance to be with anyone else when the opportunity arose, but he knew he would give up the pleasures of a single man's life in an instant if he thought he had a chance with her.

Only his mother, Sorrel, knew the depths of his feelings and supported him in his desperately understated campaign, despite being uncomfortable with the idea of introducing a man like Avery Holbrook into a family with an insatiable appetite for debating politics and religion.

Nick had been surprised to learn from his parents that the Reverend had seen active service in the war. He had been coming to Kimbanyon ever since Nick was a boy; he rode with the library lady, he helped out widows doing it hard with clothing and food from the church's charity collections – he and Mrs Van de Velt were practically an item – and he often brought in special requests like machinery parts that he would leave with Walt Grimsley for collection at the station. Yet despite the depth that the contradictions of familiarity and reserve lent to Avery Holbrook, he seemed too tied up with old ladies and cups of tea for Nick to picture him as an army chaplain. In fact, he seemed more the type to be a conscientious objector than his dad did.

And he's nothing like Kate. She's the sort of girl who could turn a train just by demanding the tracks go around her. Him I just want to run down in my truck.

'What colour are my eyes?'

The question took Nick, who had dogged the Reverend and Kate from their car to the chapel before getting caught up in his own daydreams, off guard. The girl was staring straight at him, her green eyes wide and playful and her auburn hair tied loosely in a plait, looking like melting chocolate between her shoulder blades.

She had re-emerged from the chapel to confront her stalker.

'You never look at me; all these years I've been coming here, and you still can't get your eyes off the ground. Buggered if I can see the attraction of dirt, when I'm right in front of you!'

Nick's efforts not to stumble over his words resulted in him speaking more loudly than either of them expected him too.

'Yeah, well I'm shy.'

Kate laughed lightly and responded with sarcasm. 'Really?'

She trawled her gaze up and down Nick's body, feeling a defiant, almost masculine surge in being so indiscreet. He was dressed in well worn, moleskin trousers and a cornflower blue shirt which somehow put a whimsical light in his eyes. She found his nervousness around her endearing but on this occasion, it also gave her a feeling of power, an emotion she felt compelled to exploit in some misplaced retaliation for several hours of submissiveness in the company of her father.

How am I going to stand the drive back with him? He'll be so pious after lecturing to all those poor folk he thinks are hanging off his every word. God, how do I get away from him?

With mischief written in every line of her face, Kate turned to Nick.

'Why don't you show me why you're such a great catch; do you have a home somewhere or do you just loiter around the church at night?'

Is she coming on to me?

'Sure, I've got my own place on Sturt Street, not far from here. It's not much but there's nothing owing on it. My ute's just over by the station if you want to see.'

'Slow down, slow down; I'm not giving you a Christmas present to unwrap, I just thought it might be nice to get away from the Church for an hour or two.'

'I can do that. Follow me.'

Kate took a quick look over her shoulder towards the Church, which happily seemed preoccupied with matters internal. When she turned back to Nick, his hand was extended towards her.

'God, it's hot!' Kate whipped off her light cardigan, exposing her fair shoulders to the sun, and untied her hair to cover them again in a flurry of gilt tinged tresses.

Nick suddenly wondered whether he had done the dishes at home before he had left. When Kate slipped her hand into his, her skin was like soap lather and he felt an overwhelming desire to be the only one that ever touched it again.

It was a feeling that would return to him years later when he would scoop her up, her limbs cold and unresponsive in their medicated stupor, but her cheek soft and warm against his neck.

33.

Irrepressible.

[Friday, 15 November, 1968.]

The morning after his surprising afternoon with Kate, Nick's cheer had been irrepressible, curling and purring all over his face.

'Bloody hell, would you look at him?' Matt jumped down from the back of the truck that was dropping fettlers off along the track. The driver promptly took off, leaving Davo to jump from the moving tray and land at a run, propelling into Matt who had stopped dead on seeing Nick.

'Oi, watch it you stupid bastard,' Matt said, tumbling forward himself as Davo braced on his back.

'What's up with you this morning?' Davo retorted, dusting himself off, pointlessly.

'I wanna know what's up with Nick,' Matt responded. 'I wanna know what he got up to on his day off to put that stupid grin on his face.'

'You're right,' Davo chipped in. 'What's the story?'

Nick raised his eyebrows and continued to chew on the stick he kept in his top pocket to fight off the urge to put a cigarette there, on account of his mother reading a medical report on the dangers of tobacco to health and him promising her he would cut back.

'Wouldn't you like to know,' he said, turning his attention to the rails they had been directed to inspect, his face still fresh with promise despite the long walk ahead of them checking for fissures.

'Our Nick got lucky last night, didn't you buddy? Am I right or am I right?'

Matt followed Nick, with Davo close behind, keen to get in on the stirring and coming up with a few questions of his own.

'Is that right Nicky? 'Cause I hear the Holbrook girl was in town yesterday and I'd hate for you to have missed a sighting on account of you getting it on with some other girl. And who was she anyway? How come I don't know about her?'

Nick turned and faced his friends, a smug and knowing look letting them know he was proud of something and, short of bragging, they should know him well enough to guess.

'The Holbrook girl? Really? The preacher's daughter? You nailed the preacher's daughter? Matt, did you hear that – he nailed the preacher's daughter. You lucky dog.'

Matt looked sceptical.

'C'mon now; that was never gonna happen. What's he talkin' about Nicky? Spit it out or I'm not walkin' another step. Ten trains can derail on this stretch for all I care.'

Nick crouched down to run his fingers over a section of the track dropping below those next to it, the ballast diminished underneath.

'Alright, alright, you guys. You're right; I got lucky with the preacher's daughter but it's not like you think; we're gonna get married.'

Nick didn't look up from the ballast he was marking with white paint on either side of the suspect track, which was probably just as well because he would have been offended by the exchange of looks between his friends.

'Right, mate; you and the Holbrook girl getting married,' Matt retorted sarcastically. 'And I guess old Holbrook himself is gonna do the deed. What a great father-in-law that man'll make. Tell me, when did you pop the question – before or after you had sex with the princess?'

Nick stood up abruptly, the smile gone from his face, replaced with anger and disappointment.

'An' here I was thinking you blokes would be happy for me!'

Matt stepped back, his hands in the air, defensively.

He walked off up the track, calling to Davo to follow him.

'C'mon Davo, he's in cloud cuckoo land; the sooner we can check this stretch, the sooner we can be in the pub for a bang up lunch. Looks like it might be just you and me from now on.'

Nick supposed he should have expected it. Matt and Dave had both grown up in less than ideal households. Matt was the son of a patrolman who was away for long periods of time checking his allotted stretch of the 5,600 kilometre dog fence that ran from Surfer's Paradise in Queensland to the Bight near Western Australia, keeping the dingoes on the northern side in cattle country and out of sheep country to the south. His job consisted mostly of filling in wombat holes, replacing rotten posts and rethreading wires that were damaged by the odd emu, roo or dingo that had either passed through or died in the fence, refusing to take no for an answer.

The way Matt told it, his father had such a crick in his neck from driving parallel to the fence and always looking in the one direction that he insisted people walk, sit, eat, or watch television to the one side of him so he could see them comfortably without having to turn his neck too much to the less comfortable side. After a while Matt's mother said even when she did put herself on his 'good side' he couldn't see her and if he was so happy living in a truck then he didn't need her to maintain a house for him.

She sold the house and left, but not before giving Matt, then eight years old, the choice of coming with her or staying with his father, wherever that might be. Rightly or wrongly, Matt had chosen to stay with his dad, which effectively meant long days in the truck with the occasional brief stint on stations and a broken education via school of the air, delivered by radio. He had never seen his father with a woman other than his mother – for more than one night anyway – and had only the couples on stations on which to premise his ideas of what a happy marriage was. Generally, he thought life as the boys knew it now, was pretty perfect.

Davo was the younger and better natured of the two of Nick's closest friends despite losing both his parents, with the war taking his father, and his mother taking her own life after delivering him on a 'holiday' to his grandmother's. His mates were his family now and while his good looks were always a hit with women, he had no desire to get on 'that emotional rollercoaster' with any one in particular, determinedly swaggering through life without the encumbrance of attachment.

Neither of his friends could know how much Nick wanted to be in the next stage of his life; he'd bought a house and he wanted to fill it with the largesse of the home his parents had built around him. And Kate was the one to help him do it.

She has to say yes.

34.

A room squared against them.

[Sunday morning, November 17, 1968.]

I t was 2.15am. On a mantelpiece in the loungeroom of a modest weatherboard house, a clock chimed on the quarter hour.

In her bed, seventy year old Alda Van de Velt flipped her head to the opposite side of a pillow half encased in a slip, without opening her eyes. The bedside lamp threw a shallow light across her face and showed her hairnet pulled to the side, leaving a thin indentation across her forehead where the elastic had been.

On the opposite side of the house, a breeze lifted James's shirt momentarily from his back as he hoisted himself into his bedroom through an open window. The forgotten flyscreen popped into the room, landing underneath him as he tumbled heavily to the floor.

Alda sat up abruptly and turned to the right side of the mattress, expecting in her barely woken state to see the slumbering form of her late husband.

Another crash made her jump and brought her senses swiftly back to reality. She picked up her watch from beside her pillow. It was warm from hours under the heat of the lamp.

Twenty past two.

Endless nights lying half awake, waiting for her son to come home and a tightness in her body, triggered by the aching, wrenching screams of his nightmares, had left the widow both chronically fatigued and hypertense at the same time. With some force of habit, she gathered her frayed wits and reached under the bed. Her fingers found the axe handle her husband had kept there because it had a cleave in it that had proved useful for pinning snakes.

When Derk had died, Alda had donated his clothes and books and even burnt belongings that she had not shared his affection for. The handle had remained beneath her as she slept because it kept her memories of Derk tactile. She doubted she had the shutzpah to use it but having him with her gave her the feeling that if she really needed to protect herself the strength would come.

Ignoring her slippers, Alda left her bedroom and moved slowly down the hall, gripping the handle as if it were a baseball bat.

James? James is that you?

Alda had learned over the past twenty years or so not to approach her son when the drink unleashed his demons but she also preferred to have them in her sight, rather than have them come look for her.

Blinking multiple times as she pressed herself flat against the wall outside James's bedroom door, Alda suddenly felt profoundly isolated and vulnerable. The lithium she had stolen from him was having no impact at all.

Damn the doctors. And damn that Reverend.

Tentatively, Alda peered around the doorway. She saw a bright moon through the long bank of windows and followed its bluish light along the silvery hardwood boards that had made this room sound so cavernous when the verandah sleepout had been enclosed. James had gradually been reversing his mother's renovation of it into a bedroom, removing the curtains and rugs that had absorbed the sounds of his pacing through restless nights.

Alda heard a shuffle and watched in anxious silence as a man crossed in front of her. He stood silhouetted in the corner, his head appearing to slide onto the adjoining wall and then return to his torso again as he swayed. Alda could not tell if he saw her.

She looked to other end of the room. James's mattress was on the floor. In front of it, the iron bed frame and base was turned on its side, forming a wall of wire.

Suddenly the figure was running and shouting.

'Ahhnree! Gerown. Gerown!'

James dived over the frame, thudding into the wall and falling back onto the mattress.

Alda dropped the axe handle. It landed with a reverberating boom. She put her hand to her mouth and froze.

Whether James heard something of the crash on the floorboards or felt a vibration through the thin mattress, Alda couldn't be sure. But he did respond. Gunner James Van de Velt rolled onto his knees, pulled something out of his pants and peered through the coils.

Alda decided to show herself but lost her voice. She stepped into the moonlight and smiled nervously in the direction of her son.

Crccccck..

For a second, Alda thought she'd been kicked. For another second, she remained upright. Then an unbearable heat filled her and she crumpled. Panting, she put both hands to her stomach, feeling the roll of flesh between her fingers and the wetness of her own blood soaking the webbing.

Everything felt like jelly.

She toppled onto her side.

He shot me?

James ran to the soldier and cupped the man's heels in either hand to drag him back to the bunker.

Alda cried out with each tug as the wound expelled more blood and her panic increased. James dropped the feet, grabbed the soldier's arms and continued dragging.

'James! Stop.'

He did not hear the words. But he felt the moist throw of a breath on his wrists. And then he smelt talcum powder. It bloomed in his nostrils like a mini grenade. James looked at the soldier's face – curdled in the half light – and saw for the first time that it was a woman. A nightdress was gathered around her waist and everything below was a dark wash. She had scrawny shins and bare feet. James dropped her arms. Her head hit the floor. Her chest convulsed. A balloon of blood and bile erupted from her mouth. Another followed it. A thick red line flowed from one nostril.

Confused, James looked to every corner of the room, confronted each time by seeing it squared against him. He closed his eyes, counted to five, and opened them again on the pitiful shape curling into a ball at his feet.

Mum?

35.

courtship on a claypan.

[December 1968.]

I t had been weeks since Kate's rapacious assault. It had left Nick feeling ripe with purpose and as a consequence, her absence left him hollowed out, his mind distracted and his nights unsure. When she finally called, Nick's stomach churned with the kind of sweet anticipation you sense it would be foolish to digest.

Despite his open face, ready smile and genuine nature, Nick had not been lucky in relationships and was relatively inexperienced when it came to progressing them beyond the bed. Mostly, he felt, women thought him boring, and if he was honest, it was probably because he couldn't be bothered investing emotionally in their lives or letting them into his. He wasn't aware that he had set the bar at the point of being able to impress his parents, but he was conscious all the same that most of the women in his life to this point would fail to do that. From the first time he saw Kate, tailing her father off the train, her lithe figure a contrast to his bulk, he became mesmerised by her restlessness. She exuded a petulant energy that threatened never to tire and perhaps it was this that settled Kate in his mind as a woman who could hold his attention for the rest of his life.

Yet the way in which they had come together – the thrashing sex – was so far removed from how he thought it would be that he feared they had blown the possibility of an ongoing relationship. He tried to tell himself that it was not a 'one-night stand', that he had not felt the satisfaction of total abandonment through ensuring every gratuitous need had been met and totally satiated due to being liberated from further encounters the next day or in fact, ever again. The lust of that day could have been interpreted as cheap, opportunistic sex, but Nick had come to think of it as if he was a man swallowing a drop of water from a canteen that was thought to be full on a scorching day and regretting that it had not been appreciated more for the knowing that it was the last. He also felt an unfamiliar pang when he imagined her breath in sudden bursts into his open mouth as he moved inside her, every bit of her bringing more of him to the surface of his skin. He had invested in this girl.

And yet, something about that afternoon, the way it came about, suggested to him that Kate's mission might not necessarily have been centred on him. She might even have laughed at the idea that what they had done was the start of a relationship. So, while Nick waited for her to call, he planned a courtship. Instinctively, he thought to ensconce her in his world by following the shadow of those times and places that had made him happy and reinventing the memory of them, this time including her in their bloom.

When Kate appeared off the train, her shoulders glowing with a tan not present when she was last here – accentuated by a white halterneck top – and her athletic legs protruding from scalloped turquoise shorts, Nick was waiting for her with two pushbikes.

'Can you ride a bike?'

'What do you mean, "Can I ride a bike"?'

'Never mind; everyone can ride a bike. Silly question.'

Kate put her hand in Nick's as he helped her down from the carriage steps onto the broad platform. Behind them, Mr Grimsley, a little more hunched than he had been when Nick was a boy, was pulling on one sleeve of a rather worn navy blue jacket as he left his office with an inventory sheet and clipboard slipping in snatches from under his other arm. When it fell to the platform, Nick stooped down to pick it up while Mr Grimsley got his other arm into his jacket and smiled broadly at Kate through grey bristles and moist teeth.

'Why Miss Holbrook, is that you?' Grimsely asked. 'Without the Reverend?'

Wouldn't be game to show his face after failing the widow Van de Velt I imagine. Scandalous she asked for a Salvation Army minister to send her off in her will. Still, nothing to do with the young lass.

The old station master's eyes squinted into Kate's face and imagined her somewhat sharp features soften a little as her gaze warmed over Nick's back. He nodded in Nick's direction.

'You're in good hands there you know,' he rasped, years of smoking making his words sound like they had been pushed through a whistle stuffed with grass.

Kate offered him the curt sort of smile that young women sometimes throw at older men when they aren't sure if they're being lecherous or not, a consequence of having aged several formative years since she had spoken to him last. Grimsley didn't seem to notice. He turned to Nick and took back his clipboard, searching behind his ear for his pen and setting off to the business end of the train, his wheezing in sync with his footsteps.

The ride through town was a breezy one, not that there was any breeze, just that it was light and joyful in a juvenile, romantic sense and Nick was glad that none of his mates from the railway were there to see it.

Despite not knowing which way to go, Kate was happy to race Nick, kicking her feet away from the pedals when she got far away enough to think she had him beat and cutting him off when he pretended to challenge her despite the overtaking opportunities of the main road which was so ridiculously broad as to double as a community cricket field on Boxing Day.

Nick pulled away with ease, standing up from his seat and leaning forward, his bicycle rocking from side to side underneath him as he pedalled. They raced as if they were both ten and their peers were watching them from the playground, making mental bets on who would win.

'I never knew winning meant so much to you,' Kate exclaimed breathlessly as Nick pulled up in front of her, having passed the last house on the edge of town some fifteen minutes before.

She looked around her, seeing nothing remarkable that might register as a destination you'd take a 'tourist' to. A black cockatoo swept overhead, it's wings fingered at the end, tilting and soaring in a descending arc to land on the branch of a distant tree that looked to Kate to be completely lifeless, spun grey and tapered at its ends like a watery ink sketch. The cockatoo's screech took her by surprise and even though it was far away, she ducked into her shoulders as if she had been swooped by a nesting bird.

'I used to come here as a kid,' Nick said, getting off his bike in recognition that Kate was puffing.

Kate followed suit, beginning to regret her decision to wander into the outback without at least a bottle of water. The ground crunched under her weight, feeding the smallest of stones between her feet and the soles of her sandals as they walked. Though she lost a step shaking them out, one foot at a time, she did not ask Nick to stop and wait while she rid herself of the irritation; she didn't want to appear fussy.

Where the hell are we going? There's nothing out here. It's probably a wombat hole. What if that's what they do to city girls out here? Murder them and stuff then down wombat holes.

'In summer, it was always dry. Pretty much every winter too,' Nick continued, loping ahead of Kate as her thoughts slowed her step.

Finally, he stopped, the wheel of his bike on the lip of a deep, broad claypan that appeared like a sculpted crater in the landscape. It was rectangular in shape, with walls angled inward to the base. Its floor was broken into a thousand clay tiles, heat shrunk, their edges curling in on a thousand smooth surfaces glaring back at the sky. Between them a thumb's width of shadow highlighted the relief of each segment in the vast tessellation that spread in front of them.

'I saw this filled with water once, when I was about seven,' Nick told Kate. 'Mum tried to teach me to swim here. You wouldn't believe it, to look at it now.'

Kate stared into the abyss. It looked about the furthest thing from a clean, blue, pool with its inviting bold lines urging her to the other end. She imagined a seven year old boy with his eyes crunched shut, attempting to push his outstretched arms through a caramel-coloured slurry.

'So apart from your inexplicable need to share these obviously fanciful memories, why are we here?'

Nick didn't answer her, pushing off over the lip of the dam wall instead. Kate's first response was to gasp, assuming he would come to an ugly end when his wheels jarred at the bottom, but he sailed off in front of her, legs splayed either side, feet airborne.

'Yaaaaahoooo!'

His jubilant cry came back to her from a distant place – the image of him pedalling furiously to get up the other side curiously seemed much closer than the sound. Kate couldn't help but notice how his receding buttocks moved under his shorts and was still thinking about them when he lifted his arm, now facing her from the opposite side of the dam, his bike flat on the ground, to call her over.

There's no way I'm doing that, no matter how cute he is.

Nick started clucking like a chicken and lifting his elbows, his hands tucked under his armpits, as if he were flapping his wings. This time the sound carried.

She called back to him: 'No way. You come back here and don't expect me to patch you up if you don't make it this time.'

Nick started scratching around with his feet and stretching his neck as if looking for food, all the while squawking, arching his back and puffing his chest out ridiculously. By the time he completed a circle, clucking and flapping his elbows, Kate had got herself to the edge of the dam wall.

Fine. Looks like we're doing this.

She took a deep breath, holding it long enough that she could silently count to three in the hope that she could force her limbs to take the bike over the edge and save her pride. She lifted one foot onto the pedal and looked across the dam floor. It was vast and empty. Random weeds were knee high, standing brittle and straight on the downward slope in front of her. She pushed off.

'Wooooohooo,' Nick yelped as Kate tore down the embankment. His cry was right in her ear.

Doesn't that beat everything!

'Stand up just before you get to the bottom or you'll be crutched,' he called out in a less than gentlemanly manner, before taking off himself and hurtling toward her.

Kate's whelp of delight – of pure surprise and heart-racing exhilaration – vibrated inside his chest as they rushed past each other at the base. At the top of the dam, Kate planted her feet firmly on the ground, her shoulders rising and falling with each heave of her chest, and turned her face to Nick, sharing across the expanse an open mouth gasping for air and spilling exuberance at the same time. Her eyes were wide from the simple thrill that she would later tell him she had not experienced since the age of about 10 when she won her first medal in a pool for a backstroke event, having had no idea how many might have been in front of her when her knuckles hit the edge.

Although he knew there was no way he could have told what colour her eyes were from that distance, he had it in his head that that was the day he discovered they could change with the light. Sometimes smoky green, sometimes charcoal flecked with gold, sometimes a rich chestnut. The look in her eye, probably suggested by the one he had seen after kissing her later, the whisp of her now stringy hair and the sunlight flaring off her white top combined to lock themselves together in his memory. It was one of the images that would come back to him when he was distracted or bored on the job years after they had married, and his mind would ache for missing that girl.

36.

[June 1969.]

Mel was running late, still rummaging around in her soft leather bag as she walked into the café, assuming Kate would be at their favourite table, looking across a border of planter boxes on the rim of the deck to a view of the river.

The water was a flurry of rivulets crossing over and under each other in a giant brown plait, with gusts of wind darting fitfully in and out of the weave, causing random splashes, as if birds were diving for fish. Never had the girls seen it so alive.

'What a wild day! Do you want to sit inside?' Mel asked her friend, who had just returned from one last trip to the bush with her father, despite Mel being sure Kate would have grown out of them by now.

'No, it's fine; it'll make Ricardo's day to serve us out here,' Kate said wryly, having already turned him away twice while waiting for Mel.

Despite having been regulars at the café for almost two years now, the girls were not staff favourites; with little personal income, they sat on one or two coffees for hours, never ordered food, and often monopolised the best table in the house by virtue of getting there before the lunch or after-work crowds and settling in.

Almost on cue, Ricardo, a stringy Italian man with long wrists and too-short sleeves on his black shirt, appeared at their side.

'Sorry girls,' he said with a modicum of sincerity, 'there's no outdoor service today; it's too windy.' He raised his palms to the weather as if testing for rain.

'That's okay, I think we'll stay anyway. We like the view,' Mel pipped up, changing her mind abruptly upon the waiter's appearance.

He shrugged and, as if to reinforce his point, picked up two chairs that had been blown over several tables away, turning one upside down on the other so their seats connected, as he would have done at closing time. Kate followed Ricardo inside and ordered takeaway coffees, confronting the blustery wind immediately she opened the door to return with them to their regular table. The girls huddled into their clothes and warmed their hands on their cups, determined to continue the news from their telephone conversation the night before.

'So, Kate. Getting engaged – that's wild news! Tell me about this boy. He must be pretty special to meet Holbrook standards.'

'Well,' Kate began coquettishly, 'he has gorgeous eyes, dark brown at the edges, but like honey in the middle, especially when the sun hits them, or he looks at me,' she continued in a purposefully soppy love struck tone, 'because I light up his life.'

Mel shook her head with mock despair. 'Oh spare me the Mills and Boon.'

'Hey, there's nothing wrong with a bit of Mills and Boon; my mother has the odd copy around the house. A little romance novel never hurt anyone,' Kate returned, feigning hurt.

'Yeah, but your mum isn't getting any from the righteous reverend, so she'd be an easy target!' Kate raised her eyebrows at Mel's crassness but it didn't slow her down.

'You on the other hand, could have your pick of the most eligible bachelors in town and you're lusting after some guy from the bush who'll make you live in whoop whoop. What's the attraction?'

'C'mon Mel, we've both talked about getting out before. You'd go at the drop of a hat if you got the opportunity.'

'Not if that opportunity was going to walk around the house in a blue singlet drinking beer all day and it was 500 miles to the nearest bakery. My God, they probably don't even know how to make coffee there!'

Mel turned with new appreciation to the cup in front of her and took a long sip, wiping the perfectly frothed milk from her top lip with her bottom lip, letting it settle on her teeth before wiping it off with her tongue. With only a light cardigan on, she realised her teeth were actually chattering.

'God, it's freezing, I have to walk or I'll turn into a popsicle.'

The girls drew the handles of their bags higher on their shoulders, wrapped their fingers tighter around their near empty paper cups and shuffled off together, shoulder to shoulder for greater warmth.

'Is he built?' Mel asked when they were on the path beside the banks of the river, shielded a little from the wind by a chain of tall trees between them and the water.

'Is that all you ever think about – sex? Of course he's built; he's a ganger.'

'Which is what exactly?'

'He builds railways.'

'Really. And that's the guy for you? I can see the reunion year book now: Kate Holbrook, top of her class, once expected to achieve great things, now happily married to a ganger with ten kids.

'Truly, sweetie, *this* is the guy for you?'

'C'mon Mel, can't you just be happy for me? He's a really good man; he's not afraid of Dad, he makes a solid living and who knows, I might be able to convince him to live in Adelaide. Maybe he can "commute".'

'Right, Kate, he'll commute on his little maintenance trike thing that scoots along the tracks. He's going to do that every morning to get to 'work' building railway lines that go across to the other side of the country.

'Although,' Mel added a little more hopefully, 'I s'pose it doesn't really matter where he lives, given that he's going all over the place, whereas you have to live here. Not negotiable. What would I do without you? What will Avery do without you for that matter? Talk to his wife over dinner? Not likely!'

While Kate would not have allowed anyone else to talk about her parents that way, she could only grin at Mel's insolent humour.

'Seriously, I don't know what I'd do without you,' Mel despaired, tossing her empty cup into a nearby bin and hooking her arm through Kate's.

'I'd be miserable all by myself, with only the charming Ricardo for company, and the war'll take him soon enough.'

Kate dropped her head onto her taller friend's shoulder, enjoying the girl's larger frame and thick, golden hair to rest her cheek on. She squeezed her hand into the crook of Mel's arm.

'We'll write and you'll come to see me while I convince Nick to move back here. It'll work out.'

Mel sighed like an old woman, her equilibrium still a little shaken from the phone call the night before. She kept telling herself it had been a joke and had half expected Kate to laugh about her gullibility this morning. With Kate's hair brushing her jaw and her arm hooked through hers, she thought her friend's regrets would come quickly; marrying a railways man was ludicrous for someone whose mind couldn't sit still for a moment. It had disaster written all over it.

And I always thought it would be me taking the easy way out!

37.

Our only child.

[June, 1969.]

'**I** know you're disappointed that she won't be going to university; I am too,' Gwen opened, searching Avery's face for some indication that he was prepared to hear her out.

'I know it seems like she'll be a long way away, but you'll see her regularly on your trips and she might even come back with you sometimes and stay with us for a while; it's not that far really.'

Though the courtship between Nick White and their daughter had been apparent for some months now, Gwen and Avery had quietly been hoping its bloom would wilt with time and they would not have to face an awkward moment with an over enthusiastic Nick asking Avery for his daughter's hand.

Relaxed in their loungeroom one evening, Gwen with her knitting in her lap, and Avery mulling over a half-penned sermon, Gwen tentatively broached the subject. Normally, if she chose to raise an issue or chat while Avery was writing, he would gruffly hear it out to its first natural juncture, tritely offer a solution, even if none was required, and then make an excuse to retire to his study where he could continue his work undisturbed.

On this occasion, however, Avery was unlikely to have been dismissive if not for the fact he was embroiled in an attempt to appease the growing anxieties of his congregation with a more contemporary view of faith. It was less than two years since the nation's prime minister Harold Holt had drowned, assassinations in the United States of the rights activist Martin Luther King and Bobby Kennedy were still fresh and the ballot for national service that was sending young men to the war in Vietnam was still dividing the country – students, parents, libertines and conservatives alike. The responsibility the Reverend felt to make God and the Church relevant to communal wellbeing in the midst of such pervasive social upheaval was immense.

If I go down this track, if I make it a worldwide thing, I've probably got just one chance to get it right – to choose the right words, or risk losing them.

Gwen could not have known how deeply immersed Avery was in the world's problems when she set about enlisting his help in their family affairs.

There's never a good time, but it's only Thursday, so he's got plenty of time to finish his sermon and this is important.

'She's our only child Avery and we should be concerned firstly with her happiness, so if this is what she wants …'

Avery stiffened in his chair.

'Why do you do that, Gwen? You just jump in in the middle of your thoughts and expect me to know what you're talking about.'

Avery's frown was almost painful to witness, as was the sudden withdrawal of his wife's chin into her neck, as if the remarks that she found rude, condescending and deeply personal were an actual blow to her head.

'This is serious, Avery,' she said, dropping the theatrics in order to take the moral high ground.

'We have to discuss our daughter's happiness and work as a team for once so she knows that we both want what's best for her.'

Avery, whose intellect couldn't help but be affronted by being pulled from its global orbit and asked to respond to a tantrum, came out swinging.

'Okay, I'm caught up now; we're talking about the wedding. Well, what do you want from me Gwen? The boy's going nowhere; he'll be a ganger his whole life unless his birthday comes up in the ballot – and by the way I bet Kate doesn't even know when his birthday is – and then he'll go to Vietnam and probably get blown up, leaving us with a twenty something widow who has to come home and probably won't leave her bedroom for the next decade. Is that what you call looking out for her happiness? Well is it Gwen?'

Avery was on his feet, gathering up his paperwork from the coffee table between their chairs but seemingly unable or unwilling to stop his rant.

'I suppose you'd be okay with that life for her, wouldn't you? And you're right in thinking he might come back a war hero, following in the tradition of good looking men who don't blow their brains out or take their families down with them when they come home. Didn't seem to do Elvis any harm, afterall, and, as we know, Jimmy Stewart came through his experience of war just fine for a skinny man.'

Gwen was too experienced a marital combatant to wilter in the mockery, though she found it necessary to speak gently and slowly in order not to become shrill in her response.

'This isn't going to go away just because you shut yourself in your office and refuse to deal with it, Avery. She's too smart to get bored out there and if he does get conscripted, she doesn't have to rot on her own. She still has us.'

'And what if she decides to go as well? That could easily happen you know. Just because she doesn't want to go now, doesn't mean she won't think about it if he's over there.'

'Because why would a woman go to war unless she was following a man? I remember your ludicrous ideas about why people go to war. They were silly then and just as ridiculous now.'

'Look Gwen, I don't want to talk about this marriage because by talking about it, you mean talking me into it, don't you? We always end up having to have it your way, and how does that work out usually?'

Avery was on the move, headed for seclusion, neither wanting or expecting an answer. Despite wanting to return to what he had hoped would be his best sermon yet, his mind was aswim with the faces of the outback women in his parish. Not the faces that beamed as he and Gwen pulled up alongside their homesteads because of the promise of company for dinner but the faces in between times. The ones who could not come to see him later to talk over a few things, to ask for guidance – who could not disturb the routine of their settled lives on properties where they were often the only woman surrounded by men. The still ones.

Hands as rough as fence posts, living with monosyllabic men, reduced to conversations that begin and end with a weather report.

Gwen had followed Avery into the hallway, her anger growing and her usual restraint abandoned with the knowledge that Kate was out with friends and therefore would not overhear them.

'And what if your extraordinary expectations drive her away anyway? Will we wish we'd settled for a loving daughter who comes to stay on the weekends, maybe with some grandchildren and a son-in-law she can rely on long after we're gone?'

'I'm sorry Gwen, this is just going to go around in circles until I give in to you and that is not something I'm ready to do. I'm not as comfortable taking the easy way out as you are – letting her do whatever she wants even when it's not in her best interest. Not this time. It's too important.'

Avery didn't slam his office door, but the closure was resolute. Gwen waited just one deep breath before she opened it again, her chest just a little tighter, to find Avery already seated at his desk, working on his sermon, or at least giving a good impression of doing so. He finished his sentence under her glare and then looked up, eyebrows raised over fierce eyes, as if to say, 'Are we *not* done here?'

Gwen shook her head at him, barely restraining herself from spitting on the floor in disgust. She turned abruptly before he looked away and left the door open in a blatant effort to have the last word on her way out.

Back in the kitchen, a basket of washing on the table to be sorted, she took a deep breath. She let it out in the low, drawn out way that Avery had imagined the lonely women of the bush doing at the end of a day that promised to be played out all over again the next.

If this is what Kate wants, then we'll do this without him.

38.

An invitation to the past.

[Late August, 1969.]

The lead up to the wedding was a stressful and surprising affair for Kate, marked by the clouding of her relationship with her best friend and a discovery she would make about her father.

Gwen's parents had been shocked to learn of the impending marriage, having never heard of this Nick White before their granddaughter's announcement. Mr Dalana had made a visit to see Kate the next day and, after the necessary congratulations, had engaged her in a 'casual' but completely transparent chat at an outdoor table under the wisteria that had barely dried from an earlier shower, with a mug of hot chocolate forced on them by Gwen on a whim of nostalgia.

He had been over enthusiastic in remembering his university days and the adventure of discovering what he wanted to do with his life through bettering one comedic mistake after another. Kate had informed him, with a face strained by impatience, that, though she was enjoying his stretch down memory lane, she had a lot to do to get ready for the celebration. He had reluctantly cut to the chase and asked her to consider prolonging the engagement in order to make sure an outback life was what she really wanted. Grandpa had left with the economical response from Kate that she knew what she was doing, and had suffered a patronising pat on his hand, by way of assurance.

As she lay on her bed that night, the perfume from a daphne bush, flowering early and profusely this year due to a combination of warm temperatures and lingering rains, was filling the room. It came in aromatic waves through the window, on a cool breeze that brought goosebumps to her thighs and forearms.

Many times Kate had felt pampered by mother nature in this way, soporific endorphins leaving her light of body and mind until the sandman drew a cotton rug up over her shoulders and rolled her onto her side and into a deep sleep. But tonight her grandfather's hesitancy was loitering in her mind and she began to feel keenly that her days in this sanctuary were now numbered.

Kate found herself interrogating each item in the room for its favourite memory. Though she could not see them in the dark, she knew the location and story of each of her chattels. There, on the third of her book shelves was a swimming trophy that carried someone else's name. It followed a time trial that had happened at night when she had broken into the sports complex with the head of the boys swim team. She had thrashed him but would never be formally recognised for her time. He had gallantly presented her with one of his awards to mark the feat. On the rear corner of her desk, its pages in pristine condition, was the bible her father had given her on her confirmation even though she was a less than enthusiastic convert, and in the top drawer was the engraved cigarette lighter Mel had given her as a gift on the same day, even though she only smoked at parties.

Kate tried to recall the minutia of Nick's bedroom – the sanctuary of the man her family and friends doubted she could share a sustainable intimacy with. After half an hour in which she was unable to produce ten items on an imagined list of her fiancés favourite things, Kate was forced to recognise that her relationship bore all the hallmarks of infatuation.

But it's not that. They just don't know. It's how he makes me feel, even when I'm not with him.

Kate's mind wandered back to the previous night and a still warm imprint.

She was walking from town, past several stops to a quieter location where she could wait for a bus to go home. It was overdue but it was a pleasant night and she didn't mind. She was stretching her neck and rolling each shoulder backwards, standing as tall as she could manage without feeling foolish should a dozen amused faces suddenly appear in a bus window. She was dropping her head back and looking up to a darkening sky. It was subdued by cloud cover, smothering what few stars might still have stood out through the wash of city lights.

Kate remembered now why that night sky had seemed so sad. There had been no twinkling – not like in an outback sky, not like Nick had shown her that time after dinner with his parents. He had driven her to the ruins of a stone cottage on a hilltop overlooking Kimbanyon on one side and the outskirts of the desert on the other.

It was the first time they had seen each other since Neil Armstrong had inspired the world with man's first steps on the moon. As they had chatted happily about it, the silver studs dusting the dark paddock above them blinked full of promise.

Lolling together on old grey army rugs in the back of Nick's ute, they had wondered at the spread above them. Nick had told her that, as many stars as she could see, they made up only three per cent of the galaxy and that they must be awfully lonely up there because the rest of the galaxy was made up of dark matter, and, according to a professor whose paper he'd read in a science magazine, dark matter didn't interact with light.

'Nobody talks any more,' he had said in a droll voice. 'I hate that.'

Kate closed her eyes, the childhood memories of her room fading into the background and her night with Nick in the company of constellations, filling her head.

She saw herself rolling into his chest and pointing at various gatherings, finally settling on one of three stars forming a base, a few dimmer ones running parallel to them and a distinct line angling from the corner so that it looked to form the grip on a cooking pot.

'What about the saucepan? Those guys hang around together a lot; they've got a handle on things. They must talk,' Kate replied to Nick's humour.

'Yeah, but the Greeks think that's Orion's belt, with Orion's sword just above it. See that nebula there?'

Nick took hold of Kate's bare arm and pointed it in the right direction, each of them enjoying the touch of the other's skin.

'Now the reason they think the sword's up there and the belt's down here is because when we look at him in Australia, we must be looking at him upside down. I say he's standing on his head, as Greeks do when they've had too much ouzo – dreadful stuff, make anyone stand on their head – and no-one's going to talk much when they're drunk and upside down with a sword hanging over them, are they?'

'And you'd know I suppose?' Kate laughed. 'I must remember never to let you drink with old Greeks!'

'I'd only let the young women lead me astray ... unless you take me off the market of course.'

In that moment, with the saucepan saying more in its silence than all the words on the planet, Nick had seemed simultaneously more down to earth and worldly than anyone else she knew. She had never experienced such deep contentment and peace as she had lying in his arms that night and she wanted it to last forever. Nick could not have picked a more perfect time to propose.

Kate fell asleep peacefully, the ceiling above her obliterated by the conjuring of her last romantic night with Nick and the street light filtering down the side of the house, across the daphne, like a watchful guard.

When she awoke the next day, her energy for wedding preparations was renewed but it took just minutes for her parents to bring her down. Her father withdrew from dress discussions, with her mother following him down the hall unable to let it rest. The guilt Kate felt over allowing her father and grandfather to suggest that life with Nick would be boring returned, settling on her skin with the irritation of a partially healed scab. Adding to it was the grievance that even her friends did not respect the choice she was making. She had wanted to introduce Nick to her world the way he had introduced her to his, but the rails seemed barbed all the way from Kimbanyon, as if their union were an unscheduled stop that everyone was annoyed by and wanted to put behind them as quickly as possible.

Despite this, Mel set about organising the hen's night with the confidence of an A-list socialite, shelving Mrs Holbrook's plans for a restaurant meal in favour of the younger women attending a nightclub, sleeping over at Mel's, before a day of shopping for bridesmaids' attire and of course, selection of the wedding dress. Kate had had to reassure her mother that no selection would be made without her input and, as her parents were paying, Gwen was at least assured that she would not be deprived of that special moment, though she did dread revealing the sum to Avery.

True to his last conversation with Gwen, Avery made no personal contribution toward the preparations. He even informed Kate, who had always assumed he would be the one presiding over her vows, that he had asked a trusted colleague to do the honours because he wanted to sit back and 'be a father for a change'. Both Kate and Gwen suspected his motivation in pulling out was more likely that he was unenthused by the marriage, though neither could bring themselves to say it out loud.

Nick's parents had travelled up to introduce themselves to Kate's family and spoiled themselves with a rare stay in a motel, joining the Holbrooks in an awkward dinner at the motel restaurant before walking arm in arm through a pleasantly cool Adelaide evening to see the church the couple had picked out for the ceremony. They reported back that they found the grounds large and well maintained and, from the bushes below, yellow spotlights had shone up to define the lower contours of the bluestone blocks, giving the chapel 'a grand and imposing stature'. They had stood still in front of it 'for ages', wondering how time had passed so quickly to bring them to this point.

Conversation between the Holbrooks and the Whites had been stilted outside of wedding discussions. Both Gwen and Sorrell had individually asked their husbands not to discuss the Vietnam war, knowing their strong views were likely to clash and cause Kate some distress. As neither man was particularly inclined to small talk, interaction between them was therefore limited and so facile it might have bordered on the comical if it were not so painful to be around.

Nick had not accompanied his parents; though Kate had wanted him there, she had chosen to visit him in Kimbanyon rather than have him come to Adelaide as a general rule and he chose to use work, it seemed, as an excuse to keep it that way.

Despite Kate believing that if Nick enjoyed himself in Adelaide, taking in a movie, eating in cafes, perhaps seeing a band at a pub, he might be more inclined to move from Kimbanyon, she worried that if he did visit, her father and grandfather would be so aloof, or worse, take a superior position and pose conversational challenges that he would see straight through and resent.

Mel was also no help, having already wondered out loud whether Kate was keeping Nick in Kimbanyon because he might embarrass her in front of her 'real' friends. On the hen's night, her drunken friend had even bailed her up in nightclub toilets to ask her whether she was pregnant and being forced into a shotgun wedding.

But the most surprising turn of events in the lead up to Kate and Nick's wedding concerned an invitation her father had wanted to issue but had vexed over and decided in the end not to. It seemed to Kate that he had taken more time in the consideration of that invitation than he had in deciding whether or not he would be the presiding minister on the day.

Gwen's list of guests included her parents and an aunt and uncle from her father's side. She had also allowed herself to invite a friend she had made when Kate was just a toddler and had stayed in touch with regularly despite their children growing apart. Nick's parents had also asked permission to invite a handful of his cousins and close friends.

Avery's side of the family were notably absent from the guest list. When Kate had asked once about his parents, she was told they were dead. Her father had no siblings. There didn't seem anything more to ask. Avery had two invitations he wanted included in the mailout, despite assuming both parties would be unlikely to attend. One was to Jack and Betty, whom he wasn't sure would be able to make the trip, and the other was to a Father Lucas.

'He's an old friend of your dad's,' Gwen told Kate. 'He was a bit of a father figure for him when he came here from England as a boy.'

'I thought he came with his parents.'

Gwen could see there would be more questions and decided it would be easier to send Kate in to see her father – it was his story after all, and the retelling of it in her hands would only be an interpretation and would possibly be seen by Avery as a violation of his right to keep it close to his chest. Kate knocked on the study door, never as tentatively as her mother seemed to, but gently all the same.

'Dad?'

'Mmmn, What is it, Kate?'

She approached the desk as a student might a principal's, though she didn't wait for him to look up before asking: 'Who's Father Lucas?'

Avery wasn't surprised by the question, knowing eventually Kate would go over the invitation list and see a name she did not know.

'He was an older friend when I was growing up. I thought it might be nice if he came to the wedding, but I'm not fussed really,' he said, slitting another envelope with a letter opener.

'If you weren't fussed, why would you invite him?'

This time Avery looked up and raised an eyebrow of annoyance at his daughter.

'Sorry, Dad, I didn't mean it that way; I was just wondering why I'd never heard of him if he was important enough to have at my wedding.'

Avery collected his paperwork together in a pile and pushed it aside. He sighed lightly, recognising the need for a substantial conversation that he would rather not have, and nevertheless held out a hand to her, like he used to when she was little. Kate willingly came around the side of the desk and put her hand in his, fearing for a second that the unusual gesture might mean she could be pulled onto his lap. She pre-empted the possibility by leaning over and kissing him on the inlet of his receding hairline.

'Grab that chair, will you, Katie?'

Avery came around to the front of his desk and leant on the edge, giving Kate his full attention.

'I spent some time at a farm training school near Sydney when I was a boy, with your Godfather Jack, who you'll get to know if he comes to your wedding. Father Lucas used to visit the school and bring us smokes and chat with us about this and that. He was good to me when I was homesick. Even taught me some Latin!

'But some of the other priests who came, well, let's just say the boys would do anything not to be alone with them. I think seeing Father Lucas again would upset Jack, so it's probably best if I don't invite him.'

Avery paused, looking down at his knees and lightly rubbing his hands along the smooth fabric of his trousers as if he were suppressing goose bumps on his thighs. When he raised his eyes, he wore a thin smile that might have grown into a grimace had it hung around long enough.

Kate asked tentatively: 'Why did your parents send you to the farm?'

'Not everyone grows up in a home like yours Kate. Things were pretty tight for us in London.'

'I don't know anything about my grandparents – on your side of the family I mean. What were they like?'

'My mother was pretty athletic, like you, but not so much sport as dancing. She was French and met dad when her troupe was on tour. She didn't like living in England much, and even less when she became a mother. I think I must have been a pretty dull sort of a child. She used to drop me off at the boys' home every now and then to give herself a break and dad would pick me up whenever he was around, but that wasn't as often as I would have liked.'

Kate looked at her father as if she had been perusing his features for the first time and had come across an abominable growth. She felt the presence of another soul in the room – in the way a hot flush rushes through a body and reminds it of itself – and was suddenly ashamed not to have asked her father about his childhood before.

For his part, feeling the warmth of his daughter's hand on his and a sincerity in her squeeze, Avery wished he had fobbed Kate off before the conversation had gone that far. Yet her touch reminded him of their younger relationship, of the sweet innocence of his only child. He had not been much of a father lately, and his inattention had left her bereft of guidance.

She might listen to me now and give up on this foolish marriage.

As soon as Avery raised his eyes to Kate she was ready with more questions. 'But how … ?'

'Kate, things don't always go the way you think they will. I'm sure my parents thought they were doing the right thing sending me here; there wasn't much work and I was one extra mouth to feed.'

'Maybe your mother could have kept dancing, maybe taken you on tour with her?'

Avery should have been pleased his daughter had had no experience of poverty but he was a little appalled at her naivety.

'She had little children to look after Kate. But I remember this one job she had at the butchers where she'd tie my baby brother to her back with a sheet and clean up on her hands and knees. She'd gather up the sawdust they'd put down to soak up the blood, scrub the floor with bleach, and put fresh sawdust down for the next day.

'I used to like going to the shop to walk her home and carry the bag of bones that the butcher had left for her so she could make soup. That was a good job for us because it put food on the table, but looking back, it was pretty hard on mum.'

'I didn't know you had a brother, Dad?'

'I didn't have him for long. He died of pneumonia. So you can see why my parents thought what they did for me was a good idea.'

'But you would be a whole ocean away! I still don't understand how they could be so cruel.'

'It wasn't like that for them Kate. Going to Australia was billed as a great adventure; we even had a reception with the local mayor when we were sent off, about twenty of us boys and our families. We had suitcases full of new clothes – more socks and shorts and underwear than I'd ever owned, even a nice new coat. They made a big fuss of us – the "lucky ones" from our neighbourhood off to a better life.

'I was pretty sure that I would set myself up as a farmer and that my parents would sail over on the next ship to join me.'

When Kate squeezed his hand some minutes later, Avery twitched with the surprising recognition that it had not already been removed and that he'd been daydreaming about walking home from the butchers with his mother, something he hadn't thought about for more than 20 years. He unclasped his fingers and took each of Kate's into his, resting them on his knees and returning his focus to her.

'Sometimes, Kate,' he began with sudden clarity and directness, 'the things you think are going to be big adventures don't live up to the hype. It's something to think about in your life right now – think carefully about what kind of life you want. Because you're in charge of that, Kate, and you're about to make one of the biggest commitments of your life … .'

It took a moment for Kate's subconscious to shake off the sluggishness that had set in as it had let go of its normal defences – as it had opened itself up to the intimacy of a shared past, as it had softened into the porous state most welcoming of affection and understanding. She oscillated, frowned, blinked, and slowly sharpened her eyes on her father. She saw him sharpen in turn. A profound sadness sat like heavy water in her ears, hot in her eyes and salty on her tongue.

I thought we were talking about your life. But of course, you just want to lecture me about mine.

'The biggest commitment of my life? The biggest *mistake* of my life, isn't that what you meant to say, Dad?'

Not prepared for a verbal assault so soon after exposing himself to the torment of his memories, Avery chose to protect himself. He returned to his chair and almost fell into it, causing air to escape through the stitching of its leather cushion.

'I just want you to think about it Kate – really think about it.'

With that, Avery picked up his letter opener and his pile of unopened mail, leaving his daughter still seated, confused and hurt.

He did not look up as she walked away from him, leaving the door of his study ajar. He waited until he heard her get off the phone to Mel and the front door close behind her before rising from his desk.

Avery extracted the whiskey he kept hidden behind three books with spines of an appropriate width for the task. The spirit was light and glowing but it wasn't what he wanted afterall. He wanted family – someone who knew his story and how hard it would have been talking about it. He went looking for Gwen and found her exactly where he'd hoped she'd be – waiting for him under the wisteria with two glasses of white wine.

39.

A perfect day.

[September, 1969.]

It was a blissful day with the sky a baby blue and the only clouds aloft mere impressions – strips of gauze set free in a breeze. Spring leaves were the colour of limes, their edges golden when the sun beamed behind them and still perfect – undamaged yet by age or harsh weather.

Looking out her bedroom window now, Gwen wanted to freeze the scene.

I can't believe my Kate is to be married! And on such a perfect day.

She had loved her daughter from the moment she first saw her – her special gift.

It had been such a long road to finding her. After devouring dozens of books on fertility, including some extremely technical and explicit ones on loan from Dr Bettinger, Gwen had manipulated every variable that she could to try and produce a child. And still she had failed. Initially Avery had been co-operative, enthusiastic to experiment with different positions and conditions, no matter how odd the combination or deflating the constraints she placed on him. But after some eight months or so, he had grown tired of the calendars and thermometers and 'optimisation', admitting to her that he thought it a tough world for children, and that it would not break his heart if he didn't have to witness another child battle through to adulthood. Gwen thought his cynicism was a chivalrous attempt to reassure her that her love alone would be enough.

Over the next few years Avery obliged her in bed with an air of due diligence, knowing that though she had stopped involving him in her various cycles, Gwen was still tying her hopes to them. By the time Avery was in his forties and Gwen in her mid thirties, he had informed her that it must be God's will that they not be parents.

As Gwen grew frustrated at her inability to change her fate and the insinuation of the more pious members of their congregation that there must be a reason she was not blessed with a child, Avery grew more inclined to spend longer periods on the road, getting back in touch with the further reaches of his considerable parish.

Their love life mundane at best, only occasionally firing with a lust following requited denial, eventually the Holbrooks had seemed to become little more than partners in an unspoken understanding. They smiled at each other in passing in the hallway, sat comfortably over their cups of coffee or tea and newspapers and relieved each other of the pressure of being required to be more. For Gwen, at least, the urgency of her desire to have a family had waned, but so had her ability to enjoy the little things in life. She wished she could find the confidence that Jack and Betty seemed to have that their lives would not be poorer for not having children in them.

Obsessed with seeing Gwen return to her lively self, her mother had suggested adoption. Initially Gwen wasn't keen on the idea of random genetics; she already felt betrayed by nature and did not want to suffer doubly by inheriting someone else's heart condition, sluggish intellect or dodgy chromosomes. But after watching their friends in Adelaide begin as couples and grow as families – toddlers perched on broad shoulders and older siblings chasing younger brothers and sisters around on the church lawns after services – the longing in Gwen made the idea more palatable and on occasion, even attractive.

In the end it was Kate who chose her, from her nondescript crib, alongside a dozen other babies of similar age with pale pink and blue plastic tags around their tiny wrists in the viewing room of St Mary's. Of all of them, she had seemed the most like a child they could have produced themselves, with a high brow, like Avery's, and a little bob nose like her own. She even had blue eyes like Avery, though Gwen would discover later that almost every newborn has blue eyes and they would eventually become hazel swirls.

And it doesn't matter that that bob nose disappeared by the time she was walking, because Kate is like me in so many other ways.

Gwen had stood in the narrow corridor that swept past the nursery, enraptured by the swaddled bundles and alert to any movement in the dozen or so cribs that might reveal a personality. Her face and hands had been pressed up against the glass and her breath was clouding a small space in front of her, throwing her view into a romantic mist. There was a noise of some sort and several of the babies stirred. Gwen could not recall what the noise was. But she could remember clearly how Kate had woken, without a cry, and looked directly at her. Gwen had sensed a knowing in those eyes, and a connection. And it was enough.

She was told the baby was strong and her mother was young and healthy, with no history of drinking or other bad habits that might affect the child's development. And that's all Gwen knew, apart from the fact that papers had already been signed and that the mother wished her child to go to a good Christian home.

And that's what we've given her – a good home and a good start.

It was with some anxiousness that Gwen conceded to herself that she was concerned what Kate's marriage would mean for their family. Avery seemed to be distancing himself from both of them. She wondered whether even now, his desire for a son was influencing his emotions.

Surely not.

Kate had been a good sport – a tomboy even. And she was bright; she never backed down from a challenge.

Or an argument.

They even shared a love of the bush; when school holidays allowed, Kate had travelled with Avery across his parish, the two of them spinning tall stories of their 'adventures' on their return to the point where Gwen would feel nostalgic and even a little jealous of their obvious bond.

How could he refuse to conduct the marriage service? He's so judgemental and stubborn. How could he spoil this day for me? For all of us?

As she shuffled through the choices in her wardrobe, clicking coathangers against each other as she searched for the right outfit on a day when the weather was so perfect it was incidental to her selection, Gwen tortured herself into believing Kate had been of little interest to Avery for years now.

Perhaps when her looks began to change. Could he be that shallow?

By the time she was in her early teens, Kate's dark hair had begun to lighten into an auburn colour and lose some of its sheen, streaking almost blonde with the sun in summer and becoming more similar to her own. Others with children had told her this was unusual, that generally babies start with light hair that will darken – which ensured Gwen had enjoyed the change (and people telling her she looked like her mother) even more, but Avery was constantly telling Kate to tie it back to keep it tidy.

Strange from a man who used to allow the girl to stick her head out the car window until her hair was matted with knots!

It was impossible to know really when his love fractured. If she thought back, he had given her an inkling of it when Kate was about thirteen. Her sportsmaster, who had come to her girls' school from a prestigious boys' school, had expressed a desire to see her swim against the leading boy in her age group, predicting she would beat his time in an Olympic-sized pool, as well as any other male contender. Unfortunately, her own swim coach had lamented, Kate would have to be satisfied with beating every other girl that she came across, because no formal competition would allow the sexes to mix.

That night, when they were readying for bed, Avery had confessed to Gwen that he would have liked a son. Gwen had been shocked to be hearing it for the first time. After digesting a disappointment that was unfathomable to her, Gwen had raised the subject of adopting a sibling for Kate, perhaps a boy this time. Avery had argued that Kate's school fees were already a strain on the budget and there was a possibility that adoption might prompt her to ask questions about her own arrival in their lives.

I wasn't ready to tell her either. I keep thinking we should have done it then, when she was younger and less rebellious, but there never seemed to be a good time.

Gwen buried the thought and pulled a cheery, rich pink jacket with black trim and matching skirt from the cupboard and lay them on the bed. Now that she seemed to have talked herself into being the day's malcontent, she needed to drape herself in a colour of pure girlish bliss, to revel in being mother-of-the-bride and to revitalise her spirit.

I bet Ruth and the girls would never have imagined the Engineer could look so good in pink! To be honest, I would have never have allowed it in my wardrobe then …

Gwen pulled the skirt up against her and opened the door again to view herself in the mirror on its inner side.

Is it too short? Above the knee is 'in' now; Kate will like it even if Avery disapproves. For God's sake why do we have to worry about what Avery does and doesn't like with everything we do?

She laid the skirt back on the bed, did the buttons up on the jacket beside it and laid a string of pearls that Avery had given her on their own wedding day on top of them. They complemented the outfit beautifully.

He's been a good husband. We've been a good family. It's going to be a good day.

Gwen turned back to the window, satiating her senses on the deepening blue of the sky and the tussle of the hydrangeas in the breeze flitting around their garden. She could hear Avery getting a cup of coffee in the kitchen and Kate on the phone to Mel, her words bubbling in a mix of nerves and excitement. A genuinely easy smile spread across Gwen's face as she dropped the skirt back on the bed and headed for the shower.

40.

Tales of a call boy.

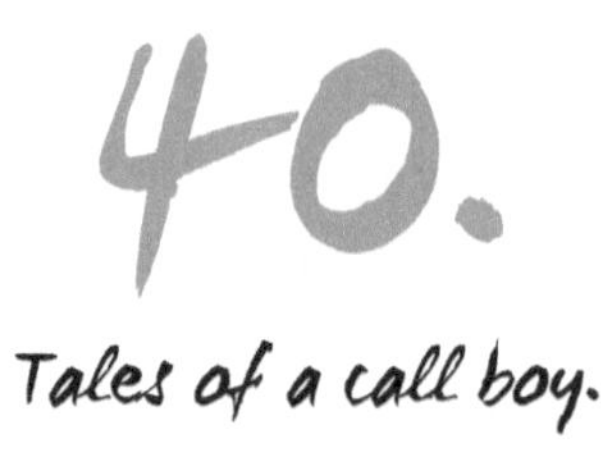

[1970.]

Nick was too tired to remember the whip of the screen door in time to stop the bang of it snapping shut.

He didn't consciously want to wake Kate but a part of him wanted her to know just how long his day had been.

He bent over, with the movement of a much older man, to kick his boots off, forcing his thumb into the back of each in turn to wedge them from his swollen feet. The sock had fainted into the flesh with the sweat and heat and would have to be peeled off gingerly so as not to take any skin off. Impatiently, he tossed one after the other back in the general direction of the screen door and headed for the bathroom.

He lifted his thinning blue singlet, the pungency of his armpits filling his nostrils as he drew it over his head.

His grey shorts, tiger-striped with dirt between the creases, and his age-loosened underwear fell easily to his feet. He stepped out of them and foot-swiped them to the corner of the bathroom. Staring into the shallow, pale yellow ceramic basin, too tired to think about what should happen next, Nick's hands seemed to move of their own accord. His gaze was blighted by a spew of water which, implausibly, startled him as it burped up the drain and then slid back down, soupy red after stealing some of the day from his face. A new ring of filth hardened against the fading enamel. His neck ached just from holding the weight of his skull.

I could really do with a rubdown.

He dragged his large calloused hands down slowly over his eyelids and across his cheeks, exhaling thinly with the relief of being home. He cupped more water in one hand, pressed what had not escaped between his fingers into the glued hair of his armpit now directly over the sink and then swapped over – other hand, other armpit. He grabbed one of the towels hanging over the shower rail around the bath and stuffed an end in to soak up the remaining water in the basin. He squeezed it, removed it still dripping from the sink and twirled it in circles until it resembled a loosely-woven rope and then slung it over his shoulder, catching the lower end dangling in the small of his back with his other hand and pulling each end alternately until enough layers of the sweat caked on during the day had been rubbed off to make him feel human again. Looking up at the unframed mirror, its reflective surface receding slightly like his hairline, Nick felt ambivalent about the face staring listlessly back at him. His eyes were dark and flat. His hair felt coarse to touch but would return to sandy and soft with a wash.

She'd probably like it better if I shaved.

Too exhausted to follow through with the thought, Nick ruffled his hair, shook the excess water from himself like a dog that had just bounded up a hill out of a creek, and put the day behind him for the comfort of his bed. His shoulders melted into his body when he saw Kate on the mattress.

How lucky am I to come home to this? My wife. Feisty Kate who fought off her father to marry me. Who gave up university, probably a great job and life with the hoi polloi playing tennis while her kids go to private schools in gloves and straw hats.

Nick wondered, as he often did, if Kate regretted the course of her life, with tedious thoughts settling in his head like flies on softening candy. He closed his eyes and opened them again, dispelling the doubt by looking at Kate's long, soft body afresh. She was lying on her side, perfectly still. Seeing her this way, not the least bit agitated, was a rare thing and despite his eagerness to touch her, he forced himself to savour it. The full moon reaching through the bedroom window was dividing her torso in two – bathing her neck, shoulders, and the curve of her ribs, to the top of her hip, in white. Only a sliver of light suggested the line of her thighs but darkness engulfed the rest of her body from the waist down.

Nick's gaze found the downy face of Kate's earlobes and traced the contour down her neck and along her collarbone. She was wearing one of his white singlets, retired before it was even worn in because it was such a long cut that it was better suited as a nightie. He froze as Kate rolled onto her back, trapping the singlet between her upper arm and ribcage and pulling it tight across her chest. Her left breast emerged through the over sized armholes. The sweep of the fine cotton ridges across her nipple had left it momentarily erect and Nick could not leave it.

He sat gently on the edge of the bed and reached for his wife. He traced the nipple with the second finger on his right hand, looking up to her face briefly to see her eyelids still closed. He wished his hands were not so rough, with grease and oil stains giving them a permanently bruised look and scars rising from unexpected places like thin white snakes.

He tried so hard to be gentle that his hand was shaking slightly. In the half light, he thought he saw Kate's eyes move under the lids. He spread his fingers and trapped the taught nipple softly between the webbing of the first and second, leaning over her and teasing it gently into his mouth. Still she did not open her eyes. Nick released her breast and rolled into the bed with her, pushing Kate gently into the middle to make room for himself. He lifted the nipple playfully back into his mouth with a gentle flick of his tongue. Kate's other nipple hardened painfully on her breast as she waited for his palm to massage the soft flesh. She turned her head towards the heat of his face and ached for his tongue to find hers.

The urgency inside her was like a weight pushing down. Her insides tightened as Nick found her mouth. His left hand cupped her chin as if to mould her face into his kiss. Her eyes still closed, she reached down to find him as keened as she was to make love. She guided him between her legs and smarted from the graze of his unshaven face against her cheek as he moved up inside her.

When Nick's body had collapsed in a state of complete contentment, Kate found she was wide awake. She suspected he would be snoring in a matter of minutes if she allowed him to slide into the deep sleep he craved and selfishly roused him to keep her company.

'What were you like growing up?' Nick's reply was slow to come.

'Why do you want to know this now?'

'I just thought I should know a bit more about the man I'm married to, and I'm curious – how does someone so gorgeous get hidden away in a little town like Kimbanyon?'

Kate drew herself up cat-like onto Nick's bare chest, resting her head on it and feeling the vibration of his heartbeat and the tickle of his wiry hair against her ear.

'I told you; I grew up around these parts.'

'You've hardly told me anything about your childhood. There has to be more to it than "Dad worked for the railways; we moved around a lot",' Kate said in a slightly mocking tone.

'I know your father was an organiser for one of the rail shops; your mother even told me he was a member of the communist party. Did you ever listen in on any of the meetings? Did he try to keep them secret?

'Is that why he doesn't want to talk about Vietnam?'

Kate asked the last question cautiously, knowing it to be a sensitive matter, with many families in the area having lost sons, brothers and friends in the war while Nick's father campaigned against conscription.

Kate had pulled herself up on one elbow, her other hand resting on her husband's stomach. She felt him flinch and then his hand came up to rest on top of hers. Had he been a political animal, Nick may have reacted differently to Kate's interrogations, but, perhaps as a reaction to the bluster and clash in the household he had grown up in, he tended to steer away from it. He had certainly fallen foul of a few colleagues and townsfolk over the war and his father's stand but if he had been thinking about defying him and joining up before he married Kate, he would not be doing it now, when all he could think about was starting a family.

'I never knew anything about Dad's meetings. I was a call boy in Port Augusta, so I was out a lot of nights. I guess that's when he had them.'

'You were a what in Port Augusta?'

Kate sounded so concerned, Nick laughed. He rolled towards her, pulling one arm up under his pillow to elevate his head. He looked at her with some amusement.

'You have no idea what a call boy is do you?'

Kate ran her finger along the modest streaks of dark hair that formed a small triangle at the centre of Nick's chest as she raised one eyebrow toward her husband.

'I know my father would send you straight to hell with a job description like that,' she responded with mock outrage.

'When we lived in Port Augusta, I got a night job out of the main station, getting the guys outta bed so everyone was on time,' Nick explained, stilling the fingers that had begun to walk their way down to his naval.

'That must have been awkward,' Kate teased. 'Did you have a special whistle or something to give them fair warning?'

'I'll have you know being a Call Boy was a very important job! You had to remember the street numbers of every driver and fireman and then memorise house maps so you don't knock on the wrong windows.'

'Oh yeah, that sounds really tough!'

'Aaaaand … after you woke the drivers up, you'd have to tell them what engine they were on, what shed it was in, where they were going and what time they were supposed to leave.'

'You mean to tell me all that relied on you?'

'I never missed a call, except one time when the driver was too drunk to turn up, but technically that wasn't really my fault; I woke him up, he just went back to sleep again … .'

Nick felt himself drifting off, even as he was still speaking.

'Katie, as much fun as this is, I'd really like to be doing that right now, just a few hours shut eye,' he said almost pleadingly.

Kate pulled back to her side of the bed, patting her husband's broad chest appreciatively with her hand as she did.

'Sure.'

Nick pulled up an end of the disheveled sheets around his shoulders and rolled back away from Kate onto his side.

'My little call boy,' she whispered affectionately, tracing a line with her finger down the middle of his back and feeling – in that moment at least – completely content.

41.

A childhood by the rails.

Nicholas White was a war baby, born in a fettlers' camp in 1942 to a young nursing graduate named Sorrell and her husband Ron White, a ganger with the Commonwealth Railways. Unlike many young boys of the day, Nicholas grew up with a father coming home most nights due to the government declaring that maintenance of the Trans Australian line was a protected undertaking.

The track began at Port Augusta – a small South Australian town at the top of Spencer Gulf from where farmers from the Flinders Ranges and beyond had sent their wheat and wool for export from a time when merchant ships were still powered by wind and sail. It traversed 1,693 kilometres across the Nullabor plain to Kalgoorlie – a West Australian town born from gold fever in 1893 that continued to provide its residents with income from mining.

If Kalgoorlie was known as the end of the line in more ways than one, with prostitutes standing at the doorways of corrugated iron sheds like dogs chained to kennels and men pouring an amount of alcohol down their throats that might kill those from the eastern states, then Port Augusta was known as a crossroads town. From there the Stuart Highway lead north to Alice Springs and Darwin, the Princes Highway south to Adelaide and the Eyre highway led west to the Nullabor and the Eyre Peninsula. Because of this, it brought together a large community of railway folk moving coal and people, workhorses looking to improve their prospects, reclusive types passing through to as yet undetermined locations and adventurous tourists with multiple options for travel.

The standard gauge line was the first significant infrastructure build to be undertaken following federation. Utilising the power of camels, iron tractors and track laying machines working at a rate of a little over four kilometres a day, it took five years – beginning at each end and completed near Ooldea in 1917.

It was a story Nick never tired of hearing from his father. If he had grown up in the city he may have had caped heroes from comic books, but as a line kid, he was in awe of the strength and stamina it took to lay 2.5 million hardwood sleepers and 140,000 tonnes of track through a hell of a lot of desert, with next to no water, apart from a few stops, with the most reliable supply having been used by Aborigines for centuries at Ooldea Soak. In Nick's mind it may as well all have been done by his father and his mates, whom he idolised.

His earliest memories were inextricably linked to the Tea and Sugar steam train that delivered vital supplies to maintenance crews, work stations, towns and the eleven camps along the route. Once a week Nick would ride in a wheelbarrow pushed by his mother to the camp stop to collect their water, meat and groceries.

He remembered the excitement of spotting the train as a smudge on the horizon and watching it all the way in. In a story Nick assumed Sorrell often overstated, she told how he would stand as close to the track as she would allow to feel the gigantic roar and 'breath of the dragon' as its steam came upon him.

The provisions wagons each had a window and a step up in those days and goods would be handed down to shoppers and passed back to children to pile in the barrows. When the carriages were opened up, Sorrell would gather up potatoes, turnips, beetroots, lettuces, carrots and apples from the produce shelves and a side of beef from the butchers while Nick would run up and down beside the train, knocking loudly on the chocolate and cream coloured sleeping car and bolting away before any occupant woke to abuse him. Sometimes he would spy into the wooden-slat wagons holding the livestock, only to be frightened off by sudden bellowing from the cows or a steamy torrent of urine coming his way.

Sometimes he got to see his father, head ganger, during the day when the men came to the Sugar stop to get their 'whips' of lunch in brown paper bags, and their pay. Nick would race up to each maintenance trike as it came in along the rails bearing four men at a time. With a big grin, Ron would lift him up onto his knee for the final leg.

When Nick and his younger sister Ruby were old enough for school the family settled in Port Augusta. Sorrell had initiated the move, hoping to go back to work, but when the moment came to leave her children at the school gate, she found she wasn't quite ready to give them up. So they would begin classes with School of the Air – education via radio – and do extra homework that their mother set them for good measure.

Sorrell was able to make her boy the happiest child in the world by taking up a position as a community nurse on the Tea and Sugar, allowing her children to come with her for several days at a time once a month. While she would tend to pregnant women, babies and old folk in the health centre wagon (no one else seemed to come), the children would play with toys or bother various 'shop keepers' in the provisions stores.

The children were given leave to roam through any of the cars on the train, except the butcher's van. Big Sol took orders the week before, slaughtering only what he knew would be sold at the next stop while they were travelling to it. Sorrell had found his presence in the health centre for treatment of a deep cut confronting enough with the children asking about his apron and the smears covering him almost head to foot – Sol having slipped during the accident.

But her intention to spare her children the trauma of witnessing the butcher at work – something many farm children grow up with as a matter of course – was futile when it came to Nick, because knowing what was happening in Big Sol's car simply stirred his imagination.

As they drew closer to the western end of the line, which featured one of longest stretches of straight track in the world, there were few opportunities for things to go rolling around or be dislodged, so when there was a thud of any kind, Nick was in no doubt where it had come from. He imagined it was the sound of a sheep or bullock crashing to its knees, blood spewing from its cut throat and eventually flying in a mass of droplets on the rush of air under the carriage to spatter the stones between the tracks in a trail of red, fast left behind. In truth, it was unlikely that Nick had experienced any of that since refrigeration came in soon after Sorrell began working on the Sugar. It was more likely that the lurid image was planted in his memory by the butcher's apprentice, Malcolm, who seemed to derive pleasure from frightening young children on the train.

Such was the power of the railways to establish itself in Nick's heart as a benevolent entity that saved him from the routines of home and school, that he could simultaneously shudder at the idea of an animal having its throat slit en route and believe it a kind of magic when people received their lamb chops and roasts all neatly wrapped in creamy paper, perfectly sized for their ovens and dinner plates.

His love affair with the railways may also have been the reason he paid little attention to an incident that infuriated his mother at the time and permanently soured her relationship with her employer.

They had been approaching the Ooldea siding. Nick was both sleepy and bored, but when the commotion happened, he had a very clear vision of it.

A number of Aboriginal men were waiting at the stop with Harry O'Reilly, a man Sorrell had introduced to Nick previously when he had come to the Sugar to collect rations and have babies from the mission innoculated. He was standing over a stretcher with an elderly Aboriginal man on it. The man's leg was wrapped in a blood-soaked bandage and he was moaning.

The train had slowed down and Pete, the postmaster, and Dimitri, the green grocer, had jumped off with an armful of parcels each that they dropped unceremoniously on the platform. Then they had run back along beside the carriages as the Sugar picked up speed. Dimitri had reached up to grab hold of Big Sol's extended hand and been hoisted back in, while Pete aimed himself at the open side of a wagon, leapt and rolled in like a movie stuntman. Kneeling on a chair by the window, Ruby had clapped wildly at the entertainment and Nick made a mental note to ask Pete to show him how to do it so he could practice the impressive move.

In their wake, a number of women waiting with empty barrows and buckets had chased or called after them. Harry and the men with him were yelling with their hands in the air. Because there was a mixture of languages, Nick had not been able to make out what they were saying.

He heard his mother talking about it when they got back at the end of the week, arguing that the Railways had no right to suck up all water reserves relied on by the Aborigines in the area for its steam train and then refuse them medical treatment. Ron said he was sure it was just an oversight that the patient was left behind. Sorrell said he didn't want to see what was going on and Nick was happy enough to forget about it, generally taking his father's viewpoint in all things and content to practice his leaps and rolling landings.

During those war years, Nick did not fully appreciate how special it was for him to be able to spend time with Ron but he would think about it often when he considered what kind of a father he might be himself.

Between trips on the Sugar and when his schoolwork was done to Sorrell's satisfaction, he was sometimes allowed to go to the Port Augusta steam sheds where Ron was busily working his way towards a new role as a fireman on the locomotives. His father's job was to keep enough water in the boiler and heat in the engines' fireboxes so drivers could easily ready them for their next journey. Nick always thought it a great joke that the trains were never allowed to actually be steaming in the steam shed. It was a tricky balance and he had great admiration for his father as he watched him jump lithely down from one engine and up to another, keeping them all just so – 'warm but not sweaty'.

During one busy time when Ron was managing several engines he pointed in the direction of a blackened billy turned upside down on a plank of wood turned into a narrow benchtop by virtue of two stacks of bricks built up under each end of it. Beside the billy had been a row of white and yellow enamel cups with the letters T, A and R on them, some with their blue trims more chipped than others. So Nick had grabbed the billy, run outside to fill it with water from a tap on the large water tank and handed it up to his dad on an engine where he was checking the pressure and lightly topping up the coal.

'How long d'you reckon it'll take that billy to boil if I put it in the middle of this firebox,' Ron had asked his son.

'I dunno. Maybe 10 minutes?'

'Four minutes and thirty eight seconds,' Ron had said with such authority, Nick had been compelled to time the event on his watch.

The driver had arrived at around four minutes and twenty five seconds, so the shovel had to be carefully slid in underneath the billy to bring it forward in the box and a steel stoker used to get in under the handle and lift it out.

'Hoo, that's hot alright,' Ron had said, looking into the billy and enjoying the fact that while it was simmering strongly, not a single drop of water had boiled over onto the coals to produce steam.

'How's the time?'

Nick had looked at his watch and said proudly, 'Four minutes, thirty eight seconds. How's it looking?'

'Boiling just nicely.'

The move from steam to diesel had been hard on his father. According to him, his boss had been looking for a way to get rid of him, tired of his union activities and the gossip concerning his association with communists. He was laid off and found himself around the house a bit more, with Sorrell becoming more in demand as a midwife and the main income earner.

In his emerging teenage years, Nick had found different adventures than those he had shared with his parents. He and his new friends would cause havoc on the wharves, playing hide and seek around the cranes and enormous wool bales being loaded into containers for export until they were escorted out of harm's way, usually by men whose backs were big enough to sow a crop on if they lay down. When he left school, he continued to get into mischief at the docks, leaving home and returning late, sometimes injured from his close escapes with security guards. During this time his relationship with his parents was fraught.

While unable to find work for himself, Ron convinced some old mates to keep his son occupied at night by putting him on the crew paid to wake drivers for their shifts. After paying off a policeman who'd come to the door asking about Nick's involvement with two men arrested for selling stolen goods, father and son barely spoke.

Then one night, Nick had burst through the door, a skinful under his belt and his shirt torn, surprised to see his father sitting in the kitchen waiting for him. Ron stood up from his chair with such vigour that it seemed unlikely his intent could be anything other than physical. Nick braced, preparing to give as good as he might get, when Sorrell appeared in her dressing gown with a baby bottle in her hand, shushing them.

'What on earth, mum?'

Ron had limped home earlier that day in a ute with a crushed radiator and produced a near hairless joey from a canvas sack. He had been horrified to see it emerge from the pouch of a kangaroo he'd hit when it darted his way in the twilight. Sorrell was only guessing, but she had appeared to know what to do, so Ron had left it to her. Now the joey was hanging in a flannel bag on the back of the bathroom door, tucked up tight with a hot water bottle. She had been able to get some sheep's milk that was now warming on the stove and had just found Nick's old bottle which for some inexplicable reason had not been thrown out.

The White family came together around the joey that night, even though they had not expected it to survive. If the railways formed Nick's fondest childhood memories, his teenage years were warmed by the presence of Roo. He had learnt to drive with Roo bounding alongside his vehicle. He recalled fair flying on dirt roads, once or twice bearing into plains and ploughing into towers of spinifex. He would look over his shoulder, the golden sun blinding his view from the horizon as Roo lifted and disappeared for a second as he landed again. It was hard to keep his eyes on anything but that elegant, giant, strawberry blonde beast, with its barrel chest, muscular haunches and regulating tail.

At full stretch, it's still one of the most majestic things you could ever see.

He understood why Matt had hated pulling the carcasses of kangaroos out of the dog fence with his father. Anyone who had seen them in flight couldn't be anything but appalled that such a creature could be boxed in, or felled by a fence, though Nick wasn't foolish enough to express that view to station owners, or any driver who had experienced the way a 'roo could turn acutely into a vehicle without apparent reason. According to Ron, who loved that kangaroo more than any dog he had ever owned, Nick was soft like that.

When the family had moved to Tarcoola to follow the growing number of jobs there, Nick had missed his mates in Port Augusta. But by the time he was employed with the railways himself and looking to buy a home, his instinct was to settle somewhere smaller, not larger, in a move that could have been seen to be nostalgic for the fettlers' camps of his childhood.

Leaving the railways, and his space, was not something Nick felt he could ever do; even when the air in Kimbanyon was a spitting, blustery clamour of heat and you couldn't breathe without it tumbling into your lungs like hot stones, it was home. He liked the way the rails cut a destination into an otherwise unmappable landscape. He liked being a part of that and working with the boys. He liked that those who lived scattered across the landscape were not needy souls and for the most part enjoyed their neighbours from a distance.

But there was something about Kate that made him unsure that he would not bend to whatever she asked of him. When he first saw her, he thought she was out of his league, but the truth was he hadn't thought about pursuing anyone before her. She had a way of finding his triggers, of getting him to think about why he did things and wanting to do things for the first time that would have intimidated him before he had met her.

Sex with Kate was the most exhilarating experience he had ever had. That first time, she had led him to his own home, without knowing where it was, and drawn from him the courtship he had planned for the next six months with her pouting mouth, soft hands and floating fingers. She had sat astride him, her flimsy summer dress slipping under his coarse hands gripping her pelvis as she thrust her hips towards him. She had made all the moves. She had pinned his hands beside him and worked every muscle of his groin into hers. He had wanted to taste every part of her but she was in charge and had only leant forward to kiss him, with her mouth open as wide as she was, when he was climaxing, and he could not think beyond his own ecstasy to return it with any competency.

When she had gone – showered and back at the church before her father had emerged – he was shaky, vulnerable, doubting himself like he had never done before. He figured it was proof that he was right to have been obsessed with her. And that it was love.

42.

[1971.]

Thbe old church had been given a fresh coat of white paint and featured a broad doormat with the word 'welcome' on it in a flourish of cursive overstatement. The concrete path around it had been cleansed of weeds and a sign had been erected in front declaring it open for business at regular times.

Services, once held here monthly by her father, were now conducted fortnightly by the Roman Catholic Church. Father Bob was an ambitious priest who recruited fresh souls as if every one of them got him closer to some mystical number that would see him rewarded with Papal colours and a seat in Rome.

The Anglicans, Protestants, Presbyterians and Lutherans in town were dwindling in number and the few that remained and cared blamed the Australian Inland Mission for reducing the frequency of its visits and 'letting the Micks in'.

Once Kate had married, Avery had given up his interest in ministering in Kimbanyon. Even though the locals, particularly Gillian Brown, had hoped they would see him more often now that his daughter had become a resident, it had resulted in them seeing him even less.

Father Bob had stepped into the void, vocal and exuberant. Half an hour before his services, he walked through the town decrying 'It's never too late to return to the Lord'. Kate discovered she was not the only one who believed he should be simultaneously swinging a brass bell in medieval fashion when a drunken fettler notoriously traipsed around behind him belting out a deadpan chorus of 'Bring out your dead'.

Sometimes Father Bob would find a string of hapless locals with other things on their minds when he approached them, not quick enough to deflect his enthusiasm or persistence without being rude, and invite them to an impromptu service. Sometimes he would stand at his podium and address a handful of the faithful with a monologue befitting an audience at the Vatican. But it was his regular chant that had become a part of life in the township as she knew it now, and the story of the drunken response was a favourite embellished by locals when visitors stopped for a pint at the Brooster.

Since her father had withdrawn from her life, Kate had found herself unsure of her feelings about God and religion in general. She used to respect, even admire, the work that he did and loved hearing stories told mostly by her mother about their travels to remote communities or stations for baptisms, weddings and wakes. It had seemed like important work – connecting people, with their pedal wireless and endless capacity for cups of tea and talk. They had even helped out a funeral director once to deliver a body after his wagon had broken down. Kate had drawn a picture of it at kindergarten.

What would have happened to that soul had they not been there, like bush angels, to collect it?

Kate had been ten when her travels with her father began, filling in a few days on school holidays and giving her mother some peace. In the early years, it had been fun to be on the road with the Reverend. Sometimes they took the train and stopped along the way. Other times they drove the car and her father lamented no longer having the Chevvie that sat much higher on the road.

She would play in strangers' front yards, mostly with their dogs, and women were always fussing around her and giving her treats. Sometimes it became boring if her father took too long 'ministering', and often she would doze off, sitting up the back of churches with her school books, but she grew to understand that it was her father's job and to appreciate why he liked it so much in the bush. Though many were stuck in their thoughts and ways, she and Avery had only one purpose, so for the most part conversations were limited to the scriptures and when there was quiet, there was an easiness and a satisfaction in it. The birdcalls travelled through the air with authority and knowing as if in some loop of nature. Everything was big – the broad streets, the horizons, the great red kangaroos that bounded in graceful leaps, even the meals.

As she grew older, she grew less inclined to join her father on his visits. She had begun training with a swim coach and there was so much more to do in Adelaide on the weekends. And by the time she was getting in trouble with Mel, Kate was also, perhaps not surprisingly, clashing more frequently with her parents. She would have much preferred to be meeting friends on the banks of the Adelaide River or going for coffee and a film when she had done enough study than getting hot and stuffy with her father bible bashing around the bush.

So while she didn't want to go and her father was reluctant to have her, her mother was even less inclined to have her headstrong daughter at home going to parties with Mel and dating boys who never left their cars to meet her and kept Kate in their cars for ages at the kerb when they dropped her back.

'Take her with you. She should see something of the country the way you and I did,' her mother had urged her father.

Kimbanyon had not been included in the Reverend's trips with Kate until she was about fourteen. When Nick had first appeared at the church, he did not behave like a God-fearing Christian soaking up the sermon in order to better his life. Nor did he appear to be attending to appease a devout mother, father or partner. He was always on the periphery, but never seeking counsel. When privacy was important to the Reverend, and Kate would be dispatched to 'play' outside the church, Nick would often happen to be in the area and attempt to talk with her, his determination to have the conversation the more endearing for its awkwardness.

Kate stood still in front of the church now, musing on memories of her father, her husband and herself – both juvenile and romantic. She wondered how it could have soured to the point that she could be accused of nostalgia in her twenties.

He always got on with people who were 'salt of the earth'. But when I fall in love with one of them, suddenly it's not good enough. I'm glad he's not here, preaching to these people. Such a hypocrite.

The chapel was glaring at her, the white cloak of its timbers harsh on her eyes. How welcoming it had seemed to her back then: the townsfolk would gather outside the heavy doors, bathed in the reflection of community pride, washed down especially for the Reverend's visit. On those mornings, the sun would illuminate the red, greens and royal blues of the biblical figures enshrined in glass so that even the most cynical found themselves compelled to try and see what might lie waiting on the other side.

I'm such a fool for thinking they were happy memories. I always thought Dad wanted me around.

Kate's mind rebuilt the church as she saw it now. The wood was splintered, the paint peeling. White, candlestick twirls of droppings, roped with brown and yellow sinews, stained the walls inside and out. Feral cats were chasing birds, swatting them with pirate paws and pinning their tail feathers to the floorboards while they fluttered and thrashed. When death stilled their prey, the felines waltzed out, light-footed in a storm of glass splinters exploding from the boastful windows.

Leaving them 'vacant and eye-like' – bestilled like Poe's House of Usher.

43.

Clever little eaglehawk.

[Friday, December 14, 1973.]

Helen had been distressed for quite some time before Carmel identified her as the cause of a ruckus in the day room of the Tarcoola Nursing Home. Residents were flapping their hands at her blocking their view of the television. It had little effect, with the cause of their frustration moving no more than a step in either direction before returning to the offending spot.

The host of the game show could be heard introducing a returning contestant as an eligible bachelor whose winnings now stood at ...

'Moooooove,' the residents called out across the semi circle of chairs fronting the popular game show.

'It's Lucky Draw,' one silver haired viewer known as Eleanor F. to distinguish her from Eleanor P. pleaded when she saw Carmel. She had a look on her face that said she would have tugged on Carmel's skirt to get her attention if she had needed to.

Linus Fenwick, a nonagenarian who annoyed most everyone with his sports fanaticism and inability to find his slippers several times a day, was urging his companions to throw their books and magazines at Helen. Luckily he was having trouble making himself understood because he had put his retired set of dentures in instead of the new ones.

'Come on you mob,' Carmel called out as she strode into the room. 'Settle down!'

Not convinced the nurse would be able to get control of the situation – being Helen's immobility in the most inconvenient time and place – Linus took aim with a paperback from a pile of B-grade reads stacked beside his chair.

'You should be ashamed of yourself Mr Fenwick,' Carmel admonished, moving between the chairs to relieve him of his weapon.

'If I see anything thrown at another resident in this home, you can all forget about dessert for a month.'

Carmel prudently steered Helen out of harm's way and took her to her room, where she guided her to the edge of the bed and took the visitor's chair for herself.

From the dayroom, a spontaneous clapping erupted. From the other end of the hallway, a dreadful howling began. Carmel took Helen's hands in hers and tried to get her attention, but Helen was shaking her head like a horse unable to rid itself of a persistent fly.

'Helen, look at me. Helen. C'mon now, you know where you are. You're with me, Carmel, and we're all safe in your bedroom. Nothing to be afraid of here.'

Helen stopped shaking her head and lifted her eyes, but she was looking past the nurse, around the room, through the doorway into the hall. The wailing had subsided and become intermittent sobs.

Carmel was used to noises that were not readily explicable at the nursing home, particularly when the doctor was rostered to visit. Patients were sometimes brought here for urgent medical attention on those days in preference to driving the vast distance to the nearest hospital. Because she was non plussed by the cries emanating from the shower block, it seemed, she mistook Helen's interest in the open space at her door.

'Cat's here somewhere, Helen, but you can talk to me; I'm a good listener,' she offered. 'You're too young to be talking to Cat. Your story's not done yet.'

Broken shadows floated across Helen's eyes and she gripped Carmel's hands with an uncomfortable tenacity. She turned the nurse's wrist so she could see her watch. Carmel sighed; Helen often expected a pickup in the latter half of the day. Sometimes it was from her parents after school, or from Avery, whom Carmel assumed to be a grandparent or family friend who had helped out when her parents had died.

'Avery would never leave me like this,' she'd say in a tone that could be either strident or faltering but rarely matter of fact.

A few of the nurses who tired of settling Helen when she became over anxious, would tease her, lifting the burden from their shift and passing it to the next by telling Helen that someone was coming for her, but that it would not be until tomorrow and that she should get a good night's rest in order to look her best. Assured as they were that Helen would forget the conversation but be comforted in the short term by the good news, it was an easy fix.

But these were also the nurses who played word games with ninety eight year old Mrs Wetherall, who was unencumbered by the real world and seemed to enjoy her prowess with the games despite her inability to hold a conversation.

'Fish and …,' the nurses would say, curling their tone upwards into a question.

'Chips,' Mrs Wetherall would predictably snap back, a blaze of pride on her face.

'Pie and…'

'Sauce!'

'Ken and …'

'Barbie!'

Carmel was one of the few nurses who hadn't resorted to popular and patronising techniques for entertaining or controlling residents struggling to hold onto their faculties, but it often meant that if Helen was disorientated, hers would be a longer process.

'You're happy and safe here Helen, with new friends and plenty to do,' Carmel would say while feeling the travesty of what was going unsaid – that it might never change for her.

She really shouldn't be cooped up with the oldies; it's just ageing her faster.

'Avery is coming for me. And my baby.'

Carmel had not heard of a baby before.

'What baby, Helen?'

'Sister Michaels says no point crying over spilt milk.'

'Helen, there's no Sister Michaels here; do you mean Sister Mendes?'

'It's three thirty; I have to get to work. Mabel's an old cow.'

Carmel grinned. While the present shrank in importance for Helen and some days did not even rate the shallowest engraving on her memory, this Mabel was a constant figure and kept alive much of what was left of Helen's capacity for abusive endearments.

Carmel had never allowed the other nurses to play their word game with Helen, but it didn't stop her imagining how it would go, on occasion, to amuse herself.

'Mabel is a ....'

A meddling, skulking, snooping old bitch.'

Carmel smiled at the thought but it only made Helen cross.

'I can't be late; I just can't be late. Can't you find my dad?'

Carmel decided to change tack.

'Helen, it's not a school day today; it's Saturday – Lucky Draw day. Do you want to go back to the Day Room and watch it with your friends? You'd have to sit quietly and not stand in front.'

'They're not my friends,' Helen said with sudden clarity and a lowered tone, looking at Carmel in a way that made her wonder whether she was being accused of condescension.

She knelt down to undo the laces on Helen's shoes.

'Helen, you know your parents are not with us any more. But if they were alive, I'm sure they'd visit you, because they loved you very much,' Carmel began, and stood up to take her hands again.

As she held them, she searched Helen's face for recognition that she was listening.

'This is your home now Helen. You're not lost. You don't need to find anyone. And nobody is coming to pick you up today but that's okay.'

Helen was looking past her into the hallway again, seemingly distracted. Her breathing had slowed a little and Carmel watched as the 'fight or flight' expression on her face softened a little around her eyes. She was accustomed to seeing confusion in old people and had even grown used to its distortion of Helen's face – in an affront to her age. But this new expression – this unreflective, flat, colourless face in front of her now – was unsettling. It was a face worn by those whose minds were losing traction – whose cogs were moving in different directions at different speeds and connecting only once in a while.

Carmel's voice was round and warm and lustrous as she tried to bring her charge back.

'Helen, did you know that you, and everyone else here, are my family now? I grew up without parents too.'

Carmel thought Helen's blink was a sign that she was listening, and wasn't sure how she felt about continuing the story she had surprised herself in beginning.

'My Aunty rescued me from the bush. She told me I was covered in bull ants, swollen and lumpy, but she took care of me and nursed me along with her own baby. That's all I know.'

Helen did not look at Carmel, but she muttered: 'Your aunt wanted you, so you have family.'

Carmel smiled at having been able to draw Helen out, rather than the words she had uttered.

'I used to have family. I got taken to a mission when I was about four. We used to hide when they came for us, but I got nabbed this time. I've tried to find Aunty a few times, but I don't know where to start.'

Carmel had not told anyone in the nursing home her story before and felt a wave of vulnerability until she noticed that Helen looked ready for sleep. She stood by as Helen curled her legs up underneath her on the bed and rolled heavily onto her side, her back to her comforter, the old coils in the mattress depressing noisily underneath. Carmel took a light blanket from a bedside cupboard to drape around her.

'You know,' the kindly nurse revealed in an intimate whisper above Helen as she spread the blanket, 'my name isn't really Carmel. The missionaries gave all us kids new names. I got 'Caramel' because of my skin.

'My Aunty, she called me 'kirrhi karrhawara' – a clever little eaglehawke – because my spirit flew to her and told her where I was so she could rescue me when I was a baby.'

That's my real name.

Carmel walked around the end of the bed now to the window, surprised at how agitated she was feeling. She pulled each curtain from the opposite ends of the rail toward each other and gazed sightlessly at the drawn blinds. She reached for a leather strip around her neck and held onto the talisman at the end of it – a small wooden eagle her Aunt had given her – as if it might warm her fingers while her eyes adjusted to the dark.

Hang in there, Helen – our memories aren't dead, they've just been stolen from us.

As Carmel headed for the door to turn off the light switch, Cat suddenly darted for the exit, startling her by slithering between her ankles. With difficulty, she stifled a gasp of surprise, then quietly scolded him as she followed his haughty tail into the hallway, closing the door behind them.

Helen lay in the darkened room. She felt so perplexed she was nauseas. Her hands were clasped across the soft band of her belly. Her eyes were half open, crowded by a frown. A bold, golden thread of daylight glared at her from the base of the curtains.

The howling from the shower block resumed. It was muffled by the closed door, but no less plaintive than the first time Helen had heard it. Her eyes travelled the length of the illuminated hemline, back and forth, as the woman's cries were corralled by more forceful voices, only able to rise above them in fits and starts.

Helen got up from her bed and pried the door open slowly to avoid being discovered by the nurses. She didn't want a needle. Through the narrow gap, she heard Faye's familiar voice, more stern and disjointed than it usually was. She was talking to the howler.

'Quieten down now,' she said taking a breath, 'because I don't want to have to hold you while Dr Bartlett does his thing. We don't want that do we?'

No, we don't want the needle.

Helen heard a scuffle that she knew from experience would end in the resident being subdued. Predictably, the squeaks of the nurses' rubber soles and the huffing and puffing dissipated.

Helen opened her door a little wider and thought she could make out the woman's last words as they tailed off and the drug took effect.

'My baby. The water's dirty but you can see him. See, he's down there. We have to … .'

44.

Blake's Worm.

[1971-72.]

Kate took the basket and slew the clean washing over the bed for sorting. A pair of socks tumbled to the floor. A pair of her underpants landed on Nick's pillow. His blue singlet, stained lime under the arms from years of sweat, landed on hers.

She sighed, then flopped on top of it all, arms by her side, face down. She imagined herself paralysed. Her breath grew hot on her face, the covers crowded her nostrils.

How long does it take for someone to suffocate?

Conceding the sentiment was nothing more than wanton curiosity but too lethargic to lift her face, she dragged both arms up through the towels and jocks and lay spreadeagled across the bed.

Like a star jump that fell over.

Life in Kimbanyon, Nick's absences – these were things she had promised her mother she could deal with, but she hadn't bargained on how fatigued her brain would become. One day last week, she had spent the day doing her chores, waddling around with her growing body exposed, completely naked. Frequently, she knowingly put the last glass or plate to be washed up on top of a pile of dishes stacked so high they inevitably tumbled onto the kitchen floor. It had become her habit to count as she walked away from the sink to see how many seconds it took for the first piece of crockery to explode and then match that with the number of pieces she would have to pick up later.

There's a useful theory of probability in there somewhere grandpa, I'm sure. Though we may run out of plates before it's properly tested.

Today, as Kate lay face down in the mud of sheets and washing, ambivalence was rising through her every cell – as if nature thought it best she hibernate through this period of her life. The shudder of sleep came with her eyelids still open and the echo of an earlier question rebounding.

How long does it take for someone to suffocate?

She heard the answer faintly as it folded into her contracting consciousness.

That depends; is the person already dead?

***

The night her milk came, the house was still and oppressively hot. Groggy with sleep, Kate pulled herself up on the side of the bed. She shuffled her right leg over the edge, cupped her hands under her second leg and dragged it to the same spot. Looking down on it, she wondered how her leg could feel so heavy.

Her foot, deadened by pins and needles, dropped to the floor. Her big toe caught an old nail which had risen like a drowning sailor's hand and remained frozen there as the floorboards sunk, one by one, unevenly into the foundations.

'Shit.'

There was a hard but cool light coming through the screen door. She aimed her belly towards it, looking for the moon. The door had a youthful spring to it, despite its shabby appearance, and it slammed loudly behind her. She jumped. Surprisingly, Nick did not stir.

In the yard, which was more salvage than garden, Nick's forgotten workhorses were bathed in moonlight. His interest in old metal had culminated in this – a collection of domestic and industrial paraphernalia that would wait so long for restoration that rust would come quicker. Nick had cleared most of the pieces that were beyond repair before they married, but gradually new treasures had come. In this quiet blue light, even the iron frames that had begun to blister were given an eerie life. If Kate squinted at the shadows, she could imagine a woman feeding wet linen through the giant rollers of the antique ringer, and another seated at the Singer, rocking the iron pedal rhythmically with her foot and guiding the cloth under an illusory needle for even stitches. She smiled at them, and the passing of her empathy through time made her feel strangely serene.

Kate smelt the outhouse before she got there – an overripe stench that used to repulse her but now seemed so peripheral as to be just part of the furniture. Shafts of moonlight filtered in through holes in the rippled tin walls, giving her just enough light to locate the toilet roll.

She pushed her pants, tight across her thighs now, to her knees, let gravity take them to her ankles and lowered herself to the seat. The urine slipped from her, almost without sensation. She dropped her head back to relieve her neck muscles and lifted her hand to wipe aside a strand of hair that had basted itself to her brow. She tilted her face and let her finger brush down her cheek. Each pore awoke with such a longing for touch, that she continued the caress, her fingers moving like warm water along the line of her neck, over the rise of her collarbone and slowly, lightly across her bloated breast.

Something wet. Warm.

The small finger of her right hand rode across her nipple like a skier crossing a wake. Her other fingers followed one by one. It was unbelievably soft. And warm. And wet. She felt a trickle. She felt a tingling. Seated in the dark, toilet paper still clutched in her hand, the house still thick with sleep, Kate realised that her milk had come.

She lifted her finger back up underneath the nipple and pushed it slightly into the flesh of her breast. Three watery droplets eased their way through, like morning dew on the surface of a raspberry.

Given this gift – the first sign that her body was preparing for the birth of her baby – Kate felt a sense of relief.

Maybe my body does know what it's doing after all.

The fear that she did not possess the right instincts for the life she was leading had always tugged at Kate. The way she stepped up to challenges – her inability to be intimidated – was something she knew her parents had always been proud of. But they didn't know how hard she worked to appear bold, to stifle a heart-racing anxiety that bailed her up at random moments and demanded answers to questions she couldn't even define.

Kate shared a great deal of the traits she observed in both her mother and father, but as far as she could tell, neither of her parents were prone to the severity of doubt that could collapse the integrity of her emotions with such effectiveness that at times it made it hard for them to regroup.

Kate thought of the squirming inside her as William Blake's worm, a creature as captivating to her as Emily Dickins' fly – poets and creatures first introduced to her by a favourite literature teacher in high school. As a teenager, when she felt the worm squirming, Kate would lie on top of her bed and recite the poem in her head. Over and over, as if it might somehow settle the infestation. Sometimes she marked her strokes in the pool to the rhythm of the lines, annoyed if her tumble turns did not fall neatly into the paraphrasing and pushing off aggressively to start at the top again.

O Rose, thou art sick!
The invisible worm
That flies in the night
In the howling storm,
Has found out thy bed
Of crimson joy:
And his dark secret love
Does thy life destroy.

She always managed to get a smile out of the memory of her teacher's analysis: The rose, she would say, that bed of crimson joy, was a vagina and the worm a great ripe penis.

A great, ripe, flying penis, no less.

Most of her students were convinced that the flame-haired, bright-eyed, middle-aged woman was a nymphomaniac who got a thrill out of shocking private school girls on the brink of their sexual awakening, though some thought she was embittered by a pending divorce from her playboy husband. Either way, whatever it was that gave rise to her teacher's interpretation was irrelevant. She had put the worm in Kate's gut and it was thriving there.

Not like a penis. More like hookworm.

Still sitting on the toilet, her fingers now gently flicking her nipple with the same movement as the twitching tail of a restless cat, Kate wondered how she came to be here. She had been dux of this, dux of that, a model student with abundant promise.

How did I become so frightened of myself?

Kate's meandering mind was interrupted by the sound of scratching.

Probably a roach, maybe a mouse. Better not be a snake.

She quickly pulled up her underwear and headed back to the house. The moon had risen higher but its subjects had not moved. The machinery was still. Even the door did not creak when she pulled it open.

Nick was still sleeping. The trickle drying under her breasts gave off a musty sweet smell. She wanted to share her news but her lover was snoring so loudly that she knew he was wretchedly tired. It wasn't worth the risk of spoiling the moment if he woke grumpily and was unmoved by her news, saying something as banal as: 'Yeah, that's great. Won't be long now!' Kate didn't exactly know what words she wanted from him. Ideally, he might search her eyes trying to fully comprehend the miracle, then kiss her breasts – lingering kisses in awe of the life they had created.

Kate stood in the bedroom doorway a short while. Even in the low light, the tan lines on Nick's bare back were evident – so defined it seemed he might still be wearing his singlet. Maybe he would have wanted to know her milk was in. He might even have been curious enough to taste a warm smear on his finger. But Kate had already convinced herself not to wake him. She climbed carefully back into bed and sank easily into a deep sleep while the moon stood watch.

Blake's worm had stretched and settled.

45.

[Rosemont Hospital. August 24, 1951.]

The stain on the blanched plastic curtain surrounding Helen's hospital bed changed colour as the intensity of the light behind it fired and lapsed. In the morning when the window frame was dissolved in the glow of a cloudless day, when Helen had arrived hunched in fear that the next contraction would kill her, it was a hand swipe of wet, rich ochre.

Her labour began quietly enough at the Benevolent Shelter for Women with a sharp stab, not unlike a stitch. Helen walked it out, pacing up and down the hallway, too scared to alert Sister Michaels so early in the morning. Others were getting up around her, jostling for the showers, checking rosters for chores, making up their beds.

With the second stab, Helen gripped her side with one hand and braced herself on the stair rail with the other, foolishly thinking it might be happening then and there and that her baby was only minutes away.

'Oh God.'

'You'd better call the Mullet,' a sullen Sybil, who was now two weeks overdue, called boldly from their room. 'You can't just stand there shrieking all day.'

Helen didn't relish the thought, recalling the Matron's lecture on the day she had arrived, particularly that she wasn't to be disturbed 'unless waters have broken or there's blood involved'.

So Sybil, so heavy that she wasn't going to do an extra trip up and down the stairs even for this, called to one of the newer residents on her way past their room: 'You, Marge, or whatever your name is, go get the Matron; Helen's baby is coming.'

The baby is coming.

'Aaaarrrrh.'

Helen doubled over as her insides shredded and rethreaded with pain so much worse than the first strike.

It turned out that the cook's husband was also the regular driver and once the matron had assessed Helen's crumpled form at the top of the stairs from the bottom, he was summoned immediately to bring the station wagon to the front of the house. Helen moved slowly, putting one foot beside the other on each of the steps as she descended. Nobody rushed her or yelled at her, not even Sister Michaels.

She was delivered to a maternity ward of some eight or so beds upon arrival at the Rosemont Hospital. Most had their curtains drawn, though the patients had little chance of getting any sleep now that yet another labouring mother had joined them.

Matron pressed a backless gown to Helen's chest, told her to tie it at the neck and pointed to a bathroom in the corner of the ward. Though she felt vulnerable without her underwear or faith that she would get her own clothes back again, Helen was indescribably happy to see that the Matron had not left by the time she emerged.

In fact, the fear that she would look up to find the Matron gone would renew itself with every contraction. But Sister Michaels would stay.

After a few hours of virulent contractions, Helen's waters broke. The look on her face made Sister Michaels laugh, despite having seen it so many times.

'For goodness sake Helen. You came to all the classes. Did you think you'd wet yourself?'

Sister Michaels got up from her seat now. She was used to her girls having to wait for attention and usually respected the hospital's insistence that only staff treat patients – for insurance purposes – but she didn't like the contour she was looking at.

'Stop squirming girl. You're going to get a lot more uncomfortable than this I can tell you,' she told Helen as she pressed her hands firmly on the right side of her belly.

'I'm just going to have a little play around with the baby for a minute. It's not going to hurt him … .'

'I think it's a girl.'

'Either way. Just try to keep still.'

Another contraction, stronger this time, spoiled the Matron's inspection and she was forced to lift her hands while Helen drew up her legs until it passed.

'I think bubby is lying on his side and that's going to make things a bit difficult,' Matron said as she resumed rolling the base of her palm underneath various bumps that only she could distinguish as particular parts of a small being's anatomy.

A tiny foot kicked up inside Helen and she gasped, grabbing the Matron's hand and squeezing it into a purple ball.

Sister Michaels pulled it back with a scowl and returned to her task as Doctor M. Sonos – according to his name tag – appeared. He was a large man with a gaunt face and a crooked nose and an athletic build that was obvious despite his knee-length white coat. He was flanked by a nurse so petite, the sight of them together amused both Helen and Sister Michaels – who shared a look for the most transient of moments.

Dr Sonos moved to check Helen's chart, which was attached to a clipboard hooked to the bedrail at her feet. Another rip through her uterus caused Helen to cry out and pull at the edges of the clear plastic cover underneath her buttocks.

When the doctor looked up, he nodded to the young nurse who perkily sprang into action. She was remarkably swift in grabbing Helen's shin and forcing the leg to bend, then whipping behind the doctor – the curtain flying up over her back – to reach the other side of the bed where she repeated the process. When both knees had been lifted into position, Dr Sonos then pushed them apart and bent down.

Helen lifted her head to see what was going on but her view was impaired by her own enormous belly and her neck began to ache with the effort.

'Knees up, head down,' the nurse quipped. 'The doctor can't see what he's doing.'

Coming from the interior of her thighs, the doctor's voice was slightly muffled, but Helen found his words no less frightening because of it.

'This one's going to be a forceps delivery I think Matron.'

'It's a first birth, doctor, so I think we can give it a bit longer, don't you? I was having some success moving the foetus into a better position and I think once that happens ...'

'Thank you Sister. I'm aware that this is a first birth, unless the policy has changed at the Shelter and you are now taking women in for their second and third mistakes.

'This is a very busy hospital and I'm not inclined to make others wait when forceps will do the trick.'

'A word, doctor?'

The conversation that followed saw the Matron speaking in a hushed tone by the end of the bed where she had led the good doctor. Dr Sonos, however, felt no need for professional discretion and was obviously losing his patience.

'Sister if I thought an epidural here was necessary I would have called for it. I don't know who you've been talking to, but it is not common practice in this hospital to give everyone the expensive drugs they think they need just because they ask for them.'

The doctor nudged Nurse Scott out of the way to swivel a metal arc attached on a pivot to the wall over the lower end of the bed. The nurse dutifully stepped back in to lift Helen's feet into the stirrups swinging from the arc on leather straps.

'These girls have got to learn,' Dr Sonos continued in a calmer but no less lecturing tone, 'that there is a price for promiscuity, and this is it.'

The doctor turned to the tray Nurse Scott appeared to have placed on the bedside table earlier and chose a scalpel for the episiotomy.

He returned to his place between Helen's knees but seemed unhappy. 'I need more light here.'

Sister Michaels filled her enormous bosom with as much breath and authority as she could muster and without raising her voice, addressed the doctor once more.

'You and I both know this is not a cost issue.'

The nurse positioned a bright lamp on a trolley to the side of Dr Sonos and attempted to push past the Matron to plug it in to a powerpoint on the wall at the head of the bed. The Matron refused to move and the nurse was forced to step behind her.

'This girl is a public patient like any other and is provided for, so if she needs … .'

As the Matron spoke, the doctor knicked Helen's swollen flesh, providing a larger opening for forceps which he deftly positioned around the baby's skull. His rotation of the cold, stainless steel pincers almost forty five degrees, was conducted with less competency and a perineal tear began. It would extend all the way through to the young mother's anus, causing excruciating pain. The world closed in on Helen in that moment, and she passed out in a nauseating spin.

Nurse Scott jumped back in surprise as Helen's right leg jumped in the stirrup beside her, a nerve inadvertently pressured by the maneuvering. Unphased, Dr Sonos began to pull, pausing once to reposition his feet. When he began again, he bent his knees and seemed to draw his strength from between his shoulder blades. His renewed exertion was rewarded with a crowning and soon the ends of the forceps emerged, pressing tiny ears against a slightly elongated skull.

One final tug and the rest of the body slipped easily from Helen's unresponsive body, streaked with blood.

'Another successful birth, Matron,' Dr Sonos asserted as he cut the umbilical cord with the kind of flourish that might be employed snipping a ribbon at a bridge opening.

'No complaints from mother or child!'

'It's hard to complain when you're unconscious, Doctor,' Matron pointed out in a sarcastic drawl.

'Now now, Matron, you know as well as I do, that she has fainted. Some women don't have as much stamina for birth as others. Your girls seem particularly lacking in willpower, wouldn't you say?'

Sister Michaels was rarely lost for words but the performance of this doctor had left her gob smacked. She vowed to herself that in future, her girls would hold out for a new shift if this man was on deck when they went into labour.

Or I'll damn well deliver them myself.

Nurse Scott placed Helen's baby into swaddling lain across the arms of a colleague who had appeared at just the right time. She then efficiently pegged the stubble protruding from the baby's stomach that flattened and withdrew momentarily from her touch. Both women then moved to the side of the room to weigh and measure the child and await a final medical sign off.

Dr Sonos wiped the forceps on the bleached linen underneath Helen's still uplifted feet, leaving a blistering crimson streak on a section unprotected by plastic. The affront to the Matron, who would be taking the bedclothes back to the Shelter, may not have been intended but it was keenly felt.

He then turned his attention to the baby, strolling over to casually draw her up from the nurse's arms by her ankles.

Helen was returned to consciousness almost at the same time her child was prompted by Dr Sonos to clear her lungs. For the baby, it was a light spank on the bottom. In Helen's case, a stinging slap to the face, delivered by the perky Nurse Scott. The shock of it opened all her valves. A jellied clot thickened in her discharge, a down of sweat filled her facial pores, her eyelids withdrew to their furthest perimeter and her ears filled with a whelp that seemed to come from deep within her and the other side of the room at the same time.

It would be another half an hour before Helen had delivered her placenta and a full three hours before the busy Dr Sonos returned to stitch her tear, complaining all the while to his favourite nurse that the ice she had applied had failed to keep the swelling down, left his workstation in a puddle and made it even harder to keep the edges aligned.

By this time the Matron had long gone and there was no one left who cared to oversee the man's manner, let alone the quality of his needlework.

Helen was relieved when she was finally alone inside the curtain that shut the world out as much as it shut her in. She gave herself permission to succumb – on the grounds that she was unlikely to be interfered with any further. She let her head loll in the direction of the window, but it was hard to sleep with the golden light glaring at her through the filter of the polyester. Sunspots blotted under her eyelids. One of them was significantly larger than the others – a flaring raspberry fist given an oxygenated vibrancy as the lowering sun bore through it. Helen remembered how she had speculated on the origins of the stain on the curtain. It seemed like days ago. Now, despite her mind feeling as dislocated as her limbs, Helen was convinced of one thing: someone had surely died in this bed giving up that blood.

46.

New eyes on the world (2).

[Kimbanyon. April 10, 1972.]

'**A**re we any closer, ladies? The boy'll wear a rut in the verandah if this baby doesn't show itself soon!'

Ron knocked on the glass. The blinds had been loosely drawn from the inside, obscuring his view of his wife Sorrell tending to the birth of their first grandchild, but he thought a verbal update should not be out of the question.

If Nick had pushed, Sorrell probably would have let her son inside to assist with the birth. She wasn't one of those midwives who believed it was better to keep a bit of mystery about the female anatomy from husbands in order not to frighten future desire from a marriage. Her views were more akin to those that would be expressed some years later by a French surgeon and childbirth pioneer, Dr Michel Odent. As he would express it, a salle sauvage – or primitive room – where women have privacy and the comfort to do what comes naturally, enhances the birthing experience and can reduce the need for interference.

Ron didn't quite understand the concept as Sorrell explained it to him but had nevertheless summarised it for his son by saying that childbirth was women's business and best left to them. Quite frankly, he had added, he was pleased to have been shut out of his own children's births because Sorrell's screams had been 'blood curdling'.

So Nick was pacing the verandah annoying his father, who was dutifully keeping him company, and swiping his dog away every now and then as it kept step with him.

'Can't you tie him up? You know Roo hates dogs,' Ron asserted, just a little irritated at the lack of response from his wife.

'Dad, Roo followed **you**. Remember? Anyway he took off hours ago.'

'We're getting close,' Sorrell finally called from behind the curtains. 'So stop asking; we're kinda busy in here. When you hear the baby cry, it'll be over. Ron, why don't you put the kettle on, love?'

Sorrell turned back to Kate, who had been sweating out her contractions for close to 12 hours now, moving around the room, rocking her pelvis forward and back with Sorrell's hands over hers on her hips. Kate was now on her back on the double bed, allowing her midwife to check the extent of her dilation.

'The problem with you young lady is you're too fit,' Sorrell chastised kindly. 'Every time we look like we've got a decent opening, that elastic door of yours snaps shuts again!

'But your contractions are regular and there are no signs that the baby's distressed, so we can keep going for a while longer before we need to think about our options. Can you do that, sweetheart?'

'I don't know Sorrell; I'm really tired,' Kate pleaded, well beyond wanting to impress her mother-in-law by searching for some elusive reserve of strength.

'I don't think I've got any more pushing in me. This baby just doesn't want to come out.'

'I know it seems like that honey. First births often take a long time; it's quite normal. But I think we can push it along a bit.

'I'm going to tell you when to push, and when to wait, and we'll see if we can't get this baby to make an appearance, alright?'

Sorrell wasn't sure that Kate, now with her eyes closed and desperate for sleep, had taken in what she had said. She blew away a greying strand of hair that had strayed into her eyes as she bent over. Her patient's thigh muscles tightened under Sorrell's hands as she struggled with another contraction that ended with Kate's cries dissolving into a swamp of tears and pain.

Nick could hold himself no longer and rapped on the bedroom window.

'Mum, what's going on in there? Why is she crying like that?'
Sorrell ignored him.

Ron gripped his son by the shoulders and drew him away from the window. It had been a long day. Sorrell had been at the house since ten that morning. He had picked his son up from down the line shortly after two thirty and had brought him to the house. Nick had watched two mugs of tea go cold and had had a beer around six with his father but had had nothing to eat since half a sandwich for lunch and his stomach was churning.

Now, with it after ten at night, Nick was alone listening to his wife whimpering. Ron had disappeared around the back to check on Long Dog who had skulked away after a particularly strident kick from Nick, who had assumed it would have dodged him, and he was left alternating between the kitchen chair and pacing along the verandah, imagining everything that could go wrong.

***

Inside the 'salle sauvage', Sorrell was concerned that Kate was becoming overwhelmed and slightly panicked.

'Okay, Kate, we want to protect your perineum here. When you're frightened your pelvic floor tightens up and there's a bigger chance that you'll tear.

'So just relax, ok – you've got at least another three minutes before your next contraction. That's long enough to work out how to make the margaritas we're going to have to celebrate when this is all over don't you think?'

Kate looked up at her mother-in-law, not sure if her mind was turning the words into gibberish, particularly since it was frighteningly close to what she wanted to hear.

Sorrell happily continued with her banter despite Kate's confused look.

'You didn't know that's what midwives do late at night, did you? Later on I'll show you how to get the salt to stick to the rim of the glass if you like. That's a secret we only share with our favourite mothers.

'And don't worry, the drinking bit will be timed perfectly so it doesn't come through in the breast milk!'

Kate looked at Sorrell, laughed at the drunken face she was pulling and then hiccupped.

'I had no idea you had such a good imagination, Kate White!'

'Alright, alright, that's enough party talk, now,' Sorrell said, wanting to put Kate's changing mood to use quickly.

'Let's get you off your back and on your hands and knees, growling like a she wolf.'

'What?'

Kate, who was more at ease now, did as she was told, rolling on to her side to get off the bed and dropping slowly to the rug Sorrell had brought with her.

A fresh, virulent wave of pain tore across her abdomen almost as soon as she set up on all fours.

'C'mon Kate,' Sorrell urged loudly, standing beside her like a sports coach. 'You're doing the grunt work and I want to hear all about it. Deep growling, between your teeth.

'And puuuuuuuuuush!'

Outside, Long Dog had resumed barking, his focus directly on the gutteral noise emanating from the house, rather than Ron who was threatening to hang him from the Hills Hoist.

'Good girl. Take a rest now.'

Sorrell had once more watched a head emerge and slip away, although it had been a much larger crown than before.

'You know, I think we're so close we can give gravity a chance to help us out here. Can you stand up sweetheart?'

'Really? You think these legs are gonna stand up – after all those margaritas?'

'You're right. Let's get some help from those useless men out there.

'Nicholas. Ron. Can you come in here please?'

The shock of seeing Kate in a t-shirt, naked from the waist down stopped Ron in his tracks at the door. Nick, who was relieved beyond belief to be summoned to the sanctum, was already crouched beside his wife by the time his father crossed the threshold.

'Alright Kate,' Sorrell said in a gentle but firm voice, 'This is the big one, so on your feet.

'You boys get under her arms and give her some support.'

Sorrell moved the towel again and knelt down. She looked up to see Kate's whole body ashiver.

'Okay Kate; it's just like before. I want you to growl like that she wolf I know you've got inside you and push with everything you've got.

'Puuuuuuusssssh!'

'Aaaaaaaaahhhgggggrrrrrrraaaahhheeeya uh uh uh grrrrrrrrrr.'

Kate found her reserve just as Long Dog found his own inner wolf. On the crest of an escalating howl and a gravelly moan quarried from nature's deepest well, a cannonball of a head forged its way to the brink of a new life and glided directly into Sorrell's hands. She let the precious skull rest on the bridge of her wrists as her index fingers stretched forward to hook under tiny armpits and ease them to the edge of the opening.

'This is it sweetheart, one more time and you'll soon be able to see the world through a new pair of eyes. Are you ready?'

Ron planted himself like he was facing a tractor pull. Nick pressed his lips to his wife's wet, salty cheek.

'C'mon Katie. I love you so much. So much.'

Kate had never been more determined about anything. The contraction rode through her like a wave and delivered the whole body in one fluid motion into his grandmother's arms.

Stay down.

[Sturt Street. November, 1972]

The nightlight threw a yellow haze around her cold, bare legs. It had only been two hours since the baby had last fed and here she was back again, determined not to pick him up and collapse into the corner rocking chair, to be found by Nick in the morning, hair plastered to the side of her face from the drool which had trickled out of her mouth as her neck gave way from exhaustion, the child on her knees, like a lap dog, ready to roll off at any minute, her over-suckled breasts with their rubbery dust-brown nipples still hanging out, her nightie roughly pulled away from them and scrunched around her waist.

She was so sick of that smell – the smell that made dogs pester women in the street. Perhaps it was that she was not wearing underwear with her nightie, or that she was also smelling the slightly sweet but dank smell of breastmilk that had been leaking slowly since the baby woke her up, but all she ever seemed to want these days was a shower.

Kate pressed herself up against the cot, pushing it, then pulling it back on its stiff castors.

I don't know why we let Nick's parents give us his old cot; the wheels are rusty for God's sake.

Sometimes the monotonous motion sent the baby back to sleep. But tonight it wasn't working. He was crying in short bursts, refusing to settle. Weary and wishing she were back in her own bed, she moved the cot more roughly and pushed the palm of her hand firmly down in the small of his back, holding it there, urging him to 'shh, shh', over and over again. His distress caused droplets of milk to spring from her nipples.

'Shh, shh.'

Kate was almost spitting it out now. The baby cried harder. She pushed down more firmly. Kate caught herself up as the baby clutched for air.

I'm frightening him.

From his lips was the sound of a distant dog barking.

She caught herself again.

Don't let this happen.

The whimpering grew louder but the child was no longer pushing up with his arms.

'Stay down': It's what boxers think when they've beaten the crap out of their opponent, what soldiers think when they're playing dead to avoid being killed. Bad things happen if you don't stay down. Would I really hurt my baby?

Kate picked William up. Exhaustion crumpled his hot little body into her arms. The night air, humid with the isolation of their shared trauma, enveloped them. His short, sharp breaths hit her face like the dirty air forced from a tunnel by an oncoming train. She realised that he had thrown up. It was her own milk, suckled, swallowed, regurgitated, yet at that moment, she didn't care about the smell. She held him to her and drew in her own air, her nose tickled by the fine, soft strands of his hair, his heartbeat double that of her own against her chest.

I'll never put him down again.

Sink floaters.

[February, 1973.]

'Eggs?'

Nick didn't look up from his paper. Kate didn't turn around from the kitchen sink to repeat the question.

'Do you want eggs this morning?'

This time Nick looked up. His wife's once glossy hair was still a rich reddy brown but its golden streaks reminded him of an old tabby cat that hung around the station. It no longer sat perky around her neck, but splayed onto her back, listless and fraying almost to the end of her shoulder blades.

When did it get so long? And why all of a sudden has she taken to wearing that old apron?

Sorrell, Nick's mother, had passed the apron on because she couldn't stand any clothing after a few washes; patterns faded quickly on Tarcoola clotheslines and she liked her colours bold and vibrant. She had kept it for much longer than most of the clothing she had bought or sewn herself because it had been more comfortable than most aprons she said. Now the paisley print was only visible in the material under the arms and on the lining of a giant pocket across its midriff.

Kate was vague and detached this morning; the last thing she felt like doing was cooking her husband's breakfast – a duty she would not have dreamed would be a part of her life five years before.

What's so hard about getting a bowl of cornflakes?

It had been a bit of a shock to learn that for 'working people', breakfast was the biggest meal of the day and that she was supposed to cook it. It regularly consisted of several slices of toast piled with eggs, bacon and sausages; sometimes it was a stack of pancakes with fruit when it was available and always, there was a big mug of black coffee sitting like a patient dog beside his newspaper. Nick would eat and then, with one eye still on his paper, he would slip his plate into the sink. She would find it underneath the water, made murky by the leftover crusts of his toast, the bit of the egg that wasn't quite cooked, the smear of the smear.

Nick always dispensed with the front part of the paper, dropping it at the legs of the kitchen table without even looking at the headlines. He only ever read the sport and finance sections – sport, because someone he had once played with around the wharves in Port Augusta was now a rugby superstar, and finance because he had become obsessed by fluctuations in the mining sector since agreeing with his mates to invest his Christmas bonus in shares.

So, after turning his back on his plate, heavy with the detritus of breakfast, as it slipped under the water, he would walk out the front door commenting on which stocks were up or down, thinking, Kate assumed, that, as their fates and finances were inextricably linked, she would be interested, or at least impressed with his knowledge of such things. Or perhaps he was just used to talking to himself.

Poor Nick. Still, it's his castle.

'Eggs?' Kate repeated for the third time.

'No thanks, no time,' he said as he gulped down the last of his coffee, tasting even more bitter because it had gone cold. Pushing his chair back under the table with one heavy-booted foot, he tipped his plate into the sink, the unwanted toast swelling in the soapy water.

'I'll be heading out today; we're working on a new siding. It'll be a few weeks. We'll do something special when I get back, eh?'

Nick looked to his wife from the front door, genuinely interested in a response.

'Yeah,' Kate said, without looking up from the sink. 'That'd be nice.'

It was good enough; the screen door creaked and slammed shut. She turned around, wondering why he always waited until the morning he was going before telling her he was working down the line. For a moment she wished she had looked into his face before he left.

'Western Mining is up 12 cents. Not bad!'

The voice already seemed far away as Nick jumped boyishly off the front verandah, raising a steam of dust around his boots and sending the ghosts of the machinery in the yard back into hiding. The sun was rising. The baby was crying. She did not rush toward either. There was no hurry; it was going to go on all day.

49.

Out of step.

[May, 1973.]

Avery was generally affronted by open caskets. Orthodox Christians were more likely to ask for their loved ones to be bared for all to see, their faces pumped with embalming fluids, their colours subtle on the palette but gaudy on death's skin, their eyelids all but ready to sink into their skulls like the buckled headstones of neglected graves. It didn't seem right to him.

That Ursula would leave instructions for an open casket surprised him a little; she had been irascible with those avoiding hard truths or sugar coating their realities, but when it came to herself, she had been an intensely private person.

He looked around the congregation to see if there was a Mr Michaels who might have made the decision for her. Having never met such a man, Avery looked for a portly, rambunctious fellow whom he thought might be a match for Ursula.

But then again, a man could easily be henpecked by a woman like that. Maybe Mr Michaels is that lanky fellow who looks like he'll break out in hives if anyone speaks to him.

A sentiment that might have been the colour of shame – had it been provoked outside of his own conscience – stirred in Avery.

Thirty years I've known this woman and yet I don't know if she was married, ever had her own children or even if her family is here today.

Despite his reservations about open coffins, Avery felt compelled to look Ursula in the face one more time. He took his place in the viewing queue. It was a shuffle he had not experienced before. In fact, it was one of the rare occasions, like Kate's wedding, where he had been part of a congregation instead of leading it.

As he drew closer, he tried to establish for himself how he felt about Ursula Michaels and whether or not, in fact, he would genuinely grieve her passing. For the most part, Ursula had given him the impression that she got on with her job because that was her lot in life, rather than her Christian duty. She did it for the pay cheque, she said, despite the fact that it barely covered the stockings straining over her painful varicose veins. She had complained to Avery about her inadequate wage on more than one occasion, as if he were personally responsible for setting it.

The woman in front of Avery was snuffling almost in time with each step of the solemn procession, the well-padded shoulders of her dark ensemble rising and falling in sync. As she took her turn in front of the coffin, Avery saw her face contort and then crumble into a man's handkerchief. He heard a deep sigh build in her throat with a rattle of her chest. Her shoulders rose one last time and then fell almost to her waist as she let her breath go. She stood just long enough for those behind her in the queue to become impatient, and then moved on, putting her rolled up order of service in her handbag and clasping it shut as she walked.

Avery realised on closer inspection that he knew the woman; she had worked alongside Ursula at the Shelter.

The cook, perhaps. Yes, the cook. I've never seen her so emotional before. Always thought she was more of a pot banger.

He looked up to see the minister entering the pulpit. Voices and movement in the church became muffled as if a blanket had been thrown over them, and the organist quietly withdrew his feet from the pedals.

I'd better get everyone seated.

Avery looked towards Ursula's body, throwing his glance across like a fishing line without a sinker, expecting a quick return. But it snagged on the gold trim of the buttons on her navy cardigan. She wore a smart white shirt underneath it with a pleated front and a long black skirt. Her feet – *I wish she'd never shown me those awful bunyons* – were clad in glossy black shoes, with a modest heel and an immodest gold buckle.

His gaze finally travelled to her face. Perhaps it was the chill of the morgue, or the morticians fluid, but there was no remnant here of the ruddy-faced woman Avery had known. The skin now had a uniformly pale pink tinge and, while her eyes had often been dwarfed by the rising cheeks of anger or laughter, the closed lids now appeared to be overwhelmed by flesh. There was an unusual bloat above her cheekbones and a shadowed valley beneath them.

Whatever they paid the funeral directors it was too much. It doesn't even look like her anymore. Elsa Timmins looked better than this.

The revolving images of the two corpses pushed Avery several more degrees away from familiarity and compassion. It gave him the same aftertaste as when he ran into former servicemen on the street, dressed in unfamiliar garb, their faces on unfamiliar bodies, in unfamiliar poses.

The skinny, nervous man who had been handing out papers for the funeral's order of service found his voice – a too-sharp voice that called everyone to take their seats, cracking at the end of the instruction like a rubber band flicking back from an unexpected stretch. The cook, who hadn't left after all, was suddenly at Avery's side.

'We'll sit together if you like; I'm over here,' she said, gently slipping her freckled forearm between his arm and torso and lifting it into the pose of an escort.

The minister leading the service forced a light cough – and those still standing began to look around for friends or colleagues with whom to sit. The cook guided Avery towards a pew at the front, 'behind Sully's family', she said. When they had sat down, she touched Avery's arm to get his attention and nodded to the back of the heads in front of them. The balding, heavy man to their left, she said, was 'Sully's cousin who stayed in touch with her since poor Richard died of a heart attack'.

'I think he might have had a crush on our Sully,' the cook noted in a quiet aside.

At the far end of the pew, closest to the aisle, was an elderly woman Avery had never seen before. Drizzles of floaty white hair barely covered her scalp of piglet pink. Her shoulders were encircled by a fox stole with a smell of mothballs that infused the air around everyone in the row.

'That's Sully's mother, Vivien Tenterfield', the cook told Avery, having followed his gaze.

'She's come down from New South Wales; she and Sully have been inseparable ever since that suitcase arrived for Sully at the Shelter last month. They were up in her room, night after night pouring over whatever was in that case.

'Mrs Tenterfield has it now, so I guess I'll never know!'

The Reverend had not been paying much heed to the cook's gossip to this point, mostly because it was being delivered on the waft of a shaving cream that seemed to have eradicated her reputation for whiskers but put him off nevertheless. But now that that the cook was done with her storytelling, Avery felt an urge to backtrack to restore the gaps in his memory of the past few minutes. Something had caught his attention but he wasn't sure what it was.

'Who's Sully?'

'Oh come on Reverend; you never heard us call her Sully? She hated Ursula – thought it sounded Germanic.

'Her family called her Sully; we all called her Sully, except for the girls of course. They called her lots of things, but I know she loved every one of them.'

The cook sniffed away a tear propelled by the last image she had of Sister Michaels at the Benevolent Shelter, talking to the girls as if nothing were wrong the day they admitted her to hospice care.

The minister began. A welcome. A psalm.

The Reverend, who always hated people in the front rows disrespecting him by carrying on with intermittent chatter while he was in the pulpit, leant down slightly to match the cook's height and attempted a hushed tone without much success.

'What did the suitcase look like?'

The cook turned to him, frowning slightly, and put her finger to her lips as the minister began his reading.

A poor choice. Why do they repeat the same ones over and over? And why does this woman who never stops talking choose now to be tight lipped?

Avery knew he was in for a long wait. He closed his eyes against a strengthening headache.

'Reverend?' Some minutes later, the cook was jiggling the arm of Avery's jacket and speaking in a fullsome whisper. 'You dozed off. You've been mumbling – quite loudly.'

'I, what? Dozed off? I'm …'

'Shhh.' Annoyingly, the cook lifted her index finger up in front of her mouth again, and frowned.

The service droned on – its lifts and lows as predictable in Avery's ears as they were to the regular church goers who stood and sat, without prompting, at all the right junctures. Her family did not speak; apparently there was only her mother left and a close childhood friend, who had had a stroke some years back, and they both waved the opportunity when it was offered.

Avery turned his gaze from the minister to the casket. From where he sat, he could see nothing but deeply varnished walnut panels adorned with cold brass handles. Not even those amazing shoes breached the top of the casket walls. He was reminded again of Elsa Timmins – the way her tiny feet had protruded from her hot cocoon.

The Reverend had seen death in a lot of forms. He felt strongly that God tended to the dying, in the minutes before they left this world. He had seen them call to Him for comfort or forgiveness and he had seen their burdens lift from their faces, as if they had been given back their innocence. But in everything he had seen, he could not conclude that there was salvation for the living. The more troubled souls Avery met, the less sure he was that God was prepared to fall in step with the walking wounded.

50.

A gunslinger and a rocking chair.

[July, 1973.]

Kate had to concede that she had become boring. She found herself without a thought in her head, her body in automatic, moving from one chore to the next, even waking the baby sometimes to give herself something to do.

She became startled by the dullest of her own thoughts, as if someone else had spoken them out loud, simply because they usually appeared in a vacuum, with nothing coming before them for the longest of periods.

Kate was falling victim to an insidious apathy, losing the will to scaffold her personality as it collapsed inside her. She found herself inclined to live through her husband, allowing her static environment to spark on his presence and dim on his absence. She began to alternately blame him for the slump of her life or gorge herself on his energy, often through aggressive, lusty and blatantly selfish sex after which she would secretly detest his presence.

When Nick was working up or down the line, Kate allowed her connection to her life to dissolve completely. She was unable to generate the simplest of intentions and chameleon-like in the way she mirrored changes in her surroundings. She often took to a post on the verandah, leant on it and stared into the sky for a sign of how she might feel about the day or respond to it in general. At her post, her world was silent: Billy did not disturb her, Long Dog's dripping tongue did not spot cold on her bare feet as he looked for attention.

Not even a plume of dust signifying a car approaching marred her horizon. Not even if all those things actually happened.

She would make up poems in her head, trying desperately to reintroduce words that had fallen completely from her vernacular since leaving school … *and civilisation.*

Today, the sky was … a whip of white – thin splashes of clouds spraying across a lively cobalt backdrop in layers of possibility …

Kate knew it was more than likely that she would end up later in the day sitting on the verandah with Billy attached to her breast long enough to fall asleep there, waiting to see Nick's ute emerge from the dust. But that would be hours from now.

The ute's still here. Matt picked him up. So he'll probably have a beer after work. I won't see him before ten. Hours and hours from now. Layers of nothing.

A light breeze brought a faint eucalyptus smell to her nostrils.

A spray of eucalyptus oil colouring the mountains in a blue haze, like the perspiration of mother earth. In the armpit of the world.

What if I just went for a drive? I could put the radio on and just ride off into the sunset – instead of sitting on my hands all day to stop me slitting my wrists …

Layers of possibility …

Kate walked back into the house, past the bedroom, past Billy's expectant noises, to the hallway hook where the keys were.

I've got nowhere to go. Endless possibilities annulled instantly by my lack of imagination. I'm a dullard!

I s'pose I could drink myself into a stupor. Or I could just go, and work it out on the way … I won't be long … .

She drove off slowly at first, considering doing a wide circle of the house and returning, willing upon herself the illusion that she had got something out of her system and seeing dutifully to her child. But her hands would not turn the wheel that way. She began picking up speed until the house was little more than a blur in her rear-view mirror, her heart beating a little faster the further she drove. At the highway, she stopped, guilt tiptoeing on her conscience, sinking its toes into eroding potholes.

Billy's probably cried himself to sleep by now. No point rushing back.

Kate roughly threw the stick shift into gear and forced the accelerator down so quickly the vehicle fish-tailed, sending up a spray of crushed rock as she turned onto the main road, her eyes glazed behind the blindfold of a truanting will. Window down, her nose filled with the smell of the smoky cloud spewing behind the ute and her thick hair shredding and stinging her as its ends slapped her face. The dead weight of her foot pressed more heavily on the accelerator.

Once Kimbanyon disappeared from the rear view mirror, Kate powered on, swaying between exhilaration, exhaustion and complete displacement as the highway opened up. About 25 kilometres from the nearest roadhouse, she slowly depressed the brake and brought the vehicle to a lazy stop on the shoulder. Her breathing slowed. After five minutes, she blinked.

Nothing. I'm empty again.

She stared through the spatter of dead insects on the windscreen to the unremarkable landscape on the other side of it. A thin vein of blood leaked from her right nostril and a weak, warm tear dampened her cheek. She waited for the first truck to pass.

Ten minutes later, the ute was caught in the pull of an enormous road train, its carcass rocking as the truck swept past then shuddering in its wake like a weary body at the onset of sleep. Kate's neck went limp, her head fell back on the top of the seat and she slipped into the sublime. A succession of trucks passed, pulling her in and spitting her out in a broken but hypnotic rhythm. She closed her eyes and became seaweed tossed in the shallows and stranded on smooth sand as the water withdrew, and then picked up again as the water rushed underneath her, spinning her spinelessly out to sea.

She woke to a blast from an air horn. The right side of her top lip, blood encrusted and tasting of dust, twitched as if a fly had landed on it.

She did not hear the thought that prompted her hand to turn the key, once, twice and turn the wheel for home. It felt like midafternoon when she approached the house. She saw Nick on the verandah and her mood, dormant during the drive home, lifted instantly, failing to recognise quickly enough the agitation he was jiggling in his pocket.

He stepped down to meet her.

'Where the hell have you been? Are you okay? God damn it, Kate, you can't just up and leave a baby like that.'

Every muscle in Nick's body appeared tense.

'The job got called off. I came home to have lunch with you and all I find is an empty house and a crying baby.'

Nick's powerful arms were arced on either side of his body, his chest heaving. Kate found herself improbably bemused.

He looks like a gunslinger about to draw.

She took a wide berth in making her way to the open front door while her husband stood rooted to the spot, his face basted with incredulity. He allowed her to pass, then followed her through the house, both incensed and anxious, as she made a bee-line to her son's room.

'He's been crying like that the whole time, Kate. I've done everything. He won't stop screaming. I was just about to call mum.'

Now he's being pathetic. What self-respecting gunslinger calls his mum in a crisis?

From a face that was stony apart from a brief tick in her temple, Kate's eyes bore into her husband's as she melodramatically tore open her shirt, several buttons popping, unsnapped the clip at the front of her bra and lifted her baby from his cot. His full-throated wailing broke immediately into gasps of relief as he smelt the milk. Kate clutched the baby under her arm like a shopping bag. His mouth searched clumsily for her nipple but when he found it he was unable to close successfully around it because of remnant sobs still pitching themselves from his mouth.

Once attached, Nick looked almost as relieved as the baby, and Kate hated him for it. She turned towards the rocking chair in the corner of the nursery and sat down, taking to it as if it were another ute she was purposefully throwing into a drift across a slippery surface. The baby pressed into her flesh as she rocked forward and struggled to hold her nipple in his mouth as she pressed her feet to the floor and propelled the chair backwards.

Nick had experienced enough of fatherhood to know that this rough feed would keep the baby up all night with colic. He leant back on the wall, his arms folded, but his voice cottony soft.

'Whatta we going to do, Kate? Do you need help, with the baby I mean? We can get my mother over one day a week, or maybe yours could come visit for a while?'

The thought of seeing her mother scratched at her eyes like sandpaper and Kate slowed her rocking. God she wanted to go home. Any home.

They never tell you that when you marry – that if it all goes sour, you don't actually have a home to go to.

She ignored Nick, dropping her eyes to the baby's skull and feeling a little ashamed of herself – her immaturity, her tantrum. She crossed one bare foot behind the other, and slowed the chair to a gentle lilt. She did not look up, willing Nick to leave the room. Afterall it was her problem, not his.

Because he can always walk away.

A twirl of milk, overflow from the aggressive suckling, wound it's way in a tickle across Kate's body in the thin ravine underneath the bloat of her breast and on top of her first rib. Initially Kate had liked the feel of her milk, of something warm and wet that was life-giving leaking from her body. She enjoyed the connection between having a rush of emotion, and leaking. Hearing her baby cry. And leaking. But something in her had broken; she no longer conceived of her baby's total dependence on her as an extraordinary gift – the gift of being the only one who is everything to another human being. She felt constantly smelly, sticky and filthy. Somewhere along the way, she had become imprisoned in this outback gaol.

51.

Avery's dream.

[Had repeatedly 1955 – 1974 and again in 1982.]

The moon is full and the light a cold blue.

My heart is throbbing in my ears. I'm frozen in her doorway, scared I am going to be forced to watch.

She is squatting in the corner of the bedroom, her back to me, her knees tucked under her chin, rocking her bruises to the surface.

One end of the bedspread is on the floor. A grey mouldy light dusts the edges of her shoulder blades. A lamp is overturned. Her underwear is strewn over the shade, obscuring the bulb.

I open a cupboard to find a dressing gown and walk cautiously toward the corner, gingerly dropping it onto Helen's shoulders. She flinches but does not turn around.

I open another cupboard and find a pair of trousers on its floor. I step out of my own trousers and put this pair on. Musty in my nostrils.

I try to help Helen to her feet, but she shakes me off, still not turning around. 'Who was it Helen?' I ask. My voice is trapped in a can.

'Helen. Who did this to you?

'Are you … violated? Helen?'

Helen draws in a pea of air, as if her lungs are the size of a baby's, as if by inhibiting her movements, her life force, she can become invisible to her assailants, to everyone.

'Are they gone?' she whispers. Another breath. 'Are they gone …..'
Her voice sharpens. 'Avery, are they gone?'

'Yes Helen. They're gone. I should get the doctor. Call the police. Will you be alright?'

No answer comes. Just the sound of her sharp, shallow breaths, drawn in as if in anticipation of a heart attack.

'Where's the phone, Helen?' Nothing. I walk through the house, turning all the lights on and noticing for the first time that all of them except the lamp have been turned off. No phone.*

'Helen. Where's the phone? You need a doctor.'*

'It's in the cupboard. It wasn't working when I moved in.' Her voice trails off, running away from me through a tunnel.*

'I'm going to go get the doctor now. Helen, will you be alright? I'll be as quick as I can.'*

I can't lock the front door from the outside and I don't want to lock Helen in. I don't even have a key.

'Reverend, don't go. Avery?' She is plaintive.*

Helen scrambles to the doorway, a watery figure, keeping her tieless gown clamped to her chest with hands crossed at the wrists, her palms upwards, her fingers curled loosely as if the tendons have been cut, or her veins drained.

'Please.'*

I stay while Helen showers. I make up a bed for her in her childhood room and then set up camp in the loungeroom. To stay. Until she falls asleep.

Is that Trudy Palmer looking in? The night is a thrash of dark veins sticking to the window pane and Trudy's face seems to be behind them.

Avery had had this dream so many times since Trudy Palmer had written to him of Helen's assault and consequent 'predicament'. It was relentless and damning in its clarity, mocking him for his failings and ultimately, his guilt. It always began the same way, changing only at the point where Helen was finally asleep, supposedly calmed by the knowledge she was under his protection.

The variations from this point were all ugly and as his subconscious dragged him painfully through them, Avery's eyes would flit wildly back and forth underneath his lids while the weight of it all would pin his body to the mattress motionless beside Gwen, a slow baste of sweat drenching them both.

Sometimes Avery found himself outside the door of Helen's house, with Helen pleading from the inside for him to stay. Sometimes she would tell him to turn around and go home. Often he would kick the door in to get to her.

Other times he would roam the house as she slept looking for the telephone. He would find it in the cupboard, plug it into the wall and call for help. He would hear his own voice on the other end telling him everything would be alright and he would feel relieved. The voice would then fall an octave, envelope itself in smoke and tell him that the girl was his – to do whatever he wanted to. Even though on some level Avery should have been able to anticipate the words coming, they always stole a beat from his heart.

If he failed to wake himself up, the nightmare would sometimes show him the face of a man sitting vigilant in a loungeroom chair. The features would be indistinct and he would lazily pass over them, his eyes roving around the room instead to pick up clues as to why he was being shown the person within this place. Then the man would rise from the chair and walk through the darkened house. He would walk for a long time, past doorways, past a garden, past a clothesline, even past a freshly painted white timber church with a tall bell tower and swinging bell rope. Then he would find himself in the room where he had put Helen to bed. She would be curled up like a small child unable to wake herself up enough to pull on more blankets against the cold. The man would stand at the end of the bed and stare at her for a long time. Then the voice from the telephone would lick at his ears: *'She is yours. What are you waiting for?'*

52.

A ridiculously elegant key.

[September, 1973.]

Gwen collected the two suit jackets – a grey, fine wool and polyester one and a satin-finish deep navy one – and their matching trousers from the back of the armchair in the sitting room. As was her habit, she draped them over her arm.

She walked to the kitchen to collect her keys from a hook inside the medicine cabinet, using her free hand to whip up the contents of the toaster she had cooked and forgotten earlier in her rush to make the drycleaners in time for same-day service. She took a bite. The toast was cold and rubbery and she scowled.

The mantle clock back in the sitting room chimed the quarter hour with a solemn but somewhat tinny authority and Gwen swept down the hallway into the bedroom for a final check. On the bed, she spotted the edge of one of Avery's waistcoats protruding from under a pile of fresh sheets.

With less care than she had taken with the first two suits, Gwen grabbed it up and tossed it on top of the jackets still on her arm. The chink of what sounded like coins falling to the floor flicked lightly off the floorboards as she crossed into the hallway.

Casually, she looked to see if the denomination was high enough to bother picking up, only to discover Avery's key at her feet. It was a ridiculously elegant one given the plainness of the desk it belonged to.

Avery had chosen to have the desk made to order when they had moved from the rectory to their own home. He had given instructions for a broader-than-usual top and a smaller than usual plain light blue leather insert in the forward middle section of the desk. It had originally formed a striking contrast with the dark wood stain but had softened as the stain faded. The insert was decorated with one thin gold line on its perimeter, on the advice of the craftsman who had argued that it would add style.

There were three deep drawers on either side of the desk – the top one on each side significantly shallower than the two below. On his modest income, the commission had been a big deal, yet the extra expense of putting a lock on the top left-hand drawer had not been open for discussion.

Gwen looked at the small, blackened brass key, with swirling metal curves forming a rather elaborate figure eight on its head and four separate protrusions of various lengths from its short stem. She thought briefly of putting it on top of the desk and continuing on her way to the drycleaners, some twenty minutes away, but on impulse slipped it back into the pocket and returned the waistcoat to the end of the bed.

After dropping off the suits, Gwen spent the morning doing the food shopping – a light one for milk, bread, tea and some cooking sherry which would inevitably find its way into the one crystal glass that she had liberated from a gift set of four. Gwen fought off the urge to buy a more expensive spirit in the vain hope that it would limit her tendency to sit in the kitchen and drink by herself when Avery was occupied in his study and Kate had similarly closed the door on her mother.

By the time she had collected the dry cleaning and returned home it was after eleven. She put the groceries away, enjoyed a cup of tea sitting on the back step under the breeze-tickled lilac nipples of the blossoming wisteria and, refreshed, headed back to the main bedroom to change the sheets.

Her eye was drawn immediately to the dark waistcoat, stark against the pale floral quilt. It had her fingerprints all over it. The deed was half done already. Gwen struggled to resist the temptation of searching through Avery's secrets.

If I asked him, he'd say it's only church business. What rubbish! As if he would have to lock those away from me.

She picked up the waistcoat and moved it onto the dressing table, making sure it did not get soiled by making contact with the upturned shoe brush that Avery had left there yesterday and Gwen had refused to move. She noticed that the silk covering of one of the buttons had lifted, revealing its crude plastic origins.

I'll have to mend it before it goes to the drycleaners – and empty the pockets before it goes into the sewing basket.

With that thought, Gwen gave herself permission to remove the key, putting it in her own slacks pocket.

By the time Gwen finished changing the sheets, the last of her planned chores, she found herself at a loose end and her resolve not to pry severely diminished.

I should confirm that it's actually the key for the desk. If it's not, I'll just hang it up in the medicine chest and ask Avery about it when he gets home. No harm done.

Gwen approached the bureau with the step of a functionary, her expression open, fortifying the illusion of her innocent intentions. And then she turned the key. Waiting a few moments until she got the courage to pull the drawer open, Gwen hoped she would feel foolish. She wanted to see those small leather bound ledger books, with a ribbon separating the pages on which Avery had last made a notation – something as simple as a generous donation, with perhaps a scribble in the margin as to a possible recipient and a question mark. She thought she might see their wedding certificate. Perhaps that was where Avery was now keeping the photos of Kate he had stubbornly removed from the bookshelves after she had married.

The drawer slid open easily and dropped forward as the weight shifted. It was messier than Gwen thought it might be. There were a few ledger books and signature stamps, Avery's dog tags from the war and, she noted with a rush of affection, a letter her father had given her husband the night before their wedding, welcoming him to the family and rather formally placing Gwen in his care.

Gwen refolded the letter and put it back in its yellowed envelope. She would have abandoned her search at this point had the drawer slid back into place as easily as it had opened. But the corner of a manilla folder had become wedged between the drawer and its housing at the very back of the cavity. Gingerly, she tugged on it.

It came free suddenly, spewing some of its contents on top of the other paperwork in the drawer. Instinctively, she looked up toward the door. Its space uninvaded, she turned back to the folder. There was an old black and white photograph, a mugshot image of a girl who appeared to be a few years younger than Kate. She was dressed plainly in a pinafore with a white undershirt and had a wilting face. Gwen flipped the photograph to see if there were identifying marks on the back. There was something written in faded blue fountain pen ink, most likely a name, though it was illegible, and a date that was more clear: March 14, 1951.

The typed paperwork inside the folder identified the girl as Helen Muldoon, who had been admitted to the Benevolent Shelter for Women it seemed, several days before the inscription on the back of the photograph, several months pregnant.

Why would Avery have this file?

Helen Muldoon? Wasn't that the name of the girl from Kimbanyon, the one Avery sent to her aunt's after her parents died? No, the grocery shop people took her on. I'm sure the name was Muldoon. She had a baby?

Gwen leafed through the file, skimming for information. She locked onto a piece of paper, a copy of the original, its lettering in blue. There was a date – 24/08/51 – the date the girl in the photograph's baby was said to have been born.

How did Avery get this file? Why does he keep a photograph of her? Why didn't he tell me she got pregnant? How did this happen? That poor girl.

Gwen flicked back through the documents to find anything else that might give her some answers. There was an address, listed simply as 'Kimbanyon, South Australia'.

Knowing she was unlikely to get access to the drawer again, Gwen abandoned all reservation and rifled through the papers underneath where the folder had been jammed.

Another envelope, fresher and whiter than the others, drew her attention. It was a long, professional envelope, marked to The Reverend Avery Holbrook and stamped in red capitals with the words 'personal and confidential'. Impatiently, she slid her fingers along the seal to find it loosely attached and easily separated.

It contained a handwritten letter. The cursive script was neatly penned at the start with small, attractive loops atop upright stems that flattened slightly toward the middle and end of the letter which was marked by uneven spacing and appeared to have been written with greater haste. Gwen sat down in Avery's chair, wheeling herself backwards, away from the desk and forgetting her initial concerns about being discovered in her husband's fiercely guarded sanctuary.

There was no signature or name identified on either page declaring the author, but the tone suggested this was someone on familiar terms.

The letter spoke of passing on a 'burden', of 'more grief than you can imagine' and an orphaned girl deserted by those charged with her care. Despite her eagerness, Gwen read slowly, sometimes taking each sentence into her head three times to make sure she was comprehending the meaning as it was intended.

It's about this Helen Muldoon.

By the time she had had wrapped her mind around the author calling on Avery to find his 'moral courage', Gwen's wrist was bereft of strength, the paper as heavy in her hand as a bag of unwanted kittens weighed down with rocks in order to be flung to the bottom of a river. The air in the study was stifling. The garden was a pulp of grey through a smeary window. Gwen steeled herself to read the letter again, this time determined to take in the detail.

'Dear Reverend Holbrook (Avery),
'I am sorry to inform you of the following matters now, when the issues they raise might seem better off behind

you, but I have been around long enough to know that unanswered questions can be like a cancer, and I wouldn't wish what I've gone through on anyone.

'I have carried around the secret that I am about to tell you of for many years because I cannot in all conscience take it to my grave. So, if my lawyers have done as I requested, you will find the burden passed to you – the person to whom I believe it most rightly belongs.

'Among the many young women you brought into the Shelter over the years was one Helen Muldoon – an orphaned girl who had no one but the both of us to look out for her.

'Helen's child was born poorly and so she was allowed to nurse her for the first three weeks of her life until the child was fit to put up for adoption. This, as you know, is not something we choose to do lightly as having newborns in the Shelter can upset the applecart when it comes to having the girls sign off on adoptions, making it distressing for everyone.

'During this time Helen grew very attached and had to be reminded that she had already agreed to relinquish her baby to a good Christian home.

'Despite the fact that Helen had no parents to support her and it seemed the obvious thing to do, the question of whether or not this was the right thing to do IN THIS CASE has caused me more grief than you can imagine.

'As I write this, I cannot relieve my memory of a distressing night in which I was called on to nurse the Muldoon girl through a fever. Due to the failure of the duty doctor at the Rosemont Hospital to remove the entirety of her placenta, she had become infected and was in a delirious state.

'She was talking incessantly, without any concern for who might hear her (though luckily I had already put her in isolation).

'Despite my best efforts I could not bring her fever down and she was returned to hospital, where she was seen to in a matter of hours before discharging herself and walking back to us at great risk of excessive bleeding.

'Prior to discharging her from the Shelter some weeks later, I brought her into my office and pressed her to repeat what she had said that night. She admitted nothing. But my memory is as lucid today as my shock then was profound. In her delirium she had spoken of you as a lover, Avery. She had grabbed my hand and begged me, as if I were you, to come and rescue her and save her daughter. Imagine my astonishment!

'You may think me foolish for believing the rantings of a desperate young woman and, had I confronted you at the time, you may have tried to tell me she was a malicious girl with a juvenile infatuation. But I wonder, as you read this, whether or not you would have been convincing?

'I sat by her bed with a cold washer on her forehead, watching her battle the fever, listening to her calling for you and sobbing in turn. I will never forget it.

'While I am compelled by my conscience to record these events, I will not take responsibility for causing further distress to the child born of such a disgraceful union and dragged into the world by the most uncivilised of surgeons.

'I write now to impress on you the need to find the moral courage you were so lacking in all those years ago to make recompense and do the right thing by this child and her mother, wherever she may be.'

53.

compatible blood types.

[September 1973.]

'**D**o you think it was wrong to hide Kate's adoption from her?'

It may have been only the second time the word was uttered out loud in the Holbrook household since their daughter was brought home for the first time. It rang in Avery's ears like the explosion of an unexpected shell.

He looked up from his desk to his wife standing in the doorway of his study, firing words at him that she wouldn't have dreamed of uttering if Kate was still living with them, even if she had been out of the house at the time.

'What if there is a problem with our grandson and we can't provide a genetic history or donate blood or …'

She had his full attention, a rarity when he was interrupted in his work. It came with a flashing in his eyes that raised up a brilliant blue. Much to her annoyance, it reminded her of how she had been attracted to her husband's fierceness, but the feeling was quickly shunted when he responded with pained restraint.

'Why would you do that now Gwen? How could that cause anything but unnecessary grief when Kate is already unhappy, as we knew she would be.'

Gwen was no longer seduced by the intensity of Avery's eyes, but saw only the glaze of I-told-you-so barely masking a stare that screamed 'none-of-this-is-my-fault'.

You just don't get it, do you?

'Have you ever thought that your negativity might be contributing to her unhappiness? You used to visit Kimbanyon all the time – one of your favourite stops.

'Now your daughter lives there and suddenly you can't fit a visit in. What is she supposed to think? What is her husband supposed to think?'

'We've been through this Gwen. I have a large parish.'

'Alright then; you don't care about Kate, or her husband. What about William?'

'Who?'

'Your grandson,' Gwen spat back at Avery.

Shit.

'Alright Gwen, the name just slipped my mind,' Avery retorted, attempting a belittling tone. 'Now for Heaven's sake come in and sit down if you've got something to say instead of barking at me from the doorway.'

Gwen hadn't expected an invitation to discuss the matter. The days since she had rifled through Avery's desk had been tense. The words of that letter had wedged themselves between her thoughts, the friction leaving them so badly frayed she could barely finish her sentences. They spilled into her dreams and moaned from her mouth, worn out and unrecognisable, refusing to wake her but stealing her nights nevertheless.

Avery had accused her of snoring and with unusual chivalry, had left her to the marital bed and moved himself into Kate's single one, retiring to her room each night for three days now. Exhausted by her own imagination and his indifference, today's confrontation was inevitable.

Gwen took herself to the visitor's chair. In normal circumstances, she would have lifted it by its curved wooden back and brought it closer to the desk from its regular home in the corner. But today, Gwen found herself unwilling to 'seek an audience' with her husband by moving into that proximity.

Avery sighed at the melodrama of her choice, a wearied frown pointedly setting his face as he looked directly at her.

'Gwen, you know I care about our daughter and grandson – I don't know why you would suggest I don't. But I fail to see what I'm supposed to do about any of this. It's not my fault she married a ganger and moved to whoop whoop. It's not my fault that she's bored out of her brain being a housewife and a mother in a one-horse town when she's been raised to think for herself; this isn't a surprise for me, and it's not like I didn't warn you it would happen.'

Already wounded by the implications of the letter to her own marriage, Gwen felt further devalued by the comment.

Because you'd have to be stupid not to be bored by being a mother and a housewife.

Avery sensed the transference in the sallow tweak of his wife's lips – a look of slight incredulity which would normally be followed by a verbal assault so virile it threatened the already tenuous grip of the plaster to the lathe surrounding cracks in the closest walls.

Why does it always have to be about you Gwen?

'You know none of what I said has any relevance to your situation,' Avery offered in a tone as unaffected as he could manage. 'It was important that you be home to raise our child; we didn't know what to expect.'

'And it's important that Kate do that as well.'

'Yes of course … she is to be commended for wanting to be home with William.'

'Oh, now you remember his name,' Gwen drawled with sarcasm.

As she moved toward the door, her desire to confront Avery began seeping away. Depression rose in her like water filling the cavern of an upturned dinghy.

'That's unfair Gwen; it slipped my mind. You're just twisting things to suit your own story and I'd really appreciate knowing what this is all about.'

'You're right of course. Because being right, and doing the right thing is important to you, isn't it Avery?'

'Why do I feel like no matter what I say to that, I'll be wrong?'

'It doesn't really matter,' Gwen said more gently, turning in the frame of the doorway to face him.

'It's just … I've been thinking about Kate. She deserves to know her genetic history now that she's started a family of her own.

'At the very least we should all know if we have compatible blood types – as a precaution for the future.'

'Look Gwen, I can't remember my blood type but if it's that important to you, you'll find it on my old tags. I've got no further use for them. They're all yours.'

Avery moved his chair backwards, stood up to make it easier to pull the key from his waistcoat, and unlocked the top drawer of his desk. Gwen walked towards him, wondering, with each of her four steps, whether or not he would notice her disturbance of the contents.

Avery shuffled through the layers of paper and retrieved the blackened tags from the back of the drawer. He held them aloft over Gwen's outstretched hand for a few seconds before letting the chain drip slowly onto her palm, followed by the tags that clanged tinnily onto the coiled links.

Why she looks so pleased to have those dead meat tickets in her hands I'll never know.

The Reverend relocked the drawer and slid the key back into its slim pouch against the warmth of his girth. Turning back to his wife's face, his own took on an overtly puzzled expression, as if he were examining the deviant behaviour of a stranger to decide if medication was necessary.

'Why are you so secretive?' Gwen challenged him, refusing to be baited. 'Why do you need to lock things away from me in your special little drawer?'

'You know I keep an old service revolver in there Gwen; I wouldn't want a burglar having access to it if you were home alone.'

The answer had come more quickly than Gwen had expected it to, and though she already knew the other contents of that drawer, she felt keenly her husband's suggestion that she had an overactive imagination.

'Now if you're not going to tell me what this is really about dear, I'd like to get on with it; I've got a significant amount of work to do before I can call it a night.'

Avery sat back down at his desk and turned his attention to his mail, using a silver opener to tear through an envelope with surprising relish.

Gwen absorbed the loathing she felt emanating toward her as she habitually did, without response. Avery could turn it on – and off – at will.

When he says it's over, it's over. Just like that. No correspondence shall be entered into.

The pun gave her a sense of having the last word. Avery's dismissive attitude was no big deal. This conversation was, after all, just one more drop in an ocean of marital dysfunction that could be diluted into a less toxic state with an evening drink and sent out on the tide before any emotional banks were overwhelmed.

She turned her back on the Reverend, clutching his tags – one small piece of the paternity puzzle – and wondering whether there was a white wine already opened in the fridge to celebrate.

God help me if have to resort to cooking sherry; it takes almost the whole bottle before it starts to taste good!

At the point his wife was about to cross into the hallway, Avery looked up, his expectation of a final retort unmet. He was mildly concerned that he did not have a handle on his wife's motivation in bringing the issue up.

In a conciliatory tone he offered: 'Gwen, I know it's been a bit lonely for you now that Kate has left home.

'Perhaps you might think about increasing your volunteer work or maybe even doing up an old car for her to come and visit us in.

'Getting back under a bonnet might be fun, or maybe if that doesn't appeal to you, you might want to get involved in the church fete; the committee could do with a good organiser.'

Gwen's slightly bemused expression, as she turned around to face Avery, could easily have been interpreted as curiosity. It put a light in her eyes that unfortunately encouraged Avery to continue on his misguided path.

'I just think you need to find an interest and get some perspective back on things Gwen.'

'You want me to find a hobby?'

'If you like.'

Well then, perhaps I will. Perhaps finding Helen Muldoon and hearing her side of the story might provide me with some entertainment and keep me out of your hair at the same time.

Gwen smiled weakly with the fast dissipating affection of a spouse who knows they have little more to share with their partner. Oblivious to the subtlety, Avery felt satisfied that he had successfully recovered the mood and that the episode was over.

'Would you mind shutting the door behind you, dear?'

Gwen silently scoffed at his poor reading of the situation, turned abruptly, gripped the round brass doorknob and whipped it towards her, letting go just before it slammed shut. She was more than halfway down the hall, her mind already on the contents of the fridge, when she heard the dull thud of a lump of plaster hitting the study floor.

Shame we were both too busy with our hobbies to fix that crack.

The Unravelling. (1)

[September 1973.]

It was late afternoon when Avery woke. He was lying diagonally across the bed on his stomach, a leg extending off the mattress like a random beam on a building site. With a moan, he pushed up on one elbow and rolled over, flopping heavily onto his back and entangling the sheet around his calf, the hair pulling slightly into the twist and the prickle of it making him feel slightly nauseous.

His eyelids failed on their first attempt to open, a sensation he inexplicably likened to having one of Mandelson's loosely knitted jumpers dragged across his brain. The gusto with which he had devoured his long-held store of Barossa Valley reds the night before was coming back to him.

Fractiously, he jerked his leg until it came free of the sheet and suffered the indignity of puffing with the exertion. He didn't remember getting undressed.

He turned toward the flimsy curtains hung vaporously over half-lidded venetian blinds. Light was sliding ambivalently over them and into the room – a pale yellow unattached to either the boldness of daylight or the subtle onset of dusk. Avery stared blankly at it, confused as to the time of day. Yesterday's breath hung over his face. He felt slovenly, his hand lying on the broad expanse of his belly as if it were a recently hooked fish on a pier.

A dead one, since I can't feel my fingers.

He looked across to where Gwen usually slept and rolled his headache into the central depression in the pillow.

The woman hates me.

As if she's blameless! As if I've stopped her telling Kate the truth all these years.

Avery's focus caught on a crack in the plaster that seemed to be crawling toward the ceiling fan.

He wondered if Gwen had considered the fallout of talking to their daughter about her adoption. Afterall, he would still be Kate's father. But Gwen would never truly recapture the sanctity of place in Kate's heart as her mother.

And where will that leave you then Gwen?

Avery allowed himself the slightest of malicious smiles at the thought his wife was opening a Pandora's box that might actually bring him closer to his daughter while pushing her away. Almost immediately it lit his face, he felt the guilt of it pushing on the wall of his heart.

He wondered how much Kate could take.

I refused her the wedding she wanted. Now her mother wants to slap her down.

Avery squinted into the pain building in his sinuses and allowed his mind to kick a can down an alley it had not visited for a long time. He travelled to a Sydney wharf darkened but for a drift of moonlight, smelling of fuel and salt, silent but for the muffled echo of dishevelled marching and the fat, slurpy lapping of jostled water.

He was twelve, in a line with bigger boys in heavy duffle coats, pushing each other's backs to move more quickly down a slippery ramp. Behind them was the ship that had entrapped them for weeks. In front of them was the promise of bountiful food and sunshine. They skidded into each other, grazing each other's heels, surging toward the unknown.

Avery could feel the small brown suitcase slip from his grasp as he recalled an oaf pushing past. He lunged for it, but it bounced open on impact, spilling its contents into the inky waters below.

Avery would lose his pyjamas, a second pair of shoes and his only photograph of his parents in the incident.

Avery rubbed his bloodshot eyes and forced himself to sit up on the edge of the bed, bashing his temple with the base of his palm to dislodge the memories he no longer cared for and instantly regretting escalating his pain.

It was no longer fun being alone in the house and out from Gwen's judgemental eyes. He had left his wet towel on the bathroom floor, turned his back on a boiling kettle and generally contrived a casualness he did not have when his wife was around. But the petty defiance – not only uncharacteristic but unwitnessed as it was – only added to the feelings of frustration and futility that had engulfed him over the past few days.

At the front of the house, the sitting room window revealed a garden, a fence and a footpath all moving in step with passing pedestrians, like a screen print on a loop. Avery blinked the chaos away and headed for the comfort of the kitchen. He sat at the head of the table. A cup of yesterday's tea was distractingly close to his hand, beside it another from the day before. Both had grey buttons of mould floating on milky skins. Crusts from yesterday's toast were similarly withdrawing from civility, flattened between layers of plates and refusing to buffer them.

Avery stretched his leg and knocked over a loose pyramid of empty beer cans on the floor. The kettle whistled, a dangerously low level of water rattling inside the metal, exacerbating the vacuous feel of the house. Though he had put it on when he first moved into the kitchen, Avery had no real desire to drink 'grasshopper piss' as Ron, a coffee drinker, had called it on their first meeting.

He could not shake the chill he felt thinking of Sister Michaels' letter in his wife's hands.

J'accuse! Three turgid pages of it. No court in the land would convict me but I stand condemned anyway. No doubt I'll see you in hell Ursula for the trouble you're causing me now.

Gwen must have discovered the letter, probably at the same time as she stole the photograph of Helen.

But why would she take one page and put the rest of the nonsense back in the envelope?

The day she had confronted him, Gwen had stormed and slammed and then gone quiet. Normally when their arguments hit a wall, it was like a building storm: you knew there was another whirlwind spinning on the other side of the first, waiting to knock you down when you got up. She had slammed the door on her way out but this time the second tempest had dissipated and they had both just gone about their business, she changing nothing but where she slept, and he palpably relieved and unwilling to stir her up again by revisiting the allegations.

Avery lifted the kettle over the granules of coffee he had tipped generously into the bottom of his cup. As he poured out the pitiful amount of water, steam fired up into his face. Any other day he might have felt its scald, but this day he simply doused it with four teaspoons of sugar.

The kitchen fell suffocatingly silent and began to feel hostile, so Avery took his cup and headed for the study.

Perhaps Gwen does deserve an explanation. She would fancy she's been living a lie – the cherished wife of a faithful husband.

Halfway down the hall, the door to Kate's old bedroom was open just enough to entice a wandering mind in. Avery paused, looking for some token of Kate that might soothe him, some echo of a playful conversation or the waft of a remembered look, chastising him for invading her private zone.

The room had changed since she had married; the Spring colours of her teenage years had been replaced by more muted tones. Gwen had moved school books into boxes and lined the wardrobe with them. Kate's pillow had been moved to her desktop temporarily, replaced on the bed by Gwen's, while his wife's dressing gown now lay across the end of the mattress. Her spare glasses were atop the dressing table and an unopened bill was beside them.

Denied any comfort, Avery crossed the bedroom, pushed a limp plant on the sill to one side and slid opened the sash window to clear the musty air. He collected the bill and took it with him into the study. He wondered at his wife, snooping around his den. He could understand her temper and distress at finding what she did, but what he didn't understand was why she had felt the need to pry in the first place.

And what of Helen's picture? Is she carrying it around with her in her purse? Surely not.

What a temptress that girl was. Perhaps if I explain to Gwen that this has all come from a deceit played on me by a wayward girl … a wayward woman … and that I never to meant to …

Even without voicing the words, they sounded hollow in Avery's head.

Isn't that what they all say, when they come to me for advice: 'I never meant to hurt anyone'?

Avery decided to write down a considered presentation of how it had all come about. It would be a letter to match Ursula's, to tell his side, to help Gwen understand, and to let Kate know how much he loved her. Gwen would read it, thrash a little and then mull it over and come back to him. She would be immovable at first – probably choose to stay with Kate longer than she had planned. But then she would straighten the tale and lay it flat. She would leave it in a harsh light until it was drained of colour and embellishment and then she would consider mitigation. And when she had weighed it all up, acknowledging the girl's part in it all, she would forgive him – for Kate's sake.

I know you Gwen.

Sitting at his desk, Avery took a sip of his coffee. It was too strong and too sweet. He put it down so that the base of the cup sat perfectly inside a crescent-shaped stain that he had rebuked Gwen for causing so long ago.

He didn't blame Gwen for leaving. After their confrontation he had barricaded himself from her, building a fortress of bracken soaked with the urine of a panicked animal. And he had been cowering in it ever since. What he blamed her for was her rush to talk to Kate about such an important thing without him.

Avery's weary eyes were drawn along the golden shards of light heralding the onset of dusk that were filtering into the study across the garden, settling on various shelves and tomes. He suddenly remembered his new hiding place for his desk key and retrieved it from behind a book on modern theology.

The drawer withdrew smoothly, the result of regular waxing. Everything he expected to see was inside, except the dog tags. And the photo. He shuffled the contents around and found a few sheets of off-white cartridge paper, embossed on the top with gold lettering spelling out 'Mr and Mrs Avery Holbrook' – part of the elegant stationary set given by Gwen's parents as a wedding present.

The only other paper at his fingertips was pre-printed with the name and address of his church and also seemed inappropriate, so Avery went back to the kitchen to search among Gwen's drawers for paper that she kept for shopping lists and letters to Kate.

The first drawer he withdrew contained neatly pressed and folded linen tea towels. The second was cutlery, which he felt foolish for not remembering, and the third had a plastic organiser in it with rubber bands, paper clips, pencils, pens, a pad of lined paper and a wooden school ruler with Kate's name on it in large capital letters scrawled over and over in red biro.

He took the notepad and the ruler from the drawer and also a heavy-bottomed glass from the cupboard and headed back to the study, turning the lights on as he went in. He poured himself a whiskey at its station on the bookshelf, sculled it and took the bottle back to the desk, his throat still smarting. He arranged the notepad and pen in an optimum position for prose, as was his habit when preparing a sermon.

The end of the pen hovered over the paper, shaking a little. Avery wondered at the movement, inexplicably failing to make the connection with his shuddering hand.

Was it this hard for my parents to write to me at the farm school? What would they have said – 'we miss you. Just write back and we'll come get you'? Mum would have been too drunk to write anything. Maybe life got better for them after they got rid of me and they just didn't feel like writing.

Avery put his pen down and slumped back in the chair, his head dropping on his left shoulder. His sight followed the roll onto the dark grey carpet and blurrily saw it churn and lap as his subconscious painted on it the waters surrounding the SS Sicilian. In the murky slappings, he saw a choppy reflection of himself as a child. He sensed the other boys were already on board. If their parents had changed their minds and come to get them, they would see their hopeful faces on the deck. But he was in the water, under the ramp.

Is that dad on the wharf? He always comes for me.

The man's coat was long. His scarf covered his neck and chin. His hat covered his face. But it looked like him. Was he searching the decks?

I'm down here. Dad, I'm under the ramp. I'm here. I'm here!

Avery felt himself bobbing, up and down. Each time he bobbed up, he hit his head on the slimy wood. He reached out to the man on the wharf but another's arm fished him out of the water and hauled his sodden mass back onto the ramp. He wrestled himself free from the grip and turned back to the wharf, but the man was gone.

Avery could have made himself dizzy with the frantic search for his father but gradually his eyes, tracking back and forth, connected with the edge of the windowsill in his study. Below it, the churning subsided and slowly Avery pulled his gaze closer, settling on the glass in his hand. Without any reason other than to see if there was enough whiskey left in it for one last sip, he tipped it backward slightly. His fingers appeared unnaturally bulbous behind the curve of the crystal.

55.

The Unravelling (2)

[September 1973.]

Gwen approached the door, taking a purposeful breath and straightening up, making her neck tall and taut. She was apprehensive and defensive at the same time, feeling like a schoolgirl who had been truanting and was now coming home to face the music, or a wasteful wife who'd stolen money from her husband to have a holiday, without the bravery to write a note or enough guilt to leave behind a week's worth of frozen meals. As she stepped inside she realised she was withdrawing the key gently and being light of foot. She had to remind herself that she was coming home to sort things out, not to leave him, or because, as a woman of little independent income, she had no choice.

She had not rung Avery during her short visit to Kimbanyon but then neither had he rung her. It had been hard not calling to share what she had encountered when she got there, despite knowing he would be curt and declare it all fixable by bringing their daughter back to Adelaide. She knew he would be impatient and frustrated and not willing to hear her out, but she had wanted to hear his voice.

The passenger train had been comfortable, much better than she had expected, and it was quicker too. Despite the fact that it had still taken the lightest part of the day to get there, the trip had seemed too short to make up her mind about whether or not she should talk to Kate about her adoption and her father's role in it all. The further away she had got from Irving Street, the less sure she was of her belief in what she had read and found in the study that day.

Kate had arrived to pick her up from the station breathy and excited and 'soooooo glad' to see her. She was wearing a pale blue linen dress – the one she had changed into after her wedding reception – but minus the matching shoes. After a hug and a seriously smoochy kiss on the cheek, Kate had lightly tossed Gwen's small suitcase into the back of the ute, which Nick had left her for the express purpose of meeting the train, mimicking a child's pout before asking if that was all Gwen had brought.

When Gwen had told her she was looking forward to seeing how much William had grown, Kate had warned her that he would not be at his best when they got back; he tended to work himself up a bit when she left him, but after a feed he'd be fine to play with and admire. Sure enough, a bellowing was bouncing off the walls of the cottage as they had entered and Kate had responded by shimmying out of her dress while still on the move.

'Help yourself to a cup of tea mum and meet me on the back step,' she had said, her bare back to her mother and her bare feet pounding the floorboards.

As Gwen had pushed open the back door gingerly balancing two cups of hot tea, a seated Kate shuffled her bottom along the top step to let her past and directed her to a small white iron table and chairs that Kate had surprisingly rejected as a spot to breastfeed.

Once seated, Gwen had not known where to look; Kate was bare breasted, her dress scrunched down to her waist. William was feeding on one side and Kate was holding a hand towel to the other breast.

'Oh, no, it's fine,' she had said, when Gwen had put her tea on the table. 'Watch this,' Kate had told her, motioning for her mother to pass her the cup.

To her horror, Kate had dropped the hand towel, taken the cup and pressed it up against the underside of her breast. Then she had moved it forward about a foot and on cue, a thin spurt of milk propelled from her nipple, arced over the intervening space and landed in the cup with a splash. Gwen's mind and mouth were agape, but then, as the arc continued and sometimes changed direction, forcing Kate to move the cup quickly, showing great judgement and barely letting any fall to the ground, she collapsed into laughter.

'Good, huh?' Kate now had her little finger curled high above the cup handle as if she were in polite English society.

'Tell me you're not going to drink that.'

They had dissolved into the moment and stayed that way, in the thin sunshine of early spring, talking about everything. Gwen had updated Kate on Mel's antics in nursing school, having heard about them from Mel's brother who had taken to doing soup van with Gwen's church group as part of his social work course. Kate asked Gwen to have a look at the ute before she left; the timing was out and she wanted Gwen to show her how to clean or change the spark plugs. Gwen confessed to having been 'impressed' by D. H. Lawrence's *Sons and Lovers* which she had read recently, years after being shocked to find her teenage daughter had it on her shelf.

Kate had put William to sleep in the middle of her bed and returned to the step with a fresh cup of tea, her dress still entangled around her waist. They had chatted like friends up until the point Gwen had suggested Kate cover herself up. She had thought Kate might laugh at her own oversight but instead she had exploded in a nasty attack.

'What, because someone might see me? Out here? Look around you mum; who's gonna see me? I can walk around naked all day if I want.

'William only wants one thing; he doesn't care. It's easier for him if he can just grab a feed when he wants. Don't worry, my husband won't see me behaving like an uncouth wench; I get about three days notice when he's heading home. He brings a dust storm with him.

'I can sit here for half an hour and watch him arrive. I could read a book in the time it takes him to reach the house; hell I could write a book, not that anyone would read any book I wrote out here. Do you see a library anywhere? A cinema? A chemist? Anything. Do you see anything at all?

'Wait a minute,' Kate continued theatrically, 'You might have seen our flies; we've got plenty of those. They're sticky – they like to stick in the corner of your eyes. Feel free to take a suitcase of them home with you; in fact take a few into the inner sanctum and see if you can convince the Reverend they're homing pidgeons – God knows they're big enough – and that he doesn't have to bother going to a post office to send me a letter or pick up a phone to call me or be anything but a total bastard to me.'

The words erupted from Kate's mouth in a rotting sluice. Gwen had been genuinely unsure of how to respond. She didn't want to turn the visit into a 'mother knows best' occasion and she certainly wasn't in the mood to defend her husband.

Fortuitously she remembered she had promised to cook her famous chocolate cake while she was there. She suggested they jump into the kitchen while the baby was asleep with such enthusiasm that Kate could only laugh at the blatant attempt at a distraction, tuck herself back into her dress, hug her mother and lead the way.

After birthday candles had been blown on the cake that was cooked using one egg less than usual because of a shortage in the fridge, Gwen kissed her daughter on the cheek and realised that even as they'd been washing it down nostalgically with milk, her daughter had been crying.

Maybe the isolation is wearing her down.

The best she could do on leaving was to offer Kate one small bit of advice, suggesting she might call on her mother-in-law for help if she needed it. She also invited Kate to return to Adelaide for a while, to give herself a break and allow Avery a chance to get to know his grandson. Her daughter told her with a sarcastic barb that she didn't wish to put her father out.

The young woman in front of Gwen had been so much more mentally dishevelled than Nick had alluded to in his letter. The house had seemed soaked in malaise – lethargy embedded into every fabric and grain of wood. The musk had dissipated a little when Nick returned with a flourish of eager son-in-law hospitality, but had then settled into the pores of Kate's life again when he left.

But as real as Gwen's concern was during her visit, it bore nothing of the weight it would amass in the coming months, when she would recall her time with Kate, trawl over the detail of her behaviour, pull each word of their conversations apart to try and find the loaded one, ask herself whether she had missed an obvious sign that should have compelled her to take Kate home, or at least recognise that her grandson was at risk.

On the train on the way home, Gwen believed she had left Kate better off than she might have been – by not revealing her adoption, and not leaning on her with her own fears of her husband's infidelity. If she was honest with herself, she would have been making herself feel better at Kate's expense and, in realising that, she hadn't been able to do it. As for Kate's mental state, she put it down to her daughter going through 'a rough patch'.

The first year of motherhood is such a shock. I don't want to make it harder for her.

As Gwen entered the house in Irving Street now, it was still – as if nothing had stirred through it since she had left. Confronted by stale air, she moved into the sitting room on her right and heaved up the rarely opened sash window. Back into the hallway, she glanced into the study and saw that it was unoccupied.

She went into Kate's old room, calling out as she did: 'Avery?'

He must be at the Church.

Rather than the tension she had expected on her return, the familiarity of place and the need for her to reset its routines relaxed her somewhat. From Kate's room she went to the kitchen, finding a small stack of plates and cups in the sink and a whiskey glass on the table. Clothes and towels littered the bathroom floor. The crush in Avery's waistcoat was almost beyond dry cleaning.

Gwen wondered if Avery would have cleaned up if she'd rung to let him know she was coming. It was a mundane thought – only lightly resting on any genuine curiosity, but in time, she would assign it the weight of an anvil: *If she'd rung, if she'd come home sooner, if she'd forgiven him … .* It was out of character – the slew she'd come home to – but Gwen had put it down to missing her, to being so completely distracted by the thought that she might not want to come back to him that everything else had dissolved in irrelevancy.

If she was a romantic – if Avery was a romantic for that matter – that would have been a valid assumption. The truth of it was that Gwen had missed him, bound as they were now in the deception, and desired only to enlist her husband in uniting their family around Kate. Against the bigger picture, the mayhem she had encountered seemed trivial at the time. It certainly didn't rate as a significant sign that another member of the Holbrook trio was unravelling.

56.

[Friday morning, 14 December, 1973.]

The sun was a punch of bronze pushing up into a hazy platinum sky through crimson-licked clouds. Nick could see it was going to be a hot one despite the lingering ease of the night. His eyes floated lazily over the red, loamy soil and low rises as he watched the landscape wake up.

The boys had been dismantling an old line alongside the Barrier Highway for just a few days now but it was beginning to feel like weeks. They'd begun at Cockburn, 345 kilometres from Port Pirie, and were working their way back to Peterborough, some hundred kilometres out from the seaport. After a night drinking at the local pub, the fettlers were now waking up – some a little slower than others in orientating themselves – at a makeshift camp between two of the fifteen stations they would either be closing or stripping back to tourist status only.

Nick kicked at the skin of a truck tyre to dislodge something that had caught his eye. The translucent peel of a snakeskin, its owner long gone, fell out. Five years ago Davo had slipped one just like it into his swag for a joke. The recollection of it made him feel old.

Only Matt had been up as long as Nick and was now stirring a stick through the remains of a fire to buffer a damper buried and cooking in the mound of coals. The others shuffled around each other, stomping their feet in their boots to wake them up, and stuffing bedding into their kits.

Abruptly the air was cut with the trill of an elegant whistle. Georgio was a young, fit, Italian immigrant who never seemed to suffer from hangovers and was prone to joviality at an hour when most of his workmates could do little more than grunt or cough up enough phlegm to make room to inhale their first cigarette. As the newest member of the gang, it was Georgio's job to get the billies boiling – three of them for tea and coffee and one for porridge. He hung them from a scaffold of tyre levers that he had welded for the task and poked his own fire a couple of times to raise the heat underneath them, whistling all the while.

Once the billies were underway, George (as the other fettlers called him) was free to practice his footwork, annoying the men by shifting and sideswiping stones around them as if he were his hero, Sandro Mazzola, whom he insisted would single handedly lead Italy to its next world cup.

The men pulled up whatever they could find to sit on and waited patiently for their tucker. Matt's damper was a favourite among them. It was a mix of his father's recipe, incorporating a bottle of warm beer worked into the flour to help it rise, and his own additions, including raisins and lemon peel if he could get them. The production was synchronised so that by the time George had filled everyone's mugs with a strong brew, Matt was dusting white ash off the crusty bush bread and breaking it up for distribution. The porridge was an added bonus, available to be spread like a thick butter on their portions or spooned out of emptied mugs where it had been mixed with brown sugar and tinned milk.

Nick had the men packed up and ready to go by six, with George the last one on the back of the truck, having smothered his fire with a sweeping kick of dirt that looked ridiculously like a final pass for goal, and tossed back his shiny black curls as if he were the last great undiscovered talent.

They had a half hour's drive to the worksite with the truck rumbling along beside the shiny steel track that was weaving its way across the country, leaving small townships to shrivel where it diverged from the old one they would be ripping up.

Just a few years before, passengers and freight moving interstate by rail were forced to use a combination of tracks involving the narrow gauge of three foot, six inches, the standard gauge of four foot, eight and a half inches or the broad gauge of five foot and three inches.

Like his father, Nick had been a great advocate for standardising the network, arguing that the country would only prosper when its rail infrastructure enabled goods to be transported to major ports without the strain and expense of gauge changes. It had taken more than a decade, but the extension of standard gauge, which could take heavier loads than the narrow one, now connected the capital cities of Victoria and New South Wales and the mining towns of Kalgoorlie, in Western Australia, and Broken Hill, in New South Wales, with the smelter town of Port Pirie in South Australia and potential for vastly increased export tonnage.

But in the same way Ron had struggled to see the romance in diesel engines while knowing the advantages they brought over steam, Nick was suppressing a feeling that something was being lost as operations in the break-of-gauge stations – with their giant turntables directing trains in every which direction – were streamlined. It flattened him to see the smaller border towns where men had met the challenge daily of reloading passengers and freight onto new engines, exchanging bogies or undercarriages of rolling stock with practiced efficiency and unspoken pride, become quiet or bypassed places with their cranes – long necked ghosts tied to the tracks by their past and facing a future of corrosion – standing as silent sentries.

The track Nick's team was tasked with pulling up had been created in the previous century, born from a vision of prosperity inspired by a discovery by station hands (who would become known as the syndicate of seven) on an isolated broken hill in New South Wales. The lease they staked out in 1883 would see the Broken Hill Proprietary Company extract ore worth more than 42,000 pounds, or $6.5 million in today's value, in its first year.

The cargo began in open wagons and was hauled to the border by trains belonging to the Silverton Tramways company. From there, engines and crews changed over to enable it to continue to one of the world's biggest smelters at Port Pirie and from there, ingots were exported throughout the British Empire. By the time the first world war broke out, it was one of the busiest lines in the world, running up to 100 steam trains a day.

Ron had joined Nick and his new bride on the last steam engine to pull a train from Peterborough to Broken Hill when it made its final run in 1970. The Class T Locomotive, one of Ron's favourites, was retired boasting more than two million kilometres under its belt. Seeing how animated father and son became in sharing stories of the Tea and Sugar and legendary gangers that no doubt had been originally overblown by Ron, Kate realised for the first time that her husband's ties to the railways went well beyond his pay packet.

The work Nick's team had been assigned now, three years later, was not the sort of job he took any pride in. Although it would be an impressive feat, it wouldn't mean anything to anyone in the long run. It wasn't the stuff of rail history or a foundation of economic progress. They were the clean up crew and while recycling was worthwhile, it would not become widely espoused for at least a decade.

As the truck pulled closer to where their work had left off the day before, the fettlers were greeted by two imposing diesel electric engines – NSU class locomotives in their distinctive livery of maroon with a silver stripe. They had been designed to work in high temperatures and dusty conditions on the narrow gauge line to Central Australia and were now ironically being put to use to dismantle the track they were built for.

A workmans' sleeper carriage was attached to the rear of the locomotive positioned to take the first load back to Port Pirie, with the engine's square bullish nose and distinctive circular light pointed toward Cockburn.

The front of the engine was attached to a series of flatbed wagons, the last of them fitted with rail-removing wedge sleds with two overhanging steel cables connected to large metal claws. The claws would tear up the tracks as the locomotive dragged them in reverse, ripping the steel from the sleepers in its wake.

The men set about getting the machinery in place, with Nick doing a quick calculation in his head to work out how many loads it would take to stay on schedule if they stacked twenty lengths of rail (at 39 feet each) five deep as they had done the day before.

Barry, the driver, warmed the engine up and then hit the air horn, deafening the men unnecessarily to let them know he was ready to go. The claws were lowered to the rail, connecting with a clang. Once hooked under the edge of each line, the cables were drawn tight and the engine muscled up and reversed with the heave of a farmer pulling a trapped horse from a muddy dam. The claws ruthlessly carved up the tracks, filling the air with dust clouds and the sound of creaking metal violently unloosed from its moorings.

After a significant length had been lifted, the fettlers got to work with blow torches, melting the bolts in the fishplates that joined each section of rail, then pounding the plates with mallets until the track separated into loadable lengths.

Nick was in awe of the logistics that had brought this operation together.

A digger had been converted to stack the steel evenly. It straddled the wagons like a jockey on a platform with giant legs arching over the edges, its wheels gliding along the length of the train on its own specially mounted rails. When the track was ready to load, the claws would be withdrawn and the driver of the digger would lower the shovel to the ground where the men would channel the tracks into specially fitted grooves on its underside. The driver would then raise the shovel, put the digger into reverse and haul the tracks up onto the wagons. Because the digger was not powerful enough to pull the weight of the steel alone, a winch had been mounted on the flatbed closest to the train engine, with its heavy cables running the length of the wagons, travelling under the digger platform and connecting with the rear of the shovel. As the steel was lifted, the winch operator would have to withdraw his cables at the same speed as the digger driver would reverse so that the cables remained taught and the operation smooth. Once in the chosen spot, the digger driver would free the track from the shovel grooves and return to the end of the train to collect more, with the winch operator loosing his cables to follow.

Nick was expecting to improve the number of rail lengths loaded per day now that they were more familiar with the interactions of time, speed and weight involved in the operation. Much of the team's success depended on those balancing on the edges of the wagons. Theirs was a precarious job walking up and down on the edges of the wagons, signalling the drivers at each end to halt or continue in order to ensure the tracks were stacked in the most stable way and the cables did not become overly slack.

At one point, George was forced to leap off a middle wagon when a length of track shot out of the base of the shovel and speared towards his ankles. In some ways it was lucky it was George; his athleticism saved him. In slow motion his stuntman-like roll into the dirt would have been as pleasurable to watch as any feat on a sports field, and George no doubt would have taken pride in its execution, but the cuts and scrapes on his face and arms from landing on the ballast, which had spread thin and wide with the ploughing of the claws, were brutal and the accident had left him shaken. Despite this, Nick had decided to leave him on the wagons, reasoning that no-one now would be more conscious of safety than him and besides, imagine if someone who wasn't a soccer star had been in his position; they'd be legless by now, wouldn't they? No one could argue with that.

By early afternoon, the men had completed one full load, looking sharper than the day before despite the rising temperature. The last wagon, accommodating the wedge sleds and the digger, was unhitched and left to be hooked up to the last wagon of the new engine and the first was sent on its way. Nick called a break, shielding his eyes with his hand to check on nature's clock. At one thirty the sky was an unbroken blue and the sun too luminously white to bear looking toward.

As the men sat now in the narrow strip of shade beside the remaining engine parked in a siding, tipping canteens of barely cool water down their throats, there was a sense of holding their own against the thickening air.

Nick didn't want to leave the men too long contemplating how draining the afternoon would be and took it upon himself to boost their morale, directing his opening salvo to the most optimistic among them.

'That was some acrobatics you pulled yesterday, mate. Keep your eyes peeled today; we don't want that kind of stunt two days in a row!'

Nick got an amused snort from Matt and a 'steady on boss' from Mother – a fifty-something, overweight and sanguine fellow who got his nickname from his ability to produce decent rabbit and kangaroo stews at short notice and had his reputation enhanced by his attentiveness in picking out the ballast from George's shoulder and cleaning up his wounds the day before.

George looked confused.

'What is acrobatics?'

'You know – like in a circus,' Matt told him.

The young man looked almost whimsical.

'I was seeing a circus once, in Milan, with elephants and women with big bouncing boombas riding white horses.'

'Bouncing boombas, eh? Well I don't think we can top that on the job,' Nick laughed.

'Not unless Mother wants to show us his,' Davo chipped in, ducking in anticipation of the bigger man's response.

Mother grinned menacingly to reveal the most appalling teeth and got to his feet.

'Yeah go on Mother, show us your man boobs,' Barry teased, looking up from his mug for the first time and drawing Mother's attention from Davo.

The heavier man sized up the skinnier one and decided, perhaps because of the steely look in Barry's eyes, not to thump him. Instead he minced comically back to his upturned milk crate, turned and sat down, cupping his chest fat in each hand and puckering his lips at Barry provocatively.

Matt snorted so loudly his cigarette dropped out of his open mouth to his feet. As the men continued to laugh at Mother, Matt darted into the dirt to pick it up and was forced to draw back hard to reignite the tightly packed tobacco into a crinkle of light.

It was too much for Nick, who couldn't get the smell out of his nostrils and reached into his top pocket for his chewing stick. He slid the mashed up twig into the right side of his mouth, letting the end rest on his lower lip. As he rolled it over his teeth like a cow chewing its cud, he scanned the group.

'Where's Wattley?'

Pete Wattley was a truculent, dried up character with sinewy arms, knobbly knees, a beer belly that looked so out of place on him he could have been pregnant, and a comb over that snaked across his tanned leathery skull in three white strands that came together in a long, thin ponytail that lagged like a fraying rope between his shoulder blades. He didn't know how old he was, or chose not to tell anyone because, though he looked ready for retirement and seemed to complain about the railways incessantly, he couldn't imagine what he would do with himself if he was forced to give the life up.

Of all the men, Wattley seemed the most reluctant to tear down the stations, often declaring them a 'lockup' job rather than a knockdown, though Nick suspected it had as much to do with saving his back as it did to do with respect for the men who had built them, or the few towns that were declining because of the new line now passing them by.

'Gone walkabout,' Barry said, winking at Duggie, who'd worked with him in Alice Springs. 'For a quiet piss.'

Mother explained that the man had a certain medical condition that made pissing difficult and he wouldn't expect him back in under 15 minutes.

'Medical condition, eh,' Nick repeated in a somewhat doubtful tone.

He tilted his neck toward his shoulder on the left side and then to the right until it cracked.

'Fair enough.'

The heat was crackling underfoot and pushing heavy against the men as they rose to get back to work. Within seconds of leaving the shade of the engine, sweat had pasted their shirts to their backs. Duggie, who operated the digger, shed his shirt, his dark skin oblivious to sunburn. A warm wind buffeted his back in sporadic puffs – like the feathered breath of a curious cow. With elbows protruding from his tall lanky form, he rolled his shirt up into a bundle and tossed it back to where Mother was packing up the mugs and water canteens.

'Don't expect me to do your washing dickhead,' Mother retorted but got nothing but a one-sided smile out of Duggie, who used his words sparingly, and sometimes spoke Pitjantjatjara to Barry, who understood a surprising amount of the Western Desert language, having grown up around Aboriginal kids.

Wattley emerged from behind the second engine, an empty enamel mug in one hand.

'D'you bastards leave me any tea then?'

Nick turned to him.

'Smoko's over Wattley; we're back on the job.'

'I had to take a piss,' Wattley said matter-of-factly, 'and now I'm gonna have smoko.'

'Look Wattley, we've got to make a couple of loads a day to get this job done in a week. It's hot as crap and I need you back on the winch.'

Nick tossed a water canteen at Wattley, who let it hit his chest and fall to the ground despite having been a fair footballer in his day.

The two men stood staring each other down, 'till Wattley spoke slowly and pointedly.

'Every smoko, I'm gonna take a piss and have a mug o' tea. You got that? Now I generally do my business away from where I eat but if you'd rather I save time by doing it all in the one place, then have it your way.'

Wattley defiantly undid his zip and winced as he urinated on the ground, the curve of it ending as close to Nick's boots as his own. He sighed with a mix of discomfort and relief as the steam rose from the intermittently dampened dust. A virile pungency perforated the air.

'Jesus Christ, Wattley.'

The wincher shook himself and then did up his zip, without taking his narrowed eyes off Nick. He then spat an enormous dollop of phlegm to the side of the pool of urine which was already evaporating in the heat, a patronising contempt for the boss who was almost half his age unfurling along his upper lip.

'Now just so's you know, I'll be takin' my tea around 2.30 and I won't be back on the winch 'til 2:50, unless I need another piss an' then I'll be a few minutes longer 'an that.'

Nick opened his mouth, but the recalcitrant already had his back to him, hoisting himself onto the wagon to work out the half hour or so left until his self-designated break.

'It's me entitlement – nothin' more,' Wattley rolled over his teeth, the words lost to everyone but himself.

57.

A morning sunshower.

[8am, Friday, December 14, 1973.]

Kate slept late into the morning, her baby breathing steadily beside her despite his face being partially covered by a sheet after a long night of flailing with colic. Long Dog had woken on the verandah and extracted a chalky mutton bone from under the house in lieu of being fed. An hour later he had given up ferreting for rabbits, flopping back down and allowing the flies to trek across him without opposition.

Kate pulled away from Billy slowly, attempting not to make a depression in the mattress that he might roll into and wake. Having successfully extracted herself from the bed, she looked at the sheet over Billy's face and decided that, as it had been there most of the night and had not caused him distress, it could be left there for a while longer. Besides, at nearly six months old, he was capable of pushing it aside. She walked barefoot onto the verandah, easing the wire door gently on its testy hinges.

Since dawn, the last of the muttony pink clouds had dissipated and the view had flattened, the skyline merging into the dirt and the dirt absorbing any element that had previously had a contour into a soft rippling heat. She stared out at the horizon, her head empty, feeling only a little anxious that she might lose her peace and quiet too soon. She stepped back into the house for a shower, walking past her bedroom with flat feet.

She turned the water on and watched it flow thinly from the showerhead into the bath at its base. After years of denial, the desire to immerse herself began to take hold until, with quiet defiance, Kate plugged the water's escape. She climbed in and stood under the shower, letting the liquid cascade over her head and pool around her feet.

When she was totally drenched and the water had risen almost to the stain that ringed the enamel, she lowered her tired body awkwardly into the water and stretched out. Kate watched with bemusement as her nightie, forgotten in the spontaneity of the moment, floated just above her stomach and legs. She left the shower running and turned her face upward, closing her eyelids to the drizzle of a sun shower.

Seduced by the fact that the underground tank had been filled the day before and that her crime was unlikely to be discovered for some time, she relieved herself of the burden of conscience and felt an almost erotic pleasure as she skimmed her fingertips across the rising surface of the water, skipping them like pebbles across a fairytale brook.

58.

Go find the hand.

[3pm, Friday, December 14, 1973.]

As he crouched down on the wagon's end to see what progress Nick was making, Duggie's leathery face was blasted by a hot wind and his eyelashes crusted by the fine sand riding it.

Everything had stopped. Matt, Mother and Davo were standing in a huddle with their backs to the spitting plains waiting for Nick to finish scraping the compacted dirt out of the runners on the underside of the shovel with his pocket knife.

Squinting against the bluster and shielding his face with his hand, Nick looked up at Duggie from his squat beside the shovel.

He called up, strengthening his voice to counter the wind.

'Is that shovel as low to the ground as you can get it?'

'Maybe go another inch or two,' Duggie shouted back, 'but that'd be 'bout it.'

'Give me a couple of minutes then get back up there and put her down as low as you can.'

'I don't think she's gonna take the extra weight much longer boss,' he warned, his words vaporising from his lips.

Nick had decided to speed up the loading of the last train for the day by stacking longer lengths of dismantled track across the wagons. He had been concerned about the strain on the digger but was confident that the winch would adequately compensate for it. So far it had worked well, with less time wasted on the mallets, fewer trips up and down the flatbeds and Wattley managing the increased tension on the cables without complaint – for once.

During the course of the afternoon, 39 foot lengths had been stretched to 78 foot for the second haul and this final load was being fed into the shovel in 117 foot lengths. Giving just enough at the fishplates to be drawn up onto the wagons without snapping, the two long lines of steel arced up onto the wagon as if they were streams of spaghetti being sucked up. The new method was saving them significant time, with George and Matt bludgeoning the already strained connections on top of the wagon while Davo and Nick worked on feeding the lengths ripped up by the claws into the shovel.

Before the wind had picked up, they were starting to get ahead of their target but pellets of dirt, floating like snow, were getting into everything now. Nick bent over and spat a mouthful of dust toward the ground but was forced to wipe away a smear of phlegm from his cheek after it caught on an incoming gust. He waved at the huddle of men to get their attention through the haze. They ran over to him, heads down and shoulders hunched against the spray.

'We're gonna finish the load, but go back down to 78 foot,' he ordered, battling to be heard against the roar coursing around them.

The men leant into the wind, marching purposefully back to their posts, George tying a large white handkerchief into a knot at the back of his head and spreading it over his nose and mouth at the front.

Duggie nimbly swung himself back into the digger cabin, shaking the sand loose from the thick wire of his grey-streaked chocolate curls and then blowing it off the controls. The shovel clunked against the ground, Duggie tipping slightly forward in his seat and edging the digger jerkily to the very end of its track to level it up.

Nick watched Matt separate the stretch of lifted track in its middle, mentally swinging each blow of the mallet with him until he could begin feeding the section into the base of the shovel with

Mother on the other side doing the same thing. He knew he was adding at least a couple of hours to the operation by reducing the lengths.

'Righto, Duggie,' he shouted back up at the cabin, waving his arm to get things going. The track went up with a jolt and the digger began to reverse along its own rails.

On the edge of the flatbed, George squinted as the thickening wind darkened everything around him. He looked for the digger through spread fingers. When it emerged, it was almost upon him. He turned to look back at the wincher at the other end of the wagons, and could just make out the dark shape of Wattley hauling himself up into the cabin.

Where the hell has he been?

George looked at the cable. It was slack. He yelled something at Wattley who had already assessed the problem and was changing gears to increase the tension. Wattley couldn't see more than a few feet in front of him.

Is that the Italian? No ... Bloody hell.

The cable was still slack. Wattley couldn't see the digger – couldn't see anything up the other end. The winch groaned. The cable pulled taut. A figure disappeared off to the left of the flatbed, swallowed up by the maelstrom. Another was running toward him, shouting something.

There was a crack like a gum tree exploding in a fire, then the whirr of a mast coming down. Wattley recoiled instinctively, saving himself from the lash of the steel cable that whipped through the cabin window, missing his face by a bare foot and showering him in glass.

A howl cut through the channel of dusty debris between him and whatever unlucky bastard had gone down on the flatbed.

At the other end, the digger, no longer tethered by the wincher and weighted heavily at the front, lurched toward the precipice of the last wagon.

Duggie leapt from the cabin seconds before it careered over the edge, landing with a thunderclap that reverberated in the dark plume rising around it.

Nick ran beside the wagons calling for his crew, detritus of the dust storm sticking to his face and collecting in the corners of his eyes and mouth.

He saw a huddle half way toward the engine. When he got closer he saw that Wattley was tearing up a shirt and lifting George's leg to get the makeshift bandage underneath it.

'Merda,' George protested, gripping his thigh as if Wattley might be going to sever his leg below the knee. A thumb of bone was protruding from his shin. His foot was twisted at an impossible angle.

Wattley's arms were a mottle of bloody smears, some redder, some darker. From behind him, Nick saw a triangle of glass protruding from his shoulder blade.

'Hold still,' he directed him, getting a grip on the edge of the shard and drawing it out. Wattley shrugged, causing blood from the newly unblocked wound to worm down his back.

'Just go get the bloody truck will you,' Wattley barked at Nick.

Its edges hardened before his eyes as the truck drove toward him. The dust storm was thinning around it, lifting Nick's hair high above his forehead before tearing over the engine and into the outback, taking its choking heart into the desert.

Matt's face emerged in the windscreen as he passed Nick, heading for the other end of the wagons. 'Oi, I need the truck over here,' Nick yelled, but Matt kept driving, leaving Nick compelled to run behind.

Davo had pushed his way behind Duggie and was now pressed up against the wheels of the last flatbed, holding the injured man's torso upright under instructions from Mother.

'Hurry up will ya, he's gonna bloody die on me.' Davo's voice was pitchy. He shifted uncomfortably underneath Duggie's larger frame, attempting to stop him toppling over.

'Hold him still you bloody idiot,' Mother barked at him. 'Where's that rope?'

Matt handed him a length of rope from the back of the truck. As Mother turned around to receive it, Nick saw immediately that it was intended as a tourniquet.

Bloody hell.

The state of Duggie's arm, severed several inches below the elbow, was ghoulishly mesmerising to him for the slightest of moments.

It's chewed up; it's, oh God, it's completely gone …

Mother pulled the rope tight around Duggie's forearm, blood simultaneously spurting into his face.

'Fucking hell!'

Duggie, who was thought to have been unconscious, began to moan, bringing Nick back to his senses.

'Matt. Get the others. Go find the hand!'

59.

[Late morning, Friday, December 14, 1973.]

I n the soft patter of the shower spray on the bathwater and the misty droplets lightly settling, pooling and sliding over her languid limbs as she pushed ripples to the edges and waited for them to come back, a kind of music was becoming apparent to Kate.

It was an ethereal sound, with no distinguishable voices or instruments and so many entwining chords it might be thought of as a hypnotic hum, thickening and thinning as it fell in curtains. The circling harmonies infused the water like a reviving oil, filling her nostrils with a cleansing vapour and permeating her through every pore. It had a soporific affect on her muscles, providing the strangely comforting sensation of melting.

Kate's fingertips, lightly pocking the surface of the water, had risen with her arms to the height of the bath rim. From her slumped position with her head resting on the end of the tub, she reluctantly pulled herself up enough to turn off the shower to prevent an overflow. The music stopped abruptly with the last sprinkles, filling Kate with a sudden and overwhelming sadness. Spontaneously, she scrunched up her knees and slid under the water hoping it could still be heard beneath. She closed her eyes and held her breath, attempting to entice the unearthly symphony by stirring the water.

When she came up, disappointed, she found the silence profound, as if she had been given a taste of something extraordinary and its cruel withdrawal had left her life mute. Unwilling to move, unwilling to test whether she was able to move, Kate slothed sullenly in the cooling water until her fingers and toes wrinkled.

Outside her oasis, the air hung low. A fly crossed Long Dog's nose and tumbled off in a daze to land on its back and make the only noise in earshot as it began a futile spin on the uneven boards of the verandah. It was the hungry grumblings of the baby in the end that touched Kate's brain like a poke from a stick, injuring it and scabbing it in the same amplified intrusion. She braced against the imagined pain of a sudden migraine and took a few moments to connect herself with the furniture of the bathroom and the noises of her home, remembering she was in the bath and that she had left William alone in her bed. If the ends of those thoughts had been soft and waxen, they may have bonded in a sensation of achieved relaxation and readiness to return to the needs of her child, but they were frayed by the erosion of doubts and came together like white noise bouncing off the sides of a stainless steel bowl.

Kate stood up and teased the plug out with her big toe. The nightie that had been weightless now sealed her pores like the skin of overheated milk. On the second pull, the straps broke, but the garment still clung, the neckline now cutting across her engorged breasts. Fractiously, Kate rolled the baste of her nightie to her ankles and stepped from it. Impulsively she turned the shower back on, but the bang of the pipes and the shrouding of her hair over her ears didn't mask William's cries. Every fibre of her was now taut – her mind an electrified space.

She stepped out of the bath, wrapped a towel around her, tucking a corner of it into her cleavage and storming toward William's now stumbling bleats. The visible portion of his face was a red, bulbous cushion of flesh. His ears were filling with tears and his arms were flailing against the swaddle of the sheets.

Kate extracted her baby from his swaddle and picked him up. She thought to calm him first and feed him after she had got dressed, but once William's hands touched bare flesh, there was no stopping him. He swivelled in her arms, flipperscratched at her chin and dragged the towel aside to get his fish-popping mouth to her nipple.

With one arm cuppling a full nappy, Kate awkwardly secured the loosened towel around her waist. Cradling William now – the greedy suckling quieter than his wailing but more visceral against her chest – Kate took herself to the verandah and sat on the edge.

Other than Nick and sometimes his pickup crew, only Sorrell ever came to the house, sometimes to bring groceries when Kate ignored the need and often just to check in on her, but she hadn't visited for weeks, probably deterred by Kate's frostiness.

With William tugging at her and occasionally butting her breast like a lamb at the udder, Kate resigned herself to sitting there until the end of the feed. She let her knees separate as she pulled the towel out from under her buttocks to bunch under her elbow cradling the baby's head and felt the release of a familiar odour.

My whole body lactates! I'm like this giant leaky, smelly orifice that weeps every time Billy looks sideways at me.

Kate looked despondently over William's now bulging belly, to the bottom step. Dozens of ants were darting erratically, sometimes bumping into each other as they crossed paths on the worn concrete underneath her feet.

How did my toenails get so long? I look like a Yeti.

Long Dog appeared from under the house, wagging his tail even though Kate seemed not to notice him. After a minute of giving her his broadest smile and nudging her under her elbow with his surprisingly moist and dusty nose, he was tickled by the sweet smell of milk and phoofed on both of them with a shake of his head.

'Go on, get out of it,' Kate said half heartedly, though the wave of her hand sent the dog trotting off to the back of the house.

William was feeding more gently now, milk leaking thinly out of the corner of his mouth as he dozed off between suckles. Kate's mind left the ants but failed to find a next rung to leap to, so it lay on its back, waiting for a thought as someone might wait for cloud formations, to entertain it. She was as invisible in her own story as she was in everyone else's.

After a time, William fell asleep and a premise did come to Kate.

I could sit here with him on my lap all day, and nothing would be displaced in the world because of it.

Over the next hour, Kate was fooled into believing time had slowed down, the sun was not burning them and the breeze was a sign that recovery from her inertia was possible.

Slowly, she began to realise that there was movement in the palette around her. She craned her neck forward to peer with greater focus on a tumble of wolf-grey balls dirtying the horizon. They were too low for clouds, yet they were not whirly whirlies either. She looked up. The sky was no longer a milky grey but was inking and squirming.

A drop of rain touched her forehead – a gentile forward scout marking the trajectory of the drought-breaking furore that was about to descend. As she marvelled at the sensation (having not seen rain since she moved to Kimbanyon), the charcoal clouds soaked up every shadow in sight.

Kate gathered William up in her arms and stood up.

Long Dog had returned excitedly to the front of the house and was barking at the sky, doing a half jump with every thrust from his throat.

In a resounding echo, the sky barked back. Thunder tore upward through the wolf balls, now alight with shock and indignation, before crashing to the ground and rumbling underneath the house with a tremulous roar.

William's eyes sprung open. Stupefied, he threw up – a curdled, variously custardy and watery bile that collected in the horizontal hollow above Kate's collarbone, before spilling over onto her breast and coating the nipple that William had simultaneously grabbed with his hand.

'Holy crap that hurt!'

Kate delicately but firmly levered William's fingers out of their lock and lowered him onto his back on the verandah, deftly pulling the towel out from under his head as she did to drop it underneath him.

The rain was now pelting against her back, spicing the air in her lungs and appearing to come out of her mouth as steam. She ran her fingers over William's pudgy chest and tummy, making imaginary tracks in his oily skin on her way to stripping him of his heavily soiled nappy.

The baby seemed to be enjoying the diffused rain splintering over his mother and misting on his face. Blinking but not upset he was jerking his arms with that short sharp motion that children have when they are happy and liberated from their clothing.

Kate suddenly thought of the dam – how it was probably filling like a swimming pool. She saw herself gliding through it, weightlessly, free as a bird.

'God damn it Kate, you can't just up and leave a baby like that.'

She rushed inside the house, slipped into one of Nick's singlets and a pair of pyjama shorts that were hanging from the bathroom door and Dunlop sneakers that she'd left at the base of the sink.

She flew out the back of the house into torrential rain. Unpeturbed, she grabbed her bicycle and ran with it to the verandah to find William wriggling with delight under the cover of Long Dog whose nose was energetically investigating the muddy moat around his bottom.

In one swooping motion, Kate picked William up and bundled him into the plastic wicker basket on the front of her bike. He would lose most of the morning's feed as he bounced along under a tumultuous, bucketing sky – a vicarious passenger on his mother's wild ride, Long Dog running alongside.

60.

Screamin' on the back o' that truck.

[3.45pm, Friday, December 14, 1973.]

An extraordinary strength could be drawn from Barry Marcombe's deceptively scrawny arms when he put them to work and he was able to uncouple the wagons in record time. He set the engine ready to reverse as the men carried George and Duggie like loosely strung hammocks between them into the accommodation van, the slash on Wattley's shoulderblade expelling a thicker flow with the exertion and awakening a clutch of blowflies from their post-storm stupor.

It was Matt who had found Duggie's hand. He had stumbled on it some twenty feet from the fifth or so last wagon, coated in dust and only given closer inspection because it had maintained a lumpy silence when his boot had shunted it under a bluebush. With a mix of relief and repugnance, he had picked it up by the thumb and walked toward the men, holding it at arm's length in front of him, his face turned away and barking that someone had better 'take it off me'. There was some relief that all five digits were intact.

It had been wrapped in a clean singlet (from George's kit), and put in a lunch tin, sandwiched between two water canteens that barely retained a chill but were better than nothing in 113 degree heat. It remained in Nick's care, between his feet, on the carriage floor, as he sat on the edge of Duggie's bunk.

'You gotta talk to him, keep him conscious,' Mother informed the men as the engine gathered speed.

Nick had never really thought about Duggie's age but riding with him laid out in the carriage, he noticed how the man's skin crinkled around his knobbly knees and barely coloured the tendons behind them – how the skinny legs that protruded from his baggy shorts were those of an old man.

In the end it was George, suffering from his own wounds, who reached out to him. On a bunk opposite Duggie's, a portion of his bone sitting up underneath the shin bandage like a badly pruned tree branch, George was a pallid ghost of himself. The oldest of eight children who sent money home to Italy to support his siblings every month, he instinctively assumed Mother was talking to him in instructing on the care of his workmate. He rose on one elbow and leant toward the older man, the blood draining from his face, his eyes struggling to maintain contact.

'Lie down mate,' Nick ordered George. 'I got this.'

'Duggie, we're going to meet the flying doctor,' he said in an unnecessarily loud voice.

'They've been talking to Barry and we've strapped you up like they told us; they're gonna try and save your hand but they want us to keep you awake. Duggie?'

'Ask him something,' Davo suggested. 'Once I got knocked out at footy and my gran just kept asking whether I was gonna get MVP that season and telling me that she hadn't seen nothin' super special about my game that meant the coach would pick me for it.

'All I wanted to do was go to sleep but she made me so mad, I told her every play I could remember that had got us goals and how I made 'em happen.'

'Yeah, well, thanks for that, but I don't think Duggie plays footy; he's sixty if he's a day,' Matt retorted. 'And as for you,' he added, grinning, 'I'd like to see what bush pigs you played that made you look like an MVP!'

Nick couldn't help laughing at the remark, but it was Wattley, who'd been sitting on the floor of the coach at the end of the small carriage, his back up against the door apparently asleep, who came up with an idea.

Without bothering to open his eyes, he muttered in the quietening carriage: 'Ask him 'as he got a girlfriend or a wife.'

'Probably both, eh Duggie?' Davo ribbed.

To their surprise, Duggie responded.

'I gotta daughter.'

The words came out clearly but were cut short by a rasping cough. A white drained tongue emerged from of his mouth and brushed haltingly across his bottom lip.

Nick grabbed a water canteen, lifting Duggie's head to help him drink from it. His boot knocked the lunch tin at his feet as he turned. At the same moment the carriage jolted over a rough bit of track, causing everyone in it, bar Wattley, to stare at the tin, picturing its macabre contents while willing it to remain unseen.

'Tell us about your daughter.'

Wattley demanded a response from Duggie, whose eyelids had closed again despite the heaving of the carriage and the water that had spilled over onto his bloodied chest.

He rolled his head away from the canteen and spoke to the men without opening his eyes.

'She be like her mother … but I never see that woman again. Tjaka.'

The men looked at Barry.

'He says that's just the way it is.'

Duggie turned his face back to the other side of the carriage and the men exchanged glances again.

'I gotta sleep now.'

Nick put his hand on Duggie's shoulder, withdrew it quickly with the realisation that he was touching the maimed limb and then, slightly embarrassed, resettled it gently like a fly returning to rotting fruit despite being swiped at. In the confines of the carriage, the smell of sweat and bloodied rags was pungent.

'Duggie, what about this daughter of yours? Does she live up north? Is that where you're from?

'Duggie?'

The injured man lay motionless.

'Duggie?'

What the men did not know about the only Aboriginal man among them seemed in that moment to be as vast as it had been irrelevant just a few hours before. They turned again to Barry, who shrugged and offered only: 'He's Pitjantjatjara. That's all I know.'

Mother rose from his corner of the carriage and motioned to Matt. 'Help me get him up; he'll sleep all the way to the pickup otherwise.'

Duggie was hauled without any assistance on his part into a sitting position and motioned for the canteen. After a long swig, he looked at the men around him. They were filthy – covered in dust, sweat, blood and exhaustion. He saw, for the first time, the protrusion from George's shin, covered poorly by a makeshift bandange. Duggie felt their eyes on him and, under the pressure of an unspoken camaraderie prompted by tragic circumstances, he resumed his story.

'My sister she rescued that baby from the anthill where the boss left her and she raised that kid up.

'I bin away long time thinkin' they was both dead. I get back to my country and I hear all the children was stolen to the mission. They bin screamin' on the back o' that truck but no rescue come – all the stockmen was away with the cattle.'

Putting it into words had drained Duggie in a way he would think later was worse than the blood loss. He closed his eyes. His voice trailed.

'All the stockmen was away, like me. An' them chil'en, they send them far away.'

'Hey Duggie,' Nick prodded as he watched the older man fade, 'maybe we'll help you look for your daughter, when you get done in the hospital.'

The other men looked at Nick, surprised they had been included in the mission and wondering about his sincerity.

'Where'd they take her from mate?'

Duggie's response was barely audible.

'Dry Creek.'

61.

Give it to me straight.

[Saturday, December 15, 1973.]

'It's Kate, son, she's been taken to hospital. The baby's fine. Kate's fine. They got caught in the storm, that's all.'

Ron looked over to his wife as he waited for Nick's reply, the chord of the telephone stretched around the door frame from its usual spot on a hall table.

Leaning against the kitchen bench in a pair of old jeans, Sorrell was nodding encouragingly at her husband, simultaneously willing him to sugar coat the news and ashamed to be complicit.

Nick had been handed the phone across a semi-circular bench of standing height surrounding the nurses' station at the Port Pirie Hospital. He looked across the head of the nurse who was now seated and reading a colourful women's magazine. She had brassy dyed hair, with a rambling track of grey along the part line. Her colleague was bending over to get something from a bottom drawer to her right. Her blue uniform pulled tight across her back.

On the wall behind them was a calendar that snagged Nick's attention as he looked up, with a naïve depiction of tree trunks and deer with stiff legs.

Ron's voice broke through the forest.

'Did you hear me Nick?'

'Nick?'

'Yes Dad! You said Kate and Will were caught in the rain and now they're both in hospital? You didn't tell me what happened.'

385

The nurses exchanged looks. Nick turned his back on them, stretching the telephone chord to its limits to give himself some imagined privacy.

'She just got caught up in the storm mate,' his father said with false surety. 'There's no bones broken or anything; they just want to let her rest for a bit.'

'Right, because rain makes everyone tired,' Nick said with unexpected sarcasm.

Ron fell silent.

'What about Will, Dad?'

Standing in the hall doorway where the morning light from the kitchen had not yet reached them, Ron shot Sorrell a pitiful look that sat incongruously on a face weathered by years of being set in a determined countenance. She returned it with an understanding smile but nodded sharply toward the phone to bring him back to the conversation.

'We've put him in your old room; he's sound asleep.'

Nick was feeling a little short of air, the adrenalin of the previous day having deserted him overnight and the air conditioning in the hospital leaving his mouth dry. Most of the last four hours had been spent by George's bedside, occasionally allowing his eyes to wander over his swollen face – bearing a gash that would no doubt leave a brutal scar – and the cast on his elevated leg, as he sat in a chair squeezed between the patient's bed and the window on the hospital's fifth floor.

He had tried on a couple of occasions to leave George's bedside and check on Duggie, but exhaustion had disrupted the integrity of the thought before his limbs could move and his subconscious had let him off the hook by registering the intent without an audit of its actual strength.

So Nick had wiled away his waking hours in a state of comfortable numbness, occasionally looking down over the intersections on the edge of the town centre. Cars would drift in and out of the traffic light spheres falling on dark roads, the colours of their roofs transforming as they were bathed in red, amber or green.

Eventually he had given in to sleep only to be plunged back into the nightmare of his day.

He dreamt he was a boy again, travelling with other children by rail to a promised seaside holiday. They were in a comfortable carriage with green leather seats and brass luggage racks. They had been excited and kneeling on the cushions, watching the world go past through large clean windows. As the journey went on, the bushes and towns and people in the fields had begun to go by faster and faster as the sun sank behind them.

Railway booms dropped and lights flashed as the train had charged through towns. Finally it slowed and a sense of excitement had filled the carriage as it approached a station. There was a commotion on the platform and several people around a man who was laid out – long and still. Nick had peered into the lights on the platform. The man was on a stretcher. His face was shrouded by greying curls and his feet were bare. Those around him were waving at the train. Railway men. Suddenly the engine had picked up speed again, lurching forward so quickly that all the children who'd been on their knees looking out the windows had tumbled to the floor.

The same scene had played out at the next stop and the next stop after that. Again and again the train had slowed down and then sped up. At Peterborough, a woman had run along the platform yelling for the driver to stop and then she'd thrown something at Nick's carriage. It was a doughy hand and it had hit the window immediately in front of his face, sticking briefly and then sliding off as the train had gathered pace. In its wake, a thick trail of blood had run in a horizontal line across the carriage window to the end of its frame.

Terrified, Nick had taken off through the train. It had seemed an eternity that he was running, leaping perilously between endless carriages and then suddenly time lagged and he was at the last wagon. The sound of a joyous whistle had flowed under the door. Then a thud that had lifted the floor of the carriage under Nick's feet. In a panic, he had turned to the door that led back to the other carriages but it was stuck.

With a wrench it flung open but on the other side a man in a bloodied butcher's apron was standing in his way. It was Wattley – mealy and menacing, under the hover of blowflies.

'That's just the way it is, son,' he had said. 'You fucked up.'

When the nurse had come to alert Nick to his phone call, she had found him slumped, with his head against the window pane. His eyelids had been bubbling with the nightmare and his face was sweaty despite the coolness of the room. She had pressed her hand on his shoulder gently, but had startled him all the same. It had taken him an awkwardly long time to orientate himself and slow his breathing.

As he held the phone now, and the comforting sound of his father's voice came to him, he found himself having to suppress tears.

'Nick, are you still there son?'

'I'm here, Dad. Where did they take Kate?'

'Your mother and I took her to Tarcoola. Dr Bartlett was staying over doing his rounds. He let William come home because your mother's a nurse but he wanted to keep Kate there a bit longer.'

Ron looked at Sorrell again to strengthen his resolve.

'They're probably going to move her to Adelaide Nick, so she can get proper care.'

'You still haven't told me how she got injured… or even what the injury is, Dad.'

Nick couldn't believe his father was being coy, when he was this beat. He turned back to the dumb deer legs on the calendar wanting to yell at someone. The nurses were gone.

'Stop beating about the bush Dad, she hasn't been herself since Willy was born. I know that. You tell me what happened or put Mum on.'

62.

A disenchantment.

[August 31, 1974.]

It annoyed Gwen that she could find herself lonely without Avery, but it gutted her that her departure seemed incidental in the course of their relationship, signifying to her that it was a love that had not died, but waned.

After 29 years, she asked herself, how does a bond that made the abominations of war bearable, that crossed a country as harsh and beautiful and vast as Australia, and raised a child with such devotion, peter out without so much as a whimper? When did the plaster-shattering indignation transform into this gormless resignation? Doesn't the discarding of a marriage built on constant companionship and mutual revival deserve to be witnessed by unruly emotions?

There aren't even wounds to lick.

Gwen had not had to consider income or housing before making the decision to go. Her parents had sold their beautiful home in the hills for a generous sum that enabled them to buy a low-maintenance unit in an inner suburban court for their old age and a second one that they envisaged might suit their much-missed granddaughter and her young family should she wish to return at some stage and continue her education.

'She had so much promise, our Kate,' Mr Dalana had lamented.

The Dalanas weren't told all the sordid details of Gwen's disenchantment with her husband, just her decision to find herself some peace without him. They offered to let her stay in the Quandong Court unit, rent free, as long as she maintained it and gave Kate the option of residency should she come back to Adelaide.

At first, Mrs Dalana believed that her daughter would go home within a few weeks, but as Gwen spent more time on her visits talking about the hanging baskets she had put up on the eaves, the fold out table that fit perfectly into the kitchen nook and how homely the place was becoming, her parents began to realise that their daughter was growing in contentment by the day.

Gwen rang Avery several times in those first few weeks ostensibly to check on him, but also to hear if the slight of her departure sounded like something more in his voice with the settling of it. Mostly Avery responded to her calls with a dialogue that was measured and blunt and a tone just short of curt. On several occasions he asked her how she intended to feed herself and pay the bills. With a cynicism born from years of lowering her expectations, Gwen was incapable of giving such questions the credence of genuine concern. She heard everything he said as either patronising or bullying, motivated by the self-serving need to bring her back into servitude, offering board and lodging up as fair reward for meals and the occasional sexual favour.

He's like a cat pawing at a half-dead mouse, not caring enough to kill it and only mildly amused by letting it live.

Sometimes in the silence, they each felt the sensation of earnest words clawing their way tentatively to the front of their minds, but pride or a sense of vulnerability prevented them ever reaching their lips. Generally Gwen was left blinking away tears and furious. Generally Avery would straighten his clothing and leave the house dumbfounded and embittered.

It was four weeks after she gave Avery her phone number, and three months since they had seen each other, that he made his first call to his estranged wife. It was a Wednesday, traditionally drycleaning day in the Holbrook household. Gwen had just come in from potting a cutting from a favourite shrub that she had cheekily snipped from the garden of her parents' former home. She didn't bother to wash the dirt from her hands in order to catch the call, and reached the telephone on the fifth ring. Avery had determined he would hang up on the sixth and was caught a little off guard.

He did not identify himself, opening the conversation with a cough that sounded remarkably like a clearing of the throat, followed by a carefully-worded query about how their daughter Katherine was faring. A little taken aback, but encouraged by his interest, Gwen lied and told Avery that his daughter had been asking after him also. He had promised to consider accompanying Gwen on her next visit to the clinic, but added that he didn't possess a shirt without grubby rings around the collar these days.

Buoyed immeasurably by the prospect of reconnecting Avery with Kate, Gwen offered to pick up his white shirts and return them in a fit state for visiting. It would have to be the following week, as she was working as a manager at St Mary's Opportunity Shop. And yes, she was aware of the embarrassment that working for the Catholics would cause him – naturally that's why she had done it! Gwen was sure Avery had stifled a laugh.

On Saturday morning, Gwen took the bus to Maple Avenue, a block from Irving Street. She had brought with her the cutting that remarkably had already begun to bud in its clay pot.

It'll look better in this garden anyway, and, who knows, perhaps I will come around and tend to it. Avery and I might get together for dinner once a week. Once we see Kate together … I hope he doesn't tell Kate I've left him, just to punish me … she doesn't need to know about that yet.

There was no one to answer the door when Gwen arrived at No. 7. She spent a few minutes looking to the windows on either side of the entrance and saw nothing to indicate her visit had been remembered. The sitting room blinds were open, with a film of dust on the glass barely inhibiting the reflective glare of the morning sun. The curtains were still drawn on their bedroom window.

The day was already threatening to become uncomfortably hot. Gwen stood before the door in a neat knee-length royal blue skirt and short-sleeved light grey top with thin orange and blue stripes. Though she had stopped short of dying her hair to cover the greys, she had recently had it bobbed and she was keen to see Avery's reaction to her new look.

After rapping the old bronze knocker – a ring through a lion's mouth – and noting that a screw was still missing from one side of the lions' mane, Gwen stepped back from the door to wait. She still had a house key but it seemed more respectful of the new arrangements not to use it. She spread her toes inside her modestly heeled shoes to prevent the sweat building between them and ease the swelling. She rapped the knocker again, wiping a finger from her other hand under her lower eyelashes to clean up any smudges from the makeup she had bought especially for the visit. When no answer came on the third rap, the cynicism that had waned over the past few days began to return.

I'm such a fool. I can't believe I offered to pick up his washing. Was he even serious about visiting Kate?

The old key turned easily, though the door was more difficult to push forward than she remembered.

My God, Avery. What have you been doing in here?

A rank odour pervaded the house.

Gwen vomited slightly onto her tongue and reluctantly swallowed it down. She knew that Avery's housekeeping skills weren't the best but this was vile! She went straight to the kitchen; it was not disastrously chaotic and it was not reeking the way the front of the house was. She looked back down the passage. The study door was ajar. Gwen dropped her handbag at her feet, put her hand over her nose and mouth and started toward it. Several large black blowflies drunkenly bobbed before her face as she entered the room. Her stomach erupted between her hastily spread feet. Luridly, her mind swung back to the unravelling of a tarp – to the stench of melting skin. Each of Gwen's heartbeats tripped over the last and got up only to be knocked down by the next.

63.

A breath caught.

[One week earlier, August 24, 1974.]

That mark had always irritated Avery. He had been so engrossed in his work that he had neither heard his wife enter nor leave his study. He hadn't even wanted the cup of tea, but she had brought it all the same, steaming and without a saucer. By the time he looked up, the tea was cold and the leather insert on his desk bore a permanent scar – nothing an agile imagination could interpret as 'character', but a milky crescent that bled into an unsightly blob.

Avery smoothed his hands from the middle to either end of the desk as if he were settling a sheet over a mattress, as if he might sweep away the blemish and everything else scratching at his mood. His fingers were hot and kinked with rheumatism but his palms were cooled by the passage.

Shards of late afternoon light filtered through the sash windows around him, illuminating random spines in his extensive library. Avery's gaze was drawn to them one after the other, as if following a bird around the room. It occurred to him that it was a dull and meandering collection – competing theological ideas interspersed with uncompromising dictum, bush ballads, largely unwanted gifts from parishoners, and war-time memorabilia.

The room was devoid of artwork or photographs, revealing nothing (beyond a reading selection) of the personal life of its chief inhabitant. Avery had lost his only picture of his parents when he was a boy. Packed in his suitcase by his father before he left England, it was gone by the time he had set foot in Australia.

Over the following years, his belief that he had been abandoned by them and an annoying compulsion to imagine expressions alternately confirming or denying this fact, had muddied his memory. It existed now as little more than a throng of grey faces looking up from the dock, their owners shifting weight from one foot to the other, slapping the cold from their coats.

What remained of his parents from that day had been conjured by his imagination. He recalled his mother burying her wet cheeks against the chest of his father, who had one arm around her and the other aloft in his direction – a wave among hundreds.

Avery had removed from display the beaming faces of those whose lives his wife seemed to hold him personally responsible for: Kate, Nick, the grandson he had never met, and of course, Gwen herself. Occasionally, he would exhume the frames from drawers or nostalgically peek at those that had been retired, face down, on shelves around the study. But there was one missing from this selection that had never been hung or positioned affectionately for the pleasure of its viewing. He could see it vividly – a mug shot of a girl on the brink of adulthood, her vacant face rising from the sepia as if emerging from a muddy river into the ink of a harried bureaucrat's stamp.

As Avery sighed, a broad roll of white flesh eased over the top of his drawstring pyjama pants. He noticed it with mild disdain and swivelled his chair to face the window for some respite from himself. The colours of the garden melted in his eyes. Shrub branches were bunching and parting in an erratic wind. Staring at the greenery lightening and darkening with each pulse – occupied him for the next twenty minutes until the vivid red spider-like flowers of the Grevillea Dimorpha clipped the focus of his gaze, appearing as they were to be gathering into the shape of a child's dress. With a perception so faint it held for barely a few seconds, he could see his daughter's pale, skinny arms in the long, silvery leaves, rising and falling as if she were jumping joyously over a sprinkler.

It's her birthday today and she doesn't even know it.

Avery heard a breath pass his eardrums and wondered where it was going. He tasted the salt of tears on his lips and left them to meander in thin rivulets through the stubble on his chin. His gut curled in on itself. A greasy strand fell across his eye.

Avery ached for his wife and daughter.

I should never have taken Kate out there.

He watched his fingers fatten and slim through the whiskey coating on his glass as he tilted the liquid from side to side. It hit the back of his throat with a chill. He swallowed deeply, catching air and spluttering the last of it onto his stomach. Avery returned to the bottle, his eyes blistering. He filled his glass a third full, and watched as night seeped out of the shadows.

A little more than half an hour later, the darkness denied him a view. A washed out, sulky reflection bounced back from the glass instead. Beside it the glowing orb of the desk lamp appeared as a phantom moon. Avery's thoughts were settling into an annoyingly circular motion of loss and loathing, regret and defiance. He lay his head on the desk to quiet them. The coiled spine of an open notebook pressed into his left temple, the ink of an unfinished letter softening in the drool that rolled lazily from his mouth as he slumbered.

Despite the intense heat of the lamp on his face, it did not wake Avery over the next thirty minutes. But perhaps it could be blamed – as the whiskey, fear and regret fermented inside him – for the return of his nightmare. But this time it would be different. Rather than evolving in a surreal and suggestive way, it would begin like a thunderclap and sustain itself in high definition – vivid and gratuitously tactile.

As in previous dreams, Helen's naked body was before him on a bed – the sole piece of furniture in a dark and deserted house – but now he had no time for the landscape. His fingers, curled around the base of the whiskey bottle, began to lift and stretch in turn as his subconscious luridly traced her outline. She was smooth and popping. He ran his fingers over hers as she cupped her own breasts, almost bursting from beneath the spread. Avery wanted her with the painful ache of a teenage boy and she responded with the palpitations of a virgin eager to become a sexual being.

She rose up and twirled in front of him, a siren before a lusty sailor, and then fell back on the mattress, bouncing momentarily towards him and receding again, pulling him down with her like the rip of a tide. Her soft flesh, her voluminous tangle of hair, her flat stomach, her long thighs, her warm breath parting the hairs on his bare chest like a summer breeze in grass – the dream gave him everything.

Avery felt himself to be young, virile, rippling and in command. He pushed himself inside the girl and felt with exquisite pleasure a slight resistance and shudder underneath him. He moved forward in her slowly, a molten heat coursing through him every time she gasped. They writhed together as he thrust himself more quickly. She pressed her fingertips into his shoulders as he came and made whimpering noises. Then her thighs relaxed around his hips, her knees falling almost to the sheets.

Perhaps it was extreme exhaustion, but for whatever reason Avery's subconscious began channeling his thoughts – his dream – through multiple points of view. At times he coldly witnessed the scene – now seeing himself naked, now seeing his buttocks protruding from a crumpled army chaplain's shirt. At other times he was intimate with it, feeling the friction of every rub, every graze.

If the anomaly was a sign that the dream was turning, Avery didn't see it coming. When the girl wrapped her arms around his broad back and buried her face in his neck, Avery gave himself over to the warmth of it without hesitation. And then it happened, as it always did. She drizzled onto his earlobe those words: 'I love you Reverend Holbrook.' With crude abruptness, the face against his became ice cold. His lover's body no longer moved with feline surety but squirmed anxiously underneath him.

His head still heavy on his desk, Avery's erection was softening and the beat of his heart hardening against his chest. His fingers startled from the bottle like the legs of a swatted spider.

Helen was taking control of the dream. She was now on her feet, standing at the end of the bed, looking down on him. Avery saw himself as she might – a middle-aged man, aflop and grossly overweight. Helen was also naked but she was no longer luscious and new; she was a waif with hollow eyes and a vein of blood snaking down the inside thigh of each of her legs. When she spoke, it was as if the words had to be dragged by a hook and chain from her throat – the effort causing her ribs to jostle.

'I waited for you; why didn't you come for us?'

To her side came an old woman, dressed in nursing whites that were far too big for her gaunt frame and glossy black shoes with ridiculously enormous gold buckles. She put one wiry arm around Helen and raised the other against Avery, pointing her finger like an Aboriginal elder directing harm through the point of a bone.

'Shame on you, Reverend. Shame,' she spat.

A hunchback then joined the women, his woollen jumper stretched and dagging around his knees, his soft leather shoes soiled and stained and his eyes shifting from Avery to the girl as quickly as a snake's tongue bursts forth, withdraws and bursts forth again.

'I always knew there was something off about you,' he said in a tone engorged with vindication.

Despite breathing fitfully, the shallow pool of saliva leaking from under his tongue and melding his cheek to the desk, Avery still did not wake.

Finally, a friendly face. A woman in oil-stained dungarees was smiling at Avery as he lay in a full military dress uniform. The relief the sight of his fiancé gave him was immeasurable. Then the others took her hands and the young woman began to age in spasms.

'Why Avery? Weren't we happy?'

Avery dropped his eyes from Gwen's shattered face but instantly regretted it. Hanging onto her leg with tiny fingers was a toddler, barely able to see over the edge of the mattress but staring at him all the same. His whole body shuddered. The sound of the whiskey bottle toppling off the desk and shattering on the floor stirred him slightly but was muffled by the stronger velocity of his subconscious bringing the noisy shuffle of a lynch mob into the room. The faces gathering at the end of the bed were terrifyingly familiar. Avery became vaguely aware of a desire to stand up.

'Am I in hell?'

As if in response, he found himself gripping with each hand, a smooth wooden rail. He was in a pulpit and felt instantly strong.

'When the wicked, mine enemies, my foes and even those that professed to love me, came upon me to eat up my flesh, they stumbled and fell. Even my own child. Katie ... Katie.'

In the dream, Avery had been forceful and impressive, pitching his words to the far reaches of a vast church. In reality he was bathed in sweat and banging his brow lightly on the desk while muttering and moaning. He woke on the anguished utterance of his child's name.

By the time he was sitting up and aware of his surroundings, Avery felt very strongly that he had been speaking with his God.

Was that a test? Did I choose the wrong psalm?

The epiphany that followed was clearer to him than anything he had convinced himself of previously in the wake of a prayer.

Edward, James, Helen. They weren't my enemies.

'They weren't my enemies.'

Avery picked up his empty whiskey glass but, failing to find the bottle, put it down again beside the bible he kept on his desk.

He pressed his hand against its soft, worn cover. He felt nothing.

The scriptures were useless in my hands. I never understood before now. You look after the dead. I was meant to look after the living. That's how we serve.

I was supposed to heal them so they could find You, not serve You up as the answer to everything.

'You wanted me to look after the walking wounded.'

That was my purpose, but I failed.

'I failed the old, the young. I even failed the unborn.'

Timmins confessed to me and I did nothing. I should have marched him into the bush and given his baby a Christian burial. I should have gone to Dry Creek earlier.

I should have baptised that young digger when he asked me to, not waited until it was too late.

I should have stayed with Tenterfield longer instead of thinking of my stomach. I should have realised that James Van de Velt was being driven mad by his mother …

'Is there nothing I have done right in my life?'

Avery's mind was rolling in nauseas tremors, feeding vicariously on pain. His heart was pummelled and exhausted.

I should have looked after Helen.

With unnecessary force, Avery pulled open the drawer of his desk, the key falling from the lock with the jolt. He reached to the back, putting his quivering hand down slowly on the gun. It was cold, its contours hard and uncompromising.

His heart pinched against his chest as he slipped his fingers around the weapon. He found in it a familiarity he had not felt since the war. The shake of his hand eased and his breathing slowed. He lifted the gun to the desktop and rolled his wrist over so that it lay flat on his upturned palm.

It's heavier than I remember.

A second thought crossed Avery's brow like a paper cut. He spun the cylinder. The smell of disturbed dust lifted to his downturned face and he saw it. One bullet. He remembered to breathe and the air came in quickly and deeply. He forced himself to look away from the gun and became transfixed on the guest chair in the corner of the room. When he breathed out, his body jerked, though he was so unaware of himself that it appeared to him as if it were the guest chair that had jumped slightly in his view.

Avery saw a man in a grey dustman's coat move forward on the edge of the wavering seat. He had kind eyes – bold blue eyes that held hope but not promise, overshadowed as they were by drooping lids. His jowls were soft and unshaven, the stubble growing through in both chestnut and grey follicles. A large hand with a wedding ring on it rested on one knee. The other lifted slowly toward him … .

'Papa?'

And then the man was gone, taking his downtrodden look with him.

Avery collapsed back into his chair, causing it to rock a little, his mouth agape at what he thought he had seen. He pushed his jaw shut with the muzzle of the gun as if it were nothing but an extension of his hand and there was no other way to get the job done. But once it was there, he found he did not want to take it away. He pressed the muzzle against his chin until it felt like it might bruise the bone. Then he dragged it down his neck until the metal pressed painfully on the top of his larynx. He looked at the empty guest chair, imploring from it some last strength. He sat upright, pushed himself away from the desk, the chair rolling awkwardly toward the window. And squeezed the trigger.

The flies are mine.

[January, 1974.]

Everything was painted a heavy cream, the kind that looks clammy even when it is not. Walking the broad corridors barefoot in a stiff white nightie stamped with the initials APC in faded red ink, Kate could see only barred windows and doors that opened like those on industrial cool rooms.

Everything seemed to echo. Staff punched and clicked keypads to come and go. Their actions were followed by the sound of a vacuum being broken, which you could hear if you were standing close, and then the clunk of the door closing snugly back into its metal frame. It was a hollow sound that could be heard from rooms away. And it was this sound more than any other – more than the sniffling, the sudden outbursts, the shuffling of slippers and the squeak of rubber soles on the waxed linoleum – that filled Kate's head and squeezed her own thoughts into the corners.

A poem by the patient.

[Included in the file of Katherine White by Dr Aldous Horwell – June, 1974.]

There are dead flies on my mantle
Burdened by dust
Lifeless by choice
My choice
Only I didn't know that I made it.

She's made a career of it
Afterall –
Emily, with her stringy hair,
Plastered in tails on her cheeks,
Her eyes swimming bright in a maudlin face.

Her memories
Dart franticly across them
Like the shadows of children
Running through a corn crop in a storm
Or the witless
Dancing in the trail
Of a funeral march.

She's like a mad woman,
Screeching
Lest she be forgotten as the poet of her age:
'The flies are mine.
'I heard one buzz – like no one else.'

Who does she think she is?
Those flies were there yesterday
And they'll be there
Long after I've stopped
Immortalising them,
Burdening them with the dust
From my rotting core,
Dust that lifts in puffs –
Spores from greying food.

Disturbed by chance,
Now spinning
On their backs.

65.

A magnet for lost souls.

Grimsley had not been a frequenter of the Brooster before that day; he took a great deal of pride in his proficiency as station master and felt himself on duty almost all of the time. He memorised the fortnightly bulletins and filed them according to month – even if they were only relevant to the activities of a certain hour or day – and he kept them until two years had passed, burning them in monthly allocations in an incinerator beside the station toilets. There was not a procedural code he did not know by heart; he was renowned for it throughout the railways.

Grimsley had taken responsibility for the telegraph when the area was connected, being the obvious choice to become proficient in Morse code. He took great pride in manning it more or less 24 hours a day during the war. When the mail service came to Kimbanyon he took responsibility for that too, building pigeon holes for north, south, east and west and a special one for transient miners or railway workers. Though a constant smoker, and often short of breath as a result, he limited himself to a port or a small glass of whiskey at night – *to help me sleep* – and in fifty one years with the railways, he had never had a sick day.

Despite getting on for sixty five, Grimsley had only given up on the prospects of marriage in the last eight years, prompted by the rejection of Miss Muldoon, whom he subsequently took to thinking of as the spinster Muldoon, despite previously admonishing other locals for using the term. Though he could justify the rebuff by acknowledging the age gap – being more than fifteen years her senior – he had been humiliated by it. To spare himself any further pain, he chose to withdraw from his search for a bride entirely.

Grimsley renewed his dedication to serving the families who had become like his own. Initially, as with most reluctantly chosen courses, his manner in doing this was perfunctory, but as the years wore on, it would become something more like quiet resolve and finally settle into something resembling genuine pleasure and pride in service to match his accomplishments as a station master.

He cooked for himself in a slightly battered frypan on a portable gas hotplate. At the mid-point of the week he shouted himself spaghetti bolognese, boiling the pasta in his broad-bottomed kettle and taking care not to let the water disappear and the spaghetti stick to the base because it affected the taste of his tea the next morning. Mostly he pan fried his sandwiches with seriously unhealthy slabs of butter. It seemed ridiculous to him to set up a proper kitchen in the stationmaster's house when he had a portable cooker in his office and preferred to be there around dinner time anyway.

Before that day, Grimsley was only ever seen in the pub when his nephew Hank came to visit him and, on demand, told his uncle of the most challenging or bizarre jobs he had been involved in as a paramedic while tucking into the house special and a pint of beer. When Hank stopped coming, away fighting the war in Vietnam, Grimsely returned solemnly to his hotplate, vowing to wait for his next pub roast until the lad returned. With the news of Hank's death, Grimsley abandoned the Brooster entirely and ate as a typical single person household does – with as little bother as possible and with only a begrudging attention to his health. With his cooking habits as dangerous as they were, it was a wonder the station office never went up in smoke. In later years, when Grimsley's drinking became voluminous, many locals thought quietly that a fire would be the way he'd go out.

Grimsley had never once considered retiring, though he was greatly attracted to the idea of being presented with the railways' parting gift of a gold fob watch, engraved with his name and years that began and concluded his service in a dignified script. He certainly never thought his career would be brought undone by the likes of the Reverend's girl; she might once have been a beguiling whip of a child but, in his view, the woman she had grown into was a dull, skittish creature who made as little impact on the town as tumbleweed. Perhaps that's why Grimsley was so unsettled by the dramatic sight of the figure that came in from the plains as the first torrential rainstorm Kimbanyon had seen for years was subsiding.

He was on the platform, hands on his knees, buckled in a coughing fit. Raindrops were hammering the back of his neck with the prick of needles, a welcome distraction to the drawstrings pulling tight inside his chest. When the fit had passed, he stood up, his eyes moist from the exertion, and his airways cautiously opening for fresh air. As his lungs filled, his eyes were caught by the tangerine and grey streaks of the sunset. The way the sky was moving was a thing of beauty. Grimsley's nostrils filled with the collision of the cooling air and the hot earth. A vapour was rising from the tracks.

It was then, through the sifting of colour, smells and sound, that Grimsley saw a dark form. It was indistinct to him as a woman or a man. The approaching stranger was trudging, bedraggled, and stumbling at regular intervals. Grimsley squinted at the shape until it came close enough for him to determine it a woman on the verge of collapse. She crossed the tracks and meandered with heavy feet, disappearing from his sight as she moved behind the outer edges of the station building toward the town. Grimsley turned toward the archway connecting the platform with the town's expansive main street, and headed for the steps in order to intersect her. He saw her appear from the edge of the red brickwork, one gangly leg at a time. She had shrunk and he realised, with painful certainty, that she was injured in some way.

Grimsley ran toward her, moving at a speed and with muscles he had not engaged for years. The compulsion in him to break her fall was so strong it pounded in his ears. But on the last step down, he fell himself, instinctively throwing his hands forward and embedding small stones in his face as his head hit the ground. The figure was now less than ten feet from him. He pulled himself up, aware of a strong pain in his left ankle as he walked toward her. She was an Aboriginal woman. No – she was smeared in clay, the sweep of it discolouring her breasts and underpants, being the only garment she was wearing. Her hair was matted around her face. Her eyes were wide – unseeing porcelain bulbs. She was carrying something. A baby. Naked. Also smeared in clay. She moaned – a leaky little moan. She dropped to her knees. The baby rolled soundlessly from her arms.

The morning after the storm, the sun streamed down in thin white rays from the centre of a cottony sky, like a waterfall spilling over silver rocks. The corrugated tin roof over the station was lit up in a reflective glare and every home in Kimbanyon carried a smattering of red dust that had been whipped up by the wind and glued to its boards by the rain.

Had anyone been looking for it, they might have seen a strange semicircular smoothing of the dirt not far from the steps of the station. It could have been made the same way as children make an impression of 'angels' wings' – by lying on their backs on sand and moving unbended arms from their sides to their heads – but if that had been the case, only one arm would have been used and only one 'wing' created; the stony surface of this spot had been swept smooth by Kate, who had collapsed onto her side and stayed there while Grimsley had attended to her baby.

While Grimsley, blinking nervously and trying to remember what his nephew had taught him about resuscitation, had put his leathery face to the blue-tinged lips of the infant and filled his tiny cheeks with his smoky breath, Kate had drawn her knees up under her chin and wrapped her arms around them. While the baby had spluttered and spewed up a filth of water and Grimsley had repeatedly pressed and lifted two fingers firmly into the child's chest, hoping not to crack his sternum, Kate had stammered quietly into her kneecaps, 'I'm coming, Billy, I'm c-coming.'

While Grimsley had put the baby over his left shoulder and given his small back a vigorous patting, Kate had remained on her side, her back to them both and her shins moving through the dirt in a rough cycling motion, her legs still pinned together at the knees by her own grasp.

The aberration in the road's surface had been made less distinct by the wide tracks of a four-wheel drive, made when Ron had turned his vehicle on the spot after Grimsley had called him to collect Kate and her baby.

The two men had mustered the crumpled and confused woman into the vehicle – her badly grazed legs leaving a swipe of blood and fine gravel that dissolved into the black of the seats – while Sorrell had wiped the dirt from the exhausted infant with a wet tea towel under the fluorescent light of the station toilets. She was relieved to hear his whimper and overwhelmed by the comfort he took from the simple act of being swaddled and pressed to her shoulder.

Sorrell had sat in the back seat beside Kate, who was huddled inside a blanket, her thoughts flickering in her eyes and restless on her face. Sorrell had all but ignored her, unwilling to confront her own sense of anger or turn her attentions from the grandson she was nestling close enough to feel him puff lightly on her neck, reassuring her with each breath that he was not succumbing in his sleep.

Grimsley would tell Ron later that he had not been able to get a word from Kate when he had pulled himself up from his fall at the station steps. He would recall, with an ashen face, that she had 'stared right through me; like a ghost delivering a child that might just suck the life out of me too'. What Grimsley would keep to himself was that he was irrevocably disturbed by the event because it was, incongruously, the second time he had saved the life of a soul that had wandered randomly toward his platform.

The halting figure of Kate White had carried with it the shadow of another night and another woman who, in his mind, had never left the tracks. Grimsley still felt some guilt about his part in 'interning' the spinster Muldoon to keep her from endangering herself and others, though he knew it had nothing to do with retaliation for her rejection of him in the years preceding. Since the railways replaced her at the store, she had become variously a recluse and a wanderer. No one blamed the railways; she could not have been kept on at the store. Though the door was open, she was often nowhere to be seen and people had been forced to help themselves to goods and leave their money in open sight or catch her another time in order to pay.

There would have been few besides the school teacher Trudy Wentworth who would have suspected that the woman was sitting in darkness behind the folds of the heavy storeroom curtain in the corner of the shop, unable to dislodge a paralysing thought in order to return to the counter to face the world.

Had the spinster Muldoon not gone on, in her hours outside of work, to wander on the railway lines or frighten teenagers making out in the old miners cottage by appearing from dark corners as if she were the living dead, she may have managed to survive somehow – jobless and alone – in her own home without the intervention of the Department of Health and Human Services and the Order to Secretary that would see her deprived of her liberty.

But Grimsely could not have let that summer night in 1968 go unreported. She had put not only her life but the lives of countless passengers and railway workers at risk. He still shuddered to think what could have happened had he not varied his routine.

He had learnt from a recent bulletin that The Ghan, an NR class engine hauling between 16 and 25 carriages of passengers was coming online for its first trip on standard gauge from Adelaide into Central Australia. It had been diverted from its run through Port Augusta and Quorn further west to pass through Kimbanyon and Tarcoola, before heading north through Alice Springs to Darwin.

The original route was built around steam engines and had been dependent on the bore water from the Artesian Basin, but, ironically, water had also been a major drawback to the route, with flooding sometimes stranding the train for up to a week and passengers forced to climb to carriage roofs to be airlifted out.

The new route was a milestone in railway history and despite the fact that the NR class engine was passing straight through Kimbanyon in the dead of night, Grimsley had set his alarm to get up, confirm the signals were set properly and witness its passage. He expected the driver would sound an airhorn and was curious to compare it with the freight trains which passed through on the journey from east to west.

Grimsley had slipped on his navy blue stationmaster's jacket, buttoning it over an unironed shirt, before discarding his long pyjama pants for trousers that he had laid out for the next day's wear. Having confirmed the signals, he moved along the platform with an excited step, the leather soles of his black shoes making a loud clip on the platform, busying himself with pointless corrections to the right angles of notices in the glass display case and the general cleanliness of the public areas.

Finally – at the expected time – the Ghan could be heard approaching. The stationmaster practised an acknowledgement of the driver, tipping his index finger to his head and waving him off again, in the event that he might be seen on duty. As he lifted his gaze back to the track, he saw movement at the point where the platform lights lost their fall.

It took him a moment to discover the outline of the form transitioning from black to white was the spinster Muldoon. The woman's shuffles, to and from the church, to and from the old miner's cottage, to and from nowhere in particular, had become a regular sight, but she had not been seen wandering at night before.

She came into the full flood of the lights as Grimsley heard the first blast of the air horn. She stopped for a split second at the noise, then continued walking. Instinctively Grimsley listened for the sound of the diesel engine slowing down for passage through a town, but he could not concentrate on the machinations of the engine while his eyes were glued to the woman stepping over the ballast between each sleeper with painfully slow deliberation.

She's not moving fast enough. She's not getting out of the way!

Grimsley had called out to her but she had simply looked up at him and smiled.

She's lost the plot. Bloody hell.

Grimsley clenched his teeth, looking at the total lack of comprehension on the woman's face.

Is she worth it?

With instant guilt over the thought, Grimsley had put his toes to the edge of the platform. Coming almost parallel with him now, the woman had turned toward the thundering train. Her feet were planted firmly and she was staring straight ahead.

Grimsley had heard the second blast of the air horn and felt an instant freeze. He had jumped down onto the tracks, his right knee giving way a little with the landing and causing him to fall heavily onto the woman.

The train had been hammering upon them, the rail vibrating underneath them. Grimsely had scrambled to his feet, grabbed the spinster's arm and pulled her up. The bellow of the air horn had reverberated deep in his bones and the urination of fear had soaked his trousers as he had pushed her before him in a dive for safety on the other side.

That night had left Grimsley a changed man in several ways: one of his sideburns was cut through with a hairless scar, he could no longer abide the horns of night trains and he believed every shadow had the potential to become a life staring down an unstoppable engine. They never stood still.

Though Grimsley would be the first to admit to himself that those shadows filled him with apprehension, they also entranced him. Saving a life was the single most important thing Grimsley felt he had done with his own. But some nights, particularly when he took to the Scotch, he wondered whether there was a connection between these women whose minds deserted them, and himself – and he feared that maybe, for some inexplicable reason, he had become a magnet for lost souls.

66.

[August 1, 1975.]

The visitors book at the Adelaide Psychiatric Clinic showed Katherine Gweneth White had just three visitors in the two years and seven months that she was a patient there – her husband Nicholas White, who had a hurried signature, her mother Gweneth Holbrook, who it was noted never circled the word 'Mrs' in the assigned space to the left of the signature column, and a friend who unhelpfully told nurses that she had known Kate in her 'wild days'.

Of the 820 days of Kate's care at that institution, Nicholas White chose to visit on just five of them – travelling to Adelaide just three times in the first twelve months and twice in the remaining 15.

By comparison, her mother, who admittedly lived in the same city, saw Kate on a weekly basis, bringing her treasured poetry books and novels while concealing the internment from Kate's grandparents. Kate's former best friend Melinda Harding (who had married without inviting Kate, and circled the 'Mrs' option in the visitors' book with a very deliberate hand) signed in for a total of eight visits, during which, staff noted, she did most of the talking and often mouthed the words 'poor thing' to them on her way out.

The various doctors assigned to Kate's case (she outlasted three of them) took copious notes regarding Kate's emotional state

411

following each of these visits and recorded phrases such as 'distressed', 'detached', 'unnecessarily cruel to visitor' and 'became aggressive when prevented from leaving with her husband'. Alongside the comments of one doctor, a Dr Horwell, in her file, it was scrawled in red pen 'changes to patient care and medication to be approved by the Director'.

The visit during which her mother told Kate of her father's suicide carried a brief notation and no indication of follow up. According to the hand-written remarks, Kate had appeared 'underwhelmed' by the news. A Dr Alice Blythe put this down to three alternative reasons: Kate was suppressing a genuine response which in this case was a positive sign that she had been learning from her therapy and was attempting to gain better control of her emotions; Kate was attempting to spare her mother further grief by withholding her own (this was also considered positive as Kate had apparently not exhibited signs of empathy to date); and Kate might genuinely not recall her father, his memory being erased randomly in the fallout from the trauma that had brought her to the clinic. In brackets, the author noted that a lack of visits from the patient's father would have compounded this scenario. There was nothing on the page to suggest anyone had made a link between the blood that trickled silently from Kate's nostrils as she slept that night, only waking her up when it flavoured her tongue, and the visit.

The material inside the manilla folder assigned to Katherine Gweneth White was as voluminous as it was obtuse. As a general rule, those treating her were more inclined toward medication than therapy and therefore tended to document her reactions to various psychotropic drugs, rather than observations about her state of mind when she wasn't under their influence.

It was true that Kate had signed a voluntary admission form when she had been at her most vulnerable and had reluctantly conceded that she may have put her child's life at risk, but she found out very quickly that she did not have the same right to check herself out.

So it happened that time passed at an uneven pace, depending on how her medical regime dampened her anger, tussled her nerves or lay her flat. She was left with little idea of weeks or months and only a passing interest in those around her. Only the change of seasons seemed to sharpen her mind.

In the end it was the sixth visit by her husband that put an end to it all. Kate had been in the gardens, dozy from her pills and mesmerised by the challenge of connecting her fingertips with the Spring buds she imagined unfurling onto her skin.

When Nick arrived, the garden was a bevvy of lime-green tips, furry undersides and glowing petals – more alive than most of the poor souls whose treatment often deprived them of a sense of smell and anticipation.

He scanned the faces of those walking, being pushed in wheelchairs or sitting in the sunshine on benches, but did not see Kate among them. In a small garden to the left of the main building, a patient had pushed her way into a large Daphne bush flourishing among weeds and the splayed remains of a red umbrella. The thin branches of the woody bush were bent around the intrusion, the friction releasing a virile perfume. Nick's attention was drawn first to the smell and then to the back of the woman who had ploughed in to be amongst it. She was oblivious to him. He could not see her face and she was completely still in her hospital issue gown, bar the slight fluttering of her fingers. It appeared as if someone had dressed a stone statue and awakened in it a scarecrow.

I can't believe I've left Kate in this place for so long.

Nick moved quickly up the stairs, suppressing a desire to reach out to her, and signed the visitors' book open on the reception desk, with a quick scrawl of his initials. He had been asked to come in to talk about a treatment plan for his wife that required sign off by her next of kin or guardian. After all this time, he had forgotten that he had taken on that role, despite his mother-in-law believing it was her right and his father-in-law suggesting Nick was somehow incompetent for the job.

As if the Reverend took any interest in her wellbeing before that day. I just don't get that guy.

The Director was a man of middle age and average height, whose features nevertheless combined to give him a scrawny appearance. His thin face fell triangularly from a broad, smooth brow crossed almost invisibly by thin eyebrows and crowned by wisps of mousy coloured hair that tufted over ears absurdly framed by bushy, chocolate brown sideburns.

When he spoke, in a deep soupy voice, his unusually long earlobes appeared to droop and rise on the sides of his head. The affect was exacerbated by a tendency to over-emphasise certain vowels, particularly the letter 'e', so that when he said, for example, 'We've taken a fairly eeeeven handed approach to your wife and proffered no punishment to her rather eeeratic behaviour', his mouth stretched unnaturally wide, his lips pulling back to reveal small pearly teeth protruding timidly from generous, overly moist gums.

Seated opposite him in an office crowded with filing cabinets and journals, Nick thought he had seen a lot of men who were as awkwardly put together as this one, but none who could subjugate it with such a presence of superiority.

He listened to stories about his wife and determined them fanciful at best and untrue at worst – stories of her antagonising other patients, scratching nurses when they tried to shower her and throwing food against the dining room wall. There were 'disturbing scribblings' about flies and funerals, he noted, passing a worn page stamped by a Dr Horwell to Nick across the desk. And on one occasion, the Director said, Kate had attempted to drag a baby from the arms of a visitor and had to be sedated.

Confronted by Nick's stony face and active larynx, the Director turned to the large manila folder and began detailing the medications that had been 'administered' to his wife, followed by a dispassionate appraisal of the affects each drug had had on her.

My God Kate, what are they doing to you?

'Ah, yes, we did have some success with prolonged narcosis,' the Director recalled with enthusiasm, his fingers landing on a loose leaf page with blocks of handwritten notes in black or blue pen, each dated separately.

Nick shifted in his seat again, his agitation growing. 'And what might that be, doctor?'

'It's a means of creating total relaxation for the patient's body and mind by depressing the central nervous system – eeeffectively inducing a deep sleep and then keeping the subject in that state for a prolonged period.

'A number of doctors liked this approach with your wife and I personally put her under on a number of occasions.

'But you can see here,' the Director went on, swivelling the page on his desk so that its comments would be the right way up for Nick to read, 'that the beneficial effects were increasingly short lived, and that particular treatment was terminated.'

Nick scanned the page, noting one doctor's comment that it might be worthwhile 'trialling a higher dosage for a longer submersion' to see if the calming affects could be extended to more than a few days.

The Director had resumed his appraisal of the remaining documents in Kate's file and did not look up immediately after commenting: 'And that brings us to where we are now; with the patient routinely medicated, at great cost to yourself and – if we're honest – not a great deal of benefit to her.'

Nick was still reading the comments on the one page in front of him and finding it hard to comprehend that his wife had been 'asleep' for up to ten days at a time, that her weight losses were recorded and her diet boosted in between treatments to allow them to continue.

The Director pressed his fingertips down on the edge of the page and drew it back toward himself without asking whether Nick had finished with it. He returned it to its former position in the middle of the file and closed the folder before addressing the anxious expression opposite him.

'Don't worry Mr White,' the Director laughed, 'we're not out of ideas yet!

'In fact I'd like to offer you a procedure we've had a lot of success with. My own assistant is a convert. She used to get terribly depressed; sometimes couldn't drag herself out of bed to come to work. She's much happier now.'

Instinctively, Nick looked around for the assistant.

'Oh, she's not in today, but I'm happy for you to talk to her anytime. Just a bad cold, I belieeeve.

'Mr White, I'd like to try ECT on your wife. It's a simple procedure; there are no side effects and this way you're much more likely to be able to take her home.

'Otherwise,' the Director paused for practiced effect that succeeded only in causing a buildup of saliva on his bottom lip, 'we're probably looking at a lobotomy.'

Nick felt his whole body tighten.

'Of course, you'll want to know more,' the Director said calmly.

'Eeelectroconvulsive therapy – or ECT – can sound scary but I assure you it's completely safe. Eeelectrodes on the patient's head deliver an eeelectric charge to the brain causing a small seizure. She won't remember a thing when it's all done; in fact it's likely we'll administer it under prolonged narcosis so there'll be no memory of trauma at all.

'We don't quite know why, but ECT smooths things out for people who – like your wife, Mr White – are emotionally volatile and potentially harmful to themselves and others.'

Nick was feeling something like panic – the same sensation he had felt as he ran blindly toward his crew in the dust storm.

'It sounds shocking I know,' the Director said with some amusement before being forced to suppress it at the sight of Nick's face.

'My apologies, Mr White. That was in poor taste; in my line of work, we sometimes forget what is acceptable and what is not. Won't you please sit down?'

Nick was disarmed by the sudden warmth of the Director's voice and returned to his seat.

'Did you know it was Dr Bartlett who referred Helen to us, Nick? He's very well regarded by his colleagues. Did you know he's been published overseas for his work here?'

Nick didn't know what to say, so he let the question hang there, as the director shuffled through a number of files on his desk.

'Ah, this is what I wanted to show you. This is a report a colleague sent me on Bartlett's work with the Veterans' Repatriation Hospital. They've had significant success with a soldier there who seemed untreatable when he first came to them.

'This soldier was a hard case. Eeemotionally, he was completely dysfunctional. But he was working a railways job without too much trouble, so they left him alone. Turned out that was a big mistake.

'He ended up shooting his own mother; they found him sitting with the body days later, professing not to know how it happened.'

Nick was growing impatient.

'What's any of this got to do with my wife, doctor?'

'I'm getting to that! This soldier you see could have been sent to jail for a very long time, but Dr Bartlett convinced them he was unfit to stand trial. Well, having done that, it really was on him to find the right treatment, wasn't it?'

The Director smiled again.

'Anyway, for years this man was medicated but he still terrorised the other patients. It was the shock treatment that eeevened everything out.

'That soldier is now a very happy fellow; he works as a gardener at the Repat – bit of a favourite now I hear.'

Nick seemed deep in thought. The Director closed the folder, stood up and turned to a filing cabinet behind his desk and began flicking through papers.

'We just need your signature, Mr White, and we can get moving with this. The sooner we begin, the sooner we can start planning for your wife to come home.

'You may need to bring her back to us every now and then, of course, but I assure you this is the best thing for Katherine right now.'

If Nick had been in two minds about what he was being told before the Director had mentioned Kate's name, he saw things more clearly after it. Before the doctor could turn around, having found the approval form he had earlier backdated by six months, Nick was gone. He stormed out of the building and vaulted lightly over the broad brick bannister. Remarkably, the woman in the Daphne bush didn't flinch when he landed. Nick slid one arm under her knees and the other around her back. As he scooped her up, her body gave no resistance at all; her head fell silently against his chest.

So light! There's nothing of you.

Nick pressed his lips against the woman's unkempt russet hair, strode to his truck with her in his arms and took his wife home.

67.

Paper cuts.

[May, 1975.]

egret is a complex emotion. In Avery it was the equivocal nature of his regret that pulled him apart, even as he did not recognise it. If he had not married Gwen, he may never have been guided to Kate, who was, in a waning selection of highlights in his life, the best thing to have happened to him. It was Gwen who connected with Kate in the nursery, finding a personality among the dozen or so swaddled babies in three rows of cribs that were, to him, largely indistinguishable apart from perhaps the colour of their hair and blankets.

But then Gwen was the reason he joined the Inland Mission, which led him to the Muldoons and taking responsibility for Helen, who ignited in him thoughts and feelings he had been largely unsuccessful in suppressing for more than two decades. Of course, if he had stayed in the Army, it was possible he would have continued to fail every poor tortured soul that was pushed into his orbit – though in the end he was fairly sure that had been the case anyway, so Gwen could not be blamed for how that had worked out.

When it came to family, Avery's preoccupation with fate and reappraisal, combined with a tendency to over contextualize, had the effect of putting him on the periphery of events, rather than at the centre of them. Because of this he had no clear sense of regret and therefore no clear way to rid himself of it.

Gwen, on the other hand, had no time for equivocation and no room for uncertainty in her life. The only rash thing she appeared to have done was marry the Padre and truth be told she had already considered what life would be like with him well in advance of his asking for her hand, though obviously not with any great understanding.

Her journey toward making peace with herself and her marriage would take many years. It began with a revelation about Betty and Jack. Her dear friends had come across from New South Wales, where they were now running their own Alpaca farm, for Avery's service and were now helping Gwen pack up the Irving Street house. She could not bear to be in it for long periods and had been threatening to 'torch it' since the service, so they had stayed.

As they moved around, quietly folding clothes, taping cardboard boxes and smiling at her generously in passing, Gwen felt a sense of relief and gratitude that she was not having to approach the task alone.

After a while the women gravitated to the same spaces so they could talk and time passed with less melancholy than it would have if Gwen were left alone, until they came to Kate's bedroom. Betty had taken down suitcases of long-stored items from the top of Kate's cupboards and was taking an inordinately long time pouring over them.

'Silly, I know, to keep such things,' Gwen said to her friend. 'You have no idea how sentimental you get as a parent!'

Betty spread several yellowed pre-school art works on top of the bare mattress on Kate's old bed. Surprisingly she passed over the one of a woman with a huge smile on her face in a coffin in the back of a truck, which had been one of Gwen's favourites despite being difficult to explain to Kate's kindergarten teacher. Betty was more interested in the one beside it, tracing the outline of two stick figures – one smaller than the other – in a finger painting of children standing hand in hand in front of a giant tree.

'Kate always wanted a sister,' Gwen explained.

'Here,' she said, extending her hand for the painting, 'we don't need to keep all her great works … maybe just a "best of".'

Betty would not release the one of the two figures. Gwen looked for an explanation in her tanned, lived in face, caressed as it was by hair that had not lost its colour or streaked grey, but simply faded to a lighter brown. She realised with some surprise, as she scanned her friend's features, that it was the first time she had looked into anyone's face directly since she had walked in on her husband's body. It was as if it would be disrespectful of such a horror to disturb the image by challenging her memory with the details of anything else.

Or maybe I just couldn't face anyone.

Gwen couldn't see how overwhelmed her friend appeared to be by the minutia of Kate's bedroom, until she spoke.

'It's hard for people to understand how it hurts; they think because I never got to see my babies smile, that it somehow hurts less,' Betty said suddenly.

'But it's the opposite: I have nothing to limit my imagination with. Every smile on every child is like the one I never got to see.'

It took Gwen a moment to replay Betty's words in her head, crowded as it was by thoughts of her own suffering.

'Betty, what babies?'

She received only a thin smile in reply before Betty returned to the packing, lifting an age-stained cloth doll from a suitcase, a muscle in her jaw popping slightly as she put it into a box marked 'keep'.

What kind of friends are Avery and I that we didn't know?

Gwen put her hand around Betty's forearm, and gently tried to ease a board book, chewed on the corners, from her grip. Betty resisted the attempt but put the book in the garbage bag herself. She mumbled apologetically, 'I'm obviously not making good choices here. I think I'd just like to get some fresh air and leave you to it, if you don't mind Gwen.'

Jack heard the front door scrape along the floorboards and caught Gwen looking anxiously through the open space after his wife.

'Leave her Gwen.'

Jack was holding a bottle of Scotch he had discovered behind a broad backed history of Victoria Cross winners that had caught his attention on Avery's book shelves.

'Betty was pregnant Jack?'

He raised his eyebrows at her and lifted the half empty bottle by way of an invitation.

'It's not too early is it?'

Gwen followed Jack down the hallway to the kitchen.

'It wasn't her fault, but she can't shake the idea that it was,' he said, his back to her as he opened various cupboards looking for glasses.

As curious as she was, Gwen had learned from conversations with people she had encountered while volunteering that silence nurtured a more revealing tale while questions could shut a story down.

She reached into a box below the tea towels hanging off the oven door where crystal glasses had already been stacked and padded with newspaper. Jack turned to see her holding one in each hand and filled them a quarter full with the golden fluid.

'You shouldn't feel any guilt over not being there for Betty,' he said after the first sip of Scotch had stung and settled in the back of his throat.

Am I that obvious?

'She didn't want anyone to know, and, as far as Avery knew, we weren't planning to have a family, so why would he ever think to ask?'

Gwen couldn't hold herself any longer.

'What happened, Jack?'

'We'd gone on one or our adventures, following the tracks of the great explorers,' he began, accentuating the tail end of the sentence as if narrating a documentary.

'We were away for months. But it wasn't such an adventure as it turns out. Bloody nightmare. No explorer ever went to that hellish place, just madmen setting off atomic bombs.'

'Bombs? You were at Maralinga?'

'Apparently the powers that be decided it was a good idea to let them off in our backyard as well.'

'Oh Jack, I didn't know,' Gwen said softly, extending her glass of untouched Scotch to him for a top up.

'No one did. Not the blackfellas, not the whitefellas, and definitely not us,' he said with a lazy wink that drizzled from his cheek.

Gwen took a gulp.

'How did you find out?'

'We discovered Bett was pregnant when we stopped in at a Flying Doctor base to say g'day to an old mate of mine and he picked it.

'Twins was a bit of a surprise though! Bett got quite large while we were away and they were really active – I reckon I saw an elbow glide across her tummy once. That's when we decided they must be boys; one of them was giving his brother a right hook fighting over who would be top dog and come out first!'

The story brightened Jack's voice but the memory was too compromised to hold any joy in his face and it soon clouded. He began packing the crockery on the kitchen table directly into a cardboard box with such a heavy hand that several plates chipped as they landed.

Gwen skulled the Scotch and put her hand on Jack's shoulder to slow him down, partly to show her sympathy and partly to save her mother's china.

'We never saw that elbow, or anything like it again,' Jack continued, with an almost cathartic rush, as if it were the first time he had spoken of it.

'There was no movement. I asked the doctor whether my crazy wife could have done herself some harm trying to break in wild camels and he asked me whether we'd been anywhere near Maralinga.

'At first I didn't get the connection; we didn't get the papers much and it wasn't easy catching the news through the static at Silver Flats.'

Gwen nodded and poured herself another Scotch as the kettle cooled.

'Apparently we weren't the only ones. The doctor said he'd heard of a family who'd walked through a crater seven months after the tests. Their baby was born dead, just like ours. Then there's been folks with brain tumours, so we might even have that to look forward to!

'Anyway, it had nothing to do with camels. Bett was just in the wrong place at the wrong time.'

Jack had another sad grin on his face and looked to his audience out of habit for recognition of his wit, only to discover Gwen looking as crushed as she had at Avery's funeral.

What am I doing? She doesn't need to hear this now.

'It was a long time ago, Gwen – long enough for our kids to have been the same age by now.'

Jack was swallowing down his own pain admirably, but Gwen was not so sure her Scotch intake would allow her to control hers, so she changed the subject.

'How did you end up in Scone?'

'We took the twins to be buried near where Betty grew up. It's thoroughbred country, so we're a little outside the social circle with our Alpacas – though I wouldn't put it past Betty to turn up to the track on one!'

Jack made a good fist of his second grin, but, fearing its fall, Gwen announced they'd done enough for the day. She ordered Jack to retrieve his wife from the Walkerville footpaths and meet her at the unit for dinner and perhaps a sherry in an hour or two.

68.

Reconciled.

[August, 1975.]

The sale of 7 Irving Street enabled Gwen to give her parents a fair price for their unit. She took only a few pieces of furniture from the house, including the two beds, and combined the rest in the sale. She had agonised over keeping the desk but in the end acknowledged the resentment she felt toward Avery every time he chose it over her and concluded that inanimate object or not, it should be discarded along with everything else that threatened to slow down the recalibration of memories that was needed to always think fondly of her late husband. The auctioneer secured the desk for himself at an agreed price and negotiated to pick it up after the two month settlement period.

The spare bedroom at Quandong Court became a repository for the boxes packed by Jack and Betty. They contained paperwork, books, photographs and other personal materials they had been reluctant to bother Gwen with when deciding what should be thrown and what should be kept. It was understood when Gwen loaded Avery's car with them that she would sort them when she was ready.

Several months later, Gwen steeled herself to the task. Still limber despite her age, she sat cross-legged on the fresh new carpet in a pair of nylon trousers and an overstretched jumper. She pulled several boxes close to either side of her bare feet. She tipped the contents of one in front of her and kept the empty container as a waste basket.

One of the piles would be for those items she would keep and the other for materials and documents to be returned to the Church for its records or to pass on to the new Reverend.

Most of the items were insignificant, and Gwen wondered why Avery had cloistered them so determinedly in his study. The envelope containing the accusations against him was among them, haughtily brandishing its legal moniker. She put it to one side, unsure of whether or not she wanted to keep it.

Avery must have wanted me to find it. He leaves no suicide note, no apology, but he leaves me his mea culpa.

Gwen continued sorting through the box of loosely gathered papers, wondering if Jack had been curious enough to read through them as he was packing. She was quietly thankful that Betty had provided a distraction for both of them. Maybe it was now Gwen's turn to protect her closest friends from her pain.

Strange I could get to my age and not have a single person I can talk to about this. I guess this is how the author of that letter felt.

Gwen turned to the envelope that had been given greater presence because of its singular status among the piles and slowly withdrew the pages.

She found the paragraph she was looking for…

'I have carried around the secret that I am about to tell you of for many years because I cannot in all conscience take it to my grave. So, if my lawyers have done as I requested, you will find the burden passed to you – the person to whom I believe it rightly belongs.'

Avery's not carrying that burden anymore … Just me.

Gwen swallowed back her tears, flared her nostrils against the moisture and tried to convince herself to consign the letter to the waste. With a masochistic compulsion, she chose instead to skip to the last page and read:

'I write now to impress on you the need for you to find the moral courage you were so lacking in all those years ago to right this wrong.'

We could have found the courage together, Avery. It didn't have to be this way. Why did you put yourself under so much pressure?

The page was unsigned – strange for such a confronting letter. Not that it mattered much; Gwen believed she knew the author to be Sister Michaels from the Benevolent Shelter for Women. The clues were not hard to find. But she had always been a forthright woman, according to Avery, and would not have shied away from putting her name to her accusations, particularly since they were to be made posthumously, Gwen thought with some derision.

She sifted through more papers in search of an answer – finding old bills, church ledgers, an address book – until she came across a single page, in the same cursive handwriting as the others she had set beside her. Gwen scanned it eagerly without taking in whole sentences and confirmed, with some satisfaction, that it carried the signature of Sister Michaels. She refolded the page along its worn crease, pressing it to her lap and then placed it atop the envelope.

After a few seconds of simply staring at it, Gwen took a measured breath and picked it up. She opened it and read with slow deliberation:

'To help you do this, I must pass on another piece of distressing news to you.

'After the birth, Helen stayed on with us for a while to recover from the hysterectomy made necessary by the infection. To prevent her ongoing medications flowing through the breastmilk, the baby was bottle fed. In this case, there was no need to risk further attachment to the child, particularly when we have reciprocal arrangements with St Mary's Mission of Hope for situations like this.

'You may well be feeling a little queasy Avery, no doubt anticipating what I am about to tell you. And it is surely ironic that you and your wife adopted from St Mary's in the belief that you would not come across the children of any of the young women whom you'd assisted through organisations set up by your own Church.

'I asked to be informed when Helen's child moved on from St Mary's in order to close our own file and was given details listing both yourself and your wife as the adoptive parents. Of course I had a choice in informing you or not of the connection, but at the time I was not disposed to the former as our drainage had completely blocked up and I was drawing on my own limited funds to get them cleared for the umpteenth time. I decided the match to be God's handy work and to let it lie.

'However, I have found that in old age one gets more inclined to meddle. In my case, this intervention might also be the result of witnessing an unfortunate number of distressed young women return to The Shelter years later regretting their decision and demanding information the law prevented me from giving them. If that ever changes, and I believe one day it might, it would not bode well for either of us if this information was to die with me.

'I can hear you Avery, waving the matter of the different birth dates in my face like a victor's flag. I'm sorry my friend but I'm afraid this, at least, has a verifiable explanation. The file from St Mary's carried a typographical error which has perpetuated as an erroneous birth date; your daughter was in fact born on 24 August, 1951, and this is on record in The Shelter's files and I have no explanation for how St Mary's got it wrong.

'If I am mistaken about your involvement with this girl, Avery, you will no doubt destroy this letter and think no more about it. No harm done. But if my suspicions are correct, then you must do the right thing by Helen Muldoon, your daughter, your wife, yourself and ultimately, your God.

'With delivery of this letter I will consider my conscience cleared. I pray for everyone's sake that you will be able to say the same in your declining years my friend.

'Sincerely, Ursula Michaels (Sully).'

In all her grieving and anger over the way her marriage had ended, Gwen had thought little about the others involved. Ursula Michaels was after all dead and Helen Muldoon, well, she was either a mother who did not love her daughter enough to keep her – in which case she wasn't worth a second thought – or a foolish girl who had 'done the right thing' in allowing her daughter to have a better life with a good family. If the latter were true, the girl's mission was accomplished and she should have had nothing to regret.

That was the way Gwen had felt about the adoption for the past twenty years or so, but after the funeral, after spending time with Jack and Betty, she no longer felt so righteous.

Am I so cold that Betty thought she couldn't come to me? Am I so heartless that I can't imagine another woman's grief over giving up her baby, or understand why an adopted child might want to know something about her biological mother?

Unwittingly, Gwen flashed back to Elsa Timmins rolling from the tarp. It offended her so greatly that she flinched.

Shaking it off, she turned back to the second page of the letter, to Ursula's last paragraph.

'I write now to impress on you the need to find the moral courage you were so lacking in all those years ago to right this wrong.'

Gwen's acceptance of those words slowly became a determination to pursue them to their natural end. Three months after Avery's death and 25 years since his transgression – Gwen thought she had found a new path for herself.

She saw it as a task that, while hard, was necessary for her own wellbeing, despite feeling something akin to hate toward Avery and even Ursula herself, because Avery was not the only one she should have told her suspicions to.

It was an odd sensation – wanting to better her husband's life in memoriam while knowing the depth of his betrayal. The resolve may have been possible because vitriol loses its heat in a one-way conversation with the dead, but ultimately Gwen believed she had dealt with most of the pain by the time she had moved out of Irving St.

I wonder if you have any idea how hard that was, Avery.

In the beginning, when you went on the road without me, I wanted you to long for me, then to want me, then just to acknowledge me when you got back.

When you were home, you allowed yourself to be swallowed up by the Church. You should have heard how Mandelson complained to me about how often you hung around the chapel, looking for mail, checking stores or whatever excuse you made up to stay away. I wasn't just obsolete in your life; you made me irrelevant in my own.

As maudlin thoughts threatened to take hold of her, Gwen found Avery alive in her head, replying the way he had done in the jeep on the way back from Dhurringile that first time. He accused her lightheartedly of overthinking things and surprisingly, Gwen laughed out loud, believing in hindsight that it was true. As she sat alone now in this room of boxes and voices, there was no cynicism born from a bitter conversation or a dismissive look. She could think only of her daughter, her husband's legacy, and that of her own. She was suddenly saturated with purpose and finding it easy to believe that Avery – the Avery spoken of so highly at his memorial service, the Avery she met by the Goulburn River – would be genuinely and deeply grateful that she might take up the gauntlet.

With only the slightest awareness that she was incrementally repairing her spirit by reimagining her husband and their feelings toward each other, she chose to move on from his death by seeking deliverance on both their behalves.

We'll find the courage together.

69.

A reluctant lady of letters.

As a lone grandmother of two, Gwen Holbrook might have called herself content. She was working three days a week as a paid fundraiser for a children's charity and had increased their profits and general sales in opportunity shops by a reasonable amount each year through new connections with churches, schools, Rotary and Probus clubs. While tiring, it gave her enormous satisfaction.

Her relationship with her daughter was also better than it had ever been. They called each other every Sunday – the day chosen because the rates were cheaper. The birth of Rachel in the summer of 1976 was a treasured memory; after missing out on William's birth, Gwen had not thought she would get another chance to be close to such a miracle, so she had been thrilled to hear that her daughter was pregnant again. Kate had come home to Adelaide, Sorrell confiding in Gwen that it would be best to have her 'monitored' after the birth.

Gwen did not perceive her own indignation at Sorrell's presumption as jealousy at the time – but she had responded in the way a mother envious of another woman's influence over her daughter might anyway. With shameful opportunism, Gwen had revealed Sorrell's attitude to Kate, and, like conspiratorial schoolgirls, they had cut her mother-in-law off, filtering what they said to Nick in the knowledge that he would pass it on.

Poor behaviour, I know.

The baby was born prematurely, but she was a good size and remarkably, her lungs well developed despite the surprise arrival. Nick had come down and stayed with them in the unit for a week, before taking Kate home. He had been elated about having a daughter, his manner taking on the swank of a man much loved and in love, the volume of him expanding with his unquestioning commitment to two human beings who would spend a lifetime calling him Dad.

He had been genuinely convivial with Gwen, teasing her about the gene pool responsible for his daughter's noticeably large ears: 'Well they didn't drag her out with forceps and those ears had to come from somewhere; show me yours again?' It seemed a long time since a man had been playful in conversation with Gwen (let alone swept her hair behind her ears for a closer inspection of her features), and she had enjoyed their banter to the point Kate had accused her mischievously of flirting with her husband.

When Kate had called her with the news of her pregnancy, the resolve to reveal her past to her daughter had dissolved instantly. Instead, Gwen drew her daughter in closer, heartened by being able to openly support her in her marriage without Avery's misgivings hanging over them. She was warmed by the sight of Kate cuddled up on Nick's lap on the one armchair at Quandong Court – something they would not have felt comfortable doing in Irving Street – sharing the cordless phone between them as they spoke in turn, and sometimes over the top of each other, to William, who was staying with Nick's parents.

There was an assuredness about Kate at that time that she did not have after her first birth; it was evident in her voice when she'd told William she'd be home soon, and Gwen had felt validated in her decision to leave well enough alone and dismiss Sorrell's concerns.

As for the imperative to reshape Avery's legacy, Gwen had let that fade with even less consternation. She still mourned her husband and could admit that she had hoped, even expected, that he would court her again in their old age and that she would acquiesce. But frequently when she was happy she concluded that it was because she was living without that mist of judgement and that she had been liberated from the belief that her husband had considered her somewhat lacking – in intellect, as a mother, as a wife. Even though she was furious with Mandelson for playing that malevolent toccata at his funeral (despite his assertion that Avery had requested it) it was this music that filled her head every time she was close to forgiving him and ultimately quelled the desire to right wrongs for fear she would be caught in the undertow.

The depth of Kate's anxiety had been revealed to Gwen as they walked around a cemetery several days after Rachel was born. Kate had decided she was never going back to that place and was bravely trying to reconcile the 'last' of her issues by her father's graveside. Despite the fact Gwen could not relate to the way Kate seemed to be overwhelmed by her emotions at times, she saw a lot of herself in the strident way her daughter was approaching her recovery.

She decided then, as they had rounded the narrow concrete path dividing the Catholic section of the cemetery from the Protestant and stood in astonishment at various crypts with their ornate angels and austere photographs behind cloudy glass in faded oval frames, that she had been Kate's mother her whole life and that Avery – for better or worse – had been her father, and that's all there was. When it was time for her own burial, she would want Kate to run her fingers over her headstone and truly feel the words, 'Much loved mother of Katherine', without the shadow of an irrelevant history bearing on the inscription or the visit.

Gwen had assured Kate many times that her father had loved her deeply despite his inattentiveness, and that where she might have considered him cruel, she should see only the misguided nature of a flawed man seeking for his daughter what he couldn't find for himself. Every life, after all, becomes more open to interpretation the longer it sits with family and friends after passing, and there was no gain to be made from remembering it harshly. Avery had lived his life answering to God, and he would surely be doing so now in his death.

These days, Gwen was a doting grandmother who had Rachel over to stay most weekends on release from her school boarding house, and sometimes even signed temporary guardianship for one of her friends. She felt more relaxed with her life than she had for most of her marriage.

It was 22 years after their cathartic walk in the cemetery when Gwen was reminded that she had once been terrified that her daughter might learn of her adoption from someone else and never forgive her the lie.

It was a phone call in the winter of 1998 that exhumed those fears and gave them back their heartbeat. She was in the middle of sorting a few bags of clothing she had brought home from the Opportunity shop and tipped onto her bed. When she heard the phone ring, she folded just one more sports singlet and allocated it to the size 14 boys' pile before heading into the kitchen to answer it.

'Mrs Holbrook?'

'Yes'

'Is there a Mr Avery Holbrook at this address?'

'Reverend Holbrook never lived here. His last residence was in Irving Street but my husband's been dead for quite some time now.'

'My apologies, Mrs Holbrook, but that address you gave us does indicate that I have the right Avery Holbrook at least.'

'Who is this?'

'Sergeant Ian Laslow maam. I'd like to organise a time for you to come down to the West Street Police Station to collect some material that belonged to your husband?'

'What material?'

'It might be better if you come down to the station to talk about this, Mrs Holbrook.'

'Why don't you tell me about it now, and then I'll decide whether or not it's a good idea.'

'It wasn't my intention to upset you Mrs Holbrook. This is in relation to the Victor Gant case. Are you aware of that matter?'

'I'm sorry, I don't read the papers much.'

'Or watch TV apparently!'

'That's right, not much TV either. Now are you going to tell me what this is about?'

'Well, it was a very successful prosecution for us, but it did involve an enormous amount of paperwork and we're aiming now to return or destroy whatever wasn't pertinent to the conviction.'

'And what has this got to do with my husband?'

'In the course of the inquiry, correspondence bearing your husband's name and address was discovered among the material collected from Gant's house.'

'He wrote a letter to this Gant?'

'To a Mrs Katherine White.'

'Are you still there, Mrs Holbrook?'

'I'm very confused Sergeant; why was a letter from my husband to my daughter in this Gant's house?'

'Victor Gant was director of the clinic your daughter attended, Mrs Holbrook.'

'Yes, yes, you're right. I recognise the name now. Surely he retired; it was years and years ago that my daughter was there. Aren't those records confidential by the way? Why is this coming up now?'

'It sometimes happens with sexual assault maam. Victims can have a sense of shame or a fear no one will believe them, which would be particularly true in this case I imagine. Sometimes they won't talk about it until years later when something goes wrong, the perpetrator comes back onto their radar, or they just can't hold down a relationship and they're ready to blame someone for that. Sometimes it happens when they get counselling and they think it will help "fix" things.'

'Sexual assault?' Gwen sounded as if she had been winded.

'I really would prefer to have this conversation at the station Mrs Holbrook, so if it's not convenient now, perhaps another time?'

Some twenty minutes later, rugged up against the rain and anxious, Gwen shook her umbrella off and walked into the West Street Police Station. Sergeant Laslow stepped forward with a warm, somewhat sweaty handshake. It had been a quiet morning and he had time to answer all her questions in his office. Gwen followed him past the reception desk down a short corridor into an open plan area with industrial grey carpet squares prone to static and six desks, two of them occupied by lower-ranked officers.

'I'm guessing milk and one?'

'No sugar thanks,' Gwen responded, noticing that the Sergeant nodded at one of the Constables by way of fulfilling the request.

'Thankyou Constable; I'll have a strong black.'

The Sergeant grabbed the back of a wheeled office chair, rolling it behind him as he headed for his windowless workspace in a petitioned corner of the floor.

He was a bulky man who appeared to have no buttocks, resulting in his pale blue shirt being taut over his torso and his dark pants falling loosely below his belt. His holster of plaid black leather was empty.

He motioned for Gwen to sit on the commandeered furniture and moved to his side of the desk, leaning back slightly in his own chair.

'It was a difficult case, for sure,' Sergeant Laslow opened before Gwen had a chance to speak.

'We took some convincing to go ahead with it, but the woman who came in was pretty insistent. She led us to another woman who corroborated her story with one of her own. Even so, psych patients don't exactly top the list of 'credible' witnesses!'

Gwen responded to the Sergeant's smile with a pained expression that went unacknowledged.

'In the end we didn't have to rely on the women; turns out Gant sacked a doctor on some trumped up grounds after the doctor saw him in a compromising position with one of the informants. It took some persuasion, but he became our material witness.'

Gwen nodded and looked down at her lap briefly, wondering how she could have visited her daughter weekly for all those years and not got a sense of what this officer was talking about going on.

'You have my husband's letter, Sergeant?'

'I suppose it would be alright to give it to you since he's passed on, though the better alternative would be to give it to Mrs White. Are you able to arrange that and save us the trouble?'

'Of course. Thank you.'

The Sergeant got up and turned to the back of the office. Gwen noticed how his thin dark hair spilt over his collar. He approached three stacks of cardboard boxes pushed against the wall and turned to a scattering of letters on top of the stack closest to the door. With one sweep of his hand to separate them, the Sergeant found what he was looking for.

He put the envelope in front of Gwen on the desk. It was yellowed, with a 25 cent stamp on it. The address was written in Avery's hand, unusually considering his preference for the typewriter, Gwen thought. It was the second time she had been confronted by the voice of her dead husband and this letter was no less unsettling for the familiar turn of its penmanship.

How is it that this one comes to me in a police station?

'Was this … part of your case?'

'No, we read almost every one in those boxes, but only about a dozen had any bearing on the case.'

'Why would you keep them then?'

'They were helpful to our investigators in establishing a pattern of behaviour,' the Sergeant answered, before adding in response to Gwen's slightly raised eyebrow, ' – how Gant groomed his victims.'

'What do you mean groomed?'

The Sergeant moved the mug the Constable had just delivered to him to one side, and slid the other toward Gwen, waiting until the younger officer had left the room before he proceeded.

'It seems the director wasn't really in the business of helping female patients get better. His MO was to keep them distressed and needy, so when they fell apart, he could pick up the pieces, or alternately, take over their medical treatment.'

A dull ache in Gwen's jaw alerted her to the fact she had been clenching her teeth. She reached for the coffee, leaving the envelope where it lay.

With some difficulty, she asked: 'Are you saying that he manipulated them so they agreed to have sex with him?'

'You have to understand,' the Sergeant said, getting up to close the door against those working outside, ' – and I don't mean to hurt you by telling you this – but most of these women already had dependency and abandonment issues.'

He continued talking as he moved back to his seat.

'Gant would prey on their insecurities. When he couldn't convince them to have sex with him, we suspect he assaulted them while they were drugged. There's no knowing how many victims there might have been if we hadn't closed him down.'

Gwen was struggling, feeling both panic and strange fluctuations she could only reflect on later as a desire to be violent. 'I still don't understand how this letter fits in,' she said tersely. 'Police collect a lot of information, Mrs Holbrook; some of it's important and some of it's not,' Sergeant Laslow said, the slightest hint of impatience in his tone.

'We found a lot of correspondence in Gant's house that had been intended for patients from family or vice versa but never delivered. Some of it, as you can see, goes back decades.

'Can I ask, was your husband particularly close with his daughter?'

'He loved her very much,' Gwen replied. 'Not that it's any of your business.'

'I don't mean to pry; I'm just trying to explain. We had a top psych interview Gant. He said his MO was to exploit his patients' weaknesses. He worked on his targets for months beforehand. For example, if your daughter felt she had both parents in her corner then Gant would have had less of an opportunity to win her trust. If she had issues with men, Gant could have got in there as a father figure or a 'lover'. He was what we call a classic predator.'

'I don't want to hear any more Sergeant,' Gwen said, and stood up to leave, her head pounding.

She stopped in the doorway and paused.

'Do you think my daughter was a victim?'

'We've got no reason to believe so, Mrs Holbrook.'

'If you find any more letters from my husband, please forward them to me at …'

'There was just that one, maam.'

70.

The kindness of strangers (1).

[Midday. Wednesday, August 19, 1998.]

It was extraordinary that despite the greater reach of bitumen from the city to the outback in the past decade, Gwen could suffer not one, but two flat tyres. She had checked the spare before leaving Adelaide and ensured it had adequate tread and air and it had definitely been useful for the past twenty kilometres, but now here she was again, pulled over by the side of the road, a long way from anywhere.

After the first puncture, caused by a remnant length of barb wire that had embedded in the rubber, she had perfunctorily changed the wheel, taking a quiet pleasure in the no-nonsense competency that few in her church circle would have seen in her before, despite the worrying strain on an old woman's back.

Gwen had used the last of her water to wash the grime from her hands, assuming she was close enough to a township for the threat of dehydration to be nebulous and reassured that the weather would remain cool. Now all she had to do was 'man up', as Ruth used to say when parts needed to be modified for the sake of expediency.

She grabbed a pair of clippers and a calico bag that she had left in the boot since helping her parents tame their small garden's Spring flourishes and ventured off into the palomino sands with her eyes on the tough protrusions of native grass. She and Avery had once travelled a good 60 miles on a punctured tyre they had stuffed with dense foliage, and she was hopeful she could repeat the feat over less than half that distance.

As she gathered the grass, sweating with the labour of severing its leathery strips from their roots and squinting against it, she found herself thinking of the younger Avery, slashing foliage beside her with his open tanned face and easy smile.

Within half an hour, Gwen had a full bag. She stood up and stretched her spine, swivelling each shoulder forward and back in turn, the dampness of her armpits spreading over her top ribs and darkening her shirt.

Across the plain, the shadows of the bluebushes were extending and corrugating across the sand ridges. The sky had softened, the pale blue fading to a washed out grey dimpled with clouds of nondescript shapes and substance.

She began walking back up the slight rise to the car and was surprised to confront a figure with the sun behind him at the brink of the bitumen.

Where did he come from?

A head of wiry, loose curls gave his silhouette an uneven shroud without detracting from an imposing stature, standing as he was slightly above Gwen on the crest of the road. He reached out to assist Gwen with her load but she refused to put down her bag of grass and clippers to accept.

'Everything alright missus?'

The voice was low, gravelly, dry and unassuming. Gwen could now see his curls were silvery white and though his hair was fulsome, he was a man of advanced years.

'I'm grateful that you stopped, though I had a plan to fix my tyre, as you can see,' Gwen said with just a little bluster as she lifted the calico bag a few inches.

'I'm goin' to Tarcoola if you need a ride,' the man said, nodding back toward a truck she had not noticed before then.

Gwen looked at her car, now sagging on one side and susceptible to being bogged in the powdery shoulders. There hadn't been much passing traffic and the day was getting on. She looked into the man's face. He had deep, chocolate eyes that carried no suggestion of malice.

'Thanks, that's very kind of you; can I just grab a suitcase from the boot?'

The stranger was already walking away from her. She quickly swapped the gardening gear and cuttings for her suitcase, locked the car and turned to follow him.

His truck was an odd sight, being an engine without a rig. It stood clean in a bold blue and white livery, apart from sprays of dirt, caked and circling the mudguards. The driver lifted himself easily into the cabin and started the engine, causing the cab to shudder and shake, and shots of black smoke to burst in thick profusion from the silver exhaust chimneys stretching upward from either side.

Gwen hurried herself, struggling to do more than a fast shuffle with her luggage. The step up to the door on the passenger side seemed awfully high. When, with a stiff creak, the door was pushed open from the inside, it nearly bowled Gwen over. Realising that would be the end of the assistance, she launched her suitcase clumsily into the cavity and hoisted herself in behind it as quickly as she could.

Thank goodness I wore pants!

The driver took the case and tossed it behind the seats into a sleeping cabin that looked inadequate for someone of his size, and had the truck in motion before Gwen considered herself either settled or safe. It picked up speed at a frightening pace.

'I hope I haven't slowed you down, with your schedule I mean,' Gwen ventured.

'Most truckers wouldn't stop to help someone out – and I understand that, because of their tight deadlines. I read once that the schedules are so tight, drivers have to urinate in bottles.'

Gwen blushed at her own nervous gabble, horrified that she had questioned the driver on his toilet habits and even more mortified that in the first minute of their travelling together, they were both now thinking about his penis. She stole a terrified glance at the driver to see if he was offended or transforming into a sexual predator, and was relieved to see that he was still relaxed and looking out onto the road with a bemused tweak at the ends of his generous lips.

Apart from guessing he was beyond his sixties, it was hard to gauge the driver's age. There was a kind of youthful energy that exuded inexplicably from his generally passive face, but the hand on the bottom of the large steering wheel was gnarled with a protrusion of knuckles that a dog might see fit to chew on.

On the right hand side of the cabin, Gwen's eye noticed a length of plumbing pipe, the size of a large fist in diameter, that was braced to the steering wheel with several metal clamps. Rivets had been used to join two sections of the pipe to form a crude curve so that its length roughly aligned with the circumference of the wheel.

She thought to ask about it just as the driver lifted his right arm, revealing a stump. The amputation had occurred several inches below his elbow, with the end of the limb covered by a brown leather pouch that extended to the man's shoulder and was kept in place by something resembling a chest holster.

They approached a curve in the road at a speed that would have made Gwen anxious had she not been intrigued by the disfigurement. To make the turn, the driver inched the wheel anti-clockwise from the bottom with his left hand, with the pipe rising accordingly on the right. At the point the pipe was high enough, the driver slipped his stump into it and guided the truck around the bend, now with control of both sides of the wheel.

Without the weight of a load, it felt at times as if the truck were not well grounded and at high speed might even roll, but Gwen's attention was only momentarily diverted. The Engineer was focussed on the ingenuity of the steering aid and how it might be improved. For his part, the driver seemed unperturbed by his passenger staring at his stump, only breaking her attention when it occurred to him she might light him a cigarette and stick it in his mouth.

Gwen had never been partial to tobacco but thought fulfilling the request was the least she could do in return for the ride, so she agreed. The driver shrugged his left shoulder to indicate a packet of cigarettes tucked into the sleeve of his faded check shirt. As Gwen pulled it down, she noticed the bottom half of a design, being talons extended as if ready to pick up a mouse or a snake.

'What is your tattoo?'

'Eaglehawk.'

Gwen coughed up the smoke she had been trying to swallow.

'Does it have a story?' she queried, the act of lighting and passing this stranger his cigarette somehow making her feel more familiar.

'Warlawurru'

'Sorry?'

'It's my totem.'

The ten minutes a much younger Gwen had habitually set herself to determine whether a person was worth investing in or whether they should be sent on their way without securing a place in her memory, had not been counted down to any meaningful extent since settling in Adelaide, where she had found most people fairly dull as a general rule.

However, the unpredictable events of this day had liberated Gwen from her life in Walkerville and returned her to a somewhat playful state in which she recalled the pastime with a juvenile fondness.

Retrospectively, as the truck ran down the distance, the hum of the road under the tyres the only sound between them, she gave the driver the honour of settling in her mind as an interesting soul in well under the allotted time. However, if she thought that today was the first time their tales had entwined, she would have been mistaken; Gwen had been locked into the untold story of this man decades before she would abandon her vehicle and step up boldly into his truck.

71

No longer your concern.

[Wednesday afternoon, August 19, 1998.]

Though the view had waned and flattened as it opened up the further they drove, Gwen had not expected the landscape to look as weary as it did, nor the nursing home to appear so still in it; she was forced to wonder whether she had romanticised her memories of the bush.

The truck cabin rocked jerkily on its suspension coils each time the air brakes engaged as they slowed to a stop beside a cluster of sapling gums in a small skirt of shade. There was a tiredness to the air.

Gwen did not leave the truck immediately, taking in the scene from the passenger window. The nursing home was a long building of mustard-coloured bricks with a flat roof and small aluminum-framed windows, giving it the appearance of having been pressed down into its stony surrounds rather than built on top of it. A thin, tawny lawn, looking more like remnants of straw from an animal's stall, crept in threads from it, edged by rocks that were painted white and spaced evenly apart. A couple of hardy bushes under the windows masqueraded as a garden, though Gwen doubted they had ever known blossoms, unlikely as they were to be given anything other than a quick dousing with the water from yesterday's kettle. She thought of her parents and how lucky they were to be able to live independently, enjoying their trellised courtyard among a tangle of passionfruit vines and the shops a short walk away.

To the left of the home, there was a carport with four spaces, three of them filled. The weathered wooden beam bracing the tin roof, too low for anything on more than four wheels, had been freshly painted with red lettering marking it for staff use only. Woken by the arrival of the truck, a skinny black dog appeared from behind the car and stretched. Its handlebar hips rose and fell as it shuffled stiffly down a concrete path beside the building, and disappeared from view.

Gwen opened the truck door and readied to levy herself down, only to be met by the driver already on the ground in front of her, offering up his hand.

'Thank you,' she said, surprised at the chivalry and wondering fleetingly whether it might extend to driving back to her car with a new tyre if one could be russled up in town.

'I'm sorry, I never asked your name.'

The man smiled generously.

'Well, I appreciate your help,' Gwen ceded, shaking the sinuous hand she had not released after stepping down from the cabin and looking to him to see that he knew she was genuine.

What sad eyes.

The slap of a wire door closing gave them both a jolt. A portly, middle aged man in overalls had emerged from the building, pulling a soft hat from his back pocket to cover a broad bald patch. He looked toward them, squinting and then lifting his chin in their general direction.

'Do you need any help over there?' he called out.

'We're fine, thank you,' Gwen called back, as her companion withdrew his hand from hers.

'If you say so,' the man replied dubiously, addressing himself particularly to Gwen. He grabbed a yard broom from beside the door and wandered off around the corner of the building. Gwen was embarrassed by the rudeness but not enough to try and redress it. The driver had already moved on anyway, and was back in the cabin and turning over the engine.

Once inside the home, Gwen was disappointed to find that it reeked of the nursing homes she had rejected when looking on behalf of her parents, thankfully without ever having to reveal to them that she did. The walls seemed to lean as if they were burdened by the duty of housing people for whom incapacity and precarious health were the only constants. Even the smell of disinfectant and floor wax, which during the war had seemed a reassuring covenant of hygiene, only served to remind Gwen of the visceral nature of deterioration.

'Can I help you?'

A plumpish, red-headed nurse in pale brown slacks and a blue zip-up tunic was walking toward her. Gwen did not wait to be asked her purpose.

'I'm here to see Helen Muldoon.'

The nurse raised her eyebrows and kept them high for a moment as if contemplating something in a language she only partially understood.

'Miss Muldoon, is it?'

'Yes, Helen Muldoon,' Gwen repeated with quick annoyance.

'I'm sorry, it's just that Helen hasn't had any visitors for years,' a startled Faye asserted, her tone somewhat defensive.

Embarrassed, Gwen collected herself.

'No, I'm sorry; it's been a long drive. Is there somewhere I can freshen up?'

'Just down the hallway on your left, but don't forget to sign the visitors book before you catch up with Miss Muldoon.'

As soon as she was out of sight, Faye scurried off to find Carmel setting cups of tea up on a table to the rear of the dayroom.

'Oi, Carmel,' Faye said as she drew alongside her, 'Helen's got a visitor.'

'Fair dinkum?'

'A woman. She's in the washroom. Bit of a git; God I hope it's 'Mabel' – that'd be entertaining. Where is the ol' girl?'

'Don't call Helen that … she'll start to think she's old.'

'I don't think she's thinking much beyond her teenage years at the moment; some days she's still at school, so I wouldn't worry about her going for a rinse and set just yet.'

Having hurriedly scrawled her signature in the deserted book, Gwen appeared at the open double doorway to the dayroom, her bob now pulled tightly into a small bun and held with an array of hair pins. The collar of her pale blue polo shirt had several spots of water drying on it.

'Is there a Helen Muldoon here?' she asked of the residents gathered in front of the television, pointedly ignoring the nurses.

'Shhh,' a wiry gentleman in an old cricket vest and pale short sleeved shirt hissed at her. A large woman in a floral summer frock and netting over her hair curlers got out of her seat and turned up the volume, without diverting her gaze from the set.

Carmel crossed behind their chairs to get to Gwen and motioned for her to follow her down the adjoining hallway.

'Just give me a minute to see if Helen is sleeping,' she told Gwen after stopping at a particular door. She opened it quietly and stepped aside. Cat strode out, stretching his front legs. Gwen peered over Carmel's shoulder to see the back of a fully dressed form curled up on the bed, facing closed blinds on the opposite wall.

'I'll wake her,' Carmel said amiably without turning around. 'She shouldn't sleep too long at this time of day anyway, but if you could wait a bit, I'll talk to her first; she can be a little anxious around strangers.'

'Excuse me nurse, before you go in, can you tell me – and I don't mean to offend anyone – but is Miss Muldoon simple minded or unwell? I mean she's not that old by my reckoning to be in a nursing home. I was just wondering ...'

'How do you know her again?'

'An old family friend ...'

'Well, she's having a pretty good day today. She has dementia, so her short term memory can be a bit problematic but I'm guessing you're not a new friend, because she's had no visits or calls for as long as I can remember.'

Carmel waited for Gwen to reveal something more about the relationship, but when she was met with silence, she moved inside Helen's room, blocking Gwen's view first with her broad shoulders and then with the door itself. Finding Helen dozy but still awake, the nurse encouraged her into a chair, took up a brush and casually imparted her news while smoothing the mass of Helen's hair. Grateful her attentions were tolerated and wanting Helen to appear at her best, she opened the blinds to brighten the surroundings and gave her her warmest smile.

'What a treat, Helen. A visitor!'

Gwen waited patiently until finally Carmel emerged saying that Helen was happy to receive her and that she would bring them a cup of tea in due course. Carmel dragged a doorstop from under the bed with her foot and wedged it underneath the door to keep it ajar.

Helen had her hands on her knees like a schoolgirl told to await the principal. Her eyes were hooded and wary. Gwen saw an attractive woman –her soft freckles suggesting a sunny youth and her hair voluminous and still rich in colour – but her features betrayed an exhausting demeanour.

'Helen, you don't know me, but I'd like to talk to you about something – about someone,' Gwen began soon after drawing her chair around to sit directly in front of her.

Helen's eyes narrowed.

'Do you remember a Reverend Avery Holbrook?'

Gwen hadn't noticed Carmel was still in the doorway until the nurse spoke: 'She often talks about an Avery.'

'I'm sorry dear, this is a personal matter and we'd like to be alone if you don't mind.'

Carmel left the room, bursting with curiosity, yet anxious on Helen's behalf. She went to find Faye, hoping she could convince her to intrude before afternoon tea and find out what relationship Helen had with this woman.

Where does she get off after so many years without a single visit, expecting I'm going to leave them alone?

Gwen got up and nudged the plastic wedge out from under the door with her toe, allowing it to close behind her slowly on its air pump as she returned to her chair. She was committed to revealing what she knew and equally as committed to discovering its veracity. Despite this and the rehearsing she had done on the road, she found she had barely begun the conversation before she lost her way. The junctures at which she felt most tenderly her husband's culpability and betrayal were like potholes, and when she could not steer out of them, she fell silent until the wheels stopped spinning and she was ready to start again.

Through it all, Helen remained hunched, her eyes shrouded so heavily by her hair even the nurses would have found it hard to judge if she was engaged or simply tolerating movement and noise until 'lights out' banished the sensations and left her in peace.

'Helen, I have something very important to tell you and I'm sorry it's taken so long. You and I, you see, are mothers to the same daughter and right now she needs us both.'

Helen straightened up as if a sharp wire had suddenly been threaded through her vertebrae. Her face and body became rigid but still Gwen did not feel confident that she'd been understood. The gaze in front of her was bald and glossy.

I should know where the emergency button is.

Helen blinked. 'Is Avery coming? Is he coming for us?'

Gwen stood up and moved behind Helen's chair, causing its occupant to veer away slightly. She put her hands on the back rest and looked down.

'Helen, Reverend Holbrook is dead,' she said cautiously. 'I'm sorry.'

Helen moved to the bed. Glaring, disbelieving. With shock, Gwen was reminded of Kate – bottled and boiling.

'You're just saying that, you manipulating old cow,' Helen burst forth, standing up and showing herself to be menacingly taller than Gwen.

'You just want him to yourself. Meddling, skulking, snooping old bitch. What lies do you tell him about me! You think we just have milkshakes in your kitchen? Wouldn't you like to know!'

Gwen bristled, perspiration dampening her armpits. She had not been prepared for this.

What a fool for thinking this delusional creature was ever a naïve child and not a cheap … She's no use to Kate. I'm more mother than she'll ever be.

Gwen moved around Helen to the window and pulled the curtains shut so swiftly the bottoms of them swung. The room darkened instantly. Helen had resumed her hunched position on the edge of the bed and appeared to be panting and in distress.

'You don't need to worry about this, Helen. It's not important. You remember I told you that man – Avery – was dead, well, you should stop waiting for him; he'll never come for you.'

Helen raised her eyes. They glistened.

'You're lying Sister! He's coming alright; he's going to rescue us and you won't be able to stop him. We're going to be a family.'

'Avery's not coming Helen. Avery is dead.' Gwen paused. 'And so is your daughter. You need not concern yourself with either of them anymore.'

72.

The kindness of strangers (2).

[Late Wednesday, August 19, 1998.]

'**Y**ou're mad,' Carmel informed Faye, as the pair of them swaddled their arms with the limp sheets from Mrs Wetherall's bed.

'As a hatter,' Mrs Wetherall chipped in from a chair in the corner of the room.

The nurses smiled as the woman who had been sitting so quietly became animated, moving forward in her seat, eager to play a word game.

Carmel put her bundle of sheets, topped with a cotton rug, on top of the bedside table.

'Why would you lend a car to a woman you don't even know and then tell her she can leave it by the side of the road for you? Likely you won't see that car again.'

'I donno; she seemed a good sort to me,' Faye responded defensively.

'Maybe I just have a little more faith in people than you do; I sold her my spare tyre an' all."

'Wait a minute. What changed since you called her a "bit of git" a couple of hours ago?'

Faye took up a fresh sheet from Mrs Wetherall's lap, where she had casually plonked her bundle of linen when they had first come into her room, genuinely pondering the question.

'And what are you going to do if you get your own flat tyre driving the car home – assuming you can talk me into taking you out to wherever it's been dumped to get it?'

Carmel stood with her hands on her hips, waiting for Faye to fling open the sheet across the bed so she could tuck it in on her side. The gesture irritated Faye.

'Come on, you can't tell me you wouldn't have taken that money; it was cash in hand,' she snipped, her face flashing in and out of Carmel's view with the lifting and falling of the linen.

'How much did she give you?' Carmel whipped her hands out from under the mattress where she had been tucking the sheet as Faye dropped her side.

'Worth two in the bush,' Mrs Wetherall interjected brightly, as if contributing some vital piece of information to the discussion.

'It's a bird, Mrs Wetherall, not cash. The saying is "a bird in the hand is worth two in the bush",' Carmel informed her as she lifted the light cotton blanket from on top of the bedside cabinet, revealing a waterproof bed liner underneath.

Both nurses frowned at the sight of the liner and the two began peeling back the crisp sheets they had just put on in order to remake the bed.

'All I'm saying is,' Carmel continued, 'this is someone who visits Helen out of the blue and leaves her angry and crying and talking about murdered babies. What on earth did she say to her?'

'Helen talks a lot of nonsense,' Faye retorted. 'You know that. And the woman had no way of getting back to her car unless I helped her. Imagine if someone left your elderly mother stranded like that.'

'I wouldn't know.'

Carmel's tone rebuked Faye for forgetting her mother had died in childbirth, but her friend was tiring of being lectured. She spread the waterproof out and tucked it under the mattress, dropping her side heavily. Faye looked for the fresh sheet, which she suddenly remembered she had tossed in the direction of Mrs Wetherall's lap.

'All I'm saying is that sometimes you have to be the one they talk about when they mention "the kindness of strangers".'

'Oh, Oh,' Mrs Wetherall interrupted, the sheet over her face ballooning with her breath and prompting Faye to hurriedly remove it.

'I know this one,' the old lady said excitedly before changing her tone to a surprisingly smoky drawl: '"I have Olways depended on the Kahndness of strangers".'

Faye raised her eyebrows.

'Well aren't you the surprising one, Phyllis Weatherall. You know, I saw "A Streetcar named Desire" in London, and you would have made a fine Blanche Dubois; your accent was tops!'

'Blanche who?'

'You're unbelievable, you know that!'

Faye plumped up Mrs Wetherall's pillow and roughly pulled the alert chord out from behind the bedhead. She turned back to her colleague who was heading for the door with the soiled linen bundled under her chin.

'Look Carmel, mistake or not, I could do with a lift to go get my car after work.'

Carmel's non-plussed expression slowly warmed into a broad grin as she twirled one of the sheets into a rope and flicked it at her friend.

'Sure – just 'cause you asked me so nicely,' she minced.

Mrs Wetherall rose from her chair, exhausted as much by listening for cues in the conversation as she was by the frenzy of activity in her room.

She ducked between the nurses' play to bring her brushes and handcreams back to order on the bedside table and mumbled at their backs as they headed off to the laundry.

'That's a wild goose chase – that's what that is.'

***

G wen was sitting just a little over the speed limit, but the rattling of her borrowed Corolla, hiccupping over every slight bump,

454

invoked a sensation of hurtling along. She attempted to wind the window down, looking for some cooler air, but the winder was stiff and by the time she had it half way down, the gust was anything but fresh and she wrenched the glass back up again. Instinctively, Gwen moved toward the centre of the road.

She had thought this might be a day of enlightenment and was carrying in her purse Avery's letter that Sergeant Laslow had given her, thinking it could be a catalyst for disclosing the adoption to Kate and then soften her perception of her parents and the years in between that might somehow seem dishonest.

Gwen thought to see the Muldoon woman first, in case she lost her nerve – as she willingly admitted to herself now that she had – but things hadn't gone as she'd hoped in Tarcoola. She had thought that by the end of the day, she would be feeling unburdened. She thought at the very least, that she would have 'corrected' a moral deviation that recorded against the merit of her own life, not for God's sake, as Avery might have wanted, but for her own – to have integrity as a mother.

I want Kate to forgive me.

But despite all her good intentions, Gwen had found herself hitting out at Helen Muldoon like a schoolyard bully.

Can a child so clever, so wonderful as Kate really have come from such a wretched woman as that?

The air in the car seemed suddenly quite stale so Gwen opened a vent but it only served to bring in a fine dust that kept her coughing for almost a minute. When finally the tickle seemed gone from her throat she noticed that her speed had crept up and the car was skimming on the surface of the road. She eased on the accelerator and instinctively checked her mirrors. To her rear, a truck that had been on her tail for some time was drawing closer to overtake. It had the same livery as the truck that had brought her into town and Gwen looked to her right to see if she could catch a glimpse of the driver as it pulled alongside, but the windows were too high.

Instead, what filled her view was the orange excavator on the truck's tray, with its large caterpillar track. The tread was rolling a little, the machinery straining against giant chains. The edge of the tray was so close to her car she moved the left wheels off the bitumen and onto the dirt to give herself some space. Wondering how much weight those chains could bear, she slowed down significantly to let the truck pull ahead of her. Suddenly something hit her window hard, and disappeared under the vehicle. The right side of the car lifted before coming back down with a thud. Something was dragging in her undercarriage. Gwen lifted her foot from the accelerator but did not brake, knowing innately that the car would press closer to the ground if she did. Slowly, the vehicle ground to a halt. Gwen took a deep breath, her heart pounding.

What have I hit?

She put the car into reverse. Initially the wheels spun atop the obstacle, then the vehicle slowly dropped. There was a crack, like a dry tree branch snapping and a guttural cough she felt in her feet. She reversed slowly off the mound and stopped the car when it rolled into view.

It's a wombat ... No, there's a tail ... A kangaroo.

Gwen moved to get out, but the driver's side door was jammed from the collision. Awkwardly, she levered herself over the handbrake and gear stick into the passenger side and got out through that door. She felt a shooting pain through the base of her neck and across her shoulders and instinctively raised her hand to squeeze the muscle.

Holding her head as still as she could to avoid more pain, she walked apprehensively to the front of the vehicle, finding her feet as if she had just got off a boat. The radiator had blown and steam was rising from between the triangular folds of the crumpled bonnet. She looked past it and put her hand to her mouth. The kangaroo was a large, sandy male, lying on its side. The fur on its midriff was soaked in blood and oil, a rib protruding through it. Its head lay still against the bitumen. Inexplicably, a rattling growl was coming from underneath it.

Oh dear God, it's moving!

Jerkily, the 'roo raised itself onto its front paws, drew its legs up from underneath and paused, hunched over, apparently dazed. Strawberry coloured saliva drizzled from its mouth into the green film of coolant on the road. In disbelief, Gwen scanned the 'roo to assess the extent of its injuries. She heard shouting from somewhere behind her but she could not dissuade her eyes from the injured animal. Suddenly the 'roo stood up. One eyeball tipped forward from its socket onto its cheekbone, held there by a stringy blue nerve. Gwen froze. The 'roo stretched taller, pushing off its tail and swaying close enough for her to feel its heat and smell its weedy breath. It reached out with its paws to either side of her neck, rooted its claws into her shoulders and kicked her thunderously with both legs.

***

Duggie had clipped the roo as it swept in front of his truck but thought it had made it to the other side of the road. It was not until he saw, in his rear mirror, that the Corolla behind him had fallen back drastically and then stopped that he realised there had been fallout. With around 100 metres between the vehicles, he pulled the truck over and got out for a better look.

He could see two figures in the middle of the road, rippling in a funnel of steam from a ruptured radiator behind them. Duggie saw the danger instantly.

He turned to the cabin of his truck and pulled a Nulla Nulla out from behind his seat. He began loping toward the car, hoping the roo would take fright.

'Gettaway! Hey, getaway!' he cried out.

He was only a dozen paces away when the 'roo lunged. He got to them, his Nulla Nulla raised, as the woman and the 'roo propelled backwards in opposite directions, each falling heavily to the ground. The 'roo was writhing, an eyeball partially dislodged, a section of its intestine protruding through a gash across its belly and the acrid smell of stomach bile overwhelming everything else.

The hapless animal died instantly on Duggie's blow to the skull. He bent down over the woman, dropping his ear to her chest. *Nothing.* He pulled back to look at her. Her eyelids were closed. Her nose broken. One nostril torn. A beard of blood caped her chin and was threading itself in two lines down either side of her neck, filling her ears and disappearing underneath her lobes to stain her collar.

Duggie recognised the pale blue shirt from that morning. As he did, he felt a strange sensation in the palm of his hand, a phantom of the woman's touch. He moved behind her head and pushed the stub of his right arm under one armpit and the elbow of his good arm under the other. Her head rolled forward as he hauled her body up under his chin to drag her to the side of the road. Her back was warm against his chest. Through it came a reverberation – a skipping stone that submerged heavily into his flesh and then bobbed up weakly against the surface of the skin between them.

A heartbeat?

***

Faye fidgeted in the passenger seat, frequently turning to look behind them, as if it were possible to miss a red car by the side of the road as they were passing it and therefore necessary to check in their wake. Carmel had driven her some fifteen kilometres out of town, about three quarters the distance Mrs Holbrook had told her she had abandoned her own car. The day was fading and evening was beginning to absorb the last of the light in uneven swatches.

'Why don't we double back,' Faye said.

'Why? The car's not there; it can only be ahead of us,' Carmel reasoned. 'It can't be much further.'

On their left, shadows behind the blue bushes were being drawn up into their darkening mass. On their right, the golden halos that had lit the tips of the bushes were receding as the last of the sun's rays slipped down below the horizon. Carmel lent forward in the driver's seat to peer into the distance.

'What's that?'

A scarlet beam was streaking across the road several hundred metres in front of them. 'It's a flare,' Faye said, 'Slow down.'

Carmel turned the lights on and braked gently. As they drew closer, the flare filled the windscreen with vivid sparks and threw everything behind the spray into darkness. Suddenly a man appeared in the headlights. Carmel pushed hard on the brakes.

'Holy crap. Where did he come from?'

Faye, her breath still held from the shock, stared at the man. His eyes were squinting against the headlights and he was waving them down, the fingers on one hand spread as the arm moved up and down and the opposite limb rising and falling against his rib cage, stumped below the elbow, like a clipped bird wing. Sparks were flying behind him and the women were also struggling to see clearly.

'Stop! he's hurt; I think he's lost an arm,' Faye said, trying to get a closer look.

Carmel steered the car onto the shoulder beside the road, pulling in behind another vehicle. The man disappeared from the headlights and in his absence, they illuminated the number plate in front of them.

'That's my car!' Faye got out and headed down the left side of the Corolla. Carmel alighted to see, to the front and right of it, the man leaning over something …

'Are you alright? I'm a nurse, is anyone else hurt?'

Carmel directed as many questions as she could toward the man's back. Small feet in women's shoes protruded from his right side.

'Stay with her,' he told Carmel, getting up, 'I'm gonna radio for help.' With that he turned and ran into the darkness.

73.

Restless.

[Wednesday night, August 19, 1998.]

Helen was sleeping fitfully, the most virile of her memories rising and falling in random succession to both rescue and destroy her in the middle of the night. Though her tossing and turning would have appeared to an onlooker as if she were wrestling her subconscious in a dream, it was actually held captive by an embrace.

She was 19 again and he had come to her. At her door. Full of want. After months of willing it to happen, its inevitability now made her anxious. Was he really going to do this? This Reverend. This man of God. Her Avery.

His kiss took her by surprise. Despite her inexperience, she had expected to be the one to tease him into bed. She had thrown it all at him, let him know she was his for the asking. But he hadn't asked. Now he was pressed feverishly up against her, the wall behind her preventing her from backing away to ease the pain of his hand flattening her breast. The friction of her nightdress, as he massaged the flesh underneath it made her nipple rigid and her mouth wilt.

He pulled back, his lips not releasing hers immediately, but sticking slightly, the dry skin moistening slowly. She pushed back into it, with visceral eagerness. He forced her lips apart with his own, turning her head to the side, his tongue finding the flesh inside her mouth and satiating the doubts inside her.

She met his lust with her own, feeling stronger for the aggression, pushing back harder into his face, releasing from the kiss and burying herself back into it in quick succession. Her naivety dissolved with youthful impetuousness. She had control again. He bobbed down, taking the kiss with him and then lifting up with it as his hand emerged underneath her nightgown and brushed over her stomach, gliding down flat along her abdomen, stretching her underwear tight across her buttocks as he moved his fingers between her thighs.

The nursing home halls were quiet now. Everyone was tucked in. Behind her closed door, Helen had stopped thrashing around in her sheets and had begun to moan quietly. On night duty, Faye noted various sounds emanating from Helen's room but was reluctant to disturb her by looking in. At the start of her shift, she recorded Helen's night on the summary chart as 'restless'.

Inside Helen's dream, inside her underpants, fingers tickled at her edges, twisting her pubic hair and causing her to forget her involvement in the kiss, her lips still being tugged at by Avery's, but falling idle and rubbery. Helen's own hand joined Avery's and pushed memory's fingers inside her. The lobes of her vagina were swollen, moist and warm. Avery's knuckles pressed hard up against her pelvis as his fingers delved deeper. Helen's moan seeped limply from her like ice-cream melting around a cone.

Avery turned her from the wall and began to push her gently in the direction of her parents' bedroom, his fingers still flicking thickly inside her as they moved forward, coupled in an act where each movement sent vellications through her body and sapped her of the strength to remain upright.

At the edge of the bed, he lay her down, withdrawing his fingers slowly from her swollen edges and making her feel faint. He stood up and undid his belt buckle while she lay like a wet towel, her face to the wall, her eyes closed, seeking out her own breasts, wishing he had more than two hands to play with her. Her excitement was tinged with fear.

Faye continued on her rounds, only breaching Helen's privacy when the whimpering grew so loud it threatened to wake the other residents.

'Helen? Helen? Is everything alright?'

She opened the door slowly. Helen had her back to her, lying on her side, one knee raised slightly, her sheets dishevelled around her feet and her nightie swaddled around her waist. Faye walked around the bed, so as to approach her from the front and not frighten her. Helen's face was turned into the pillow. She was sobbing into it, her wrist arched between her thighs, her knuckles pumping vigorously. Too experienced to be shocked, Faye pulled the sheets and a light cotton rug up over her. Helen's hand fell still, though her chest was still heaving. She swallowed her last sob but it left a trail in the form of a high-pitched whine.

'Helen. Helen!' Faye snapped at her in a harsh whisper.

'You need to be quieter love or you'll wake everyone up. I'll have to give you something if you can't settle. D'you hear me?'

'Wake them all up, I don't care,' Helen snapped back unexpectedly, her eyes now popping and her thin arms rising against Faye's ready hands.

'Wake them all up. They're all going to leave anyway. If there's no one here, then no one can hear me crying and if no one hears me crying, then maybe I'm not crying at all. Isn't that right Avery? Maybe you never loved me and maybe I never cried. Not one bloody tear. Why shouldn't everyone hear me? Wake them up!'

Another night nurse was suddenly on the other side of the bed, pushing an elbow into Helen's upper arm, pinning it to her body with her full weight as she tapped a bubble out of a syringe with her other hand. Faye clasped both of Helen's arms to allow the other nurse to remove her elbow and deftly slip the needle into a vein.

74.

A day of firsts.

[Thursday, August 20, 1998.]

As a psychologist of quiet acclaim, William would reconstruct December 14, 1973, as a day of firsts – the first time he had felt rain, the first time he had been on a bicycle and the first and only time in his life (he predicted) that he would come close to drowning. He had no recollection of that day and despite his grandmother's discomfort when he had asked her about it, there was nothing to suggest to him that he had suppressed a memory too confronting to process. He only knew that it was a significant day, as they are for everyone when fate takes on the disquieting role of guardian after it is relinquished by a parent.

William had decided on the approach while studying for his degree. He had accepted that it was unhealthy to deny the event a place in his timeline, so he had labelled and lodged it. He had done this without serious analysis, apart from the time it took to reject the obvious alternative that would consign it as a 'day of lasts' – the last day he would see his mother's face for two years, the last day he would be totally submerged in water and the last day he would have perfect hearing – because he could not accept these thoughts as dispassionately.

Kate's homecoming was clearer in William's mind. He remembered his father bobbing down and talking to him very seriously about the importance of being on his best behaviour. He had been curious to see what his mother looked like and frightened she might try to hug him.

William had been living with his grandparents, spending his days helping Grandma around the house, sometimes learning his numbers or letters on a special stool at the kitchen table, always with biscuits and milk, riding shotgun with Pa in his truck, visiting the library bus and playing with the dogs. He saw his father back then mostly at dinner. At the time, he thought he had all the people in his life that he would ever need.

These memories came back to William now as he looked out the window of his east facing office on the 26th floor of Macquarie Tower, a shimmering monolith overlooking Sydney Harbour. He had taken the office because it was close but not too close to the legal precinct that spawned most of his work, and because he loved the view, as he did from his home on the Bondi rise, where he was one of the few fit young men who regularly ran along the clifftops and down to the beach who didn't toss himself into the surf afterwards. He preferred to keep that pleasure at shin level.

Despite his relatively young age, Dr William Ronald White was sought after by a certain type of clientele – people whose issues had less to do with their mental health and more to do with managing stress and time and the extraordinary pressures of leading corporate and legal missions while underwriting the demands of high achieving and spending families. Remarkably, for a boy who had grown up among outback men, he had proven to be adept at aligning the thoughts of those unaccustomed to taking advice with his own, lightening the weight of their high octane lives and relationships through his expensively unique viewpoint.

The office view – glittering and shimmery in summer, grey and brooding in winter – usually filled him with calm and perspective and gave him confidence in his approach on clients' issues. His habit was always the same after an appointment; when the client had left, he rewound his tape recorder and played the session back while taking in the breadth of the sky, the harbour, the boats, the odd flash of red or yellow travelling in congested lines across the bridge. Movements caught his eye and glare intruded occasionally but mostly the largesse of it all soothed his eyes and allowed him to concentrate on the audio. He never stopped the tape to write anything down – he had already made notes as the client spoke – but when he swivelled back to those notes after the voice and the pauses behind him had stopped and the view had become translucent with the waning of his attention, he could modify his assessments with a flourish of certainty.

As he stared today over the rooftops of lesser buildings toward the choppy grey water reflecting a cloudy, indecisive sky, he could think only of the three phone calls he had with his father that week. Despite not having spoken to his son for close on six months, his first call was brief: Grandpa had died and it would mean a lot to the family if Will would come home for the funeral.

In the cool, evenly circulated air of Macquarie Tower, smells and physical fluctuations rarely intruded. Now William's nostrils tickled with the sting of a random dust storm. He could smell the strong black tea awaiting his grandfather at the kitchen table and the thick gravy his grandmother would pour over mounds of mashed potato, the slightly charred sausages and the mint peas awaiting him on his dinner plate. Even after his mother had come home, he was a regular for dinner and weekend lunches with his grandparents, putting out dessert bowls hopefully as he set the table.

He must have been ninety if he was a day. That's not a bad innings.

William was not prone to nostalgia but when it came to his grandparents, his memories, once prompted, came back in floods. Still, it seemed years since he had even thought their names. From the tone in Nick's voice, William felt sure his neglect of his grandparents was on his father's mind, particularly his absence at Sorrell's funeral. He had been in the middle of his exams when she had had her heart attack and had been given a chance to re-sit one on compassionate grounds. Ironically, the university set it on the same date as the funeral, with administration staff shrugging by way of confirmation that the timing was unnegotiable.

When Nick first told William about Ron's death he had seemed calm. He had found Ron in his bed. It had been a good way to go – in his sleep, he said. But then he'd had a conversation with his sister, Ruby who had lived most of her adult life in the United States after marrying an American tourist. She had returned for her mother's funeral but could not see her way back to Australia for her father's because of 'critical' work commitments. It had offended Nick to hear it but then berating her on the phone when she was obviously upset had made him feel guilty – all the more so because he didn't feel it was something he should apologise for and so it would likely linger between them.

So by the time Nick rang William to give him the details of the funeral, the calm had well and truly gone. He told William he was no longer sure Ron had died peacefully; he had been dead for several days and his face had had 'a look to it' he would never forget. By the end of the call, it was the quiver, the vulnerability, that had swayed William in deciding not just to go to the funeral in Port Augusta, almost five hours from Tarcoola, but to stay a while with his parents first and perhaps even drive them.

'We had to have it in Port Augusta,' Nick explained. 'That's where his old mates live and most everyone who's on the railway and unions and ...,'

William stayed quiet while his father recovered himself.

'It would mean a lot to your mother to see you,' Nick said finally and hung up before William could respond.

He's going to miss Ron more than he knows – He'll have no parents so no escape from mum and she's such hard work.

Since leaving Kimbanyon, even Adelaide, William had acclimatised slowly to the bombardment of city living. At first he had found it hard to sleep with the intrusion of lights and conversations from the sidewalk. His grandmother had said he was like Pavlov's dog when it came to bedtime – no matter what the day had held, when the light was switched off and the room was totally dark, he'd be asleep and stay that way until the sun came up again, without fail. At first, he had also missed the magic of the night sky in the outback. In the city it became almost incidental to the life below it, with the glow dissolving all but the brightest stars and only a few that his father had pointed out to him being visible, often without the companions that gave them their identity. He had also grown accustomed to being able to meet all his wants and desires now that he was on a good income, while being unaware of how his expectations of gratification had been heightened and his tolerance for ineptitude lowered. Much like his clients.

In Sydney, he walked briskly along footpaths flanked by office towers, so encompassed by glass and concrete that the reflected heat made it easy to forget that his skin was only infrequently aroused by the touch of sunshine during the working week.

He remembered when he first moved here and was living in a basement unit of an old colonial building converted for tenement living on Bridge Road, in the inner suburb of Glebe. He hadn't noticed that he always walked to the milk bar on the corner taking only shallow breaths and never talking in order to avoid excessive intake of pollution until a friend had visited and pointed it out. He felt foolish when his friend noted casually that there was obviously so much traffic, so much pollution because, after his street rose and fell though the suburbs, it became the main thoroughfare across Sydney Harbour – that's why it was called Bridge Road. His friend had laughed that it was a revelation to him after two years. That seemed a long time ago now.

William turned away from his musings and harbour view to his computer. He sent an email to his personal assistant, despite hearing her arrive as he typed, asking her to clear his schedule for two weeks, to provide his mobile phone number to several clients, and book a hire car for him from Adelaide airport. He rang his stockbroker and left instructions about purchases he wished to make if the market reacted the way he predicted it would. The broker, apparently, was already onto it.

Not to leave it to chance, William brought his assistant up to speed as he left his office.

'Morning Jenny. I'm just on the way out – family matter interstate – would you follow up on the email I've just sent you, oh, and arrange to have my car picked up from the airport. Spare keys with the others in the tearoom. I'll let the hire car company know where it is, so get the driver to go straight there. Thanks Jen.'

In the lift down to the car park below his building, he opened his briefcase, pushing it against his solid abdomen (a product of regular gym visits), to hold it while checking that it contained his wallet, iPad and mobile phone. He tossed the briefcase into the back seat of his black BMW and swung the car up the ramp toward the exit. As he climbed the steep drive and paused at the top, he saw Srijay, who regularly busked around the corner. He was setting up with his guitar and stool to catch the morning arrivals, his harmonica already attached to its hands-free steel frame around his jaw. William nodded to him from the driver's window. He pushed the button to withdraw his window so he could hear the music while he waited for a break in the traffic. He felt happy to be acknowledging the work of buskers now that he was no longer taking the train. There were so many in the city that he had gotten into the habit of avoiding their eyes so as not to feel compelled to make a contribution as he walked past. Then, probably through the guilt of it, he would leave their music in his wake as quickly as possible so as not to get something for nothing.

Overthinking it as usual.

The drive to the airport was typically congested but William had allowed an additional hour to get there and arrived in good time for his flight. He had packed only carry-on luggage, and was on the road from Adelaide in an 'executive' level Commodore organised by his secretary – *Nice pick Jen* – with a takeaway beef and gravy roll from an airport diner – *watch the suit, I'll need it for the funeral* – just as the midday news came on the radio.

William waited until he turned onto the Stuart Highway to put on a new CD he had not yet had a chance to play so he could listen to it without distractions. With the open road and hundreds of kilometres in front of him, he immersed himself in music that, as he had hoped, gently subsumed his surroundings and allowed him to glide through time without any of reality's 'glitches' interrupting the flow.

The harmonies wove around him in a caress so smooth, he could see why the composer had titled the album 'Porcelain'. And while the stereo system in the car was not as good as that in his BMW, it still enabled a connection with the strings and piano that was intimate enough to endear in him a kind of whimsical yearning as the kilometres slid away underneath him.

By the time the CD had run through six times, the intimacy had gone and each track on the album had begun to sound the same. Fearing he might actually doze off, William stopped it and turned on the radio. Reception was scratchy and after a while he switched that off too, leaving a silent car cabin in which to startle himself with a sudden burst of flatulence.

I knew that airport diner was suspect.

Despite all the road improvements, there was still a sparsity of services in the region, William realised as his discomfort grew increasingly vocal on the lookout for a roadhouse. He saw nothing by the old highway but a dead roo, his passing causing two ravens to lift momentarily off its ribs and then resettle to continue feeding, and a mangled red Corolla.

Wonder if the driver survived that.

Finally, on the very edge of Tarcoola, he came to a squat building with enough vehicles parked in an adjacent carport to suggest it might be for public use. He turned the Commodore in sharply. A skinny black dog emerged, sneezing. After taking a moment to shake himself off, the dog ambled awkwardly down the side of the building.

Someone ought to put that thing out of its misery.

William's stomach rumbled noisily. He swore he felt bubbles bursting in there and was growing alarmed at the prospect of having to drop his pants behind a tree. Once inside the building, he realised quickly that it was a nursing home and he could possibly masquerade as a visitor in order to use the bathroom but as he didn't know where one was and the issue was pressing, he chose to ask a casually dressed woman at the reception desk.

'Well, it's not a public toilet; there's one of those at the Tarcoola railway station,' she said curtly.

'I'm afraid that's not going to be possible, if you can help me out just this once,' William said in his most charming voice.

'Sure buddy. But you're going to have to sign in like a real visitor first.' The large woman with jowly cheeks and thinning hair was intractable.

'Seriously?' he asked.

She slid a large visitor's book across the counter to him, open at the day's date and handed him a pen with a chewed lid on its end. He looked at it with some disdain and scrawled his initials quickly in a corner of the page.

'Full name please, under the last one,' the woman said. It seemed to William, though her face was droll, she was enjoying his discomfort.

'You'll be wanting directions,' she said, her words following him down the hall as he looked left and right for the appropriate graphic on a door.

'Or maybe not …,' she added to herself quietly, with a shrug.

William's sigh of relief was gratuitously loud as he emptied his bowels in the pristinely white and surprisingly broad bowl of the nursing home toilet. Anywhere else he would have been embarrassed by his lack of inhibition, but as he had no intention of ever seeing these people again he saw no need to restrain himself unduly. The stench, however, was appallingly organic – *might even kill an old person!* –and he drove the door back and forward several times in an effort to diffuse it.

William stepped out of the bathroom to a different kind of commotion, erupting in the community room down the hall.

'I don't know her; get away from me; I don't know you.'

As he came to the entrance, he glanced in to see a woman probably in her early seventies skirting the edge of the room, her hands pressed flat against the walls, her eyes squeezed shut and her face turned away as if from a pending attack.

She seemed genuinely distressed, sometimes calling for assistance, sometimes addressing her perceived assailant directly.

'Get her away from me. Just go away.'

'Helen, it's alright. It's just me, remember? I'm not going to hurt you.'

William thought momentarily that it might give him some satisfaction to step in in a professional capacity and calm the situation down. It might even be good for his practice to help someone who wasn't wearing designer clothes for a change, but the day was getting old and he was keen to get to his father's place before nightfall, so William chose instead to walk past the disruption, nodding pleasantly at the grumpy receptionist, and head straight for his car.

He turned the radio on without any expectation of entertainment, and swung back out onto the main road.

75.

New turns in familiar stories.

[Friday, August 21, 1998.]

Despite the long drive to her father-in-law's funeral service awaiting her, Kate chose not to disrupt her routine; preparations were taken care of and there was little chance she would be missed at home for the next few hours at least. Nick was surrounded by friends from the railways – some of them his father's, some of them his, but all of them rusted on for the purposes of farewelling the legendary Ron. Rachel had arrived by train two days previously and had barely left her books. William had appeared in the doorway late yesterday, dressed incongruously in a suit and visibly unsure of where to settle himself in the chaos of the house, laden as it was with amicably inebriated men whose ease in his childhood home made him look like a stranger in it.

Eventually he had been seduced by new turns in familiar stories – how they thought Ron would have gone from a heart attack years before one took Sorrell, particularly as he was the one who could be counted on to blow his fuse. William heard for the first time how Sorrell had stood by him when he had suffered for being a conscientious objector and how not everything Ron did as a union organiser was 'exactly above board'. William seemed enthralled by the stories of Ron ranting 'virtually non-stop' for three days after Gough Whitlam was dismissed by the Govenor General, about how the country should be a republic to stop the Brits meddling in its affairs once and for all. William, despite being only three or four at the time, had thought he remembered that. And he laughed with the others when Nick told of how he had arrived at the house one night to find Ron half asleep on the porch, drunk as a skunk and crooning to Roo because he hadn't realised Sorrell had gone to bed.

Kate had enjoyed William finally soaking up the matey warmth radiating from Nick, whom he seemed to have been expecting to be maudlin and unapproachable. As she left the house, she smiled at the unlikelihood of seeing her husband and son, who had fallen into quiet contemplation over their beers in the early hours of the morning, draped over opposite couches, comically snoring in sync.

I hope he's not wearing that suit to the funeral!

Kate felt strangely buoyed as she drove to the nursing home where she volunteered. Perhaps those who gave their time to be an extra set of hands to change sheets, wash dishes or prepare meals got a sense of satisfaction from it, but Kate couldn't see how! She had offered instead to read to residents, much to the annoyance of the bedpan crew who hadn't thought of it first. She had unpacked the last of the books her mother had brought up for her soon after she had married and dispelled their musty smell with the emergent tales of adventure, renewal, challenge, love and hope. Some of her captive audience had appeared disinterested or distracted and had wandered off from the group but soon many could tell her exactly where she had left off in any given narrative despite a week passing in between chapters.

Kate had begun, unnecessarily, to defend her increasing commitment to volunteering at the home to Nick as if it were an essential service but the feeling that it brought her was that of a secret indulgence. She was coming to realise that she had inadvertently allowed her love of literature to slip under the tread of her married life and that exhuming it was fundamental to her wellbeing. Though she would never have admitted it to her mother, whose charity work was tied inextricably to altruism, this was all about her.

A surprising convert to the new activity in the home was Miss Muldoon, whom Kate had been told when she first came was unable to remember things from one day to the next and could be confused by simple instructions, written or otherwise. Because of this, Miss Muldoon had been denied the opportunity to choose a book when the library bus stopped there once a month – It would just frustrate her, staff had said, and if not, she would probably lose it.

Anything for an easy life.

So Kate had taken on Miss Muldoon and had been pleased so far with her response. She would accompany Miss Muldoon to her room when the afternoon shows came on – with appreciative smiles from the other residents warming her back – and sit in the corner to wait for her charge to plump her pillows up and climb onto her bed. Miss Muldoon would thank her for visiting, often addressing Kate as Trudy, and sometimes tell her she wasn't sure she would be staying in the home long enough to hear her story from the start, so perhaps Kate should begin closer to the end.

She was a strange woman, but Kate knew from the nurses that it was better not to contradict her, so she usually read from the chapter previous to the one other residents were up to, to make it easier to keep own her place in the book.

As Kate pulled into the driveway, she gave some thought to what choice of literature and audience might allow her to be home in time to drive with Nick to Port Augusta, where they had been invited to stay with friends overnight, leaving Will and Rachel to drive up together for the funeral service at midday the next day.

She might read a chapter or two of Charlotte Brontë's *Jane Eyre*, a book she had held no affection for in high school but had since appreciated for the pervasive eloquence that set it apart from modern novels. Or perhaps she might finish reading Katharine Susannah Prichard's *Coonardoo*, a battered paperback she had found in a second-hand bookshop about a white landowner who loves an Aboriginal woman but denies the relationship with horrible consequences. Both novels were intense and breaking for convenience would easily kill the vibe.

On poking her head into the dayroom, Kate was immediately calmed by the sight. A cool morning light was filtering through four windows on the opposite wall and sitting lightly on the heads of those already seated at chess boards set up the night before, or doing crosswords. Miss Muldoon was fixing herself a cup of tea to the rear of the room and frowning over the empty biscuit tin. She had on a knee length pleated skirt that looked too heavy for the warming weather and a plain cream blouse. She wore odd socks and men's slippers.

'Miss Muldoon, it's lovely to see you this morning. I'm Kate.'

'I know who you are,' came the response, 'You're the woman with the stories about that Aboriginal girl – whatsername?'

'Would you like to hear more about Coonardoo, Miss Muldoon? I wasn't going to read that today but since you remember the story…'

Miss Muldoon's eyes were shining.

'She let that Sam Geary have her, didn't she?' Even though she didn't like him. It's Hughie she loves isn't it? She slept with Sam because Hughie wouldn't be with her. Why wouldn't he be with her if he loves her? It doesn't make sense. But then I thought it was like Ed. Maybe she just got with Ed because she got sick of Hughie hiding her away, being ashamed of her. Probably he'd come in the night and she'd leave the door open for him. That's the way it works when they visit. Like a consolation prize.'

Hearing a rush of sentences – even as it bordered on jibberish and seemed this morning to be mixed with her own version of events (real or otherwise) – was as exciting for Kate as it was for Miss Muldoon.

'Well, the relationship's a little complicated and not really well explained,' Kate said, eager to help out. 'Why don't we sit over here and see if we can find an answer.'

Kate moved to put her hand under Miss Muldoon's elbow to guide her to some chairs by the window, but her charge lifted her arm away, tilting the tea a little from the cup she was carrying.

The women settled in a corner of the room that was vacant due to the armchair cushions being sunken by age and somewhat difficult to get up from for most of the residents. Kate began flipping through the book looking for a passage that might express why Hugh, the station owner who raised an Aboriginal girl Coonardoo up to be his housekeeper, does not acknowledge his love for her, despite being the father of her son Winni.

'Here,' Kate said, finding what she was looking for, 'I think Phyllis – you remember, Hugh's daughter to his wife who has left the station to live in town – might provide us with an answer. Phyllis is talking here to the man she wants to marry, defending her father.'

Kate began to read, while Miss Muldoon sipped her tea, her attention unusually fixed.

'I know of course, what the countryside thinks of Hugh and Coonardoo,' Kate began in an affected voice that she thought the character of Phyllis might use.

'There's nothing in it as far as I can see. There might have been once. Winni's a sort of stepbrother of mine, I suppose. Hugh says as much himself. It seems to me Coonardoo and Winni, as far as Hugh's concerned, were an accident.

'Hugh's been decent about them,' Kate continued reading. 'So decent people would hardly believe it if he told them, and he wouldn't bother to explain. He's like that, Youie – awfully decent inside. He's got a high standard of his own. "I believe in honour," he says, "Honour, courtesy, and keeping yourself clean."'

Helen was nodding. 'An accident. Coonardoo and Winni. Hmmm. I can see that. Hmmm.'

'Are you sleepy Miss Muldoon or do you want me to keep reading?'

'We haven't even had morning tea yet,' Miss Muldoon snapped, 'Why does everyone want to put me to sleep all the time?'

Kate suppressed a smile.

She's really on the ball today!

'Tell me more about Hughie's honour and keeping clean,' Miss Muldoon requested with affable insistence. 'He must always have a handkerchief with him for that.'

Kate had not wanted to leave Miss Muldoon while she was so lucid. Given a choice, she would have stayed to finish the book, if only to see how an evolved ending looked on Helen's face.

What a shame; chances are she won't remember a thing tomorrow.

'Miss Muldoon, I don't want to tease you but I can't stay very long today and the ending deserves some time. But I will come back – I promise – and we'll finish it then.'

Miss Muldoon smiled at her and nodded, simply remarking, 'Okay, if I'm still here'. The casual nature of the response evoked a surprising sense of pity in Kate.

'I guess I could leave the book with you. Do you think you might read it yourself?'

'Oh yes, I've always been a good reader; Miss Palmer always said so, but she doesn't bring me books anymore and there never seems to be any around here … .'

Kate handed her the worn text, hoping she would not regret leaving it at the home despite the gratifying glow on Helen's face as she flipped through its pages, lighting on a phrase here and there and refreshing herself with the story.

On her way out, Kate looked for Carmel, the nurse who had originally asked her to read to Miss Muldoon, to let her know she had left a book and to ensure it was not abandoned before she came to collect it. The girl at the desk told her it was Carmel's day off.

'Would you mind signing in before you leave; you forgot, and it's policy that everyone sign in.'

The girl at the desk was young, thin and unusually pale for someone living in the outback. Kate had not seen her before. She held up a pen expectantly. Kate took it, though she hadn't signed the visitors' book since her first visit six months ago. She flipped through the pages of scrawled signatures to find the last page for the current date.

'You know, you've got the same coloured hair as Miss Muldoon, without the grey streaks of course! It's kind of like a tabby cat. That's weird!'

Kate lifted her gaze to the girl, who appeared not to think her comments rude. She did not respond but turned her attention back to scanning the names. Something had caught her eye – a familiar combination of letters.

William! William was here. Yesterday!

'That's funny.'

'What's funny?'

'My son, he was here yesterday. Do you remember a young man, mid-twenties, fairly tall?'

'Well, there was this one guy in a suit; I didn't get a good look at him. I was helping the others with the cat lady – sorry, Miss Muldoon – in the day room. He didn't visit anyone; I think he was just using the toilet.'

Kate turned back to the book, flipping again through the pages. It hadn't been the letters forming the word 'White' that had caught her attention. It was …. There: 'Gweneth Holbrook'.

Mum?

'Excuse me, were you on reception yesterday?'

'Yes, I told you, I didn't see the guy in a suit, except on the way out. I think Faye did though.'

'No, not William; this woman.'

Kate swivelled the visitor's book back to face the receptionist, scanning the names again and pointing to the one she was interested in.

'Gweneth Holbrook: do you remember her?'

'That's not yesterday, that was a few days ago. Why, did you know her?'

'She's my mother. Do you know who she visited?'

The girl looked as if someone had stood on her fingers. She closed the book and pulled it off the bench, swivelling on her chair to face a drawer to her left, open it up and slip the book in.

'You're just s'pposed to sign the book, not read it, you know,' she said without returning her gaze to the bewildered Kate.

'Why was my mother here? Who did she visit?'

The girl shifted uncomfortably in her seat and began fiddling with pens in a tin cup in front of her as if arranging flowers.

'I'm asking you a question,' Kate said impatiently.

'Look, there's some bad news, but I'm not gonna be the one that tells you, so you're gonna have to find Faye, she's the one that found her anyway.'

'What do you mean "found her"?'

The girl stood up from her seat, clearly flustered.

'I have to go to the toilet; I'm really sorry,' she said, before scampering off down the hallway. Kate went in search of Faye.

***

Rachel woke with a start, butting her chin on the spine of an open textbook splayed face down across her chest. Her room was saturated with light, despite it being barely six, and she regretted not closing her curtains before she had fallen asleep. She pulled herself up on one elbow, letting the book slide to the floor. She looked to the window, intending to stretch her eyes over the landscape, but could not lift them above the partial and whole bodies of dead flies forming a motley line along the sill beside her pillow.

Why does mum leave them there? I don't know why I had to come here first. I should have just been able to meet them in Port Augusta.

She sat up in bed, and ran her fingers through her thin, stringy hair, lifting it up and letting it fall, as she did habitually when she first woke, before heading for the bathroom. In her student dorm, there was a shower for every four girls. Here, she thought, there was every chance she was going to run into a large, hairy, drunken – and probably weepy – male if she ventured out.

This whole funeral's going to be one giant hangover. Grandpa would've loved it!

76.

Drunks and little children.

[March, 2000]

The skinny one was hot. He was wearing full leathers and had foolishly spiked his hair with a significant amount of gel that morning. His friend Dan was dressed more lightly in blue jeans and a denim jacket, but he was also ready for a pit stop. As they rode their motorcycles abreast on the old highway, Shane caught his friend's eye and thumbed toward the edge of the road. The riders slowed in unison.

'You've got a woman's bladder, mate,' Dan asserted, removing his helmet as Shane strode down the embankment from the road to relieve himself.

He took a packet of cigarettes out of an inside pocket in his jacket. Turning his back on Shane, he leant on his bike and tapped the filter twice on the case as if to pack the tobacco hard up against it. He put it in his mouth, cupped his hands around the end of the smoke and flicked a flame from his lighter with his thumb. Shane continued to urinate in a torrent that could be heard by Dan despite being close to five metres away.

'You're gonna have to watch how much you drink or this road trip's gonna be a lot shorter than we thought,' Dan called to him half-jokingly without turning around.

Looking absent mindedly across the open plain as he shook the last drops and zipped up, Shane spotted the shell of a small car. A white cockatoo was walking around the base of it.

He called back to Dan. 'Hey, need any car parts?'

'What?'

'There's an old wreck over there might have some parts for Mandy's car.'

'Oh yeah?'

'I'm gonna check it out.'

Dan identified his target – assessed its partially crushed front end and tyreless rims – and decided instantly that it wasn't worth the walk.

'It's not even salvage mate; I'm gonna wait with the bikes.'

'Yeah, no worries,' Shane called back, 'but when Mandy wants to thank me for getting her little Corolla back on the road, don't expect me to be a gentleman and refuse her ….'

The idea of his friend having sex with his little sister was not something Dan wanted to dwell on, so he drew his keys from the ignition, gathered up Shane's from his bike and trudged reluctantly down the shoulder to the wreck.

Just a few metres from the vehicle, the dark bulk of a hunched figure became apparent through the clouded glass.

'Hey, there's someone inside.'

'Bullshit.'

'I'm serious. There's an old codger in the car.'

'It's a ghost, mate – no other explanation,' Dan mocked, his curiosity aroused nevertheless.

The coating of webs, dust and bird droppings deterred the friends from trying to clear a view closest to the inert shape. Instead they peered in across the row of glass teeth that was all that remained of the driver's window. The men were alarmed to see the body of an old man slumped in the back seat. His eyes were closed and his mouth agape, revealing teeth that even a dentist might revile from. With some relief, they noted that under the motley stubble covering his jowls and extending down the folds of his neck, was skin the colour of windburn.

Having determined the man to be alive, or at least not long dead, Shane canvassed his clothes. He was shirtless, with a formal navy coloured blazer open and revealing a bare, fleshy chest with a dark ring of hair around each nipple.

'From the smell of him, I'd say we've got ourselves a drunken sailor,' the biker concluded.

'That's not navy, you idiot, that's a railways insignia,' Dan asserted on closer inspection.

'Yeah, well, I think you're right about the ghost thing,' Shane quipped, before adopting a spooky tone as he circled around the car. 'Maybe he crashed here a hundred years ago and he's haunting the outback.'

The man remained inert, oblivious to their speculation. The only movement inside the vehicle was the blinking of the sun on a half empty bottle of Rum loosely held in the open curl of his fingers.

'Check this out,' Shane called to his mate over the car roof.

Dan stepped back from the window as the car suddenly lurched toward him. Shane was rocking the chassis, drawing his elbows into his slight torso and throwing his shoulders and back into an action made more difficult by collapsed suspension. Wads of newspapers, plastic bags, bottles and condoms were dislodged and spread throughout the car as it creaked noisily.

Shane rocked harder, yelling 'Wakey wakey, hands off snakey!'

The Rum bottle fell to the car floor, disappearing under the front seat and reappearing in a sea of rubbish with each sideways motion.

'Leave it Shane; he's just a drunk,' Dan urged, still shocked from the car jumping at him while he was thinking about the supernatural.

'Nice fella you are,' Shane retorted. 'He might be dead, for all you know. It's our duty to try and wake him.'

With that, he shook the car more violently, causing the man's head to loll side to side, without waking him but eliciting instead a muddy burp, followed by a gutteral moan.

'He's a bloody long way from town,' Dan noted with some relief at the sign of life. 'I don't see another car and it would be a bloody good effort if he rode that bike,' he said, nodding at a woman's bike with a rusty chain and partially attached front basket that lay on it's side not far from the car.

Shane soon tired of the exertion, his sweat now uncomfortably gluing his skin to the lining of his leathers and the smell of his labours rising pungently from his armpits. He turned his back on the old man and leant against the door. In between heavy breaths, Shane thought to settle his heart rate with another cigarette.

On his second puff, he saw with some annoyance a familiar frown on Dan's face.

'Don't you go getting any ideas, mate. We're not taking him back,' Shane said, as if Dan and the moaning man had made a joint request.

'There's no way he's throwing up on my jacket. Anyway, he'll be okay: God looks after drunks and little children, right? Or is it madmen and bums? I forget. Either way he's in good hands and hey, he can always cycle back the way he came in.'

'You're probably right,' Dan said and surprised Shane by walking off toward the road. 'But get that radiator will you? Looks like it's got a bit of life left in it. Mandy'd really appreciate that.'

Shane snorted: 'Smart arse!' He turned back to the old man who was now snoring, and sized him up, his attention drawn from his soiled pants to the shiny brass buttons of his jacket.

What a sad excuse for a human being.

A glint on the man's hip caught Shane's eye. He pulled the car toward him, gently this time, the motion coaxing the object from the man's pocket. A gold-plated fob watch rolled onto the seat. Shane let the car down slowly and gingerly reached in through the window. He pilfered the watch, looking up briefly to see whether Dan, who would have disapproved, was watching, before slipping it into his jacket pocket. He took a last drag on his cigarette and casually flicked the butt into the car, mouthing the words 'Sweet dreams grandpa' before jogging up toward the sound of Dan's impatiently revving engine.

Misfits.

[March, 2000.]

Helen had been sitting in the hallway since around four in the morning, her breathing shallow and the floor cool underneath her. Around her it was all grey, flat, quiet. The silence was cottony and encompassing – not that Helen registered the emptiness or a desire to fill it, or the fact that she could no longer summon the words to describe it. Her mind and body required nothing from her.

She blinked. It was still grey, flat and quiet, apart from Cat, who strolled toward her shortly before sunrise, from the end of the hallway to her right. When he got to her, he shook one paw as if to wake it up. Helen was looking vacantly at the wall opposite. Cat pushed his head under her hand, then his bony shoulders. He dropped his body to the floor. His fur was tufts of grease. Some of it stayed on Helen's skin.

By 8am, Cat had been long gone.

'There you are Miss Muldoon, it's time to get dressed now.'

The unknown nurse spoke directly to Helen and put her hand out to help her up. Helen behaved as if she had been struck, her arms rising to protect her face.

'Come on now. You and me, we're friends. We met yesterday, remember?'

Remember. Remember. Remember.

Helen would not take her arms down. She made a sound, like those that profoundly deaf people make, having never heard their own voices or the sounds of normal speech. It was an uncomfortable mix of yelling and moaning.

'Just leave her; she's okay for now. If she hasn't soiled herself, she can wait till breakfast.'

The voice came from somewhere distant. The unknown nurse wandered off. Helen felt something warm spread underneath her thighs.

By 8.30am, feet were trudging past her in a procession to and from toilets and breakfast. Slippers. Soles. Slippers. Bare feet, some with big toes bent across the others like hooks. Squeaky nurse shoes. Slippers.

At 10.20am, Faye arrived and spotted Helen in the hallway. She looked around for her colleagues.

'Why is Helen here? She's soaked. How can you not smell this?'

The other nurses got busy with manufactured duties or real ones that appeared to have extraordinary urgency.

Helen allowed Faye to lift her to her feet. The smell starched her nostrils, despite its familiarity, and a pool remained on the floor.

It's a wonder her urine smells at all; she barely eats.

'Helen, we may as well shower you love.'

Faye walked Helen down the hallway to the showers. The other residents had been indignant for some time that 'the cat lady' was given the privilege of being washed and dressed by one nurse, rather than the production line of stations the majority of the residents were subjected to – stripped by one nurse, sponged by another, dried by yet another and for those who needed assistance dressing, helped into their clothes by whoever was available at the end of the line.

They asked pointedly as she was led off to the showers first or last in her allotted time: 'If I scream, will I get the personal service too?'

Faye directed Helen to a spot in front of a tiled cubicle, the first shower in a row of six. A long channel at its base ran the length of them to a drain at the far end. Helen's gaze settled on the gutter and the shallow snake of soapy water that had not completely drained from it.

From a large cupboard with white louvre doors, Faye selected a towel that retained some colour and a respectable amount of thread, and a washer. She rejected a yellow bar of soap, reaching to the back for a smoother, creamier one that she then placed on the towel atop a chair beside the first shower.

Faye turned each tap with a practised hand to get the right temperature, detaching the shower hose from its prop and letting it rest in a metal bucket at her feet. The bucket began to fill with the warm water.

'Helen, I'm going to help you get that nightie off now, alright? Can you put your arms up for me?'

Wiry limbs that bore the bruises of mishap were dutifully raised. Faye lifted the nightie, bunching it as best she could in her hands so the soiled material did not touch skin as it traversed Helen's face.

'Thank you for not resisting, gorgeous. We'll get through this much quicker now, won't we?'

Helen blinked a couple of times to let Faye know she was thinking it over.

Helen doesn't resist. Helen doesn't exist.

'We'll just get you to sit down in the chair now, so I can wash you properly,' Faye continued, happy for her small talk to be ignored as long as things were ticking along. 'That's it.'

The affable nurse dipped the washer in the bucket and soaped it up. She smoothed it slowly over Helen's body, creating a thin, bubbly lather.

Helen doesn't resist. Helen doesn't exist.

Cupping Helen's left breast in one hand, Faye lifted it and briskly moved the washer underneath with her other. She swapped the washer into her other hand and repeated the process with the right breast. She dropped the washer back into the bucket and withdrew the shower head from its warm waters. She lightly pushed Helen's right knee and then her left knee toward the extremities of the plastic seat and directed the shower head between her legs. Helen blinked furiously as the pressurised water pelted her and then drained through the fist-sized hole in the seat.

'I'm going to need you to stand up now love.'

Helen turned her face to where the voice had come from. She allowed Faye to help her to her feet and stood still while the nurse hosed down her buttocks. The purple of the veins in the back of her legs rose with the warmth of the water.

Faye dropped the shower head back into the bucket. It overflowed onto the tiles at Helen's feet.

Boy those nails need cutting! I should do that while she's calm. Or maybe Carmel could do it tomorrow.

As Faye towelled Helen down, a commotion began in the common room. Mr Fenwick, who had overdone the deep heat treatment because he missed the smell of menthol and clubrooms and no longer had a sense of what overwhelms, was arguing in favour of having Mrs White read the finer print of his new almanac of Australia's finest footballers and was likely looking to legitimise it with a conversation in which he could impress the others with his broad knowledge of the game. He had some support from a number of residents, but there was strong opposition from those who had been waiting for the latest instalment of *Tess of the D'urbervilles*.

Faye smiled to hear it, moving more quickly now to press dry the strands of Helen's hair between her towel-wrapped hands.

Kate walked out of the common room, promising to return only when a decision had been made on what she might read. She decided, in the meantime, to go looking for Helen.

She found her sitting in her customary spot in the hallway, dressed neatly as if she had somewhere important to be. She had on stocking socks that did not reach her skirt. Her shoes, and one random man's slipper, sat beside her outstretched legs. Her hair was damp, a mist of water sitting lightly on the frizz of it and she smelt of lilac, or was it lavender? It reminded her, unfortunately, of the women's toilets at the Wily Rooster.

Kate didn't bother introducing herself. She didn't ask Helen what she might like to have read to her, but slipped silently down onto the linoleum beside her. She reached into her satchel to find a particular novel, her fingers identifying it by the width of its spine and the dog-eared cover. She sat with it on her lap for a moment, pausing to look at Helen and to wonder at how imperceptibly the fight to retain her faculties seemed to have been lulled.

Do not go gentle into that good night dear Helen: Rage, rage against the dying of the light.

Various feet passed them by. Some residents scowled at the thought that the cat lady had commandeered Kate's attention, others seemed pleased that she was out of their hair, sometimes even thanking Kate conspiratorially with a whisper or a wink, while others took no notice of them.

Despite being over familiar with Helen's favourite story, the tension was now beginning to leave Kate's body as subtly as sensation returns after numbness. Her heart rate was slowing, only seeking her attention by sighing in between beats, and the scent of Faye's labours now shifted in her mind from the Kimbanyon pub to the garden at Irving Street.

Kate skipped across the pages of *Coonardoo*, deciding where to pick up the story. She did not feel like spilling the tragic end of the novel into their peaceful hallway. She did not want to tell, yet again, the story in which Hugh, lashing out over another man having his way with 'his woman', pushes Coonardoo away from him into a campfire, causing her to wander from pillar to post with abhorrent wounds and scarring and a broken heart.

She glanced at Helen. Her skin was returning to its normal colour after being flushed from her shower but her eyes still reflected little more than the cream wash of the walls opposite them. Kate turned to the novel, skimming blindly over the type on each page. On her 'good days', reinvented storylines unfolded from her imagination like long blades of grass reviving in the wake of a bounding dog, but today they weren't coming easily.

'Hugh looks out over his property,' she began, glancing at Helen to see if she was listening. Her gaze had not moved from the wall opposite, though she was blinking less as the movement in the hallway had slowed and people began to settle into their morning's activities. Kate went on, thinking one word ahead of each written one, attempting to craft a gentler narrative.

'It is blessed with ancient Boab trees, giving the landscape a sense of timelessness. From his verandah, Hugh can see it all clearly – the life that he has built, its place in the natural order and his place in it.'

Kate paused, unsure of where to take the story.

I should have started with a plot line, not a description!

She turned back to Helen and thought of her sitting alone in this corridor, hour after hour, while other residents of the nursing home bustled around her, settling in groups for activities or meals. It occurred to her after all these years, that she liked reading to Helen, because, ironically, it also gave her a chance to be alone.

Misfits, the pair of us. Or maybe we've just got a different perspective on things ... Like ...

***

Kate renewed her version with fresh confidence. 'Though she shares a life with Hugh, Coonardoo does not have the same pride he does in how the station has grown and how the homestead within it is regarded by other pastoralists.

'To Coonardoo, the land has always been there and will continue long after the station is gone. Her home is not marked by the fences that Hugh has built, but by places of ceremony and dreaming.'

Carmel walked past them, catching Kate's eye to wink at her as she carried sheets off to the bedrooms down the hall. Kate wondered at how Carmel sometimes spoke about her 'mob', though she knew from a discreet conversation with Faye that Carmel had no brothers or sisters and that she had grown up on a Christian mission.

She thought of how her own father had been sent from England as a child and, despite being settled in Adelaide for many years, had always seemed to her to be quite restless. He had lived comfortably with his family and enjoyed the respect and loyalty of a regular congregation, but none of these things had tied him to his life. Even his Faith had failed him in the end.

It seemed to Kate that the human spirit would always be restless if it depended on a common definition of 'home' because people and places could be tarnished or taken away so easily. It made more sense to her to love the moment, be it fleeting or prolonged over a period of months or years, and to love those people in it as part of that moment. The pleasure of it all would be a pure one, because you would not have planned your future around those people and therefore your time with them would not be coloured with the fear of losing them.

And maybe that's the way it's meant to be and we should still value those people who are with us for a brief time because of what they bring to our lives: here for a reason, if only for a season.

Kate suddenly remembered that she was 'here for a reason' and was momentarily fearful of how long she had been 'off with the fairies' as the nurses put it. She looked down at the open book that she had let fall limp in her lap and realised that her musings on Hugh and Coonardoo were redundant today and that her audience of one would likely be called on for morning tea, having missed her breakfast, or a sleep soon enough.

She slipped her hand into Helen's, prompting no response beyond a brief shiver. She chose to let her thoughts float in their mutual silence and fell quiet unless someone walked past, reading a passage from the book out loud if only to avoid them thinking that she was similarly afflicted by Helen's inertia. She stretched her back and noticed from the corner of her eye that Cat was with them, needling the slipper mischievously with his claws.

She wondered if it might be possible to take Helen out for a walk, perhaps even to get 'day release' and let her sit on her verandah at home in Kimbanyon for a while, like a special family guest.

Surely it would be kinder than letting her waste away here day after day, losing her mind.

It was not difficult to withdraw from the corridor, though Kate's back protested a little as she got up. Helen did not acknowledge the departure, still rigidly fixed as she was on the wall. Cat was now under her hand, purring. His frame was vibrating so hard that as Helen's fingers parted, spikes of fur stood up between them like weeds in fissures.

***

Outside of town, Grimsely lay on his side in the back seat of the car wreck. At his feet old newspapers variously sodden with alcohol or bone dry were igniting from the discarded butt of Shane's cigarette. The corner of an envelope protruded from between the black and orange curls. Grimsley began to cough.

He raised himself up on one elbow and waved away the thickening smoke. His eyes were burning and his toes were impossibly wet inside his boots. As flames took hold, Grimsley pushed open a back door and fell out, landing on his head, without support from his slow-moving arms, and drawing his legs out subsequently.

He lay on the dirt beside the car for a few moments, his lungs seemingly unable to hold air. He closed his eyes against the shooting pains in his neck and found his body lumbering and unresponsive. He patted his hip instinctively. He pulled himself to his feet and pushed each hand into each pocket. There was no watch.

It must have slipped out.

Despite smelling the foam combusting in the seats, Grimsley steadied himself and his resolve on the open door, his inebriation masking the scald. As he crawled back inside the car, the smoke and heat was intense. He closed his eyes and pushed his hand, already blistering, down the crevasse at the rear of the back seat. He stabbed his finger on buried glass, and hastily withdrew. He turned his attention then to the car floor and saw a glimmer among the flaking newspapers under the driver's seat.

Grimsley pulled a handkerchief from his jacket pocket, mopped the sweat from his face and chest and wrapped the damp material around his left hand, the one that wasn't bleeding. He flopped his whole body down on the backseat and reached forward, losing sight of the shiny object as he lay his head on its side to get a further extension. He touched something smooth, very hot. *My Bundy.* He pushed the bottle aside and rummaged blindly through the rubbish for his watch. After a long minute of coughing, it felt like his larynx had been dipped in cotton wool and he was forced to give up the search. On impulse, he retrieved the Bundaberg Rum, swinging it out the open door before it could meld with his skin.

Falling backwards from the vehicle, Grimsley lay there a moment before bringing himself to all fours, his last convulsion profusively vomitous. Casually he looked over at the bottle, glaring at him now under the bright sun. Something was stuck to it. He dragged himself to his feet, wiping his mouth with his jacket that was now making him unbearably hot.

It was an envelope. Though its edges were rimmed in a saliva of gold and orange and coloured by swirls of grey and black, it was remarkably intact. He liberated it gingerly from the glass and pushed it with his poorly swaddled hand into the dirt, suffocating any remaining spittles of fire.

His curiosity aroused, Grimsley looked sadly toward his preferred reading spot to take in the extent of the damage. A fiery glow was infiltrating the smoky haze, rising through it like fingers on outstretched arms. So it was with vague but unsettling thoughts of the Devil, that Grimsley turned to the envelope.

It was addressed to Mrs Katherine White. *The Reverend's girl.*

He peeled the letter open. In parts, the ink was diluted beyond legibility, and at one juncture, the script had been swallowed by a charcoal fog that remarkably had not yet destroyed the paper. Grimsley felt compelled, if a little sickened by the effort it required in his addled state, to read it. This is what he was able to make out:

'Dearest Kate,

'It seems the world has caved in on both of us, and I suspect you have no idea why. Certainly you should not be in that clinic without support from your father and, for this, I feel you deserve an explanation.

'You should know I am deeply ashamed of …' (here the words faded away) ' … and do not want my absence from your life to upset you further or lead you to rely more heavily on your mother, who carries burdens of her own.

'You bear no fault in any of this Kate, and you must remember that so you can return to health for your sake as well as your son's.

'I don't know the details of what happened to bring you to this point, but I do know that you have a good heart and would not purposefully seek to harm your child. I truly believe that.

'I also believe that you would find great comfort in the Lord, if you would just let Him in, and that in times …'(the black smear intruded here)

'In the spirit of progressing your recovery, there are some things your mother believes you should know and that I should tell you. Your mother and I have grown apart and I have no idea what she has told you and what she has hidden from you.

'I'm assuming that you are aware …' (Here the ink had disappeared) 'and this news is a shock to you.

'Your biological mother resides close to your home town, in a nursing facility in Tarcoola. Her name is Helen Muldoon. I cannot vouch for her mental health or wellbeing; she was a brave and feisty young woman, much like yourself, when she gave birth to you but it has been a lifetime since I have seen her. I expect she might now be the worse for wear as there is a history of dementia …'(Grimsley attempted at this point to clarify something in brackets about an 'assault on the functions of the brain' but after a brief effort and doubling of his vision, he skipped it.)

'Your natural curiosity, if it has not been dampened by your marriage, will probably lead you to seek this woman out. I have been told by others it is your right to do so, though I believe your life would be none deprived by not taking this course of action and may even be diminished by the torment such contact could bring you.

'If you do go down this path, you might hear things that surprise you, but I can't apologise for the actions that brought you to me. Gwen and I adopted you not just in the spirit of charity, but with genuine desire for a family. You were raised in a Christian home where you wanted for nothing. In judging me, you should remember that any unhappiness you might feel as an adult is more likely to be rooted in your own choice to shun your education and deny your potential, rather than anything I have inflicted on you.

'At the risk of making the same mistake twice, I would advise you to consider how much happier you might be if you pursued a life of ambition rather than mediocrity.

'I want you to think also about what a good mother Gwen has been to you and know that she has always blindly taken your side. Telling you of your adoption would have hurt her greatly, but in this too, she believes ...' (Here, frustratingly, the words again disappeared.)

Already weary and bewildered, Grimsley found his head aching from trying to put it all together.

So the Reverend's daughter is adopted! Kate Holbrook – Kate White. And the Spinster Muldoon is her real mother? Jesus. How did that happen?

Grimsley could not fathom why he had been marked for such torture. For years he had managed the town's mail. All the telegraphs during the Second World War had come through his tiny station office. He did not want to be intimate with anyone's pain anymore. And he didn't want to know now what he'd just read in that letter.

Behind closed lids, he could see Kate's staggering form, near naked and smeared with clay. He fingered the scar he had got crashing onto the ballast and a fixated Helen Muldoon to drag her from the path of an oncoming train. It had been easier for Grimsley to accept his part in locking away these women – to being a first hand witness to their mental collapse – when the coincidence was too random to explain.

But this! Mother and daughter. Why couldn't they leave me alone?

Grimsley also struggled with the Reverend's 'fall from grace'. He had seen him come and go through his station and town for almost 30 years. Avery Holbrook was a calm and righteous conservative – a dependable man of God ... *who killed himself, if the rumours are true.*

The old station master shakily reinserted the pages into the envelope, which now barely held together. He got up awkwardly and turned back to where the bottle lay on the dirt. The glass was now cooler in his hand. He swayed a little from the rush caused by bending down too quickly, and then headed for the car. It was smouldering still, but the smoke had thinned. He reached for the rear door, forgetting to let go of the handle when he pulled away from the heat, dragging it off its hinges and falling back underneath it. Gruffly, Grimsley pushed it aside, and staggered forward again with the letter and the bottle, to climb into the back seat.

Amidst the smoke and stench of near melting vinyl, Grimsley looked at the two items in his hands. The letter seemed the more evil. He let it fall from his grasp to the floor, leant his head back and tipped the last of the warm Rum down his throat only to bring most of it back up over his chest. As embers flared around his trouser legs (liberally soaked as they were in alcohol), the smell of panic mixed with his earlier vomit in his nostrils and Grimsley leant forward over his knees, expecting to purge.

In spasmodic coughs, his breath shot holes through the smoke and fanned the flames darting around his feet. Through them, Grimsley's watery eyes caught glimpses of the letter and he suddenly felt – with all the integrity he had shown previously in delivering bad news during the war – that he must witness its destruction. And when Avery Holbrook's confession had become nothing but ash, and Grimsley could barely breathe, the proud stationmaster slowly rolled himself into a foetal position on the back seat of the burning car and closed his eyes.

78.

Fate's wild card.

By his 20th wedding anniversary, Nick finally felt comfortable with his marriage. Kate no longer tugged at his conscience by seeming to him bigger and brighter than her surrounds – a constant reminder of her family's belief that she had been 'wasted' in marrying him. Finally, she seemed settled and sure of herself and he had not felt anxious about how he might find her when he came home, not for years now.

The only other great worry in Nick's life – Duggie's injury and his role in it – also lingered less often and less painfully in Nick's thoughts, despite the stunted limb being so overtly present in his everyday life. Their partnership in a long haul business had given them both some closure on that day. Nick had invested the proceeds from the sale of his parents' house on a second rig and Duggie had invested what he had saved from his injury compensation on a third. Their timing had been perfect, capitalising on the rapid expansion of a new mining venture with back-to-back contracts. It hadn't been easy at the start watching how difficult it was for Duggie to manage with one hand, but he never complained and business was profitable for both of them, so, for the most part, Nick was able to put it behind him.

At first Nick thought Kate might not accept the relationship with Duggie, given his part in Gwen's death.

And Roo's. That was a blow.

But his wife seemed less intense these days, easier to be around. Perhaps she appreciated that he and Duggie were a good team and that this business meant they could be relaxed about the future and their ability to support their adult children when they needed it.

We've got great kids. I still can't believe Duggie found his daughter right on our doorstep, at Gwen's funeral of all places.

It was funny how all their lives had aligned, almost like it had been pre-destined – something Sorrell might have suggested in the way she had of instantly accepting things as they were and dealing with them on the spot.

'People who blame and question and regret just end up with spastic colons,' she used to say.

Sorrell had been a fixer – of bodies and minds. She did it without fuss or fanfare and Nick missed her more than he could put into words.

He felt he had done his best as a husband but he could not convince himself that Kate had spent a tenth of the time he had invested in their relationship thinking about him or his wellbeing.

She doesn't have the capacity to deal with anyone else's problems. She's not interested in the business or how the portfolio is doing. She loves her books and talking about the weather, which is crazy because it doesn't change much out here and it's not like we're farming. I think what she's doing at the nursing home has been a good thing for her; they tell me she's really sweet with old folks. It's a shame mum and dad never got to see that side of her!

The thought that Ron and Sorrell would have been proud of the changes he'd made to make his marriage stronger, sustained Nick when he was low. He knew his wife was pleased that he had left the railways and that Duggie took the lion's share of the road time so that he could work in the office overseeing the other drivers. The irony wasn't lost on him that he was finally able to be home at a time when he no longer had fears about leaving Kate alone … or with their young children.

I don't know that I ever really thought Kate was a risk. I never wanted her to feel that I did, anyway, and it's noone's business now.

Despite some shortcomings as parents, somehow their children had proved themselves capable of forging a future without them in it. Rachel was enthusiastically overworked as a surgical intern in a Sydney hospital. How she had done so well in the sciences was still a mystery to Nick – perhaps she was a throwback to Sorrell – though he was quick to acknowledge her doggedness as a trait she had got from him.

That is, afterall, how I won her mother.

Nick was proud of the fact that Rachel had held on in her studies at junctures where others had dropped off, even confessing to her family that she enjoyed working with cadavers in the hospital's teaching morgue. She had not yet had a significant relationship and both he and Kate feared she would never possess a good bedside manner, but Rachel would be a fine surgeon.

With any luck Grandpa Dalana will live long enough to see her graduate and then he can claim both my kids have his genes!

William? Nick knew that boy would do well wherever he landed. He'd never molly coddled him and though he'd been disappointed at first that Will had no interest in the family business, he respected his very early determination to be independent.

He's worked hard to be living among the fat cats of Sydney, even though he'll never know a blister and his mother thinks he's doing it by preying on the weak!

For her part, Kate also considered herself content in her marriage. When she looked at Nick, she didn't see a man who had drawn her into an environment where she could not survive, or a man who, for all intents and purposes, had abandoned her when she needed him most; she saw a husband who came for her, who carried her out of a garden bed where she had stood day after day, stupefied. She loved him for being a good father to her children. She loved him most for never mentioning that place or that time since. Before it, she had despaired of the monotone of their conversations, now she genuinely took an interest when he spoke of floating his company and what the shares might be worth. Where once she perceived herself as languishing into oblivion staring out from the verandah, she had come to see that movement in the sky and talk of the weather had bearing on their days and that Nick genuinely seemed interested when she predicted dust storms or rain. The drought had passed.

Kate had learned to live with a lot of things, including her parents' deaths. If William had asked her to describe how she felt about Avery's suicide, all these years on, she would say she was 'quietly angry', that she considered what he did to be infinitely selfish and that he was undeserving of her sympathy. It was an honest appraisal for the most part.

Over the years, Kate's children had been a welcome focus, dominating most of her time with Nick when they were young and now, as they led eventful and ambitious adult lives, giving her fodder for contained conversations when called on to have them with residents around town.

Kate phoned Rachel once a month and enjoyed hearing how William took his sister out for a feed every now and then, or how she might catch him at his favourite boutique pub with his friends if she needed to borrow money from him which both of them knew she would never pay back. Kate listened with bemusement as Rachel spoke condescendingly of her brother's silk-suited friends and their over inflated opinions of themselves but then played on his generosity to go see the latest Star Wars movie.

The White children hadn't always got on, but that was to be expected. Rachel was William's half sister, something Kate barely condoned as a thought let alone a reality. The real father was suppressed in her thoughts, only ambushing her when random expressions transformed her daughter's face, sometimes revealing teeth better sized for the mouth of a toddler, or her attitudes showed an audacious lack of sensitivity, such as when she had asked Duggie to let her remove another section of his limb in order to fit a new prosthetic – not because it would help him, but because she thought it could help her secure a placement at a prestigious city hospital. But then Rachel was also distinctly her own person and because of this Kate could think of her abruptness with affection, like when she had offered her very practical grief counselling along the lines of 'Do or do not, there is no try', a line she learnt later was first issued by Yoda in The Empire Strikes Back!

At first Kate had only suspected that her daughter was not Nick's; though she was at the clinic for years, much of her time there was thankfully a blur and she had little stomach for sharpening her recall once she had left. Nor did she have the will to join the class action proposed to her by a lawyer, whose call came as a bit of shock initially. What would be the point of being one more name on a long list of his victims? Gant would be punished, or at least deregistered, without her help. And as far as Kate was concerned, keeping Rachel oblivious to the fact that her real father was a man who raped drugged-up mental patients was a smart way to prevent her from becoming one herself.

Kate would continue to protect Rachel's relationship with Nick, cognisant of the loss she had felt when her own with Avery deteriorated. She thought of what an awkward and, toward the end, detached parent he had been and wondered whether it was because he had suffered from growing up without family. Regardless, Kate would not deprive her own daughter of the unconditional love of a father, or the opportunity to make of herself something more than the scars of her past would allow her to be.

Of all that Kate had been forced to deal with, the death of her mother had probably been the hardest for her to reconcile. William had been wonderful as she had struggled to cope with the suddenness and brutality of the accident. With some pride in being able to support his usually cloistered mother, he had encouraged her to be open about her grief.

So Kate had told him how, at the sink, driving, sometimes lying back in bed wondering what season it was, she had been disturbed by violent daydreams in which Gwen was repetitively pummeled until she lay limp on the road. At night the visitations had bathed her in sweat.

Her son had helped her get past the sensory assault and to ask herself whether there was more to her distress than the physical nature of her mother's death.

Why didn't she come and see me? Why was she here? What did she want from Miss Muldoon?

William had told his mother that the 'less visceral' questions would soon replace the maulings of her dreams and, in turn, become 'less febrile in the subconscious'. They would be easier to deal with in the long term, he had said, because questions that could be answered with a multitude of possibilities and theoretical outcomes became less threatening over time, even while remaining unresolved. It had seemed to Kate at the time to be an absurd proposition but she clung to it because at least this mystery did not bring guilt to the doorstep of her slaughterhouse the way her father's death had.

There isn't a sword sharp enough to slay that dragon.

William had been generous with his time, staying on after Ron's funeral to attend Gwen's in Adelaide, where he held up his sister whom he had not realised was so close to her grandmother, and then bunked with his folks in Kimbanyon for a few more weeks after that. Despite this, he was gone before Kate was ready for him to be – just when she felt she knew where the edge of the cliff was, but not how to step back from it.

What about my mother's secrets? What am I to do with them?

With Gwen's death there were plenty of scenarios but no explanations. Duggie knew nothing of why Gwen had come to Tarcoola or even that she was Nick's mother-in-law. As he told it, it was a coincidence that he had both picked Gwen up when she had broken down and had been on the road at the same time Roo had swerved in front of him and ended up totalling Gwen's car. All Duggie could tell Kate was that Gwen had seemed 'a very nice lady' but not a chatty hitchhiker.

There were no clues in her mother's abandoned car, which Kate had given to Faye by way of replacing the one Gwen had borrowed. Nor were there any answers to be found in her recovered handbag or single suitcase. The red Corolla now stood as a vandalised shell, a loveshack for teenagers and a shelter for drunks just outside of town. She suspected Nick, Matt and Davo had pushed it further away from the roadside, so she would not be confronted by it if she drove to Port Augusta or Adelaide, but there was little she could do now about being confronted by her mother's car in the staff carport when she volunteered at the nursing home.

I guess I should have thought about that before I gave it to Faye!

With William's help, Kate had succeeded generally in getting on with life after her mother's death. She was sleeping at night now but she found herself prone to outbursts that she blamed on her upset stomachs, as if the niggle of not knowing lay in wait like a pinch of gunpowder in her gut.

William's parting advice had been to use a technique that Kate could only think of as a 'catch all' solution – no more complicated, in her mind, than seeing something good in something bad. And while it felt ugly to be pursuing a 'silver lining' in such a bloody affair – Kate had to admit that the one that emerged was truly remarkable. As the second death of a parent in a week had tested her own family, it had brought another together. The two most out-of-place people at Gwen's funeral – Duggie and Carmel – had begun talking behind the service and discovered a connection. It turned out that Carmel, whose mother had died in childbirth, had been taken to a church mission for 'half-cast' children when she was a girl, just like Duggie's daughter.

Seeing Duggie and Carmel in each other's company had a calming affect on Kate. Once Nick and Duggie established their business, Kate would invite them over frequently for barbecues. Unbeknown to them, she thrived on the distraction of being in their presence as they discovered new things about each other, like the necklace Carmel's aunty had given her matching the eagle Duggie had tattooed on his shoulder. They would sit on the White's verandah and Carmel would tell Duggie stories like how she and the other kids would beat down the seedballs from the Mungata trees around the mission in Spring and eat them raw, or stew them up to make pies and Duggie would teach her language that the missionaries had denied her speaking. Nick told Kate that they also called each other by different names when they were alone.

Kate discovered the other person who could be relied on to calm her restless mind over a long period of time and with some surprise. When she was first introduced to Miss Muldoon, the woman had been shadowing Carmel to the point of grazing her heels and was in dire need of an anchor. She was erratic, panicky, often abrupt and increasingly suffering from a vaporous memory.

Frustrated residents who wanted Kate all to themselves in her new role as literary entertainer suggested Miss Muldoon could be distracted with a picture book. Deciding not to deny her the liberations of adult fiction was possibly the first truly altruistic thing Kate had done, but that did not mean her temperament was suited to the compromise it required. Hearing her own voice convert the elegant words of admired authors into simplistic and sometimes clumsy phrasing was something that had embarrassed Kate. She had liked even less the idea that Miss Muldoon wouldn't notice or be slighted by the disrespect shown in 'dumbing' down the prose. When she finally changed tack and superimposed her own creations on existing storylines – it marked not only a change in Kate's understanding of Miss Muldoon's condition but also the level of her own enjoyment.

When she opened those novels now, rather than butchering art, she would embellish the pathways and projections to take the tales in more adventurous or mellow directions, depending on the moment. Her voice became the herald of a freshly stimulated mind, and would transcend the sterile monotony of every routine and space in the home.

Kate felt enormous satisfaction that Miss Muldoon was capable of being lost in a fictional world without panic of the unknown, for trust in her guide. The story was everything between them and Kate was vigilant in keeping herself or anything she knew of Miss

Muldoon from dictating its evolution. There were only words, and while they were offered and received in this purest of forms, the two women were at peace.

The relationship had come close to being ruined when Kate understandably crossed this line. Within days of her mother's death, she had questioned Miss Muldoon about Gwen's visit. She was capricious. According to the nurses, who were curious themselves, it was not a sign that she understood or was harbouring a past relationship with Mrs Holbrook, but that she was being frightened by Kate's insistence. On the advice of the nurses, Kate had then waited for a 'good day' to resume her gentle interrogation. But on this subject, at least, there didn't seem to be one. Over almost a year, she had had it at the back of her mind, bringing it to the fore when she thought it opportune. Miss Muldoon would become distressed and confused, dismissing her queries casually or raging at her, calling her Mabel and spitting that none of it was her business.

In the end, pursuing it was too much for both of them and eventually, with more relief than Kate cared to admit, she conceded defeat and allowed them both to retreat back into the innocence of unburdened readings.

Kate had also found some peace in being back in the water again. She taught swimming at the local pool, built with royalties from a mining company that had, to the great surprise of the locals, found what they were prospecting for and brought new wealth and working families to their edge-of-the-desert town. That was a remarkable day – when water had been railed in to fill the pool. The whole town had gathered to watch the level rise, thumb by thumb, until finally it glimmered full, the gentle sounds of lapping at the edges enticing the first brave few to jump in clothes and all.

With it, Kate had enjoyed a fitness she had not experienced for years. She swum laps most mornings in summer and took classes three afternoons a week after school. She was generally popular with the children and newer families in the area, with her role compromised only once by the intrusion of gossip from a grandmother who had warned a couple that it would be foolish to trust Kate alone in the water with their young ones. An embarrassed mother passed on to Kate the whispered words of the meddlesome crone: 'She tried to drown her own child, you know.'

Numbers had dropped off significantly as that rumour had spread through the parent group, but most of them came back the following summer. No one had said anything – about why they had left or why they had come back – and Kate was not one to indulge them. What was there to say? She was still confused as to why something so innocent had resulted in making her husband, her parents and her in-laws so fearful that they had abandoned her to strangers and a languish of meds.

For years she had sat torpidly in front of her counsellors, never offering an explanation, never accounting for her 'crime', never revealing how exhilarated she had felt in that watery ampitheatre and how much, in her loneliness, she had wanted to share it. It didn't seem to matter to them.

Even Nick had not seemed interested in an explanation during those first years back home. Not once did he ask, either out of a misguided sense that his silence would ensure her ongoing 'recovery' or because he knew deep down that it had been nothing more than a storm in a teacup and felt some guilt over what had been allowed to happen to Kate while he was away down the line. As William had grown into a confident teenager and she and Nick had got on with the business of family life, Kate had nurtured the sense of being safe that her husband's position had allowed to grow in her mind, until the reason she had needed to nurture it was near forgotten.

But with the threat of the poolside gossip spreading from the mothers to their husbands at the mine, Kate had feared Nick would find himself amongst it and finally come to her, confessing his doubts. She had forced herself to think clinically about what she remembered of that day, of what could possibly have forced the hand of her family in interning her and taking her from her child.

There was a storm. I'd never seen anything like it in Kimbanyon; the rain was torrential, blinding. It filled the dam: it was empty for years, then it was full. We rode on the bike, to have a look. I took Billy out of the basket and lay him down at the top of the dam. Long Dog lay down beside him. He was licking him. I remember he smelt so bad, like wet dogs do. I looked to the water. It was incredible. I kicked off my shoes. I dropped my shorts. I ran down into the dam, falling at the bottom and coming up with a mouthful of mud. I strode in. The water was cool on my shins. It got deeper as I walked, my fingertips dragging behind me. I crouched to feel the water against my belly. Silky below, jumping on the surface. The rain was drumming into the dirt at the lip of the dam walls, plucking at the water and raising a giant halo of steam around me. Rivulets had formed in the embankments. Streams were entwining and coursing into the rising waters. Limy clay squelched between my toes. I looked to the sky. I had to close my eyes. I could feel every single drop this way. I held my breath and let my skin breathe. I bobbed down so the water could cool my breasts. My singlet lifted and ballooned. I took it off and threw it up. The rain beat it down. I twirled again. I wanted to share this feeling. I looked back behind me, to the edge of the dam where I had left Billy and the bike. I left him with Long Dog. Long Dog was still there, barking. He was on the edge barking at me. He was dripping. He looked half his normal size. The bike was there. Billy wasn't. I ripped through the water toward the bike. The water dragged heavily. I got to the edge of the dam and screamed at Long Dog: 'Where's Billy?' I turned back to the water. I called out: 'Billy.' I shouted: 'Shut up Long Dog!' I looked to the other sides of the dam. Then Long Dog was in the water. His head was bobbing back and forward. He was reaching out, paddling in a circle. I ploughed back into the water toward him. He was still swimming in a circle. I dived under, in the middle of it. I opened my eyes. It was murky but I could see swatches of pink floating in and out of my reach. My hand encircled a limb. I lifted it; it was Billy and he wasn't upset at being under the water; he was peaceful. He seemed happy. He's a natural, I thought, like the first time my mother swept me through the water by an arm and a leg. Like I would skim Billy. He became part of the flow. He wasn't upset, or hurt; we were both laughing. But Long Dog wouldn't shut up. I was moving Billy so fast, he must have thought it was a game. I wanted Long Dog to shut up. He was spoiling it. Billy's head was trailing his body as I pulled him by the arms, left and right, sending up a spray and leaving a wake. The rain wasn't hard anymore; it was falling softly on us and making us sleepy. My arms were sore then, and Billy began to sink under the water as the skimming slowed. I pulled him up onto my chest. He was definitely sleepy. I carried him out of the dam. I passed the bike. I didn't want to ride; I liked the feel of Billy's skin on mine. It was warm where our bodies touched. But he didn't snuggle into me. His head flopped. He didn't pop his lips, even though milk was leaking from my breasts.

I remember when I saw Long Dog alone on the embankment that day, I had the sensation of an icy needle skewering quickly in and out of my heart. I know that, in giving Billy back to me alive, Fate chose not to damn me but to play its wild card. I got my baby back, but somehow, no matter how many ways I re-imagine it, something is still lost. I close my eyes and Billy comes up from the depths, but when his face emerges, it is blank. I look up at my own face – as if through his eyes – and it's blank too. I look down into the turbulence and there, in front of me, are our vagrant masks, the features variously wistful or tortured, depending on how they tilt and bob about the surface, drifting further from my reach …

Nick was right not to ask.

79.

A conversation with John Doe.

A month or so after her return to the family, Kate had visited the library bus. She found it galling that, after years of chatting about literature, Gillian Brown had chosen to wait until she returned from the nut house to proffer her the book that would give her the following sage advice.

'He who fights with monsters should be careful lest he become one. And if you gaze long into an abyss, the abyss will also gaze into you.'

It was from Nietzsche's 'Beyond Good and Evil: Prelude to a Philosophy of the Future'. Gillian had taken it from a rack, dog-eared the page on which it was pointedly underlined in pencil, and handed it to Kate without saying a word. Her almost apologetic smile and overly intimate squeeze of her hand as Kate accepted the book was the only responsibility she took for the presumption.

Kate shared her thoughts just now on what happened that day in the dam – a metaphorical abyss if ever there was one – partly because the telling of her story here required it, and partly because of Gillian's gesture.

I stared it down, rather than stared into it. But I'll never talk about it again, because I have a family to think about and it's no longer relevant.

For some, it may not be comprehensible that something so pivotal in a life could be put to rest so resoundly. Boxes unopened, photographs in locked desks, a suitcase of letters – these are reminders of the baggage that can build up over a lifetime and potentially follow a new generation around, or see one off – like a cat that smells death.

Perhaps Kate did 'stare down' her questions to find peace in a way Gwen surely didn't get the chance to. Perhaps Avery, who lived as a failed salvationist and died reimagined as one of the walking wounded, was staring down the contradictions of faith to make peace with his God. Perhaps Helen's disinterest in fighting her slide into dementia, sometimes even using it to mask her inclination to 'sleep talk', was her own form of stare down. It did, after all, allow her to leave her regrets and bitterness behind and find her way instead into 'day release' and a rocking chair on Nick and Kate's verandah to join their small, irregular gatherings. It could be argued that it allowed her to achieve the family she had been denied when she was, by common definition, capable of rational thought and purpose.

But, by way of letting the current generation have the last word, I'd like to revisit a conversation between the White siblings that began as they drove from Kimbanyon to Port Augusta for their grandfather's funeral.

It was prompted by Rachel, a young woman with little interest in philosophy and even less in hindsight who nevertheless made a discovery combining the two one night when she was allowed to fly solo on an autopsy at the Coroner's Court morgue.

The cadaver was an unidentified man in his early thirties whose death was most likely mishap rather than murder but it needed to be ruled out. He'd been found behind a dumpster by police an hour earlier. Given the level of putrification, the chief pathologist had speculated on his way out that 'John Doe' may have been there at least three days.

'It's amazing Will,' Rachel recounted for her brother. 'In the wet lab at uni, we get bodies that are yellowy or pasty brown. Their faces are kind of shrunken in on themselves. They're so prepped for us that they barely leak – maybe a bit of faeces in the intestines, the odd pocket of congealed blood or fluid where you don't think it will be. It's not hard to work on them; it's almost like they're aliens.

'But then I worked up this overdose at the Coroner's morgue last week. He was all bloated, with that greeny, charcoal colour on his legs and face.

'But it was the smell Will. I've been around a lot of preservatives in the wet lab. It's a strange thing, but the smell of whatever they put in formaldehyde just makes you hungry after a while! But the guy at the coroner's smelt so foul if I hadn't smeared Vicks under my nostrils, there's a good chance I would have thrown up!'

'I might just throw up if you don't get to the point soon, Rach,' William warned.

'It hit me when I cut between the intestines. When you're alive you've got this bacteria in you that's pretty much benign but when you die it becomes this almighty carnivorous thing, decomposing tissue and organs and producing this god awful gas.

'It started me thinking about the whole idea of something dead housing something alive and how these innocuous microbes can cause such amazing destruction. They just need to be activated.

'And then I started to think about entropy, a term we learnt in physics that didn't really make sense to me before. It's a measure of thermal energy that's not available to be converted into anything useful. Can you believe you can quantify that?

'I asked the lecturer about it and he said it's about the degree of randomness or disorder that's in every system. He said it was a law of thermodynamics that entropy – this energy that's not energy, this random chaos – always increases with time.'

Will hadn't been looking forward to the drive with Rachel, partly because he wasn't sure what they'd talk about over the hours. And here she was, speaking to him sincerely, as an older brother, and giving every indication that the subject matter was important to her and that she would, at some point, value his opinion.

He turned from the old road at the junction where the giant miner had once stood as a beacon for the tourist attraction that had been torn down decades before, and weaved his way toward the highway.

'Why on earth were you thinking about this stuff?'

'You're the psychologist – you really need me to explain? And why is that, Will? Why **are** you a psyche?'

Rachel immediately regretted confronting William with what she had long considered to be the heaviest elephant in the family room; it wasn't the day for it.

'I just think there's always been this tension with mum,' she continued hastily, 'but she behaves like everything's okay. And I think Dad worries about her constantly, maybe that she's going to do something crazy, and yet everyone thinks he's pretty laid back. There's this rot in the marriage only they don't even know it.'

'It's just dysfunctional families kiddo,' Will said, trying not to think about his day of firsts.

'I thought that too for a long time, and then I wondered what you'd say if you took me seriously,' Rachel replied teasingly.

'I thought you might tell me it's a "primal scream" thing,' she went on, 'but I don't think that's right either, because not everyone has a childhood trauma they're repressing; from what I can gather, dad had a near perfect family.'

Will was so diverted by Rachel's ideas that he failed to notice how heavy his foot had become on the accelerator.

'So what's your theory?'

'I talked it over with John Doe and I think everyone has this inside them, all the time – dead on the outside, wild on the inside. But that wildness is, for the most part, a dormant turbulence, maybe even a suppressed turbulence, if that makes sense. It's energy we're not aware of, so we've got no control over how it might be activated or even if we can stop it from totally destroying us when it is.'

Will thought for a moment before offering: 'I think I know what you're saying. Like in nature – there can be a calm inside the storm, but with people, it's really the other way around.'

He straightened his fingers to relieve a grip he hadn't realised had tightened on the steering wheel and caught his sister's eye before continuing. His words quickened as he sharpened the concept.

'Even though this "storm" appears to be inert, it's fundamentally unstable so it's only ever going to intensify. The important thing to recognise is the potential trigger – which of course will be different for each patient and ...'

Rachel moved to the very edge of her comprehension of the world as the car slid smoothly into the powdery shoulder of the old highway. She was listening to her brother, but felt the need to cut him off before her own understanding lost its way.

'The thing is, I think it's random. Whether it's alive or dormant is a matter of chance. That's why we don't see it coming – it's settled and then the universe tilts to destroy the equilibrium.'

She looked to see if William had caught up, but her brother was already several steps ahead of her.

'You're missing something here, Rach. It's not the universe that tilts; it's our minds that trigger everything and that's okay. That's what makes us human.'

'Sure, it's okay until we lose our grip on things and we implode or explode because there's this ignitable ...'

William interrupted his sister, sensing he was on the verge of an epiphany he had been waiting for, for most of his life.

'Who we are isn't determined by whether we've got a strong or a weak grip, it's determined by the act of pulling and tugging.'

The building authority in Will's voice filled the car with a sense of anticipation while simultaneously, it seemed, transferring adrenalin to the engine.

'Our humanity is most real, most raw, most pure at the points where we shift our weight to balance the known against the unknown – to stay standing while we're buffeted by unanswerable questions and the compulsion to keep asking them.'

Rachel looked at William's glowing face. She wondered whether her brother was experiencing a personal breakthrough but decided it was more likely he was imagining his carefully chosen words appearing in some prestigious medical journal likely to be read by his peers.

'So you took my theory, padded it out with psych-speak and now it's all your idea? Wow, you really are worth $300 an hour,' she teased.

'And the rest!'

With their grins still childishly loud, William pushed a button on his armrest and watched his sister jump as the wind rushed in, lifting her hands to her head to stop the pull of her hair.

Unexpectedly, he thought of his mother and how they had been flying along like this when he was just a boy. All this time William had convinced himself he had been scared that day, kneeling on the seat, his fingers gripping the door across the frame of the open window – forced to the brink. But the memory of it now made him feel profoundly happy. They were whooping and breathless, their hair whipping their faces and their eyes shining as if to say to the other that being in this moment together would be the highlight of their lives.

'Stick your head right out Billy. The wind won't hurt you. Just lean into it.'

Author's note.

Many of the places and events included in this novel are based on historical fact (that is expanded on in the following pages) but the primary characters and their interactions are entirely fictional.

Warmest thanks!

I want to express my sincerest gratitude to my friends and family who have helped me with the ins and outs of telling this story – listening to my ramblings, reading over chapters, advising on 'likely' language and scenarios and most of all, having the faith that it would all come together in the end.

Special thanks to Di Bone, Shirley Pandolfo, Jan Fraser, Alex Loefstedt, Karen Woolsey, Patrick Hamilton, Keith Scott, Mark Ragg, Amanda Westoby, Jo Sinclair, Mitch Pincus, Blaise van Hecke and Megan Low of Busybird Publishing and my thoughtful, talented and generous sons Jack, Jesse and Sean Rintoul. I'd also like to thank those I have lost along the way - my aunt Robin Giesecke and grandmother Helen (Dick) Harbutt for their support and author Calton Younger for his professional advice.

Scheyville Farm School

The Lord Mayor of Sydney's Dreadnought Fund was set up in New South Wales (NSW) in 1909 to purchase a Dreadnought battleship to contribute to Great Britain's response to Germany's growing naval capability in the lead up to WW1.

Around 90,000 pounds was donated by the public over the year but when the Australian Government decided to establish its own navy, around 80,000 pounds of it was put into the Dreadnought Trust. Half of this went toward establishing a naval college at Jervis Bay on the NSW south coast and the other half was allocated to bringing teenagers from Britain to bolster the state's rural workforce.

A 2,500 acre farm north west of Sydney, named Scheyville after a then member of parliament William Schey, was utilised to train the youths aged from 16 - 19. Differing reports estimate the scheme, which ran from 1911 to 1939, saw between 5,595 and 7,500 'Dreadnought boys' arrive in Australia.

Many British families saw the scheme as an opportunity for their boys to improve their life chances. What they experienced was very basic conditions, employment over vast distances and often exploitation.

During WW2, the farm school became a military camp, training members of the 73rd Australian Anti-aircraft Search Light Company and the RAAF 244 1st Parachute Battalion. From 1965 to 1973 the land and buildings were used to train officers heading for the war in Vietnam. The area is now a national park.

All characters in the novel who are named in association with the Scheyville farm are fictional.

(Further reading: Gill, A. *Likely Lads and Lasses: Youth Migration to Australia 1911-1983*, Marrickville, Sydney. Big Brother Movement Ltd, 2005)

Forced adoptions

'**A** mother whose child has been stolen does not only remember in her mind, she remembers with every fibre of her being.'

Personal accounts like this are included in the report of the Australian Parliament's Senate Standing Committee on the *Commonwealth Contribution to Former Forced Adoption Policies and Practices*.

The inquiry resulted in the Prime Minister of the day, Julia Gillard, apologising in March 2013 to victims of those policies and practices that created 'a lifelong legacy of pain and suffering'.

The committee estimated that up to 250,000 babies of unwed mothers were adopted by married couples from the 1950s through to the mid 1970s.

The painful stories and submissions made to the inquiry and to contributing researchers have revealed that those in maternity homes were often isolated and put under extreme pressure to sign adoption papers.

Some were told not to use their real names, they had possessions and clothes taken from them and if taken to hospital to give birth, were often put in different wards to married women. One Melbourne hospital was found to have forced the young women to endure longer labours to avoid Caesarian sections.

'The Benevolent Shelter for Women' identified in the novel is a fictional amalgam drawn from research into homes for unwed mothers run by religious organisations in the 1940s and 1950s and from residents' accounts.

The Stolen Generation

By 1911, the Northern Territory and every state except Tasmania had adopted 'protectionist' laws that gave a Chief Protector or Protection Board power over the welfare of Aboriginal children that dismissed the rights of their parents.

Governments and police officers enforced the removal of children from their communities and distanced them from their families on missions where they were prevented from speaking their own language and had Christianity imposed on them. In Tasmania, many Indigenous families were forced onto Cape Barren Island, off the northern coast.

The following is from the *Bringing Them Home Report (1997)* resulting from a national inquiry by the Human Rights and Equal Opportunity Commission into the separation of Aboriginal and Torres Strait Islander children from their families.

'During the 1950s and 1960s even greater numbers of Indigenous children were removed from their families to advance the cause of assimilation. Not only were they removed for alleged neglect, they were removed to attend school in distant places, to receive medical treatment and to be adopted out at birth.

'As institutions could no longer cope with the increasing numbers and welfare practice discouraged the use of institutions, Indigenous children were placed with non-Indigenous foster families where their identity was denied or disparaged.'

In 2008, the then Prime Minister Kevin Rudd made a formal apology for the laws and policies of successive governments and 'the pain, suffering and hurt of these Stolen Generations, their descendants and … their families left behind'.

In 2007-08, the rate of Indigenous children in out-of-home care (removed from their parents or communities to live in state-run residences, foster or kinship care or group homes) was seven times the rate of non-Indigenous children. The Productivity Commission's *Report on Government Services 2018* reveals that, a decade later, that rate has increased to ten times.

(There are many good books on The Stolen Generations but for first hand accounts on this and more, I'd like to recommend: Rintoul, S. *The Wailing – A National Black Oral History*, 1993, William Heinemann Australia. This book was nominated by Pat Dodson for inclusion in Egypt's New Bibliotheca Alexandria which describes itself as 'a place of dialogue, learning and understanding between cultures and peoples'. Unfortunately this book is out of print but still available in good libraries and worth the search.)

Dhurringile Prisoner of War camp

During WW2, there were eight prisoner of war (POW) camps established in regional Victoria, most in the Goulburn Valley where food and water supplies were reliable. Four of them, built near Tatura, were for civilians who originated from countries that Australia and its allies were fighting against.

The 65-room mansion Dhurringile formed part of that network and was used to intern German officers and their batmen (personal servants or 'orderlies').

The crew of the German raider the Kormoran was among those imprisoned in the camps, with their commander, Theodore Detmers, interned at Dhurringile.

The Kormoran had been on a mission to lay mines off the coast of Fremantle, Western Australia, in November 1941 and was reportedly flying a Dutch flag when it came across the HMAS Sydney on the afternoon of the 19th.

A letter sent after the war from one of the Kormoran's crew, Otto Wendroth, to a nurse who had looked after him when he was a POW, told how both ships were ablaze within 45 minutes of the Kormoran opening fire. While the Kormoran was abandoned, the Sydney slunk off over the horizon, his letter asserted.

Around 315 Germans survived, picked up in the water, on boats and onshore, but all 645 on board the HMAS Sydney perished.

Detmers suffered a stroke in Melbourne before being transferred to Dhurringile. While a prisoner, he was promoted by the Fuhrer Adolf Hitler to Captain and awarded the Knight's Cross of the order of the Iron Cross for his sinking of the Sydney.

Detmers led 19 other prisoners in an escape from Dhurringile through a 120 metre long tunnel under a false floor in a music room in January, 1945. He was among the last recaptured, eight days later near the border with NSW.

All other military personnel, prisoners and guards described in the novel as associated with the camps are fictional.

The Tea and Sugar supply train

The Tea and Sugar (or slow mixed goods train) ran on Australia's east-west Trans Australian Railway line from Port Augusta in South Australia, across the Nullabor Plain to Kalgoorlie in Western Australia for 79 years from its completion in 1917. It serviced the fettlers and gangers who maintained the track across almost 1,700 kilometres (the distance from London to Minsk, according to a Commonwealth Government promotional film in 1954) and the steam trains as they used it. Around 345 men and their families resided at 11 stops along the route and relied on the Tea and Sugar for health services, water, fresh produce and groceries. Sheep were slaughtered on the train as needed and the meat sold through the shop front window of the butcher's van when it stopped at stations. Refrigeration didn't come until the 1940s, with the butcher's van dropped in 1982. In the sixties, by which time the Tea and Sugar was a diesel powered locomotive, there was even a 'picture theatre' car providing rare entertainment for those living and working in isolated areas.

During the steam era, the railways pumped up the only natural waters along the line from Ooldea, on the eastern edge of the Nullabor Plain, to keep engines running and deliver water for households. Ooldea Soak was a waterhole thought to originate from an underground river and to be used by Aboriginal people from the Western Desert culture for centuries but by 1926 the source had been drained.

The Trans-Australian line used by the Tea and Sugar was the first standard gauge line built in South Australia, making it a three-gauge state. Before standard gauge became the norm, transport of goods and passengers across Australia was difficult with 'break of gauge' stops a necessary delay. It wasn't until the 'One Nation' project of 1995 that each Australian mainland capital city was connected by the preferred standard gauge lines. While the narrow gauge line between Broken Hill and Port Pirie was abandoned in 1970, the description of its removal in the novel actually reflects the operation to remove the old Central Australia Railway between Oodnadatta and Marree in 1982.

522

www.ingramcontent.com/pod-product-compliance
Lightning Source LLC
Chambersburg PA
CBHW032153180726
48284CB00001B/33